Benevolent

a novel by

DEVON TREVARROW FLAHERTY

Owl and Zebra Press
Durham   Detroit

*Owl and Zebra Press
PO Box 62412 Durham NC 27715
owlandzebrapress@gmail.com
Visit our website at owlandzebrapress.wordpress.com*

*First paperback edition, March 2013
ISBN 978-0-9889651-0-2
E-book available, ISBN 978-0-9889651-1-9
and 978-0-9889651-2-6*

*Cover photograph copyright © 2013 by Devon Trevarrow Flaherty
Author photograph copyright © 2012 by Dwight Knoll
Cover design by Owl and Zebra Press*

*This book is a work of fiction. Names, characters, places and incidents are
either products of the author's imagination or used fictitiously. Any
resemblance to actual events or persons, living or dead, is entirely coincidental.*

Design by Owl and Zebra Press

Printed in the United States of America

ଔ

for Grandma (in memoriam),
Aunt 'Nette (in memoriam),
and Aunt Caroline (with much love)

౪

4 BENEVOLENT

Benevolent

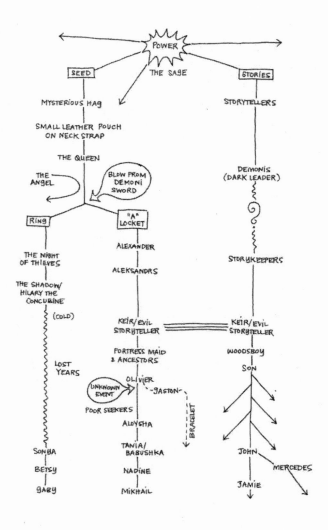

CHAPTER 1
OUR HERO DISCOVERS A MORAL IMPERATIVE
℘   ℭ

Tow-headed Mikhail bent over the lifeless, flattened, bloodied chipmunk. Then he squatted next to it and studied it hard with steel-blue eyes that were tearing up.

In the gravel next to the road lay Mikhail's discarded spade, his bucket, his wool mittens dug out from the recesses of the hall closet. Beside that, his bike, thrown onto its side in the grass. The roadside was quiet. Tall grasses whispered and trees shimmied in the light breeze. Green permeated the landscape, silvery-green on the undersides of grass blades, bush leaves, tree branches. The sky was blue and Midwestern-wide up beyond the scraping of the branches. Occasionally a car whooshed by to disturb the still: a mechanical groan of motor and tires eating pavement with a "Shhhrrrrwwwooosh!" And then gone, more quiet and breeze. There were no houses around this bend. No church, no store, no anything. Just a boy and a dead chipmunk; one lying splattered on the pavement with a paw over the glimmer-flecked white line, the other squatting and staring at the carnage.

Nine-year-old Mikhail Aleksandr put on his gloves, took up the spade, and wedged it under the body. He lifted the chipmunk, still held together in one piece, and lowered it very gently and a bit awkwardly into the bucket. Then he stood up the bike, applied the kickstand, loaded bucket, gloves, and spade in his bike's basket and peddled up the gentle slope of the road.

He knew of a quiet wood, which might have been private land, but no fences or garish neon signs told him to stay away. It was crisscrossed with dirt trails, one which eventually led out to the end of Mikhail's street. To this trail Mikhail rode, through high weeds, navigating around rotting logs and stray rocks. Then he shouldered the bucket and the spade and walked a little off the path, into the sparse wood. He dug a shallow hole in the ground at the edge of an overshadowing bush, dumped the chipmunk in, covered the hole, smoothed the dirt. He marked the grave with a stick, bowed his head, and steered his bike homeward.

"Mikhail?" His mother called from the kitchen. The house smelled of boiled green beans, baked chicken. Nadine rounded the corner. "Mikhail! Where have you been?"

"Nowhere."

"You can't just be 'nowhere,' Mikhail. Where were you? And go wash your hands for dinner."

"Nowhere, mom." Nadine looked at his pale face, the bleak shadows in the depths of his irises, and then padded off to the kitchen, banging around plates and pans, her hands oven-mitted in gross shades of brown and orange and green. She was sitting at the table with her hands folded under her thin chin when he came in extra-scrubbed for dinner. The kitchen was lit by the light of the dusk diffused around the drawn curtain and two yellowed bulbs in two brown-shaded lamps. The refrigerator hummed. Mikhail lowered himself into his chair. Nadine took the posture of prayer and quickly snapped off "God is great, God is good. And we thank Him for our food. From His table we are fed. Give us, now, our daily bread," her eyes on Mikhail the whole time. She served him a chicken breast, some beans, some rice, and let him push them around on his plate. "Sweetie, what is it? What's wrong?"

"Why do we have to eat animals?"

"Oh, not this again!" She threw her hands up and then set one to re-aligning her napkin, the other to picking up her fork. She cut at her meat for a while and lifted a bite to her mouth, stopping just short of it. "I still don't know where you were and why you won't tell me."

"It's just nothing."

"If I had a nickel for every time you told me 'nothing' or 'nowhere!' That's truly exasperating."

Mikhail thumped his feet against the legs of his chair.

"I'll quit asking when you communicate with me. Remember about communication?"

"I wasn't doing anything, Mom." His fork traced the flowered pattern on his plate, slowly looping around the chicken and green beans and rice. "Look, I'll eat some chicken." He cut off a piece and shoved it in his mouth, chewing with his mouth open so she could see. "It's good. Yum."

Nadine worried some of the fine lines of her face into creases. A lock of hair found its way stray from its tight, low bun of chestnut hair. "Seriously? I just ask you these things because I want you to be safe. You know what it's like when I don't know where you are…" She bit at her lower lip.

"I was riding my bike."

"Where?"

"In the woods, behind the Thessinger's house."

"What were you doing?"

"Mooo-oom!" in two long, defeated syllables.

"What? Were? You? Doing?" Each word came with a nod of the head and an unswerving glare.

He cleared his throat. He coughed. But in the end the stare won and he mumbled, "I was burying a chipmunk."

"You were *what*?!?"

"Mom!"

"I mean… Could you please explain?"

"I just saw it from the bus window. And I went back and buried it. That's all." His eyes watered and he wiped at snot with the back of his sleeved arm.

"Well, I... Just... Next time tell me where you're going. And does that mean you were riding in the busy street? How far away was it? And how did you— did you— pick it *up?*"

"But—"

"But nothing. Your father would never hear of you riding out on the highway or handling diseased carcasses, even at your age." Of course, she never really knew what Alexy would have thought; he never got to have a nine-year-old boy. But still. "You are my baby, Mikhail." He was so disgusted at her calling him a baby he hung his head until his nose nearly touched the chicken sauce. "But you're my little man, too. The man of the house. Like your dad." She took a bite of rice and gave Mikhail a reassuring smile.

CB   BO

Across town, in the same duskiness of that summer evening, Gaby lay on her bed, belly-down, feet swinging. Her windows were thrown open to the first few stars off the pale horizon, her room lit up and vibrating with a light and ceiling fan combo, her radio at level five to compete with the radio downstairs. She sang down at a drawing tablet, colored at odd angles with fluorescents, "Oh bay-bee, do you know what I mean? Being with you is like havin' a dream!" She picked up a turquoise marker, colored more.

There came a banging at her door. "What!?" she continued to streak the paper. "Bein' with you-oo is like havin' a-uh dream. Ooooh."

Annie swung open the door, hand on hip. This meant, *Mom made me walk all the way up here to get you because we've been calling you for dinner and you can't hear us!* "Turn down your radio! You're in trouble!"

"Am not."

Gaby capped the marker, threw it on the bed with two pinched fingers, swung her legs over the side of the Rainbow Brite festooned bed, and exaggerated a strut to the door. Looking at Annie with her head jutted forward on her neck, she switched off the light. The din in the room stopped with the pop of the switch: light and noise. The fan whirred slower and slower in the dusky dark. "There," she said. "Happy?"

Annie sang, "You're in trouble."

"By the power of Northwyth!" Gaby bent one arm behind her head and straightened the other, holding an open palm out at Annie.

"Oh, puh-lease! Nerd. Why did you even think of that?"

The two girls went crashing down the stairs two-at-a-time to a familiar scene: all a-hum and a-buzz with gold light and noise, the clashing of pans, dishes, silverware on the dinner table. Bette Midler crooned in the foreground and background and off the walls. Stellar crooned along as she shuffled herself toward the table, a pan of meatloaf balanced on an oven mitt. She set the meatloaf on pot-holders, danced with her oven mitts around the end of the table, and kissed Adam on the head as she sashayed by.

"Gross, Mom," said Annie, trailing in behind Gaby.

"Gaby!" Stellar simultaneously pointed a remote at the radio and scooted her chair in to the table, all while looking intensely at Gaby. "How many times do I have to tell you not to play your music so loud and close your door?"

"I can't hear my radio over *yours*."

"And Bette Midler too!" said Annie.

"You two don't be smart with your mother." Adam was a number of bites into his scalloped potatoes.

"Yeah, you two"—eyebrows raised and pointing her fork first at one and then the other— "don't be smart with your mother." Stellar scooped up meatloaf and then rested her hand back down. "Plus, Bette Midler is cool. And plus, *you*" at Gaby, "are still in trouble."

"For what?!?" Hands flung down to her side, a pouty face.

"For playing your music too loud and keeping your door shut. I've warned you enough times."

Annie stuck her tongue out.

"Mom! Did you see that? Annie stuck her tongue out at me!"

"So did not." Another roll of those hazel eyes.

Aside to Annie, "Cut that out. And you—Gaby, look at me—are grounded from your stereo for the week."

"That's not fair!"

"That way you can hear when I call you to dinner."

Adam shoveled in three carrots at once. "You heard your mother."

ca ꙮ

Mikhail was back at the bush in the woods a week later, with another pail and another bit of roadkill. It was a damp day, a nip from lake wind digging right into the bones. Mikhail finished burying a flattened turtle with loose dirt and sat down on the ground several feet away, rubbing his bare hands against the back of his thighs. He watched a few darkened leaves fly from the mostly green and clattering branches high above and did not hear the foliage crunching nearby or see the red plaid move among the brush.

A gruff voice startled Mikhail, "Hey, you!" Mikhail jumped to his feet and stared. He waited for a cue to grab his bike and run off.

"Now just you wait a second." The man strode closer to Mikhail. "What are you doing here?"

"You— I— Just sitting. And riding my bike."

"You look harmless enough. Not smoking or anything?" He stopped ten feet back from Mikhail.

"No, sir. I'm just a kid, sir."

The man had a grizzly ring of brown hair and a large, shaggy mustache cut low around his lips. His brow was heavy but the lines around his eyes were worn deep and friendly. He wasn't a big man, but exuded masculinity through ashy smells and mended bootlaces and patched, flannel hunting coat. He carried nothing in his half-fingered gloved hands, his nails mere stubs: clean hands but with deep lines of dark. "Yeah. Sure. So you come back here often?"

"Sometimes, yeah."

"Where you from?" Mikhail didn't think he was in trouble anymore, but he was itching to get away from a protracted conversation. "You seem sort of fidgety."

"No, sir."

"No? Well—" Just then there was a low rumble as the whole forest lurched in one direction and a deafening boom cracked the autumn still. Mikhail and the man looked around with hurried glances, and before they could think what on earth would have done such a thing, there was another, more localized crack above and a bustling of tinier cracks and swishes as a branch plummeted through the canopy. Mikhail did not see it coming and he was thrown, sprawled and pinned to the side, as the man stood watching, helpless.

The man was not sure just how Mikhail lost consciousness, but he knew that the scrawny, pale boy was not awake anymore. He lifted the slight boy and carried him through the woods the short walk to the tiny cabin at the end of the crazy dirt road that separated him from the onslaught of suburban sprawl. He had a truck there, but it was propped on cinder blocks and in the middle of some undefined "work." More usefully, he had a wife there, who looked up as he came thunking the only door back on its hinges and stomping unceremoniously in with an unconscious child. "Man alive,

John!" she gasped, before expressing no little confusion: there had been a boom and a lurch that shook the whole cabin, and now here was John with a baby in his arms.

"Hardly a baby, Mercedes."

"Ah, tut, tut, tut." She shushed him with the wave of her lean, brown hand and gathered Mikhail into her own arms, cradling him and bobbing, taking in the smooth visage, the lay of his white eyelashes on his pale cheek, the scuffed tennis shoes and relaxed fingers with fresh dirt under the nails. She hummed a quiet chant as she bobbed, which seemed only a muffled craziness, as she carried him the few feet under the loft's rafters. There it was a dimmer dark and a couch sagged nearly to the ground, layered with furry blankets and furs. She nestled him under a wool blanket of intricate, colorful weaving and sat beside him on a low stool.

John and Mercedes knew nothing about the boy; where he might live, who he might belong to. Before John could articulate this Mercedes hummed to herself, and rhythmically rocked as she dispensed the only remedy she knew to make him better, or perhaps just to kill the time, waiting. This is the story that Mercedes told Mikhail as he journeyed from unconsciousness back to consciousness, a story that would begin a relationship of boy to Mercedes to story, and perhaps even infect his soul with romance:

"Sand sprayed across The Queen's body like thousands of needles. White linen wrapped her head to protect her ears and nose and mouth, and she remained silent as she approached the tall, slim stranger, even though any noise she made would have only been ripped from her and flung skyward out against the empty desert, anyhow. Only the top of her face showed between the folds of fabric to reveal her gem-blue eyes, big and clear and windows into a quick and pondering, discerning soul; the linen clung with the wicked wind to the curves of her slender body, first one way and then another.

"The stranger watched her fight against the wind, toward him. She was young and he saw her tenderness peeling away quickly to reveal steeliness. He saw everything clearly with a vision that is unknown to humanity, as unknown as the feel of passing between dimensions or the knowledge of creating something from nothing. His clarity extended to her disarming eyes, her camel bobbing its long neck away from the spray of the sand, her hand tucked under double-thick fabric. In that clenched hand—he could see this in both her thoughts and also in the skeletal, dynamic, colorful, rainbow that was his vision— she tried to conceal from him a small leather pouch with a long, slender thong, able to fit neatly in her hand. And in the pouch, fastened so tight that the knot would not give without great force, was a small magical seed, extremely ancient and powerful enough to take up much more room—in his way of seeing—than a small sliver of a seed had any right to take up. The Queen had managed somehow to disguise herself and remain incognito through various boundaries, travel across dangerous and hostile environs to meet him in the middle of the largest desert at a terrible time of year, alone, and yet what impressed him the most was with what stunning composure she held the pouch in her tiny fist.

"They stood in the middle of a great expanse, the sun infernal, intense, and throbbing through the golden haze of whipping sand. Her gaze met his intensely, and she stood solid, unblinking. As soon as their bodies aligned and their eyes met, he was keenly aware of something, and he wondered how she could not be. A burst of searing heat exploded in their midst and shot out in a widening circle of magenta that ripped up more sand as it flew away from them. The Queen showed no sign of noticing. As a matter of fact, neither did he. But he pulled a bit of it from the air and pocketed it to ponder later. He was terrified he might know what it meant.

"'What do you want?' he asked her. His voice was clear and soothing, even though The Queen had the distinct impression that he was reining in the sheer extent of his volume and wrath with every syllable. She had the same impression about his body, as if he could flex and his body would come tumbling out of his clothes—or maybe even his own skin—in every direction. She also noticed that he was not without handsomeness and magnetism of the most devastating sort.

"She chided herself for thinking of it at this moment.

"She stared at him still, thinking about her mouth bound up against the desert, and how her every muscle and limb were bruised, sore, and stinging with thirst and abuse. She came all this way and now she could not imagine how she would be able to speak to him. All the miraculous strength of mind and body that she was blessed with seemed to scatter like a bush of butterflies taking off in flight and she realized at once that her eyes must be betraying her frustration.

"All at once, she was aware that she was stringing thoughts together as cohesively as the Germanic language that she spoke out loud. The thoughts moved swiftly from her own mind and appeared—she could see this so clearly—in the stranger's mind or behind his eyes. She was startled by this, and wondered if her thirst was affecting her mind. Surely it was nothing like this when the castle's Gypsy girl read your mind; just a fleeting uncertainty about a color on a card hidden in your bedroom.

"*What do you want me to do with it?*

"This time, The Queen was sure that the stranger had said nothing with his lips, but his thought was as tangible as a cuneiform tablet in the front space of her head.

"*I have never spoken like this before*, she tried.

"He did not respond, but she knew all the same that he understood her and was keeping his own council.

"*This confuses me—in other ways, too. How is it you speak in my mind? How is it you...* she hesitated; suddenly she knew that she was standing dangerously close to a raw segment of history. How did she know that? This went beyond telepathy.

"He knew the curve of her thought, even though she snapped it off defensively. The question hung unfinished between them, stretched over the desert, emblazoned like a sword that pierced through his heart, through her heart, and out like a bloodied ship mast rising on sandy waves. He surrendered to what was happening, and a loud crack sounded in his ears, renting all the time before from all the time after.

"She was looking at him, questioning.

"*You want to finish your question?*

"She clawed at fabric, peeled cloth from in front of her mouth, revealing a long, slender nose and a wide, ruby mouth which the stranger hungered to kiss. She stood with the wind whipping the white linen across her strong, straight thighs, her blue eyes gleaming over her sunburned, high cheek bones and a lock of red hair escaping to blow curling out around the side of her narrow face. 'How do I know you?'"

CHAPTER 2
OUR HEROINE DISCOVERS A
MORAL IMPERATIVE
FIVE YEARS LATER

ᔥ   ᔥ

The sound of slush under the tires continued, uninterrupted, as the LeFevres traveled down Woodward Avenue into a far-flung borough of Detroit. Inside the minivan it was dim: the sky was water-color gray and the windows tinted. Gaby sat with a plastic bag of clothes on her lap, looking at her reflection in the window. A car-window reflection was a soft thing, only curved lines and the absence of pimples and bumps. She admired that kind reflection. But really, there was no need for erasure; she was wiry at a blossoming fourteen, long and lean and upright. She was pale with a curly, full head of dark hair and large, shadowy eyes, cinnamon in color but flecked with a hint of Egyptian blue.

Annie had headphones on over her bobbed, blonde hair and blunt bangs, her Discman loud enough that everyone could identify the ghost of a song. She looked out the opposite window, mouthing words to Mariah Carey and breaking out with a line or two. Adam (an older, male approximation of Gaby) was driving. Stellar (with blonde-gone-dirty-blonde hair which she wore eternally, gloriously long) sat in the passenger seat, her chin in her hand, her elbow against the door.

"That's it, right up there," Stellar pointed to a cinder-block building painted a bland cream on a long street of brown and tan and cream buildings. Between a flower shop and a bridal shop, behind a narrow parking lot of broken pavement: The Salvation Army Soup Kitchen. The patrons were already loitering: standing against walls and sitting on curbs flanking the entrance with shopping carts and back packs. Adam maneuvered the minivan down a tight alley to a back lot.

Annie switched off Mariah and removed her earphones, stuffed them in the seat-pouch in front of her, and craned her neck to look out the front window. The minivan came to a stop and Stellar's and Adam's doors clicked open, their jackets whispered with movement, but the girls stayed seated, looking around them.

"Gaby," Stellar poked her head back in the door, reaching for her purse. "Go put that bag where it goes. And you too, Annie. There are another two bags in the back seat."

Annie rolled her eyes and reached into the back seat to get the plastic bags. She came back with only one. "Gaby, you get the other one."

It was frigid with earlier-than-usual snowfall. Dirty snow clung to the car, the curbs, the sidewalks. Slush stuck to the gutters, the corners of things, the fences, the tufts of dead weeds and cracks in the pavement. Gaby yanked a fur-lined hood up over her curly mane and walked toward a high, slatted fenced-in area with the sign "Donations Collected Here" and lifted the latch on the gate. The enclosure was stacked with toys, some of them too abused to be of use. *That's the Christmas spirit*, she thought. Many bags, boxes, and crates hadn't quite made it to the collection bins, but littered the ground and were sprinkled with the snow. A ten-speed bike all but blocked the gate from opening.

It was calm and hushed inside the fence. City noise sucked into netherspace and gave the impression of peace among the debris. Annie and Gaby threw their bags into an open bin and Gaby loitered at the bin's entrance, peered into the dark corners of the container. She saw lots of clothes, a box full of used toothbrushes, a rotary phone, before turning to walk away.

Inside the building it was warm and full of fluorescent light and hard surfaces and a bit dusty. Linoleum floors, cinder block walls, exposed ceilings: all cream-colored. The main room into which the LeFevre family entered was basically a small gymnasium with scuffed, taupe walls and hung with giant lights and fans in basketball-repelling cages. It was set with rows of brown industrial tables and hundreds of brown, metal, folding chairs. Stellar stomped off her boots and led the way to the far end of the room, where a large window opened into a restaurant-style kitchen from which drifted the banging of pots and women's voices. It smelled of turkey, gravy, instant mashed potatoes.

Stellar framed herself in the doorway and Adam, Annie, and Gaby stood lined up in the window. "Hello?" Stellar leaned into the din.

"Oh, hello! So glad you're here!" One woman wiped her hands on her apron and approached, assessing them. "Four of you?" She was joined by another woman and they stood looking and grinning behind a stainless steel island-counter where a giant pot stood idling, a greasy smear of butter in a swirl that disappeared below the surface.

"We just sent the prep crew home. We'll put you right to work, then."

Gaby was expeditiously stripped of her winter jacket and stood at the stove with her sleeves pushed up past her elbows. She bided her time watching the bubbles pop on the surface of a veritable tureen of canned gravy, stirring and listening to the women talk passionately about Black Friday deals and whether or not they would go shopping and why or why not. Adam and Annie clinked plastic forks down on the tables, shuffled chairs around to accommodate more people. Stellar mixed punch from powder and was trained in the operations of the coffee machines as they whirred and spat and stared unblinking a single, orange eye a piece, at her.

The building was industrial, sure, but it smelled like Thanksgiving would just about anywhere in Detroit. At the LeFevre home, today would have been a day for gingered cranberry sauce and homemade pumpkin pie, candles and soft Muzak, a crackling fire and the building of an elaborate gingerbread creation like a mammoth teepee or a Southern mansion or a whole village decked out in gumdrops and rainbow jimmies. It was Stellar's idea for the family to work the soup kitchen instead. She wanted to be the mom that exposed her kids to philanthropy, but somehow, besides the occasional clothing donation, the years had gotten away from her. Annie protested. Gaby took the matter to the school quorum, and, when worked out in the labyrinthine conversation of teenage girls, she concluded that volunteering was good (in the abstract) for character-building or would look good on a college resume or something like that. What would Jesus do?

Gaby had been coming home from school to a routine: microwave a bowl of Cheese Whiz; grab the saltines; watch cartoon re-runs until dozing off for a cat nap; rouse to the smell of spaghetti and ragù. For cartoons, there was the perpetually present *Flintstones*, now followed by old episodes of her childhood favorite, *Avengers of Northwyth*. On the day before Stellar dropped the Thanksgiving-Soup-Kitchen bomb, an episode aired in which The Queen and The Sage joined forces to save a Northwyth populace plagued by malnutrition and starvation (due to the Demonis' severance of the traders' routes and their burning of the kingdom's fields). Oh, those Demonis.

In the end, all four avengers united to drive the Demonis away and dispense with nurturing compassion for the masses (Queen Northwyth) and re-grow the crops at an incredible rate (The Sage and his magical staff), and Gaby was properly inculcated with a humanitarian spirit.

Every little bit helped.

Now Gaby stood at the industrial kitchen window, scooped out stuffing on Styrofoam plates with dividers, only one scoop per plate as the prescriptive had been given.

"Can I have another scoop of stuffing? Stuffing is my favorite," a woman asked, pointing with a thick finger, black under the ragged nail.

"Yeah, sure. It's Thanksgiving, isn't it?" Gaby piled another scoop on the plate and the stuffing spilled over into the section for mashed potatoes. She smiled at the woman and handed the plate to Annie. As Gaby moved on to the next patron, she heard, "Can I have another scoop of mashed potatoes? Mashed potatoes are my favorite." She glanced sideways at Annie and they giggled.

"Sure," Annie said. "It's Thanksgiving, isn't it?"

Once everyone was served and the last wave of patrons were tucking into their turkey and rolls, the kitchen staff encouraged Stellar to have the family sit down and enjoy the meal themselves. Another teaching opportunity rose large in Stellar's mind and she ushered each of them to different spots around the room, insisting that they sit separated for this special Thanksgiving. Gaby, Annie and Adam stood alone for a long while, eyeing the tables in front of them and looking absently down at their divided Styrofoam plates of vittles. Adam gave his daughters an encouraging smile before sitting down.

Gaby slid quietly into the closest vacant seat, on the end of a full table. She was suddenly enraptured by her corn. She moved kernels with the tines of her fork. After a few minutes she looked up to see the stuffing-and-mashed potatoes lady directly across from her. She was eating, but soon reciprocated Gaby's stare.

"You like what you see?" the lady asked.

"I'm just a little uncomfortable. Sorry." Gaby pushed her corn around a little more and dropped her eyes.

"Oh, I see. Don't normally work here, huh?"

"No. First time."

"Congratulations." Then offhandedly, "Runaway. Drug addict. In and out of rehab until I just went to panhandling. That's my story."

"Oh. I'm sorry?"

"No you're not."

"Oh. Oh. Well, I just don't think I would like that."

"Of course you wouldn't. What are you going to do about it?"

"Well, I gave you an extra scoop of stuffing."

"I think I'll nominate you for a Nobel Peace Prize."

"No need for that," she snickered.

A TV fizzled to life around black and white snow, and Gaby could just barely see it around the kitchen's gleaming, stainless steel counter. She watched without watching the distant, muted picture as she sighed her way through her meal. "Hey! I love this show!"

"What?" The woman across the table—the one with the Nobel connections—swiveled her shoulders and craned her neck to look back in the direction Gaby was facing.

"Yeah. This is *Avengers of Northwyth*. On TV there, in the kitchen." In response to a vacant raising of the eyebrows, "I used to love this show when I was a kid. They just started playing re-runs after school and I saw this episode the other day. But I fell asleep right before the ending. Actually, right about now." Gaby leapt up from her chair, which scraped back across the linoleum. She ran across the room and leaned into the kitchen window, seating her chin in her palms and her elbows on the counter. "Hey, can you turn that up?"

A startled woman shuffled over to the ancient TV and nudged the volume just a little.

Gaby stood there for another five minutes as The Queen and The Sage defeated the Demonis, and eventually Annie joined her. "You were always so into this show. I remember all your Avengers dolls. And the castle."

"I know. I wonder if they're in the attic."

"I think we got rid of them at a yard sale."

"No! I don't think so. Maybe I should find them and give them to someone."

"You mean some impoverished kid? What, are the soup kitchen vapors going to your head?" Annie threw her body into Gaby's until she started to tip.

"Whatever." Gaby leaned back, a little harder, and Annie bumped into the side of the service window. As she did, her arm flew out to catch her weight and her hand knocked into a tall container of massive cooking utensils. The container rocked a few times until, top-heavy, it tipped away from Annie and onto the busy counter, making quite a racket and sending one particularly rambunctious spoon flying rocket-like at a large pitcher of iced tea. The pitcher shattered as the spoon hit it, exploding tea and ice in an a-bomb tidal wave that took out a bowl of garden salad and splashed right on the red "Pull in Case of Fire" switch. It sputtered and shorted. One by one the alarms all over the facility started to scream and to flash their epilepsy-inducing, white bulbs.

In the dining room, most diner's hands flew up to their ears as their faces scrunched in dismay. Chairs scraped and people exclaimed as the sprinklers up in the rafters spurted to life and started raining down on the meal of hundreds. Gaby's eyes widened, and she turned to gape at Annie but Annie was already gone, making her way across the room to the Exit sign. "GO ON!" yelled the woman from inside the kitchen. "*WE* BOTH KNOW IT'S NOTHING, BUT WE STILL HAVE TO GET OUT OF HERE!" She grabbed Gaby's upper arm and shoved her into the confused throng. The woman went off yelling for people to be calm and make their way to the closest exit. Over the din, she was heard by only those closest to her. Gaby stood still as she watched her go, then caught her mother's worried look as she swiveled it around the room. Their eyes locked together, but just then something shoved into the middle of Gaby's back, sending her lurching forward. Her legs caught on an abandoned folding chair and her torso sprawled forward over top of it. Her chin hit on a table as she went down, disrupting a plate of food which splattered forward over the falling Gaby. She was only down a moment before someone tripped on her and sprawled out on her. The stranger struggled to his feet and moved on before more feet stepped on her and kicked her, bruising her shins and forcing the air out of her lungs.

Gaby lay on the floor, bleeding from her chin, covered in gravy and corn kernels, and rolling in toward her stomach, which she was grasping with her forearms. She settled on her back, looking up at the gymnasium-style lights as they seemed to dim and brighten to the beat of the fire alarm's flashing orbs. People moved all around her, oblivious to the clear pattern posted on the Fire Evacuation Plan; a man walked slowly by with his plate close to his mouth and his spoon still shoveling in turkey and potatoes. The world seemed to pulse with chaos and violence.

Then there, in the blaring light and the scream of the alarm, The Sage went walking by, his arm around the woman who had sat across from Gaby at supper. His arm seemed larger than life and wrapped around the woman like a blanket, rather than sat on her shoulder. She eased forward through the crowd with him, curiously focused and undaunted by the panicked commotion around her. Then into Gaby's periphery shone an energy which was followed by The Queen of Northwyth, galloping through the room on her steed, and rising up on Quicklander over Gaby's sprawled body, the bright light now splaying out behind her in iridescent rays, silhouetting her crown and her lively mass of long, red hair as she looked down at Gaby. Gaby cowered and gawked under Quicklander's giant, pawing hooves.

"Gaby, do not be afraid."

Gaby continued to gawk as Quicklander steadied and The Queen dismounted, came to kneel beside Gaby. The Queen smelled of cinnamon and myrrh and flowers and she gently moved Gaby's black curls out of her eyes, wiped some gravy away with the hem of her battle skirt. Then she smiled a terrifying, comforting smile at her. "Gaby, it is time to get up and help." Gaby blinked up at her, drinking in her alarming beauty.

"Gaby. Get up and help."

⚃ ⚂

In a post-trampled and vulnerable state, Gaby saw The Queen, long-since dead according to the legends, and she heard her say, "Get up and help." A believer and a literalist, Gaby listened and obeyed.

By Christmastime, Gaby spear-headed an Angel Tree at Butter High School. She told Stellar, "I don't want anything for Christmas." She borrowed a copy of Schumacher's *Small Is Beautiful: Economics As If People Mattered* from the Butter Public Library. She made Stellar drive her back to the soup kitchen once a week, on Wednesdays for dinner service. On Thursdays she answered phones and filed papers for the Butter Community Center.

"Come on, guys, take an Angel Tree form. How much do you *get* for Christmas? Why don't you *give* a little something this year?" Gaby passed out red and green slips of paper, watched them litter the floor a ways up the hallway.

"Turn them in with your gift before Christmas break! C'mon. Take an Angel Tree form, people. Give some cheer to needy children this year!"

Melodie Polejski tossed her permed, auburn hair as she navigated the hallway toward Gaby. She carried in her slender hands the majority of the green and red slips Gaby had handed her twenty minutes earlier. Gaby looked down at Melodie's hands. "Come on Mel. Why aren't you handing 'em out?"

"Come on, Gaby. Let's just leave them on a table by the tree and let people convict themselves. I'm not everyone's fucking conscience."

"Melodie." Gaby rolled her eyes and then forced a few more red and green slips at a gaggle of students leaving the cafeteria. "Here, guys. Make sure and buy something for the Angel Tree this Christmas." She smiled at them, then turned a cross face at Melodie, one shoulder up, head tilted to the side. It said, "See? Not so hard."

"I'm going to class." Melodie thunked her slips down on the table adorned with a red paper-roll banner on which was painted in green and white, "TAKE HOME AN ANGEL TREE SLIP TODAY! GIVE THE GIFT OF A SMILE TO A NEEDY CHILD!" Melodie stepped around Gaby. "You're a psycho," as her backside retreated down the hall in tight jeans and a bright red sweater.

The white light of the Angel Tree's bulbs flashed rhythmically off Gaby's face as she watched Melodie scooting to class. But before Melodie reached English Hall, Gaby set her own slips beside Melodie's discards and shouldered her backpack. She jogged down the hall, calling "Melodie! Melodie!"

"No! Look," Melodie swung around to meet Gaby, her green eyes invading Gaby's personal space. "I don't want to do all this 'Save the World' shit! It's so…" she looked around at peers streaming by, teachers manning their doorways, lockers slamming. "So abnormal."

Gaby made peace: "You want to come over after school today? I've got a new CD. And we could work on that stupid math project... *after* the MTV Top Ten."

"Sure." Melodie rolled her eyes and turned, receded down the hall, swarmed by peers as she called out, "But I'm not going with you anymore to that soup kitchen."

CHAPTER 3
OUR HEROINE AND HERO MEET
MID-HIGH SCHOOL

ℰ᾽   ℭℛ

It happened at an all-ages show. Darkness, except where a thick shaft of light escaped the restrooms and except for the pulsing of stage lights red, blue, yellow, white, red, blue, yellow, white. Movement from all four walls inward; a mass of bodies standing and dancing, jumping on toes, swinging arms wildly. The smell of punk: sticky-soda floors, smoke, and sweat, but mostly smoke and sweat. Raw noise, making words inarticulate in the bass, the throbbing. The floor shivered. Kids screamed at their friends and were not heard.

Gaby lounged behind a folding table, in a "Save the Trees" T-shirt. The table was littered with magazines, brochures, pamphlets, for all sorts of important causes, and with band paraphernalia. Her head rested back against a display of posters for The Hired Assassins, Strike Back, and Wally's Toothbrush. Her left arm rested on a ripped cardboard box, brimming over with black T-shirts splattered with "John's Punkstraviganza," and on the back, "Vote Nader/LaDuke."

Gaby mostly watched, waited. If someone's hand should even accidentally brush the "Why *You* Should Help the

Homeless" brochures she had put together, she would pounce. Until then, she was nonchalant, observant, here to take money for merchandise and answer dumb questions.

Mikhail came to the show alone, but you wouldn't know it as he was sucked into the giant, pulsing organism. He looked familiar: tent-like, dark pants studded with safety pins, a fitted T-shirt, back pack, chunky black boots, plenty of hardware, ruffled hair stuck ruffled with Elmer's glue, thick-rimmed glasses, plastic frames. Tall, scrawny, wiry, pale; hair dyed dark to accentuate the paleness.

He bobbed his head for awhile letting it fall loose at the neck and be led by the ears, concluded that The Hired Assassins weren't quite what he wished, and made for the band table.

Mikhail's fingers slid over the covers of things, his head bent down at a ninety degree angle. He read the titles in the second row, the third, the first. His fingertips deflected off a brochure: "Why *You* Should Help the Homeless."

"YOU INTERESTED?" he heard.

Mikhail looked up into a face lit with some sort of excitement, big eyes bigger with interest, brighter with answers to questions he wasn't sure he had. "Oh," he managed. "ABOUT WHAT?" he yelled back through the auditory mess of The Hired Assassins, squinting at her (as if that might help), leaning in with one of his ears and upper body.

"ABOUT THE HOMELESS." Gaby looked down at his fingertip just barely resting on her brochure.

"OH! THIS." He read the title. Picked it up. Feigned leafing through it under her scrutinizing eyes. "YOU?"

"HELL YEAH I'M INTERESTED. I PUT THAT THING TOGETHER." Gaby nodded toward his hands, where he looked again, having forgotten for a moment that the brochure was there, having forgotten everything except for the big eyes on this little alien.

"I see."

"WHAT?"

"I SAID, 'I SEE.'"

"IT'S FREE. YOU CAN TAKE IT." She looked hopeful.

"Yeah, I'LL TAKE ONE." *What was the brochure even about?*

"BUT I'LL EXPECT TO SEE YOU AT THE BUTTER COMMUNITY CENTER THIS WEDNESDAY. THAT'S WHEN I'M THERE. THAT'S LIFE-CHANGING SHIT." Another nod at his hands.

"YEAH, SURE." Suddenly he had to go to the restroom, or out to smoke (which he didn't even do), or *some*thing.

Mikhail managed the rest of the first set out on the curb, the brochure stuffed in his pack, inhaling second-hand smoke and tracing the X on the back of his hand. He squeezed himself into the swaying knot of kids front-of-stage for the second set, and enthusiastically discussed Strike Back with a guy at the band paraphernalia table during all of Wally's Toothbrush, with the occasional acknowledgment of Wally's out-of-this-world vocals. Secretly, Mikhail had hoped to have a re-do conversation with that spunky homeless-person girl. He conversed looking over his shoulder, but she eluded him the rest of the night.

Gaby spent the second set in the bathroom, retching from the smoke and three foot-long chili dogs with fries she'd consumed that afternoon. She was being deposited on her bed, courtesy of Melodie, by the time Wally's Toothbrush mounted the make-shift stage.

଴ଓ   ଞଠ

Mikhail didn't go to the community center that Wednesday. He just couldn't bring himself to do it. But by the following Wednesday, he had read the brochure seventeen times, memorized whole passages, and peddled toward the community center straight from school.

He leaned back over the rear tire of his bike, coasting down the hill toward the center. The wind pushed against his back, an inertia-breeze smoothing against his face and chest. He ate it in, with the cloudless sky, the manicured lawns in every direction, Irish green and fat with spring rain. He smiled despite himself, his stomach knotted against his purpose, and his hands tingling with the thought of a skinny, cute, interesting girl.

Butter Community Center, like all the buildings around it, had a manicured lawn, square-cut bushes along the front façade, interspersed with geraniums in un-natural (but somehow natural) shades of yellow and orange. A white-washed wood-clapboard fence, waist-high, ran between its front yard and the un-pocked sidewalk. The parking lot was tucked away behind; more un-pocked pavement, black, with neat white lines delineating the car spaces. An overhang on the side was broad and tall enough to hold a bus, which it did, a refurbished blue affair.

Butter had few citizens needing the services of a soup kitchen like the one Gaby was familiar with on Woodward. Instead, if you wanted to feed someone hungry, you could join an outreach project at one of a few local churches or the community center. Meals were bunched around the holidays, and there were other services to manage, like clothing give-a-ways, winter jacket collections, Christmas toys for kids, social service awareness days, after school technical education programs, sports health initiatives, and grocery collection and distribution, to name a few. The local wealth-to-poverty ratio kept the community center's Community Outreach coffers full, and working there was really quite rewarding.

Back to Mikhail, coasting into the parking lot of the Butter Community Center on a fine, spring day when he noticed that alongside a few, shiny mini-vans was parked a practical, two-door sedan with a few band stickers cracking on the bumper, and some fresh window-clings neatly lining the rear window.

Among them: "You Gonna' Eat That?" A shiver went up his spine and back down into his groin.

He found the back door locked, made his way past the geraniums to the front door and into a reception area, carpeted with flat Berber laid right on the cement foundation, hung with cheap brass chandeliers, lit also by daylight shifting through the dusty, rubber tree leaves that flanked the doors in terra cotta pots. He maneuvered around the lacquered-wood couch with gaudy cushions and its matching coffee table set with magazines. He stood lopsidedly in front of a wall-mounted pamphlet display, stuffed and color-coordinated. He picked out one about Butter Community Outreach, started wandering clockwise with it around the room. On a painted concrete wall which joined the room in a T with two opposite hallways, a bulletin board hung: trimmed with pale pink, backed with pastel blue, and edged on the bottom with shredded green. Among the green nestled a few construction paper cut-outs of eggs.

Mikhail stood, taking in the precision of the green fringe, when someone addressed him from the right side. "Hello?"

It was her. Lucky break?

"Hey, I…" *memorized your brochure? Came to volunteer for the sole purpose of asking you out?* "met you at John's Punkstraviganza. I… You gave me a pamphlet and told me I better be here."

"Oh." She looked through him, her elbows out to the side and hanging, her hands folded around little stacks of white cut-out letters. Her mind went searching.

"Sorry I didn't come last Wednesday."

"Yeah…" She moved around him, "Here. Just let me set these down." She set the letters on the floor in front of the bulletin board, navigated around him as he swung his upper body and his gaze after her.

She straightened back up and he tried again. "I came to volunteer. To, uh, 'do what only I can do.'" He was shocked by his own nerdiness; his eyes popped open and he gave her a half-mouthed smile. Gaby noticed the smile, and the direct quote of her own brochure was not lost on her. Digging her hands into the back pockets of her jeans, she smiled back.

Gaby and Mikhail, having been properly introduced to one another—and Gaby under the misconception that Mikhail was *way into* the helping-the-homeless thing—spent the late afternoon working on the Easter-themed billboard. Mikhail decorated the paper eggs with crayons, Gaby stapled the white letters into a configuration that announced an Easter meal that needed donations.

Mikhail, if we be fair, was interested in a whole lot of causes, homelessness and hungry people not being the least of these. He showed at the community center to get the girl but he contemplated social issues mostly in the shelter of his own room and during particularly drowsy chemistry lectures. He adopted issues only in his aversion to meat, loose asceticism (no smoking, no drinking, loosely constructed celibacy), and in his closet-hobby of burying roadkill. But his heart was deep enough, his hands as strong and able as his feet were unable to carry him out to the public without a little persuasion.

Gaby was happy to provide persuasion.

The two looked sideways at each other more than once while Gaby toured Mikhail around the community center quarters. Kitchen, dining room, a few random rooms with couches, folding chairs and tables, that were sometimes loaned out for meetings and used for storage of random donations; floor-to-ceiling food in the pantry. She took him in to the fridge, opened the janitor's closet, walked with him right into the men's restroom, as if he had no idea where a urinal might be.

The front door swung shut with a little thud and clack as Mikhail left for the evening, his hands full of papers Gaby had stuffed into them. He had begged off for dinnertime at home, promised to return the following Wednesday. He didn't glance back at her, inhibited by the desire not to appear over-eager.

But she was waiting with an unsure smile, should he turn. Gaby stood in the middle of the lobby facing the door, hands on hips, and sighing, biting her bottom lip.

βͨ ʘσ

Mikhail returned the following Wednesday and Gaby invited him to the Easter meal. He barely dodged Nadine's protests when he excused himself from their two-man family Easter dinner to work at the community center. Annie and Melodie joined them for the meal, slicing ham (Mikhail skirting this task), scooping steaming casseroles and cooling, marshmallow-studded ambrosia, thwacking down rolls, serving up coffee, water, sherbet punch.

The less-fortunate and lonely of Butter were lined up at brown, Formica folding tables neatly draped with paper tablecloths, set with mismatched pastel colored paper cups, plastic silverware, Styrofoam plates. Jaunty saxophone music piped in, quiet under the din of meshed murmurs. Chairs screeched against linoleum, feet shuffled back and forth from the kitchen window, mouths were silenced by green bean casserole. The room was warm with lots of cooking and lots of bodies, stuffy with the smells of mingling foods: cheeses, creams, cooked mayonnaise, breads, soggy vegetables, salty ham.

Mikhail was handed a pan of cheesy potatoes and told to offer seconds around. He made his way to the corner, eating up time, and stood still at the end of a table, the pan resting on his copious belt buckle. He watched people eat, waited for someone's bent posture to straighten up and ask for more potatoes. His shoulders rose and fell.

"You a meal-service virgin?" Melodie was standing at the end of the table next to him. She balanced a coffee pot in her left hand, with a tray of ham propped against her right hip. She looked at him with her head cocked, but her body still hovering over the table of eaters.

"Yeah. I…"

"Hey, don't sweat it. I was just staring at the table and sighing, myself." Mikhail dropped his chest forward and looked grateful. "I've done a few of these meals with Gaby, ya' know, but I'm still not used to them. She does this like every day. It's her thing." Mikhail looked like he wanted to say something but it hurt his head. "Yeah, she drags me along. And her sister too. That's her," pointing with the coffee pot. "Annie."

Mikhail looked in the direction, spotted Gaby around her sister, a plate of food on each hand, maneuvering around chair backs with her hips. She set the plates down in the center of a table, bending over two people. Then she placed a slender hand lightly on the shoulder of one of them, leaned in toward them, answered a question with a smile. She took off again for the kitchen window, sneakers squeaking on her pivot.

Mikhail dropped his gaze back on Melodie. "I like it, though. It's interesting. I'm just not… not real outgoing."

"What you got there?" A man not two feet from Mikhail's cheesy potatoes gestured at it with his spoon.

"Um. Well, looks like cheese and potatoes. A casserole."

"I'll take some."

"Great." Mikhail dug at the corner of the potatoes with a slotted spoon, plopped them next to ham skin on the man's plate. "Enjoy."

"I most certainly will." The man looked Mikhail squarely in the face, his eyes twinkling and his cheeks tightening; which Mikhail took to be a smile buried underneath his liberal mustache. "Hey, Ms. Green Shirt," he called to the woman across the table from him and gestured again with his spoon, which was this time filled with cheesy potatoes. "Do you want some potato casserole?"

Ms. Green Shirt looked up at him and then at Mikhail. "Sure," lifting a plate in Mikhail's direction. "Sure do appreciate it." Mikhail spooned out more potatoes.

The man with the mustache leaned in toward Mikhail a bit, "Psst!" and crooked his finger for him to come in close. Mikhail leaned in and the man softly said, "Now why don't you try? Your lips work, don't they? Friendly is catching."

Melodie snickered and walked away.

ᕯ   ᕘ

Nadine re-scheduled their Easter dinner for late evening and informed Mikhail that she appreciated his bleeding heart and all, but he had better be home by seven. She rattled and cut, shook and stirred over the stove all afternoon, making as much noise as one woman can make when filling a silent house. Children ran around the yard next door, a neighbor cut their grass ("On Easter Sunday!" Nadine exclaimed), but inside the house was all thick smells, warmth, and Nadine's thin arms flailing, spastic, octopus-like. It was a warm Easter. Nadine perspired with the heat of the oven, furrowed her brow at lumpy gravy until it was smooth, fidgeted her hands in her apron when drying them, bumped against things and deflected off them without bending at the waist or altering her rigid posture.

At six-thirty, the meal refusing to be fussed over any more, Nadine sat gingerly in the family room chair closest to the kitchen. Her mind wandered across years as a single mother of a boy who was now a young man. She imagined she was a watchdog-mom, a be-prepared mom. She had always tried to pre-empt Mikhail's questions and his needs. After all, she was all he had; the feminine and the masculine and the exhausted.

Nadine dug her elbow into the arm of the chair, cradled her chin in her folded hand, and sat there, chin slightly higher than was natural for most people, staring across the fastidious and polished-wood room, out the window which abutted the front door.

Nadine thought about Mikhail, about night times when he mumbled something to her as he slid sideways out the front door. About the pile of dark clothes—always dark—piled on the chair in his room and smelling of smoke, of body odor. About the X's on his hands, drawn in marker (*Pre-cursors to tattoos?* she wondered). About the lack of friends invited for dinner or hanging out in his room, or parking noisily in the driveway waiting to take him somewhere and leaving oil puddles on the cement. The few boys that did stop struck her as acquaintances.

She assured herself that this was a stage, that at least his pants didn't hang so low she could see his underwear. She let herself dream of what he might become; a doctor, a lawyer, an engineer, a veterinarian. A vet. That's what she thought he really might become, if he kept up his grades. And yet, despite the fact that she secretly knew he was still burying dead animals and would never let her kill even a spider in the house, she couldn't help but notice the absence of pets, no ambition to take horse-riding lessons, no mention of a future career.

When Mikhail was seven, Nadine coaxed him into the car with a few hard suitcases, a picnic basket brimming with sandwiches and cookies and a Thermos of lemonade. She climbed in the driver's seat, her sunglasses perched on her forehead, a sarong tied around the waist of her bathing suit, and aimed the nose of the car at a distant Great Lakes beach. His smile was longsuffering. She rolled her window down, he emulated her, and they sang along to oldies stations all afternoon. They stopped for lunch at a rest area picnic table, where Mikhail was stung by a bee. But he was fine. A detour to the drug store and they were on the road again, wind in their hair, crooning down the highway.

Nadine sunk in to a Nadine-shaped dent in the sand, on her towel, and smiled up at the sun. She was hot, and pulled herself up on her elbows to flip over to her stomach. The book that she propped open on her chest slid off to the side. She looked around a moment to check on Mikhail, craning her neck to peer around the many sun-worshippers and their children. She did not see him. She straightened her spine and lifted her chin and her eyebrows. She stood up and dusted her backside with the palms of her hands, looked back at the towel to make sure anything valuable was hidden in her beach bag.

She paced a few feet, observed a group of kids gathered nearby. She drew closer. They were playing in singles and doubles and triads, building sand castles, digging large holes. A dad let himself be buried in the sand. With red face and smile, he was threatening in a mock-booming voice, "When I get out of here, which won't be long, I'm GOING TO *GET YOU!*" The children closest in proximity squealed with delight. The others rubber-necked the commotion. A few girls on the crowd fringe perched in gallinaceous disinterest. They were tightly flocked, hands to their faces in different postures, leaning in to form a crested cylinder and whispering. Their gazes fell elsewhere.

Nadine followed their gazes to Mikhail, although she figured that their whispering was not meant for Mikhail when she saw the boy with him. Mikhail was on his knees, sandy from head to foot. His pail and shovel lay abandoned next to him, a castle and moat only partially complete and partially dissolved in the encroaching tide. The other boy also kneeled in the sand, same sandy, tan, boy's body, same page haircut, same innocent, full face. But where Mikhail had a weedy, right forearm and hand, the other little boy had nothing. His stump was red scar tissue, grooved in tight, red lines on his baby skin. The boy looked down at this stump, his elbow balanced on his knee, the stump out in front of him. Mikhail held the stump gently in both of his hands, examining it. Both boys wore the same expression: interested, curious.

As the memory faded, Nadine shifted in her chair and cleared her throat. Still no Mikhail. She worried the dinner was getting cold.

When Nadine was seven years old, she accumulated a chest full of her mother's and aunt's old clothes, jewelry, make-up. She believed that she was a French Princess mistakenly deposited on American shores and saved from the orphan life by an eager, young couple (her parents). As such, she smuggled an evening dress, heels, a tiara, and a pocketbook of makeup and rings to school during the long, mostly uneventful winter of second grade. Before the school day, she detoured between bus and classroom to convene with four other orphaned princesses (of various countries) in the lavatory. After a few minutes of nervous, hushed conversation, it came down to this: one of the princesses forgot her fancy attire; one was too frightened to sneak it in her bag past her mom; one—in all her excitement—left her bag on the bus; and the last one was chickening out right then and there.

Nadine reasoned that she was too smart to reveal her true identity to the classroom and Ms. McNeil without her friends. However, a bag full of girlish delights was a bag full of girlish delights. So they all stood by, on tip-toes in front of the mirror, as Nadine applied pink rouge, red lipstick, greenish eye shadow, pulled her hair back with "pearl-encrusted barrettes" (as she explained to her cooing friends), and donned a gold necklace. This is as far as she would go, but didn't she look extravagantly beautiful?

The girls slunk tardy into class in single file, Nadine at the end of the line with head dropped and avoiding eye contact with Ms. McNeil. Ms. McNeil paused in her lesson, asked them where they had been, gave them a brief lecture while they took their seats, and wrote all five of their names on the blackboard. She continued ticking away at sums. She asked a question of the classroom, set down her chalk, dusted her hands together, looked around at the eagerly raised hands.

Nadine felt Ms. McNeil's gaze snag on her own face, high with bright smile. "Nadine Duval!" Ms. McNeil exclaimed, her mouth dropping into a horrified O, her body stiff with her hands still together in front of her. Nadine felt a rush of shame engulf her; she too stiffened, her hand still in the air, her ankles still crossed beneath her desk, her eyes wide.

"Nadine!" Ms. McNeil regained her composure. "You march right back to the restroom and wash your face this instant!"

Nadine felt the burn of sixty-two eyes on her. She sunk into a ball, her hands on her lap. "But... but Ms. McNeil!" she protested.

"Nadine, I don't want to hear it. You do as you're told."

"But, I'm a... a..." Nadine's lower lip began to tremble. She rushed out of the room and ran down the hall (another demerit) before throwing herself into the restroom door and standing in front of the toilet in a quiet stall, whimpering, her make-up streaked across her face and down her arm in bright pinks. She was found there, in the stall, by Ms. McNeil (while the other students had snack time) and was instructed—Ms. McNeil's arms folded, her legs set wide—to go straight to the principal's office, her mother was on the way.

At the Aleksandr household, the older Nadine sat in reverie while a glint of sunlight off an approaching car flashed through a front window and momentarily highlighted her gold wedding ring, her blue-veined hands. She thought about her princess fiasco, how she was scolded, grounded, and vigorously scrubbed from hairline to chin. All the regular acquiescence, and it still took weeks of servitude before she drew the best picture of "Christmastime" and had her coloring placed on the bulletin board in the hall, outside the classroom for the whole school to see.

The front door opened and Mikhail slid inside, only cracking it enough for the width of his body, belt buckle to barely-there butt. Nadine looked in his direction but her eyes glazed over; she had not seen him approach through the window. "Hey, Mom."

She looked over at the clock on the mantelpiece. "It's seven-ten Mikhail. Dinner's been ready for twenty minutes."

"Sorry, Mom. It took longer than I thought to clean up."

"To clean up! Why don't you try taking longer than you thought cleaning your room?" She pulled her chin back with the exclamation.

"I said I'm sorry." He made his way to her chair, bent and kissed her on the cheek. "Happy Easter."

"Well something's cheering you up, today." This was usually enough for her, but she noticed just then a twitch in the vicinity of her heart. She rose from the chair, led the way to the kitchen.

"Smells good."

"There's asparagus, pie, lamb…"

"Mom, you know I won't eat it."

"Just this once, Mikhail. It's Easter Sunday. You're so scrawny! Look at you." She turned toward him as they approached the stove, grabbed his wrist in the circling of her forefinger and thumb, held it up for them both to see.

He raised his eyebrows at it. "Yep, too skinny Mom. Just like you," and poked her in the side with his finger. She skirted the poke, smiled at him, and swatted him limply with a dish towel. "And *you* eat lamb! Seems like there's nothing can be done for me. Genetics win."

"Genetics!" Nadine raised her eyebrows at the bowl of mint sauce she was carrying to the buffet. "Genetics."

CS &

The day that little Mikhail came home accompanied by the hairy woodsman, Nadine rushed to her room and shut the door as soon as John left.

She pulled her jewelry box away from the back of the dresser where it abutted the wall and—with a glance at the locked doorknob—turned it around. She pushed against a segment of the wood detailing and it popped back out at her, just a centimeter or two extra. How long had it been since she last opened this compartment? She had to give the panel a little tug as she removed it and it was followed by a small drawer. She pulled the whole thing out and tipped it over her open palm.

What a strange visitation. She could have sworn she knew that woodsy stranger. What did he say his name was? John? That certainly didn't ring any bells. How many Johns lived in this town, anyway? Dotted history? And what a crazy story, too. Mikhail off in the woods (he didn't mention burying animals, but she figured that was sensitive information), there's the sudden apparition of a back-woods man and a loud noise that shakes the ground and Mikhail is knocked unconscious by a rogue tree! Then the man takes him to his house and his wife takes care of Mikhail until he can tell them where he lives and walk on his own. Meanwhile, Nadine was sitting at home watching the TV news reports of the residential gas explosion that had shook the earth, imaging Mikhail caught in the blast. Mikhail said there was porridge (porridge!) and cold water and that the wife was a great storyteller.

"Well, I'm the real storyteller, but my wife has quite the knack for retelling a yarn."

There was something about what he said, it seemed suddenly mysterious but perhaps it was really just polite, random conversation. Nadine sent him on his way with the urgent intention of running upstairs to the jewelry box and the secret compartment. Now she held the locket in her hand and remembered what Tania said. "It should stay in the family. But it belongs somewhere else, too. Time will tell."

CHAPTER 4
ZYGOTES

Annie was short for Anibel, which she never *ever* went by. Anibel and Gabrielle were fraternal twins, born on the same day, to the same mother, in the same master bed. They shared the same small, dark, place, the same amniotic fluid, entangled their limbs for nine months straight. And they had been making up for it ever since.

Even on the day they were born, Stellar—her long, hippie hair slicked with sweat, her boobs swollen over her swollen stomach—looked at Adam with his arms full of one dark, naked bundle, one light, naked bundle, cocked her head to the side, squinted her eyes at him to make sure, and practically yelled, "Honey! Are they *both* mine? Aren't they *twins?*" She birthed them at home, with a midwife, and there were no other purpley-tinged newborns to be found in their house. It was a legendary story, one that the aunts and uncles and grandparents, old family friends, and Adam too verified the moral of: the two little girls were stubbornly independent from the beginning.

They asserted their independent identities "every day," Stellar claimed. They breast-fed differently, cried differently, smiled differently. Gabrielle had a head of curly, dark hair, Anibel had a fuzzy baldness for the best part of a year. Anibel crawled at four months, Gabrielle never did crawl; just walked long before Anibel. Anibel sucked her thumb, a pacifier, anything near her mouth; Gabrielle made too much noise to stick anything in hers.

By kindergarten, the girls never liked the same foods, never wanted the same clothes, even had their own circle of distinct playmates. In first grade, Gabrielle asked to take piano and drawing lessons. Anibel joined the junior soccer team. Stellar observed to her friends, "They're like night and day."

In second grade, Gabrielle and Anibel marched off the school bus one day, accosted Stellar on the way up the driveway, where she was ready to greet them. They stood, hands on their hips, feet planted, faces upturned at hers. They informed her they had altered their names. Theirs, they claimed, were much too alike. They thought it over, talked it out amongst themselves and made an executive decision: from now on they would be Gaby and Annie, and they wouldn't settle otherwise.

After a few months of receiving awkward silence when Stellar or Adam (or an unsuspecting relative or neighbor) referred to one of them by their *old* names, everyone forgot to call them their given names anymore. Gaby and Annie it was. Modern parents were such pushovers.

In third grade, Gaby and Annie held a mini-conference at the dinner table with their parents. This time they wanted separate rooms. "Annie's such a slob," argued Gaby. "Gaby likes the color *brown*!" argued Annie. And, they both argued, the family didn't need both a den *and* an office. Stellar and Adam agreed amongst themselves that they were now a little overdue for more kids. They whispered to each other in the night of deliberation, "Our hands are full enough as it is." "What goofs, the two of them, *demanding* their own names, and now their own rooms!" "Like very cute little negotiators."

The next day Gaby and Annie were informed that one of them could move into the upstairs office. Arrangements would be made for the computer and bookshelves to retire to the den that very weekend. But that night—a Wednesday—Gaby slept in a sleeping bag on the office floor, and kept it up Thursday and Friday. Never mind that she at first couldn't fall asleep, Annie's breathing absent from the darkness.

Within a year Gaby convinced Adam to help her paint her new room brown. The two gallons of paint she received as a special-request Christmas gift from her grandmother. In retaliation, Annie—as a birthday gift—had hers painted fuchsia.

"Those girls!" is how everyone responded.

Annie liked fuchsia, even though it was clearly not the color for a soccer player, or a lacrosse player, or a wrestler (especially one who had to petition the school with her mother to be let on the all-boys team). On the lacrosse field (in high school), she could be seen running hard down the field with lacrosse stick, compact and sinewy, an intimidating look on her face (well, she was trying hard anyhow, around her classic cuteness), sweat in her eyes focused fiercely on the game, her short, blonde bob pulled high into two little pigtails, tied off with fuchsia ribbons, fuchsia shoelaces in her regulation black cleats. Her nickname: Pinkie, to which she responded, "A color does not de*fine* me," arms crossed.

One wintry day of Annie's junior year of high school, she came home splotchy-cheeked, sniffly-nosed, mascara running down her face and smudged under her eyes.

"Jeez!" Gaby said on encountering her in the upstairs hall. "What happened to you?"

"Nothing." Annie slumped into the bathroom, ripped a yard of toilet paper off the roll, sank down onto the toilet lid.

"Nothing, my butt cheek!" Gaby kneeled on the linoleum in front of Annie. "You've got mascara all over your face, your…" she ran her thumb on Annie's cheek. "You don't wear mascara!"

"I know," Annie sniffled. "I just…" her face puckered into a frown, her eyes squinted, she let out a sob. Gaby held her.

"Girls, what's going on in here?" Stellar thudded barefoot into the bathroom, slipped quickly from curious into somber upon encountering the scene at the toilet, awkwardly imposed herself into the small area, and held both her girls in her large embrace until Annie was ready to talk.

Annie dictated the day's events from atop the porcelain throne, toilet paper handy beside her, Gaby and Stellar sitting cross-legged with their backs against the bathroom counter, wet mascara wiped across Gaby's T-shirt.

Ashley and Jasmine were players on the lacrosse team. MVPs. Their mothers were members of the PTA and Ashley and Jasmine dominated student government. Their fathers practiced in the same medical office. Ashley and Jasmine had been in Annie's third grade class, where the three were inseparable. When they re-united in a crisscrossing junior high schedule, the three re-fastened the Velcro. In high school, a large student body and plenty of extracurriculars helped them each spread their leaves, branching into the complex social system that is popularity.

Every year (as everyone who was anyone at Butter High knew), Ashley's and Jasmine's families took off a week from school in the late spring (having super-involved parents to negotiate around tests, assignments, too many absences, or maybe just bully the vice principal) and headed up north. Year after year, they rented the same two cabins, side-by-side, had the same evening barbecues, used the same rent-a-boat company to take all the kids out tubing. The kids were each permitted to bring a friend to stave off their pre-teen and then, teenage, boredom. The last five years, Annie went along, a guest of both Ashley and Jasmine.

This year, Annie was informed, the car space filled too quickly. Between all the brothers and sisters, their friends, and Susie and Rachel…

"Susie and Rachel?" Annie gaped.

"Yeah," unified. Ashley and Jasmine stood, shifting about uncomfortably (for this is the time when battle lines are drawn), shoulder-to-shoulder, trapping Annie up against her locker. Annie gripped her books to her chest.

"Susie Whiteman?" looking for a new tactic. "Can't I come along too? It'd be us and Susie. The old foursome. The four amigos. We could…"

"The four *amigos*?" Ashley and Jasmine raised their eyebrows at each other.

"What about Rachel?" Ashley asked. Jasmine nodded her head emphatically.

"Rachel who? Rachel *Sandborne*?"

"Yeah," in unison again. "Who else?" Jasmine added.

"But you hardly even know Rachel Sandborne. She's totally new!" Annie was losing ground, shifting in dangerous sands. "And you said she dressed like a slut!"

That would not get around! "Annie, we're just trying to be *nice* to the new girl. We've talked to her. She's cool, you know." And that was the legitimate end of the conversation. Annie understood; the new girl was throwing elbows up the social ladder and those at the top were re-organizing. Ashley and Jasmine preceded Annie to the conclusion that today's requirement was to make friends with her quick or face possible extinction. Sacrifices had to be made.

Annie managed a, "That stinks, you guys," but she knew the school buzz would now declaim: Ashley and Jasmine Reach Out to Poor New Girl! Annie Rejects New Girl, Trying to Steal Her Place from Annual Vacation!

Whispers anticipated Annie down the school halls and she was shot more than one ill glance. She was quickly ousted from the lunch table ("There's just no more *room* today!"), dethroned from her seat in math ("He just sat down before I could say anything!"), forced to ride the school bus ("Paul really needed a ride home today because…"). Not that anyone believed the stories, but no one was willing to throw themselves under a bus for Annie, as it were.

Thus, the mascara-streaked face.

After more hugging and sympathetic nods, Gaby said, "Wait a sec. That doesn't explain why you're wearing mascara."

"I ditched my last period, all right? *By myself*," (invoking more sympathy in case Stellar was ready to ground her on that last confession). "I was bored, in the bathroom, and found some mascara at the bottom of my bag." She shrugged.

Annie was permitted to stay at home the next day, but she went to school anyhow. She slumped home for weeks looking beat, her clothes in disarray, her eyes hollow. Gaby nonchalantly offered her a ride home every day, with her and Mikhail and Melodie. Annie accepted when she wasn't staying for sports. And in the spring, Annie was suddenly whisked away for a long weekend to the world's largest roller coaster park by Stellar and Adam.

C3   80

Annie slouched into her room, hair a disaster (felt like hay), catsup stain on her T-shirt, and bags under her eyes. She was exhausted and it was very late. She tripped across her dark room in the shadows cast by the half-moon and clicked on her desk lamp before dropping her duffle bag in the middle of the floor and sitting down in the chair. She thumped her elbows on the desk and buried her face in her hands, rubbing at her eyes.

She needed to get ready for bed: brush her teeth, wash her face. What she really needed was a shower to wash away all the French fries and other people's perspiration. One thing she never liked about roller coasters was sitting on those plastic-y seats and grabbing those metal bars and buckling up in those nylon belts... which thousands of people had nestled into, sneezed on, and—let's face it—vomited on as well. And now, with the smell of axle grease and onion rings in her hair, she was going to slide into some PJs and contaminate her bedding just so she could go to sleep.

She was drifting off just now, with her cheekbones rammed into her palms. Was she drooling? Gross.

She forced herself up out of the chair and across the room to her dresser, where she picked up last night's pajamas off their dangling place on top. The PJ bottoms caught on something and she reached up to snag it off. The little box came with them, sliding to the front of the dresser before Annie caught it. Absentmindedly, she set it on the bed and after changing, flopped down nearly on top of it. She reached over and laid an arm on it, drawing it close to her.

She groped her hand over the top, without looking, and lifted the lid back on its hinge. The box ticked and then whirred quietly before a tinkling song began to play. Annie loved music boxes. She loved this music box the most. She'd bought it at a street fair; painted with intricate scenes of princesses and knights and woods and trolls and fairies, with such a simple tune, lilting, alluring, and exotic. Perfectly crafted so that all the notes sounded just when they were supposed to, the tiny, flat arms pinging back over the knobs on the brass cylinder as it moved round and round as the spring released its energy.

She liked it anyhow, but then she took it in for fourth grade show-and-tell and Mrs. Sullivan got a puzzling look when she started up the music. When the last, uneven notes died out, Mrs. Sullivan gathered the class to the story corner, seated them on the rug surrounded with bins of paperbacks, and told them she knew that song. The song was really a story. And lucky for them, she knew the story.

"Once upon a time there was a very beautiful queen with long, shining hair the color of polished copper. She was the queen, but there was no king, for she inherited the throne as the very last in a long line of kings and queens and their children and brothers and sisters. She was alone, and she was a strong ruler, all by herself, because she had a long history of faith and hope and love. What she did not have was a future.

"It was a time of various wars and constant warfare, and many times her kingdom came under attack from one way or another. One of these times, The Queen was forced to abandon her kingdom, leaving it under the uncertain care of her advisors and a loyal, look-a-like maiden, while she ventured across countries and through other wars to the remotest place you could imagine, seeking a lost treasure of the kingdom and then seeking council to understand it.

"She survived her dangerous journey, and returned to her castle in the Branderby Wood with the treasure—a potently magical seed—inside a pouch she wore around her alabaster neck. But she returned with something more dangerous than the monsters and madmen that she had faced along the way: she had fallen in love with an unreachable man.

"Sure, he loved her, and sure, the kingdom scrolls told of days forever ago when women and angels were together and bore children strong of limb and mind. But those were days long past, and angels must move in spheres invisible and do the bidding of God, not bend to the beauty of women. The Angel assessed the treasure. He disappeared in a tidal crash of sand and an overwhelming heat and a look of agony. In The Queen's confusion, she searched for his body there in the stifling heat before she realized that it was magic and it might destroy her. Even her, wisest and strongest of rulers, kindest and most shrewd (well, usually. But what was shrewdness to love?)"

Mrs. Sullivan stopped here and looked at the class, their faces upturned and mostly blank. She would have to bring it down a notch.

"When The Queen returned to a kingdom under siege, she used the treasure to save it. No one knows precisely how, since magic is by nature mysterious, but all witnesses attested the turn came when the lead Demoni fell inexplicably dead from his dark horse. Near the end of the determining battle, a Demoni struck The Queen in her upper arm, his weapon sliced the leather pouch in which the seed lay nestled, cleaved first through the leather, then the treasure—as small as the moon hidden on a baby's smallest fingernail—splitting it right down the middle into two pieces, and then piercing The Queen's white flesh.

"The queen mended, and took the broken seed; supervised her most trusted and skilled jeweler to encapsulate one half inside a strange locket emblazoned with the letter "A" and the other half deep inside a gem of rarest ruby which was then set in a golden ring. Both pieces of jewelry were immoderately ornate, swirled with curlicues, and encrusted with chips of a rainbow of gemstones and pearls. She placed the locket away in a secret hiding place in her castle, and placed the ring on her slender finger, on the finger from which blood flows straight to the heart, and she went about the business of ruling the kingdom.

"Many, many times men and knights and kings and rulers of other sorts came from other far-away places and sought to marry The Queen. Advisors advised her to marry, and soon. Some advisors advised her to marry *them*, and soon. It was entirely possible that the factions caused by her dying and leaving no apparent heir would break the kingdom, would bring war and this time from the inside. A queen was a servant to her kingdom. Forget whether she liked any of the suitors. Choose wisely.

"But The Queen asked herself this: what is love? She searched the scrolls in the kingdom library, sought the council of the sages, and of one sage in particular. Love perseveres, he said. Love hopes. Love is patient. And, she heard him say, love is not afraid."

Annie smiled to herself as she remembered the midget uprising the open-ended ending had caused in her fourth-grade class. Now, in high school, modern stories were praised based upon their ambiguity, it seemed. The weirder, the better. Well, good for you, Mrs. Sullivan.

And as the last notes sounded their tentative pings, Annie snored.

CHAPTER 5
TWO TO TANGO
ℬ   ℭ

Butter High spread out on a hill overlooking the town of Butter. It was, in fact, at the peak of the legendary Butter family hill. On the crisp, clear, chilly nights of fall it shone like a beacon, the football field lit up like Christmas, the cheers of the large crowds and the ring of the announcer's voice wafting down to the streets of Butter. On holidays, the kids of Butter filled the streets with parade floats, the clang of cymbals, the march of feet, the painted faces and fancy dresses of pageant. At 7:30 on weekday mornings and at 2:15 on weekday afternoons, traffic clogged the veins of Butter hill, creeping up and down, honey on a tablespoon.

Butter High was the hill around which the ants danced.

The buildings of the High were clean and extensive, the grounds green and manicured, the computer labs impressive. The morning and afternoon announcements broadcasted enthusiastically, the principal attended events with a smirk of pride. There were students on grounds from 5:00 AM to 10:00 PM for every type of suburban sport and club you could imagine. School pennants, award trophies, painted banners, club fliers, lined all the neatly swept and amply sunlit hallways.

This suburban mecca of social elite education nestled out on the fringes of urbanity where other suburbs touched the metro borders over lakes and around rivers, towns where each cracked jokes about the other's inhabitants driving tractors to school and cow tipping (which no one really did). For families to whom Butter Country Club wasn't enough of a social life, they could wander across these borders for various doses of reality in other more urbane suburbs and towns. If they were especially brave, they could even step into Detroit itself, into Greektown, into Motown, slip into the slums, the grit, the under-belly of American society along the alleys (with their doors locked and windows up, instructed not to look anyone in the eye), in the theaters and stadiums with the scalpers and hookers outside, hookers with their panties considered outer-wear below short skirts.

Like movie characters who spend their youth maturely longing to get out of it, to escape their suffocating or dysfunctional family or their backwater town, the misfits of Butter High hunched their shoulders against each other in the school hall corners, lined the chain-link fences around the perimeter in a cloud of smoke. They bummed cigarettes, wore black, toted skateboards to grind the stoops of local shops. This was their rebellion; waiting for adulthood like waiting for a jail break. But as anything glamorized, in reality they appeared as anything but movie characters. They were an anomaly to soccer moms, who spent lifetimes clawing for and hanging on to their gold necklaces with one charm for each baby, their knockoff purses, their cruises to Mexico.

These kids rebelled for rebellion's sake, jumped on various bandwagons to swim out of the main stream. Most of their causes grew out of their own selfishness, their own desire for uniqueness, and ultimately: fame. But these were the darkest corners of their motives. Many of them were also altruistic, lonely, restless-legged for the wide-open, foreign shores, different views of the same moon, and curious. Anything but mediocrity. Let's allow our hero and heroine all of the above in varying degrees.

Gaby, Mikhail, Annie and Melodie were all inmates of Butter High, all in the same year. The sole high school on the west side of Wallen County, the school district engulfed all of Butter Township out to a couple smaller dales and glens of otherwise unclaimed students. Three thousand was a really hefty number of hormonally-challenged people to police, guide, and train, and so outside of specials (built around interests like shop and computer design), cliques and bus routes, students could go unnoticed one to another for months or years at a time.

Once they met, Mikhail quickly fell into line with Gaby's cause: the homeless. He accompanied Gaby to her outings, assisted her with her projects, without conflict of heart. He made friends with those around her: the ladies at the community center, the classmates she gravitated to and orbited around, the yearbook and newspaper professors, Melodie, Annie, Stellar, Adam.

They exchanged phone calls, walked in to each other's front doors with only a brief knock and a "Hello!?", rode with each other every day to and from school. Gaby helped write Mikhail's papers, he tirelessly explained her math lessons to her. Gaby left Coke bottles of wildflowers for Mikhail by his mailbox, he fried her eggs when she got in late from the soup kitchen. They became a way of life for each other, a habit, special friends. They slowly unfurled their secrets, went beyond awkward silences, their roots mingling deep within the earth.

Mikhail became surer and surer of the lack of erotic interest from Gaby. But he secretly loved her, more and more with each day, as is the habit of heroes of the ilk of Mikhail: sensitive, deep, surrounded by powerful women, and easily melted by his lack of self-confidence.

CR   RO

Mikhail wandered into Violet Monkey, a record shop on the main stretch of Butter. Violet Monkey housed an extensive (and tightly packed) selection of new, underground material and dusty, old faves. It was equipped with three racks of great T-shirts (Johnny Cash, The Pixies, Violent Femmes, and Bob Marley) and a display case of not-for-sale merchandise: original Beatles, Jimi Hendrix, The Ramones. Over these Mikhail drooled (on multiple occasions, with and without accomplices) from behind the counter.

Mikhail buried his hands in the front pockets of his navy zip-up hoodie, adjusted his eyes to the dark, den-ness of the store. The light that filtered in through the glass doors accented a wall of flying dust with gold sunlight and then spilled on the first display. Everything else was dim, smelled of attics and old trunks and abused carpet. In a weak attempt to unify the smell, a stick of incense trailed its tendril of smoke, suffocating the store in sandalwood. A man stood behind the glass counter (covered with stickers and taped-on fliers and paper fragments: "My Other Ride is Your Mom" and "Goonies Never Say Die!"), arms shooting down straight in front of him and his palms pressed against the streaked top. He turned toward Mikhail as the hanging doorbell dinged and clattered against the glass. Then looked uninterested; adjusted his focus outside.

Mikhail dodged into the back of the shop, started leafing through thousands of filed vinyl albums, then slunk his way to the CD section. There was a proto-punk band, one of the forefathers of all later punk bands. Mikhail wanted their debut album, and he wanted it bad. He mentioned it in passing to both his mother and Gaby when his birthday approached, but they both later complained that the album was nowhere to be found. He figured they hadn't wandered in here.

After a thorough search of the vinyl titles in even the sections that were very unlikely, even outrageous, for the album to be filed in, he resolved himself to the CD section. Still nothing. So Mikhail wandered back out of the shop, grabbed a couple fliers from the table by the door, squinted in the sun. There in his hands: ads for the upcoming rock shows, punk shows, ska shows, and a flier for Violet Monkey. Near the bottom of the Violet Monkey flier: "We will order any album or CD for you, if we can find it, no matter how obscure."

That was it then. All Mikhail had to do was turn around, walk right up to the counter through the wall of golden dust particles and sandalwood smoke, and ask George or Joe or Mike or whomever to look for that album. He knew that they would probably be able to find it for him. But here's the thing: Mikhail stood there, stared down at the ad, shrugged his shoulders, and stuffed the fliers in his satchel. Then he walked down the road, mounted his bike, pedaled away toward Gaby's.

A ritual had begun. Mikhail repeated it maybe once a week, often more. He wandered into Violet Monkey, leafed through the obvious sections, then the not-so-obvious ones, in search of the holy grail of Mikhail's current album collection. He eventually gave up and pedaled home smelling of patchouli, mildew, lavender char.

After a few weeks, George or Joe or Mike or whomever— whose name actually *was* George—started keeping his eyes on Mikhail, afraid he was one of the kids lifting records from the shelves. George hovered over Mikhail during Mikhail's ritual, pretending to dust the shelves (an obvious cover and a laughing matter), to re-organize the alphabetical order, to check inventory of necessary albums. When George became convinced Mikhail was a harmless kid, George still continued his farce, peeking over Mikhail's shoulder to see where he was looking, what he was picking up. It became a game for George, and he would say to his friends later, "I think it's Pink Floyd's *The Wall*," and the next day, "No, no, no. I was way off. It's the early *The Clash* single. I just know it." And if George didn't have what he guessed Mikhail was looking for, George ordered it and stocked it; watched to see if the fish bit. George would even play the album in question afternoon after afternoon until Mikhail wandered in, watching the expression on Mikhail's face as he entered.

This became such a sport for George that it didn't really matter if he made a sale, as long as he *guessed it right*. Mikhail noticed George hanging around, figured he was creepy or lonely, and resented his shoulder being looked over. The one thing Mikhail never did: say a word in Violet Monkey.

Eight months into the silent dance of Mikhail and George, Gaby, Mikhail and Melodie were walking downtown Butter, looking for a place to eat, a used book for Gaby, and a place to loiter. Melodie turned as they passed Violet Monkey, pressed her nose to the window. "Hey, let's go in here!"

"No…" Mikhail stuttered.

"Yeah. It looks cool. C'mon." She opened the door with a loud tinkling and clanging of bell on glass. "Gaby?"

"Sure. C'mon Mikhail."

The store transformed. Smoke parted around waving, long, thin arms, the dimness scattered by lighted eyes and flashes of skin, the still of Violet Monkey went hiding: Gaby and Melodie chatted, cursed, yelled, laughed as they made their way from the front of the store slowly to the back.

Mikhail scooted away, made his way back to his usual section, dodging George's look of desire and disbelief. (George stayed firmly planted behind the counter this crazy afternoon.) Mikhail began leafing through the records, looking for the usual.

"What're you looking for?" Gaby's head appeared over his shoulder, her chin resting on his collar bone.

"A record. It's called *The Stooges*, by The Stooges. But they don't have it. I already looked."

"Oh." She reached out her arm around Mikhail to flip through the albums herself, then stepped beside him.

"What're you looking for?" he asked.

"Nothing particular. You know, just lookin'. This place is pretty cool, huh?" She pulled a few records at random to examine. "Anything you recommend?"

"Ummm. Give me a minute." Mikhail bit his lip and strode to the back of the shop, his eyes narrowed over the stacks. Gaby wandered the shop, making offhanded remarks to Melodie over The Beastie Boys.

Melodie purchased a T-shirt while Gaby fidgeted by the counter, leafing through the fliers scattered about. Then Melodie exited to the ice cream shop, yelled that she would meet Gaby and Mikhail there when they were done.

"Find anything for me yet?" Gaby popped into Mikhail's personal space again, barely touching his left thigh with her right hip.

"Yeah, I think I did." Mikhail weighed a record each in his two hands, then slid one back where it went in the stacks. "Here!" He turned and handed her a record.

"The Beatles. *Abbey Road*. You think I'll like it?" She took it in her hands, held it against her waist.

"Yup. But that's only the beginning."

"Okay, deal. But I have something for you too." She handed him a flier and pointed to the bottom. "Here. It says that you can order any album that our man George can find."

"Who's George?" Mikhail furrowed his brow down at the paper.

"Guy behind the counter. Just talked to him. Let's go order your CD or whatever."

And they did, just like that: approached the counter, made their request to George, filled out a form, and got a "great album!" from George. Mikhail stopped in daily, afterwards, to see if it had been found, then if it had been shipped, then if it had been received. When it was in his hands, he thanked

George and disappeared from Violet Monkey for two weeks before returning to browse the shop with Gaby. George's game was over.

СЗ   ВО

The growing Polejski family was a little tattered around the edges. Their white saltbox house stood just as tall, the siding just as shiny, the pavement just as straight, orderly, permanent, as the proverbial Jones' house. Inside, people had *pasts*, they had *memories*, they had *issues*. And while things inside their saltbox house were sometimes messy, sometimes loud, sometimes downright *musical*, they were also passionate, fertile, rich. Melodie was a real, live girl, splattered decidedly on a long line of plebian history. All the Polejskis—mom, dad, Melodie, two brothers and two sisters—were a stretch for Butter. And what should have been a breath of fresh air sometimes blew around the neighborhood making the neighbors' milk curdle in the porch bottle.

Melodie was born into rock 'n' roll, of the variety: sex, drugs and. She could have been any number of rockers' daughters, but a certain bassist (no one you'd know) named Dave Polejski accepted paternity and even married her bewitching, waif of a mother, Barbara. Melodie's earliest childhood years her parents spent in twin stupors: Dave on the road, buzzed with cocaine, a long line of women waiting to have I-couldn't-snag-the-lead-singer sex; Barbara, still a roadie, but often with baby on hip, mingling with various bands as they swooped through Nashville. She was smokin', in more ways than one, but she considered her daughter and abstained from the hard stuff.

A couple more kids later—any of which could have been, realistically, Dave's or some other band member's—and the sand of youth and rebellion settled. Dave left the road life with a fist full of money and bags under his eyes, admitted himself to a rehab center. When he was a determined clean, he turned his energies to family life, with force, fury and concentration. He went studio musician until he made enough dough to buy a house in the suburbs, back home in Detroit.

Melodie was five when the Polejskis uprooted what they had in Nashville, loaded up a maroon '75 wagon with mismatched luggage, a cherished lamp, an inherited medal-of-honor, and three kids (plus one on the way), and waved to the retreating lights of the city. A day and seventeen Coca Colas later, Dave pulled into his old Hamtramck house, hugged his parents with tears in his eyes, and introduced them to Barbara—a startling beauty at eight months pregnant—and his wide-eyed daughter and two sons. Grandma Polejski pushed her ear up against Barbara's belly, ushered them all in out of the snow, which the boys were busy throwing at each other in glittering, blue arcs through the blue air.

Melodie sent coloring book pages to her old friends, and postcards with the Ambassador Bridge, the Joe Louis Arena, on the front. But with kindergarten came all new friends and all new enemies, finger-painting, recess, counting bears. She lost her ache for a familiar life in the Dukes of Hazard, in the haze of second-hand smoke, became fiercely loyal to her grandparents, was sad when the family moved into a house of their own in the rapidly-developing Butter. A year later and Dave settled into lucrative work at the GM factory.

First grade in Butter's Saint Thomas' Catholic School for Children again brought with it all new friends and all new enemies, all new things to do. Melodie intuited that this was the settling place, the place to build a foundation, grow upward on it, sky's the limit. There were open places here, with few trees and close-clipped grass, no cracked yards, no crumbling porches, no honks and sirens and laughter outside her window. She could sometimes hear a couple walk by in the night, hear the crickets, the frogs singing steady in the distance, a train whistling far away. She would watch headlights arch around her room, watch them disappear, followed by the long darkness, the cicada-drone.

In bed at night, Melodie developed a sophisticated ritual based on a fear of monsters. Preparing for bed, she would first shut the closet door, making sure to push all her weight against it and double check its snugness. She would then open her bedroom door until the knob hit the wall, lining up her change jar and her record player—both of substantial weight—in the path her door would have to make to shut. On top of that, she placed her stuffed dog Buddy on the record player (and safely off the floor) to act as guard. Then she would turn on all four of her night lights (one on each wall), turn them off again, and on again. She would switch off her overhead light from outside the bedroom door, straining around the corner on tiptoe, in the light of the hallway. And since she would by no means actually touch the floor in the dark (or the under-the-bed monsters would grab her ankles and suck her under the bed for a late night snack), she climbed from dresser to desk to bed to get there and tuck herself under and pull up snugly to her ears more blankets than could be comfortable on a summer night.

After the ritual was performed one night and Melodie was peering suspiciously into a certain corner of her room, Dave's shadow darkened the doorway. He looked across the room, Melodie's fingertips and eyes peeking over the edge of her Care Bears sheets. *What if,* Melodie contemplated, *that shadow is not my dad, but an alien pretending to be my dad?* She decided she'd better play it safe.

"Melodie, sweetie, it's a little warm in here. You all right? You're all covered up with about a hundred blankets." Dave eyed the four night lights, the record player and change jar with Buddy at his post (this was all explained to him before). "You scared again?"

Melodie shook her head no, her eyes wide with terror.

"You are, I think." He crossed the room and sat at the foot of her bed.

She thought, *He crossed without being grabbed by the under-the-bed monster. He IS an alien!*

"You gonna be okay? You want to come have a mug of warm milk? Watch some TV with us for awhile?"

Melodie could take it no longer. Dave reached out to her and she jumped up out of the bed, screaming a steady blood-curdling note, ran across the floor, down the hallway, down the stairs, through the family room (where a bewildered Barbara-alien watched her run past), out the front door and down the street. She thought she might run to Hamtramck, but considered that Grandma and Grandpa might also be aliens.

Melodie hyperventilated a block later, passed out in the cool, dewy grass of the corner house, and was scooped up by Dave and Barbara and carried home. She slept that night quietly between her concerned parents and could forever remember what it was like to wake in the still of a shut-down house at night, her parents rising on either side of her like mountains black against an early dawn, protecting the valley, impenetrable.

CB BD

One fair fall day—all deep blue sky with small, particularly cumulus-y clouds and trees on fire with raucous colors and a fresh, smoky smell even in the suburbs—Mel's parents had a couple over for dinner. Mel happened to answer the loud ding-dong, and welcomed them into the home, wondering why her parents couldn't invite any *normal* people over to the house. All the soccer moms a Jonesing family could want, and Mel would bet Frances Bean's life that these two—wielding their ancient Corningware casserole dish and a peasant skirt looped with chain after chain belt—did not have a tree full of plastic bats or a "Happy Halloween" wreath anywhere on their premises.

The woman had a calm, breathy voice and she smiled her way into the foyer with a, "Hi, you must be Melodie?"

"I have no idea how you knew," sarcastically. "There's only like twenty of us."

Mercedes plowed ahead, as if teenage angst was a thing not to be bothered about. "Ah, but you're the oldest. And I remembered your name because it's such a wonderful one. Melodious. Melodie."

"My parents are really into music."

"So I hear." Mercedes looked piercingly at Melodie. "I also believe that we have a friend in common; Mikhail Aleksandr."

"You know Mikhail?"

"I see he doesn't go around telling stories about *us*. Yes, we have been friends since he was, oh, I don't know, about eight or nine. He first came to us unconscious. A tree branch fell on him in the woods by our house. Quite a story, really."

Just then Barbara swooped into the foyer from the stair landing and roped the woman into a hearty hug, ignoring the giant casserole and defying the rules of physics pertaining to it. Melodie, forcing apathy at the woman's effusive compliment, too-friendly knowledge of the family's history, and surprising revelations about Mikhail, wandered off toward the dinner table, spread full of hot food and burning candles and crested with vases of fall foliage.

During dinner, Barbara and Dave chatted incessantly to the guests—John and Mercedes—with whom they had so very much in common. All of them were artisans of some sort. Besides being particularly handy as a mechanic and in almost every other conceivable way, John was a storyteller. Mercedes was a "healer, mostly intuitive," she said. She also made things. Crafty, you might have called them, but Mel assumed her creations were quite different from the painted ceramics of her friend's parents' "crafty." Mercedes said last week she made a wind chime from salvaged silverware, pinecones, and crystals.

"Lovely!" Barbara exclaimed.

"Now what do you mean that you are a storyteller?" Dave asked, a bite of roast paused at the end of his fork.

"Well, I collect stories and I remember them, and sometimes I tell them. I come from a very long line of storytellers. People of oral tradition."

"Fascinating. Where do you collect these stories from?"

"Well, to be honest, that's a bit of a misconception. The storytellers a long time before me were really the ones generating the stories—if that's what you would call it—and I am more in the business of story*keeper*. I make sure they stay around. Sort of like each storytelling line has its own specialized library, and I am the sole librarian of this library."

"The sole librarian? That sounds serious."

"Again, a bit of a misconception. My son has been entrusted with the stories. He exasperates me by wanting to write them down for his kids. But Mercedes is very good at telling them. She knows every word and can relate them better than I do. And of course I have told them around, and so have the storytellers before me. The stories exist, even if I am gone and my son is gone, here and there: in a short story, in a song, and an immortal poem; in a *loose cannon*, to play with words a little." It took a moment, but then everyone over the age of eighteen laughed.

"Could you tell us one?" A gust of chilly wind came up under the barely open sash and swept across the table, snuffing out the tallest taper. Barbara jumped up to close the window and relit the candle.

"Of course. Let me think about it." And then dinner continued. The story that he told was so mesmerizing and perfect in its telling, that Melodie would never forget it.

"Storytellers are not always honest, you see.

"Sometimes storytellers lie, but it is truth. That is mostly okay. Sometimes storytellers tell the same old stories, but they make them a lie. This is dishonesty, or insincerity. For many years, the stories that I tell were held captive by a wicked storyteller. His story has become part of the stories I tell. This happens, sometimes, too.

"Tonight I tell you about a good storyteller. A benevolent storyteller who was wise beyond his years, and odd, besides.

"He was only a small lad, living deep and secluded in the Wood of Branderby. He knew that he was not like the other children that he met on his rare trips to the Wood's small villages, but it did not bother him much, because he was mostly his only companion. The birds and small game that chatted among the dense trunks and played peek-a-boo with him in the deep shadows were looking only for seeds and nuts and never minded or rumor mongered when the boy knew unaccountably what they twittered only amongst themselves. Sometimes they carried messages from sparrow to squirrel to hoot owl and the boy would learn that a hunter was soon to cross the mossy, gray brook he was drinking from or that his mother was looking for him to come home and wash up for unexpected supper guests.

"One cool day in the forest, the sun strong and golden where it filtered through the canopy, the boy bent over a bubbly stream, searching for smooth pebbles and talking to the minnows caught in the eddies. The boy squatted in a strong, golden ray of light. A tall and ominous man came striding through the gloomy parts of the forest. This man was especially good at being sneaky, and he strode almost silently through the shadows, nearly tripping on the boy as he paused at the base of a tree. He towered over the boy, stiff and straight, glaring down at him with his heavy eyes, but never lowering his chin, and the boy talked on to the wildlife, still searching for stones.

"The man's patience was sustained and sure when it served just him, and fiery and fierce when it did not. He stood a long time listening to the boy, whose patience was almost always simple and gentle, especially when talking to the animals or waiting in secret to find one. When the man heard enough, he spoke suddenly and startled the boy and the fish away.

"'Boy, I've been watching you,' he said. And he offered the boy something intriguing and frightening and wonderful. He asked the boy—the boy who spoke to fish and they answered—to come to his vast estate and he would apprentice him as a magician.

"Soon after, the boy went to live with the magician in his vast, dark, buildings and his curious corridors, with the few other servants.

"The boy lived and worked in the castle with the magician for a long time before he saw many of the secret rooms in the magician's winding sprawl. One particular day, he found himself in a still, small annex behind the magician's personal study. In this closet-sized room stood a cupboard, just taller than the boy's head, polished to a shine, decorated with impressive, delicate engraving, and filled with line after line of thin, narrow drawers with shining brass pulls. The man shooed the boy aside as he stepped around him and swished his long, graceful hand over the drawer fronts to where he casually pulled out a drawer and removed a phial. The phial—narrow and corked—looked common. It was not.

"Every drawer contained a story, bottled by magic and filed away for future use. Many of the stories were stolen, most of them from the same line of storytellers, and was kept captive by an incantation which made of them prisoners, here in the darkness of the smallest room of a maze of a castle at the edge of a mountainous gloom. The magician dropped a bit of the chosen liquid onto his own tongue before he told the boy the story he had wanted to tell. From then on, the phials haunted the boy, but more so the stories.

"It was not long after that the boy found an opportunity to slip unseen into the annex and stood staring at the magical cupboard. He reached out and down and his hand rested on the very last drawer in the last row. He opened it. He uncorked it carefully. And even more carefully he let a single drop of liquid fall to his outstretched tongue. It was cold. Sour. And when it absorbed into his muscle it hit his veins and he felt the cold spread through his body and quicken the speed of his heart. When it hit his brain, it frizzled and then fizzled, and he had the story there.

"The boy was surprised to realize that the story he had ingested was a story about him, the story of his being found in the woods and coming to live with the magician and apprentice with him. How odd. He carefully returned the phial, slid the drawer into place, and spent the rest of the day and night lying in bed, the covers up to his chin, telling himself the story and wondering about the rest of the stories.

"When he returned to the cupboard—it was quite some time before the magician took another trip away without him—he went to the drawer directly above the last one and tried one taste of that. This time the story was about the magician and about the time he hunted a white deer to saw off its antlers, which he powdered and used in a very powerful sleeping potion. The boy knew about that sleeping potion. How odd.

"Each time the boy saw his chance, he took it and drank from the next drawer up. The boy learned more and more about the magician through his own stories, unveiling his cruelty and despicability with each story. He was terrified to discover that the magician was a thief, a murderer, and a villain. The boy believed these things, because the magician was often terrible, and always threatening.

"As the boy grew into a young man he continued through the stories, keeping his knowledge and his infatuation buried deep inside him where the magician could not see, or so the boy hoped. He had moved far back in time, and long before the magician's own life, to where the stories sang of brightness and sadness, of heroes, love, and honor, and of all sorts of people living and thriving; getting lost in a gingerbread town; pulling a baby from a rushing river; making stew for a husband returning from war; joining forces with an unrequited love to keep the Demonis hedged outside of the kingdom.

"The boy—now a man, as we said—had become adept at moving in the shadows and being still in the corners of the magician's study and his laboratory, and even his room. The boy learned well what the magician taught him, but he also waited and watched when the magician was occupied elsewhere, augmenting his education with observation and what he heard in the twitterings of birds. He learned things this way that the magician would hardly have approved of. And it came about from his waiting and watching that they boy-man learned how to bottle a story, cork it, and file it away. And it came about from his listening to the animals and their rafter gossip that he learned how to make a story before it happened. And it came about that the boy-man knew what he had to do.

"The magician returned from a long and arduous trip to the green shores of Ireland (where he hunted faeries and tortured them for their secrets). He strode into his study and with the wave of his long, slender hand lit the hundred drippy stubs of candles set about. He peeled off his coat and its clinging ice and dropped it to the floor, sighing as he emerged into the warmth, the wet hem of his long robes slithering with him across the floor. He saw a phial out on his table. He looked at it curious, an insidious glint of anger in the icy calm of his iris. He uncorked the phial, he tipped it, and he took one small drop on his outstretched tongue. It was cold. And bitter. And in a moment of rare indiscipline, he shivered as it hit his veins.

"When the story wrapped around his brain there was only a moment of uncertainty before his eyes widened with terror and disbelief. The boy! That insignificant boy! The one who hugged obedience and acquiescence and skulked in the shadows like one of the mice! The magician had read his own demise in a story admirable for its simplicity. The boy did not even have to be the hero of his own story, in which the magician simply died suddenly and mysteriously as he stood in his own office. The magician clutched at his heart and the maid found him sprawled there when she came laden with wine, soup, and papers.

"The man-boy took only the peculiar cupboard full of drawers with shiny brass knobs when he left, a sparrow perched hopping on his shoulder and the cupboard tinkling as his wagon hit ruts in the road on his way home.

"Let it be said, that it never sat well with the boy—who became a great man and a wonderful storyteller—to have stolen the stories and tricked the magician, even if his thievery and treachery had produced a sort of goodness. It took a son and then a grandson before he would even let his story be told, and as for the cupboard and the phials: *that* he destroyed and sent piece-by-piece floating down the river. He kept the stories in the conventional way, talking them, singing them, and mulling them over on sleepless nights under full moons, and his children would become storytellers, and their children after them, and so on."

೧೫   ೮೦

The story was still echoing around Mel's head as she sat in class the following day. She was propped up behind a computer screen, being requisitely bored all the way through technology class. Her screen was at a DOS prompt and she stared right through the blinking green box, her hands sitting still and lightly resting on the off-white, gunked keyboard. Students moved about the computer lab, completing an assignment with the teacher peering at them, filling the room with a quiet murmur.

There came a quiet knock at the door, to Mel's back. She didn't respond, but she heard the door click open and saw a blur move by reflected on the black screen in front of her and stand at the teacher's desk. Hey, ho! Who was this tall, lean silhouette in her computer screen, standing just over her shoulder? She could hear his deep voice muffled in between all the other voices, almost lost in the other voices between them. It was deep, and quiet, too.

Then she saw the shape turn and make its way past her and reach out for the doorknob. There was something oddly familiar about the distorted boy in the reflection, whose few details sketched themselves together as he drew closer.

She turned to look over her left shoulder just as Mikhail disappeared around the open door. Mel flushed. This was a new development.

CHAPTER 6
COMMENCEMENT EXCERCISES
ℰℐ   ℭℛ

The festivities were coming to an end. Senior skip day. Exams. Last day of school. Prom. Ashley-Jasmine nominated Annie for prom queen and darned if she didn't win. She floated across the stage in a sequined, fuchsia gown, her short bob pulled into two pigtails; the undulations of the popular crowd an enigma to the bleacher-sitting onlookers wallowing in the wake of the rituals.

Later, Gaby, Annie, Mikhail, Melodie lay sprawled on the grass in the front yard, graduation caps resting on stomachs, graduation gowns wrinkling under their prostrate bodies, their paper-thinness dirtied, grass-stained. They all laid face-up, picking out shapes in the clouds.

"Mmm!" Melodie cleared a Starburst out of the way of her teeth. "Dragon, right there." She pointed straight up into the air, everyone else squinting and trying to follow the trajectory of her point eight thousand feet above their heads.

"Don't see it," said Mikhail.

"Right there?" Annie sounded skeptical, added her own arm and index finger to the air.

"Noooo. Closer to *right above our fucking heads!*"

"I got it," Gaby smiled and traced the sky as she detailed: "Head right there. Neck. Wings. Tail."

"Still don't see it." Mikhail.

"Never mind. It's already going." Melodie relinquished. "Now it looks like an old man." Melodie noticed that her arm happened to be just barely resting against Mikhail's arm. It tickled when he moved the slightest and she held her own arm very still in the itchy grass.

"Oh, oh oh! I've got God over here," Annie jabbed her finger into the sky.

"What the hell does God look like?" asked Melodie.

"You know, white guy with beard," she painted the cloud with her hand as she particularized, "mustache, two eyes, a nose. And a robe and sandals, but that's not important here. It's just His face. See?"

"Yeah, I kinda do." Mikhail cocked his head to the side.

"What else does God look like?" asked Melodie.

"A smile?" offered Annie.

"No way!" answered Melodie. "You're thinking of Santa Claus. I always picture God with a grim look on His face. Arms sorta crossed."

"I always picture Him sad," said Mikhail, searching the clouds for more shapes.

"Why the hell would God be sad?" asked Melodie. She chided herself for her brusqueness.

"The condition of the world, I guess."

"Then why doesn't He fix it, if He's *God* and it makes Him *sad?*"

Mikhail didn't answer. Gaby said, "I just picture God as Jesus. You know: brown, curly hair, brown beard, robe with sash, dirty feet, sandals. Like real placid."

"You see that in the clouds?" Melodie asked.

"No, but I do see a camel."

Annie giggled. "Where is it? One hump or two?"

"Right there, one hump." More pointing, more eyes searching as the sound of a warm car engine sidled near, car tires eating the dirt on cement and brakes gently squeaking.

"Well, my ride's here," said Annie. She and Gaby stood up. "See you at the graduation." She set her left cheek against Gaby's left cheek, they kissed the air beside each other's ears. "Good luck everybody. Don't trip." Annie saluted a wave to them, ran off to the car, the homecoming king behind the steering wheel ducking to watch her under the visor. She climbed in, they backed out.

"Yeah, whatever." Gaby and Melodie watched the car pull away, Melodie making a distasteful face at the receding hot rod. Mikhail lay still in the grass, looking up at the clouds, the blue sky, the brightness, the wind.

"Well, let's go." Gaby picked up her car keys from their discarded place on the lawn, wandered toward the driveway and the car.

"C'mon Mikhail, or you'll be biking to the ceremony," Gaby said over the top of the car.

"Wouldn't mind," he blinked at Gaby.

Melodie sang out, "Shotgun!"

 C3   80

Butter High School Valedictorian's Speech to the Class of 1997:

"Good afternoon class of 1997! [cheers, hoots], parents [a few lame claps], friends and family, teachers and administrators. [nodding to each, enunciating every phrase, leaving time for each to sink in].

"It's a beautiful day here in Butter. Blue skies [the wind thudding in the microphone with the sound of flags snapping in the background], sunshine, warm breeze. And all our loved ones gathered to witness this momentous occasion: the rite of passage we Americans acknowledge as the change from childhood to adulthood. When we walk onto this stage in a few minutes to receive our diploma, we will mount the stage children. When we walk down those stairs, right there [he pointed his robed arm], we will be men, women. Some of us will immediately strike out on our own. Others of us will successfully live off our parents for an entire college career [some laughter]. Some will leave Butter High with ties that last a lifetime. Others leave here unfettered, to blow forth on this windy globe and lay roots with other friends, other places.

"Which leads me to the point of my speech: no matter where you may go from this stage, make sure you leave yourself wide open. 'What does he mean?' you may be asking yourself. [*No shit*, thought Gaby. *Do I have the option of not knowing?*] What I mean is this: Many people move about life numb, paralyzed by fear, worry, bad self-esteem, or too much esteem over what others think of them. [He smirked at those silly people in the last group.] But to enjoy the great joys—the highest mountaintops—that this life has to offer us, we must OPEN OURSELVES UP to *EVERYTHING*. This includes the pains, the stresses, the disappointments, the disasters and the tears as well as the triumphs and the laughter. Without opening up to both, without descending into the dark, difficult valleys, we cannot truly experience joy. So OPEN UP class of 1997! [He raised both hands in a victory pose, fists clenched toward the audience.] LET LIFE IN!"

Near the rapidly approaching end of this short-and-sweet speech, Gaby heard Melodie cough, then Mikhail. She passed her fist over her mouth and coughed too, a code that meant, *We're in this together.* The class of 650, their parents, their siblings, their teachers, applauded, the band erupted into the first measures of a Souza march, a cloud rolled over the sun.

CB   BO

The bonfire snapped and licked high into the night sky. It was a clear, summer night, full of scopic views of faint stars, orange flame casting orange glows off young, tight, skin, wet grass wetting jeaned bottoms, bodies close together (exposed to a slight chill where they were not), empty plastic cups melting in the fire, clothes and hair smelling of ash. A few loners circled in close to the blaze, reached out sticks to the embers, blew them out, watched them smoke, started again the ritual. Otherwise, graduates grouped in circles, semi-circles, knots, avoiding silence with talking or looking away. Some circles passed around a water bottle, their breath smelling suspiciously of alcohol. A few couples sidled up on the tree line almost in the bushes, slowly leaning into one another, sliding hands in the dark, bodies tingling as they rolled around in the brush. Even further off, in the woods, the ones who were just twenty-four hours ago waiting to bust out of here were now only a bobbing red ember in the pitch black and the rustling of leaves. Freedom was still settling down and in.

Gaby was in the woods, had seated herself on the leaf-strewn ground, hugging her knees to her chest, her back against the rough bark of an old tree. Mikhail was nearby, offering some lucky kid a free lesson on the terminal effects of smoking. She could hear his voice rising and falling, the leaves whispering loudly overhead when the wind would drop through. She watched the fire through the trees, black and orange in a tango; movement and still, watched shadows dancing around it, the murmuring of distant voices.

Leaves crunched behind her, to her side, the feeling of warmth on her left arm, left cheek. Ben sat on the leaves beside her, drew his knees up to his chest in a perfect mirror. He nudged her with his upper arm. "You lonely?" he asked.

"No. Just looking." Gaby continued to look. She was acquainted enough with Ben to distinguish his voice. "You?"

"Just wanted to sit down. Saw you over here." He looked at her profile in the firelight and moonlight. She noticed he smelled like campfire, cigarette smoke, bottled cotton, skin, warmth. She remembered suddenly how straight and white his teeth were, how tan his hands.

Ben came to Butter halfway through the whole high school experience. In California, he must have been popular with his sun-streaked hair, his disarming smile, the essence of sea, lemons, the Santa Annas, salad greens, clear skies. His compactness; his pervading bleached-browness, from hair to skin to eyes, as if God used one paintbrush, one paint, on him. But in Butter, he was too foreign and too late: his look was too new, too magazine, too edgy; his coming before junior year was too post to save him. So he fell in with those kids longing for school to end. He skateboarded, dreamed of the surf, of surf-boarding, of orange trees and women with Latina hips. He wanted to rent an apartment in an adobe building within walking distance of a Jack in the Box and a second run theater. Take art classes, join a community drama troupe.

Ben didn't quite know why he was at the bonfire. He should be packing his bags, catch the first bus out in the morning. "You know where I'm going tomorrow?" His eyes and voice got lost somewhere way outside Butter.

"Where?"

"California." He turned his gaze to her again. "I'm going back home. I'm just gonna hop on a bus, ride it to the coast, look up my old friends and see if one of them can put me up for awhile."

"Then what?" Gaby entered the conversation.

"Get a job. Get a place."

"What kind?"

"What kind of job or place?"

"Job. And place, too, if you know."

Ben smiled at Gaby and she felt a drop of the stomach. "Anything, really. I just need money. Want to come by it honestly. Could work at a surf shop, or at a local theater."

"That sounds exotic." Gaby smiled at Ben.

"It's not. How about you? Where you going tomorrow?"

"Tomorrow?" She raised her eyebrows. "Well, I'm actually headed to Cedar Point. Going to eat a bunch of crappy food, namely a frozen banana, cheese fries, ice cream, and then go on all the tallest roller coasters until I get sick."

"Super. But then what?"

"Alford College. Not a big deal. I'll still live at home. I just want to study sociology, travel around to cities to volunteer and stuff."

"Oh yeah, I almost forgot. You're the homeless guru."

"What does that mean?" Her pupils shrunk, her hand retreated on the ground a half an inch.

"Nothing, nothing. I volunteered at a soup kitchen in California." Gaby quickly forgave him. They started talking the homeless, Democrats, Republicans, welfare, food sustainability, and by the time they got to vegetarianism, they were leaning over into each other until their shadows were one, their ideals one unified entanglement.

Mikhail noticed Gaby's voice rising for a half hour until it soared, her arms energized with persuasion and excited agreement, her eyes lit up, even in the dark. Ben's voice rose too, he laughed, smiled, squirmed around on the ground in reaction to Gaby. Then Gaby went to Mikhail, told him that she was going to drive Ben over to the community center and show him around; she had a key to the building, could Mikhail find a ride home? "Yeah," he said firmly, to buttress back all that he wouldn't say. Wasn't this going to be his night? His special memory with Gaby, filed away with prom and senior skip day and baccalaureate and their future first kiss? Perhaps he had started taking her for granted.

Mikhail watched them going, disappearing in the dark, both still chattering enthusiastically, Gaby gesticulating against the trees, the moon, the retreating circle of kids and a very persistent gaze coming therefrom.

ぐ な

In a ring of street lamp light, Gaby fished her keys out of her purse, rattled them around until she came to the one for the Butter Community Center. She looked a little apprehensively at Ben, then took it back with her smile. She thrust the key in the knob, turned the doorknob, opened the back door on a dark hallway. To the immediate right: the kitchen. Into this Gaby stepped to let Ben in behind her, the fire detector light blinking in the darkness, the yellow-whiteness of the streetlight glinting off pans, spatulas, the chrome countertop. Gaby shut the door, groped for the light in the weighty darkness.

When the kitchen lights came on in all their florescence, they both stood half-in, half-outside the doorway; half in shadow, half in light. They looked at each other with gravity in their eyes, in their pensive, apprehensive posture.

They quickly escaped each other's gazes with a glance at something more pressing: the coffee pot, the water spigot, the tiles on the floor. Gaby found her voice, looked around and steadied herself. Then she walked Ben room to room, expounding on the operations of the building and its volunteers (the mission statement, the budget concerns). It was obvious to Ben that Gaby was an expert here; trusted, passionate, at home with her theories. They wandered room to room, stepping in and out of shadows, the silence disrupted only by their voices echoing in the hollow rooms, their tennis-shoe clad footsteps, and the hum of the air conditioner keeping the place at a perfect, arid equilibrium.

At the bend in the staircase leading down to the overflow pantry, Ben called Gaby's attention and she stopped to turn toward him. "Gaby. You want to come with me?" He looked suddenly like he wanted a friend, like he was a little more anxious to leave the next day than he let on. He reached out and took Gaby's left hand in both of his, her arm now on fire with sensation, her lips tingling. He raised his left hand and set it lightly on her cheek, like a kiss.

Gaby staggered a moment, her left foot catching on her right, and teetered there for a clumsy moment, her center of gravity irritatingly *not* over her hips where it should be. Then she fell backwards, and kept falling, her feet flying over her head, her head flying over her feet, her arms in a wild, looping pattern all the way down the linoleum stairs to the impersonal linoleum-on-cement floor at the bottom. When her body came to rest, her head just barely propped against a metal door she'd hit hard a moment before, she looked up at the ceiling, at the flood of light and the long, yellowed, light fixture there.

"Gaby!" she heard, and the smack of feet all the way down the stairs. "You all right?" Ben's face was above her. "You all right?" again.

"Yeah, I think so. But," and she moved her twisted leg to be sure and moaned, "I think my leg may have problems."

∽ &⁓

Annie was at the bonfire for less than half an hour when Rick (her illustrious, homecoming king, hot rod ride to graduation) snuck up behind her, tickled her in the sides, and said "Come on." They drove to the starting quarterback's house, where most of the jocks were having a party, the quarterback's parents mysteriously gone on the weekend of his graduation. Beer was flowing, the back deck was lost in a cloud of cigarette and marijuana smoke. Lamps were thrown over with red shirts, towels, place mats, the bassed-out, Monsoon System stereo in the family room pulsing the house and shivering the Lenox china in the Omega cabinet.

Seeing that the couches were already loaded with neckers, Rick made the rounds with his buddies, secured a few brewskies, and then led Annie away again, by the hand. He took her through a bedroom, ignoring a couple interlocked on the bed, and out through the window. He climbed out on the roof, assuring Annie that it was all right, he and Bill did this all the time: you could see the lake from here. Annie relented, said she wanted to stargaze, and they climbed to the pinnacle of the two-story house with walk-out basement. They could see the lake, shimmering under the moon, and a sky filled with stars. The roof thudded beneath them, to the beat of the bass. People laughed below, yelled, slurred their speech, made *carpe diem* entreaties.

Rick lay flat on his back, his legs out in an inverted V, one arm folded behind his head, the other extended toward Annie, with a couple wet beer bottles. "You want one?" he asked. After sighing at the dark lake and the black tree line around its amorphous edge, she sat down and took one. "Sure, what's another?"

She sat like an M beside his V, feet flat on the roof, knees bent, arms out behind her, supporting her sit. They talked a little, about who had done what, about graduation and where they were going, about their parents, about what they had done in high school. He was going to the University of Michigan to play football, where he would eventually get very little play time. She was going to Michigan State, to "branch out" without leaving the state, to study what, she didn't know. There was silence, here and there, which she was almost comfortable with, but which he was spending in an agony of decision.

After emptying his beer, he convinced her to "relax" and lay down "like me." But no sooner had she bent her arms behind her head and relaxed out straight, her ankles crossed, than Rick was on top of her, pushing her mouth open with his lips. His hand was heavy on her stomach.

"Rick! Shit! What are you doing?" she pushed hard against him and he jumped off to the side.

"What do you mean, what am I doing? Kissing you."

"Slow down a little." Annie sat up, wiped her lips with her sleeve. "I was just sitting here, a whole world away, and you just decide to *jump* on me, like that. Whatever happened to subtlety, to *wooing?*"

"This is no fucking fairy tale, Annie. We've kissed before, you know what it's like."

"Well, maybe I don't feel like making out tonight. It's a big night." The gravity of the situation did not escape her, the plausible intentions. "You need *permission* to pull shit like that."

"Oh I do, do I?" The patronizing tone in his voice struck a sour note with Annie, propelled her to her feet.

"What the hell are you talking about?" Annie asked loudly, then looked over the edge of the roof, thinking of all the peers—or were they former peers?—who might hear them below.

"You've already given your kisses away, baby." He gave her a disarming smile and reached out to touch her arm as he, too, stood. "I just want a little action tonight. It's *graduation*, for fuck's sake. I might not see you for a long time after this summer."

"That's just it, Rick." She spit the words out at his honeyed pleas. "This isn't going anywhere. And if I don't feel like it, I don't."

"Well, I do." He brought his face in close to hers, tightened his grip on her arm until it hurt.

"Rick, don't." Tears were mounting in her voice. She stepped back away from him with her right foot. It never met solid footing, but came down in midair, out over the edge of the roof. The foot acted as a weight, propelled out into nothing, and dragged the rest of her hurtling over the edge,

Rick's grip not enough to hold her; but enough to leave a bruise forming even as she went flailing through the air and into the landscaping three stories below.

⌓ ⌒

Dispatch was quiet that night, a lot of noise disturbances from Butter. Around one in the morning, two calls came in, ambulances were sent out, as well as cops, to Butter Community Center and to a residence on the north side of Butter. What could be disturbing the honestly-purchased peace of Butter?

Around three in the morning, Doctor Les went on duty, his ears perked on entering, straightening the pen in his pocket, smiling at the nurses, waiting for the news of the night. The buzz was this: a set of twins—fraternal, not identical, just graduated that day—had *both* fallen—two separate incidences—from considerable heights, at about the same time that night. One had broken her back. The other had escaped with a broken leg, a sprained wrist, a bad bump on the head that had them currently monitoring for a concussion.

Doctor Les lifted his eyebrows as he entered Gaby's curtain-partitioned area, pulled the clipboard from the end of her bed. "So, you were the lucky one, huh?" He asked her.

Gaby turned her face to him, her face strained. Stellar was sitting on the edge of her seat, by the bed, Adam standing awkwardly nearby. They all looked question marks. It was then he realized that they must not know much about the other twin.

He scrunched his face in concern, frustration. "Have you heard much about the other twin?" He asked.

"No." Stellar answered for them. "Do you know anything? Can't you tell us something?"

"I'll go see what I can find out." He put the clipboard back and pointed at Gaby as he left. "*You* are fine, you already know. Broken leg—which I see we've already set and splinted—sprained wrist, bump on the head, and I'll be right back."

Time became sticky—slow—as they waited, avoiding each other's eyes. When Gaby could wait no longer, she said, "She's fine, Mom, I know it."

That was all that was said until Doctor Les re-entered. "You have been told she's broken her back?" Nods and a nod back. "The good news is that she is awake, responsive. Her only significant injury seems to be the back. And if I had to make a determination right now, I would say that she has minimal or possibly no neurological damage. The questions are still: will she be in pain and how much? Will she have full functionality? This may be a long road, but there are many ways in which we—and you—can help her recover, if not one hundred per cent, then pretty close to it."

"Yes?" Stellar's mouth pulled straight.

"And she will be needed for questioning by the police as soon as she comes to. She was at a party?"

"Yes, with underage drinking," Stellar finished, her tone flat, lifeless. "Could you be more specific about the *pain* and the *functionality*?"

"Well, no, not yet. Like I said, still a lot of questions. We can expect quite a few tests and plenty of rest and maybe even medication and physical therapy, but that's all down the road. Right now she is in testing and there is an MRI on her near-horizon."

That night Gaby lay face-up in her hospital bed in a cold room (only starched sheets and a large-knit, factory-made blanket to fend it off), making out strange shapes on the ceiling and listening to beeps and whirs and hums. The narrow bed, the chill, the noises kept her awake and when she fell into a fitful sleep they woke her back up. There was very little pain in her leg or wrist, thanks to an IV running into her other arm. The night replayed in the dark.

She fell asleep. She fell down the stairs in her brief dream; she startled and woke. She flushed at the thought of Ben rushing down the stairs to her and cradling her in his arms. Her stomach swooped as she tried to move her leg, dropped when she thought of Annie, somewhere in another room of the hospital. Mom and Dad must be there, pacing the room or curled up awkwardly on the plasticized recliner. They wouldn't be asleep either. This night was lasting forever.

Adam wandered down to a vending machine and snarfed a Coke, a Snickers, and a bag of Lays in the hallway. He felt hungry. And sickened. What could he do here but pace? Behind the lacquered door, Stellar wore a path back and forth in Annie's room; the only real light a dim line along the headboard meant to assist the nurses on their checks. There wasn't much to check. She should be resting, she told herself. There were days or weeks or months of stamina needed. But she was hopeless. First of all, the whole dual-twin-falling thing made her feel *confused*, on the edge of some kind of magic. Voodoo. Second, her empathy threatened to engulf her, take her down and drown her. How could she rest when Annie was laying there, her dreams shattered with her back?

What was a mom to do?

The door slowly moved open, the light from the corridor slashing across the room. There was a bumping around the door and Stellar looked up to catch Adam's eyes, but she did not see Adam. Instead, a man hobbled in, leaning on a carved and highly polished cane and draped so thoroughly in a hooded coat that Stellar could not see his face. As she moved to see his face he turned his back to her and shut the door gently behind him.

"Excuse me," Stellar said quietly. "I think you have the wrong room."

"Oh." The man turned at that and Stellar caught glimpses of his face. He was quite old, if his leathered skin and generous wrinkles were any indication. But he also had a young look and a twinkle of patience in his eye. A mild smile spread across his face, still shadowed by the hood. "Oh. So I do." But he made no move to leave.

"Can I help you? Are you here to see someone?" Stellar hoped he wasn't a patient escaped from the senile wing. Okay, so that wasn't really a wing, but surely there might be a dementia patient on the loose from somewhere.

"I'm here to see someone, yes." And there he stood, unmoving. He even seemed slightly amused with himself. Or her. A tingle went up Stellar's spine as she thought of the Angel of Death.

"Oh, no. That's not me," the man said. What on earth was with his random phrases? He didn't seem harmful, but he didn't seem meek, either. His body exuded power, perhaps a life of labor or deep sea fishing.

"Well, I can help you find where you're going."

"This will do."

Stellar was too tired to really help anyone. Exhausted, and starting to feel the dawn creep up on her foggy confusion. She collapsed into the chair behind her and slumped forward with her elbows on her knees and her hands framing her face at the brow. She sighed and looked up at the man.

"I was just looking for something; seeing if it had shown up yet." He was peering down at her, and then peering down at the room, at Annie. "But I think not. Then again, I see that I might be of some help."

"Sir, please. I am too tired."

"Oh, this is not the worst of it, Miss. Not for a long time, yet. Still, it is sad. You hate to see something so illuminated and pristine broken like this." He moved toward the bed with a heavy gait, thumping with the cane as he came. Stellar made to stand and intercept him, but then she settled and found herself wondering if she were asleep, if this were just a dream. The thought of anything threatening Annie strangled her. Fear.

He stood beside Annie's bed, near her head, lost to the whirs and beeps and the flashing numbers on the displays; silhouetted against the line of light. "Were that The Angel were here," he mumbled to himself and he looked down on Annie's face and gently touched her forehead. "He always makes a joyful mess of things, but…" With his hand shaking just a little on her head, he lifted his chin and let his eyes fall shut.

Still in this pose, he spoke to Stellar; "You're a fan of Blondie?"

"Yeah, I guess. Wait; how did you know?"

"You're humming."

"Oh. I didn't know." Was she that tired? She didn't feel *that* tired.

"She's going to be okay. Her back will heal with time. There is nothing wrong with her mind." He gave a gentle sigh of relief and opened his eyes, took a step back from the bedside.

"Sure, sir. Thanks for the advice."

"It's not advice. You'll see. With time, too."

"What good would that do us?"

"It will, or I wouldn't have come."

"Who *are* you?"

"You may call me The Sage. Everyone does."

☙ ❧

Ben did not leave Butter that morning. He got most of a night of heavy sleep, extracted himself from his blanket tornado, and went in the afternoon to Gaby's room with flowers and a card. He kept up the afternoon visits all week. Often he wandered between her walls with a nervous expression on his face, his hands in his pockets, pacing. Gaby mostly sat on her bed, her leg buried in blankets and pillows, a faint smile on her face.

"You need to go, Ben," she said to him, after a few days of his pacing and their chatting.

He suddenly looked up at her, face like a trapped animal.

"You don't have to worry about me. I just broke my leg. And it wasn't your fault, I'm just a klutz. And I'm pretty sure we're not dating. At least we don't *have* to be."

"But..." He walked the floor toward her, gently rested his hand on her leg (his name signed right on the front of the lime green monstrosity) and sat down on her bed. "I mean, I like you Gaby. And I feel responsible."

"Maybe in another life I'd make you wait and then get on that bus with you in a couple months. But I have Annie to take care of. And that's okay 'cause I'll have school, too."

Ben hung his head a moment in thought, then up at her. "Gaby, you're a great girl. In another life, I'd wait those few months for you. We could have fun out west, together. It'd be good to have a friend along." He leaned forward on the bed, kissed her lightly. She kissed him back, a few moments of softness, their eyelashes brushing, the electricity between the soft skin of their faces mingling.

Gaby smiled. "That's quite a goodbye."

"Oh! I have something for you!" Ben jumped up and crossed the room, rummaged around in the backpack that he had not gotten used to leaving behind. "Here it is." He took out a paperback and crossed the room to hand it to her. "I know you love those old *Avengers of Northwyth* re-runs, so I got this. You know some guy is writing a new series? It's supposed to be really popular. So maybe it will be good. But there's only a couple so far."

Gaby turned the book over in her hands and starting browsing the back, although her mind was far, far away from book jacket copy.

"The first one is about Jaden when he is a little boy. He's really poor, but his super strength and agility set him apart and he rises in service to The Queen, like her right-hand-man. And he gets all wealthy and somewhere in there he does something that re-unites The Queen and The Angel and they're so thankful that when they are separated forever by the wiles of the Evil Storyteller, The Queen marries Jaden and he rules with her. But I'm pretty sure I just gave away the ending. Or maybe even the ending of the next book. Sorry."

Gaby tossed the book casually and it sunk into the fluffy comforter. "It's all right. It's a great gift. I could use some more reading." Both their eyes wandered to the stack of library books next to her bed. "More *casual* reading."

They shared a smile. "Goodbye." Ben looked down at her. "You take care of yourself, and Annie. And come visit me in California." He grabbed his jacket off Gaby's chair, crossed the room slowly, opened the door, closed it quietly, walked the hall, down the stairs, out the front door.

CHAPTER 7
GENETICS

ఏ೧   ೧ఐ

After falling down their stairs in the middle of the night on their property, with a handsome boy standing at the top, Gaby was forced to part ways with the Butter Community Center. During her days in bed, hobbling around her room, peeking in on Annie (asleep in the next room, grunting her way to a sitting-up position with her physical therapist), she thought about life and death with a vengeance. She thought about her own tumble down the stairs, the radiator at the bottom that could have cut her jugular, the face-smack to the landing that could have permanently blinded her. (Perhaps she was a bit imaginative.) She thought about Annie and her plummet from the roof and normal adolescence. Gaby judged that she deserved Annie's fate. From the way the story ran in the paper, Annie fell when she was drunk and screwing around. From the way Annie's bruised arm told the story, Annie had been mostly sober, backing away from the jerk all the non-jocks accepted Rick to be.

The house was eerily quiet that summer. Even the grandparents, the aunts and uncles, the cousins, and friends and neighbors that trekked through the kitchen dropping off balloons, cards, casseroles, said loud things in their most hushed voices, afraid to disturb anything. The truth is, Annie was going to be laid up for at least a few months, but was ultimately going to recover—*mostly if not completely*, like Doctor Les said. But there were complications, nonetheless. She delayed her entrance to Michigan State and didn't want to talk about her lacrosse scholarship. *But*, her physical therapist assured her, *It would be beneficial for you to take yoga or pilates, when you are ambulant.* "Yoga?!" Gaby's grandmother exclaimed for all of them.

When Gaby was alone in the house, she hobbled down the stairs (usually sliding on her butt, but sometimes—when Mom wasn't around—hanging onto the railing so hard she was sure she was going to yank it off the wall). She tinkered in the kitchen—in all her crutched glory—and made snacks for Annie, hot teas and homemade smoothies with curly straws. She made Melodie or Mikhail carry them up the stairs, and Gaby threw open the door on Annie, cracked the curtains and the window and asked, "How are we today, sunshine?" She made Melodie or Mikhail drive her to the video store, filled her arms (or Mikhail's) with *Monty Python, MST3K,* John Candy, and hauled it home. Annie's room was now equipped with a TV tray groaning under the weight of a TV-VCR combo. Gaby popped in video after video, hopped on one leg to Annie's bedside, squished down next to her with a careful nudge, and disappeared into comical scene after potty humor after ridiculous situation as the summer of 1997 slid by stealthily.

They had favorites that they watched again and again, mostly new movies that Stellar picked up on her way home from some errand: *Forrest Gump* and *Jurassic Park, Beaches* and *The Eighth Day. The Sound of Music* and *Annie.* They also got into Nickelodeon re-runs; *I Love Lucy, Green Acres*; and the perennial favorite, *The Price Is Right.* As the months went by, the physical therapy progressed and the pain in Annie's back lessened. She could distinguish the price of a bottle of Windex or a…new…car!, dreamed of planting a little kiss on Bob Barker's orange-glow face, jumping up and down, squealing over the unveiling of the second—and *always* better—showcase.

Melodie left for Northern University in the "fall," which was really in the middle of the long heat of August. She promised to return for Thanksgiving, despite everyone's insistence that she return *only* if it were safe, only if the snow had not yet made a shut-in of her in the God-forsaken cold boondocks of the Upper Peninsula. (Did people really go past Mackinac?) Mikhail was left alone to juggle the newness of his own academic career at Alford College with supporting Gaby as she hobbled to her new classes, to the school and local libraries, where she lost afternoons in the philosophy section, searching there amid the smell of book glue and the yellowed pages for the meaning of life, and more importantly, the particulars of death. The twin fall had her wondering, had left her epistemologically morbid.

On leaving the library one such day—Gaby limping through the theft detectors, Mikhail hefting a stack of her books and his own CDs in his arms—Gaby veered to the flier board, stabbed through with a thousand staples, littered with torn corners of varicolored paper. There, front and center, was a flier for a nursing home in the town over. Gaby ripped off the phone number tab at the bottom, stuffed it in her jeans pocket.

"What's that for?" Mikhail asked, stepping into the sunlight and looking at Gaby over the leaning tower of books.

"A nursing home. I thought, *What better way to learn about life and death?*"

Ꮳ   Ꮙ

Safe Places Assisted Living Community was set back from the road, lost in jungle-like foliage on a wooded road, in the town of Brandenburg, Michigan. It was away from the city, which allowed for extensive grounds. The back yard, a large, rambling green thing bordered by trees and dotted with a man-made pond, made it look to the casual observer (if a casual observer happened to wander into the back) of the typical psychiatric home of Hollywood, as opposed to a nursing home. The people who lived there, in addition to being rolled over in bed or dragged out of their rooms for a weekly puppet show, were taken for hobbly walks, scooted in their wheelchairs right up to the edge of that murky, little lake, and left for a time under the elements of sunshine and cool wind. Nurses fed the ducks, the charges cried, "Get those filthy animals away from me!"

The front of the building was French palace-esque, if such can be said for the cement, metal, plastic, and veneer structures that dominate United States architecture. It looked a little like old archeology, lost in the ramble of trees, bushes, vines. Its sign was neatly placed near the dirt road on which it was located, reading "Safe Places Assisted Living: A Community of Care."

Gaby nosed her car into the circular driveway, matching the name on the paper to the sign and then throwing it aside and letting it flutter to the floorboard as she navigated the paved loop up to the front doors. She parked in the conveniently located visitor's parking, threw her satchel over her shoulder.

She signed into the office of the center, guided by signs which stated in tall, red, letters: ALL VISITORS MUST REPORT TO THE OFFICE, FOR THE SAFETY OF THE COMMUNITY. For safety, then, she turned to the right, entered the glass-fronted office, speckled with antsy loiterers. She checked in on a lined and nearly empty log, had a seat on a plush, floral couch, surrounded by silk floral arrangements, home decoration magazines, the soft flip of pages and murmur of voices embedded in Muzak.

Within the week, Gaby watched other people do just the same thing: sink uncomfortably into the over-stuffed couches, sign their names on the registry with forced calm or long-suffering reservation. They turned around to fold themselves neatly away in the plush, or they languished beneath the brass and glass chandeliers, waited for neatly-uniformed women with smiles plastered around their big teeth, quiet, sane, orchestrated.

Gaby began parking in the employee lot, came in the back door. She performed odd jobs. Sometimes she helped out in the front office, giving reassuring smiles, using her low, warm voice, or making photocopies, stuffing envelopes with letters, inviting family members to upcoming events. Sometimes she drudged in the kitchen and dining room, helping whip potatoes, dish out carrots, spoon-feed those who needed to be spoon-fed. She helped in the leisure room, adjusted the communal TV to an audible level, passed around little Dixie cups of snacks. And at other times, she walked the floors, kept the "community" company, assisted nurses in pushing medication-distribution carts, supported the aides in changing diapers, giving baths.

Between her evenings at Safe Places, her days behind the desks of Alford and studying in the computer labs, her weekends working at a Butter bakery, Gaby still managed to visit the library, spend hours and hours among stacks of books, and later with Mikhail, among more stacks of books that piled up and littered her room. Mikhail deejayed for them using Gabbie's stereo, became agitated about particular drum breaks, or guitar riffs, about somebody's commanding vocals. Or he sat silent as she shuffled, and he read Kurt Vonnegut Jr., John Irving, Gabriel Garcia Marquez. Sometimes he even ventured into the new world Gaby was creating for herself: quiet and careful, suffocating with its intensity and density, he leafed through the books she was reading, read the covers, the introductions, random paragraphs. But Mikhail knew he did not want to drown there, so sometimes he escaped to Annie's room—she would leave for Michigan State at the new year—and played video games until Gaby emerged or until the night stretched too far toward the next day's classes. On these nights Mikhail slipped out of Annie's room, quietly, through the shaft of light that escaped Gaby's door in the undisturbed dark of the house, down the stairs and out into the crisp of night. There on the porch, he took a breath of icy air into his lungs and exhaled steam in puffs that iced on surfaces and twinkled with the neighborhood lights, cracked his knuckles and stretched toward the clear, blue-black expanse and tiny-bright stars wheeling above him.

Mikhail went with Gaby to Safe Places now and again. The boss knew him by sight, the workers lifted their eyebrows when he came in, smiled, teased Gaby behind his back until she threatened to leave the room. "Touchy, touchy," they lamented. He helped where he was needed, as well, but because of the smaller number of male volunteers, he usually worked with male patients.

Mikhail broke his heart with helping, went home and placed his hands over his face, ran them back through his hair, looking at his far wall paralyzed, stunned. He loved to be with Gaby, to be near her, to create history with her riding, listening to wind in the car or drinking Slurpees on the porch. He even loved helping at Safe Places, loved ladling steaming bowls of soup at the soup kitchen, hawking fliers at one exuberant function or another. Because he wanted to, because altruism brought him joy and satisfaction. But also because of her. Always because of her.

Cʒ ꙮ

Stellar hit the garage opener button on the driver's side visor of her minivan as she crept through the 15 mph streets of her neighborhood. It was fall; cool, crisp, clean, and airy. She coasted into the driveway, bumping over the curb, the noisy machinery of the opening garage door creaking and screeching, the cool, stuffiness of garage, the dingy, grimed fluorescent light combating the blueness of a chilly dusk. She gave a few short beeps on the horn; *Come on out and help me!*

She gathered into her arms her open purse, her cell phone, her large, lidded plastic coffee mug, empty and splattered with sticky, brown dots. She walked into the house, smiled at Gaby as she lowered all her things with the click of Formica and the muted shiver of keys, discarded her mug in the kitchen sink. "Where's your dad?" she asked as Gaby pulled on her sneakers and disappeared out the door.

"Dunno."

"Adam!" Stellar called up the stairs, leaning over the banister so her voice would project upwards with the slope of the ceiling. "Adam?!"

"Yes?" came a muffled response from the recesses of the master bedroom.

"Groceries!" she responded. And then she yelled, "Annie? How are you doing sweetie?"

Another muffled response; "Fine, mom."

Adam emerged from his room, pulled a white T-shirt over his head as he padded down the stairs with little thuds, white-socked, jeaned, hair ruffled and hands freshly washed of a day of ink and labor, in advertising, cold droplets of water still clinging to the webs between his fingers. He hurried out to the garage, skipping across the cold pavement on the balls of his feet, trying to keep his fresh socks fresh from the gritty garage floor.

Adam, Stellar and Gaby fumbled through the grocery bags; crinkling paper; whispering plastic; the smell of food, grocery store and of chilly autumn escaping the creases of the bags. They dug into bags up to their elbows, threw bags on their sides, disemboweled them, looking for any surprises that might be shadowed in a corner somewhere. "Mmmm. Beefaroni." "Look. A new flavor of Doritos!" And other similar exclamations that were uniformly interjected across the continent on grocery night, when all the feverish marketing paid off.

They ricocheted around the room in zigzags, sorting and filing things away, their voices reflecting off countertops, absorbing into carpet, drapes, light fixtures, in between couch cushions. Faintly, a bell rang.

"Annie's ringing!" yelled Gaby.

"Who wants to get her?" Stellar asked, her head buried in a paper bag, her gaze focused on matching bottles of shampoo and conditioner.

"I will," and Gaby bounced off and up the stairs in the direction of the tinkling of the bed-side bell, which was ringing without ceasing.

"What do you want for dinner, Adam?" Stellar asked, her head now in a cupboard, re-organizing the canned soups.

"What did you get?"

"Umm," she looked around her at the leaning towers of food. "Um. Um. Couscous? Spaghetti? Pork chops?"

"Are the pork chops frozen?"

"Sort of." Stellar held up a partially-defrosted mound of squishy-solid white butcher's paper. She made a sideways face at Adam.

"Mmm. No, then." Adam opened the fridge, scanned with his eyes. "How 'bout spaghetti then? That's a classic."

"Sure." Stellar walked to the cupboard, thunked a jar of spaghetti sauce and a box of pasta on the counter. "You make the salad?"

"Okey-dokey."

Ten minutes later, the house smelled like raw meat, just browning and becoming fragrant. The fat sizzled and sputtered in the pan, steam billowing from the range. Twenty minutes later, steam was also rising from the soup pot, bubbles pop-

popping on the surface of the starchy water, ripples rolling over. Half an hour later, the kitchen smelled of tomato sauce beginning to char to the bottom of the pan, the tiny bubbles on the surface of the sauce emitting little vents of steam and sending spittles of red grease flying over the stove top and onto the tan counter.

Stellar slid the pots and pans onto the table, Gaby set the dishes out, Adam cut cucumbers, onions, tomatoes, for the salad and threw them all on top of the cool paleness of iceberg lettuce. Gaby lined up the dressings (ranch, Italian, Thai-peanut), the Bacos, the croutons. Stellar filled a plate of spaghetti for Annie, asked Gaby to run it upstairs with a glass of milk. Gaby carefully balanced up the stairs and a minute later came flying down with a residual limp, putting most of her weight on her good leg as it slid on the carpet.

They ate dinner in relative silence; the clink of silverware on porcelain, glasses on the polished wood table, the TV droned on the news, Adam's eyes on the condition of the world. Stellar hummed to herself. Gaby was absorbed in her dinner, working on her third heaping plate.

"I can't believe you're still eating three plates of spaghetti for dinner," Stellar looked over at Gaby, shoveling in her food, then back down at her own salad.

"Fast metabolism."

Everyone in Butter has fast metabolism, Stellar thought to herself. She looked down at her hands, the elasticity slackening, her skin thinning, her veins blue-ing, her rings plumping out her skin in tiny billows around her knuckles. She thought of herself naked, in front of the mirror; of her breasts stretching toward her waistline; of the soft pad of her stomach pillowing in front of her curved hips, curved thighs. Everything once taut, once firm, curved downward, outward, in gentle lines, even her cheeks, her chin. Not that she gained much weight over the years, it had just gotten *looser* and *redistributed*, somehow.

Stellar played basketball in her high school days, and was captain of the Science Olympiad team. She played volleyball, and was a member of the debate team. She starred in the high school musical, and a month later soloed in the orchestra Christmas concert. Only when in college did she catch the wave of hippies, free love, save the world, as it surged across the country and lifted her away from her dotted-and-crossed, school girl days. But forever, she was always wildly popular, always more than competent, always had a clear head, traveled through the room in the spotlight. She was respected, adored, depended upon, and intensely hated from inside the secret atriums of many small hearts. She wore a crown that everyone but her could see, Vaselined teeth, shiny lip gloss of character. A halo of light around her long bones and humongous smile.

Stellar took a break of indefinite length from college to travel the United States in a bus with a fistful (constantly expanding and then shrinking) of other college drop-outs. (Stellar would return, later, and finish up a double-degree in art history and French.) She loved the whole transient-hippie thing. One day, she could be washing cars in Toledo and the next week she was making dinner for a commune in San Francisco. Her friends loped around in whorling circles. Sometimes old faces re-appeared. Everyone took Stellar in, made her their queen, let her take the lead in so many things: in cooking, in washing cars, in driving vans across the country, in rolling doobies.

After a year on the road, Stellar found herself in Seattle, with a group of kids that did some smuggling up to Vancouver. It was a freezing night, and in the shuffle of a panic and a bit of a joke, she ended up crated with disguised bundles of weed, squeezed in the silence, in the dark. She jostled around helpless in the crate in the back of a noisy, smoky van, stashed with the illegal and the decoy items. Once in Surrey, BC, the driver pulled onto a sandy spot on the coast of Mud Bay. He and the passengers hunched themselves up against the freezing spray, and jumped around back to open the doors and let Stellar out of the latched crate. She emerged, covered with straw, the smell of stuffiness. She was freezing cold, packed in with her faux-fur-trimmed hood, her hand-knit cap, her mittens, her bell-bottoms, her hiking boots. She unfolded all her amazing limbs, looked up at the driver as he extended a hand to her, and said that she had been thinking she would stay in Vancouver.

It occurred to Stellar somewhere in the no-man's-land of a dark crate and innumerable road bumps between the United States and Canada that she was like a secret. She had been smuggled in, unknown. It was a little like freedom: no one knew where she was. She decided to keep it that way, see how the cards fell. So she walked away in the darkness, the snow, during the holiday season of some year in the early 1970s, in Canada, smoking a cigarette.

In Canada, Stellar spent a few weeks in a homeless shelter until she found a commune of sorts. In her work with the commune, she fell into the UBC academic life. And with them, she volunteered to do some nature research at the far edges of daylight, in the north wilderness. She loved it: the air so cold it felt purged of all impurities. The landscape was the cleanest thing Stellar had ever seen; no power lines, just grays and whites and the blue of sky. Daylight dipped in and out at unpredictable (to her biological clock, it seemed) times. Darkness, too, sometimes came in the middle of the day, sometimes not at all. Stellar paid no attention to the turning of the years, just flowed with the hypnotic, mystical dizziness of it all: big nature, hard work, the steeliness of the earth, the fragility of her freezing cold self.

In the wilderness, she lived with a family of two sisters. She had an unassuming little garret bedroom, furnished with a bedside table, a single bed, a water pitcher, a rug, and many, many quilts. Her room had a small window, pointed up at the blue-blackness of wilderness sky, at the mess and tangle of quasars, meteors, planets covering every millimeter of unadulterated view. It made her think of her legend, of the story her mother would tell her about herself.

Stellar's mother was naive about a lot of things. She was naïve about sex, about men, about women, about Robert—a perfect storm. She held juvenile fantasies about Robert and marrying and vacuuming and baking cakes and pinky cherubic babies. Her gaggle of girl friends concluded: she just needed to crook her slender, manicured finger the right way, throw a few of the right (crystal blue) eyes at him, meet him at a drive-in and get her straw-blonde hair tousled *just a little*, get his class ring, and happily ever after would be irresistibly set. Robert— the handsome roughneck—didn't lead Julia to believe anything different. So with things moving along swimmingly (the crooked finger, the eyes, the drive-in, the ring even), Julia surrendered more ground than she intended, assuming he would win it all someday. She gave him all her time, every dream of the future, every inch of her body and every rentable space in her brain. He took it all in stride, which is how Julia ended up pregnant and abandoned. Robert didn't take to a shot-gun wedding, no matter what disasters awaited the scrawny girl he had taken advantage of.

Julia disappeared underneath obsession and passion and desperation (although that's hardly the way the neighbors put it). She was a fire burning to destroy. She was found more than once walking the wood between their two houses in her pajamas, crying, moaning. As her stomach grew bigger, Julia's parents tried harder to confine her in the house, but the rumors only grew more wild, and more accurate. Julia was losing her hair, cutting her legs up wandering the woods at night barefoot, like a ghost of a person eaten away by handsome roughneck Robert.

At one o'clock AM, Julia stood in front of the mirror in her room, her room incandescent with an overhead light, a bedside lamp, two table lamps, a vanity mirror light. She stood tracing the fabric over her enormous stomach with the palms of her hands, standing silhouetted. Her inverted belly button dotted the long, flannel nighty on the taughtness of her distended body. Without thinking, she wandered down the dark hall, down the dark stairs, out the front door, the wooden screen door slapping behind her in the quiet, unnoticed. She walked over the dirt of the family farm, soft furrows squishing between her toes, into the woods, and the mile or so to Robert's parents' house, where Robert would be sleeping behind his screen, behind his curtains, under his blankets. She stood outside his window, her feet caked with mud and blood dry in the scratches on her feet. She called to him while she cried. He woke up.

Normally, he would stay in the dark room, not moving, barely breathing, until she left or fell asleep and was gathered up by her parents in the morning; a lost animal. He felt so distant from her, this wild beast surely not the pink flesh and girlish laugh he had given his class ring to, his condescending kisses and earnest groin. She was a stranger, one who made up a past that hadn't happened or was bleeding things from him that he didn't have to give. He usually cowered, laying still in the dark. But this night he wanted to sleep, wanted to shield himself from her insanity, for once. He bound out of bed at the sound of her wailing rising up to him over the siding and lifting the curtains. He rushed out the door and over the yard, at her. He grabbed her awkwardly and roughly around the chest and steered her back toward the tree line. He pushed at her until she started resisting, crying things out in his face. Then he pulled at her, at anything he could grab: her hair, the hem of her nightgown, her sleeves, her arms. She thrashed against him, yelled louder. They moved deeper and deeper into the woods. The chaos that was their struggle, their hot breath, their mess of mud, tears, spit, anger, turned thin and quiet in the big, night air, only a hundred yards away.

He yelled, "Go home, damn it! And don't ever come back!" She moaned at him, her face streaked with tears, her hair stuck to the sides of her head, her face in a twisted, open frown, exposing her bottom teeth and a rolling tongue. He yelled it again, close to her. She clung to him, and he tried to shake her free. Her nails dug into him, he took his right arm and brought it down hard against her head, dropping her to the ground in a ragged pile, the mound of belly to the side and her limbs splayed out in the moonlight, white.

He left her there (for which he would be arrested and questioned), unconscious. She woke up later, cold and confused in the dark. She rolled over on her back, disoriented, a pain in her head and more between her legs, which were sticky with wet. She looked up at the night sky, at the clearness, the vast darkness, the beauty of the constellations. When her back and abdomen exploded in a pulse of pain, she writhed her back into an inverted bend and screamed. She continued to writhe and scream for the next three hours, through the night, pushing her baby into the world with no one to help, laying on the forest floor, looking up at the stars.

This was how Stellar received her name; a strange name that marked her for the hippies, twenty years later. Julia raised Stellar at home, amongst her parents and her sisters, emerged from insanity crystallized, worked in a tailor's shop, and eventually married Bill, who was more than a decent young man. Bill was Stellar's savior. He lifted her out of embarrassment, raised her from the level of bastard child, into the refracted light of legitimacy. And more, she wanted more, so she spent fifteen years being *more* than legitimate, being perfect. And Bill adored Stellar. Stellar adored Bill. Bill bought Stellar bikes, pony rides. Stellar made Bill lacquered cookie ornaments, macaroni drawings.

Stellar returned from the wilderness of Canada two and a half years after she disappeared in Vancouver, her hair in dreadlocks, her eyes more blue than brown, walking over the Ambassador Bridge in Windsor, Ontario in the dead glare of summer. She hitched back to her old family house in Detroit.

The cryptic letters that Stellar jotted from the garret room and sent in greasy fragments had left Julia and Bill haunted by a shade of Stellar and Bill forlorn. And now there she stood among the lilac and the spruce, in the solid form. Bill wouldn't be home from work for hours yet and Julia, she stood framed in the front doorway, a damp dish towel over her shoulder, her white arms crossed over her wildly beating heart.

$\text{os} \quad \text{so}$

Annie lay flat on her back, stared up at the ceiling. And stared, and stared, and stared, and looked and scrutinized and watched and focused and gazed and glared and inspected, until she wanted to scream, except that it would hurt. So she lay on her back, stared at the ceiling, and wanted to scream for a long, long time. Clumps of time went floating down the dammed river of her life, eddying in pools, snagging on river sticks and lollygagging through slick patches of pond slime. She had nothing to show for all that meandering time, but that it was gone, almost unremembered in the way that memories truly are formed (in brief flashes of movement, sound, smell). She could feel the hot breath of inanity in the room. It was flitting over her face and bubbling around the hazy horizons of her peripheral vision. And she lay on her back, stared, wanted to scream.

Occasionally, alone by herself in the night and after she tired of Nick at Night and the TVs buzz popped into a deep silence and then darkness, she cried quietly, unable to sleep because of the physical pain. But the crying only made things worse (tears backing up into her stinging eyes from her prone position, no facial tissues close enough to reach, her pillow wet, warm, itchy behind her head). She really needed to wail, to gasp, to scream and rail against the pain with it. Instead, railing caused pain so she lay flat and still in the heat, sticky with sweat, screams like rocks in her gullet, swung heavy down her back, crippling.

The bruise on her arm healed, dipping into various colors of the spectrum and exploding in inhuman green before fading. Rick had gone to visit Annie briefly in the hospital, slicked down and primped within an inch of his life, gave her carnations and sat for a tense ten minutes in a chair before saying goodbye. He never returned, not to the hospital, to the house, to anywhere that might count as Annie's bedside. While seeing him squirm and realizing that he must have felt some degree of guilt, Annie reached no catharsis. There was another metaphorical bruise that would take much longer to heal than the fading purpling or the cooling shadow Rick had cast on the hospital linoleum. Trust bled out on the floor.

CHAPTER 8
FAMILY TIES
ॐ   ॐ

It was Easter week. Gaby drove the old Colony Park station wagon, Mikhail sang to himself, his right elbow resting on the window frame, his right hand out tracing the wind clearing around the car as it advanced. He bobbed his head, watched greens flash by.

"I have someone I want you to meet," Gaby interrupted him.

"Oh?" He looked over at her side of the windshield, head still bobbing.

"Yeah. One of the 'community members,'"—a little smile of recognition from both of them. "Her name is Sonja. Have you worked with her?"

"Not that I remember. I mostly work with the guys."

"Yeah. Well, I'm really taken with her." Gaby navigated the car off the freeway. "They've got me on a little project with her. I write letters for her."

"Really?" He could tell she liked it by her vocal inflection.

"Yeah… yeah. I like it." The corners of Gaby's mouth twitched. "But anyhow, she's great, just great. She's got this incredibly huge collection of boxes of cards, and she loves to write to old friends, family, famous people, whoever. But she can't actually write anymore. Arthritis and other things. So she dictates, and I write it out. She's a great letter-writer; interesting stuff. She wants to fill all her cards."

"That's cool. What kind of collection is it? Like Hallmark greeting cards?"

"No. You know those nice boxes of cards you can get, like at the bookstore or at a gift shop in a museum? Like maybe ten inside, with envelopes? And they're usually blank inside? Like those kinds. She's got floral ones, artistic ones, ones with jokes on the front, Barbie, Van Gogh, airplanes, golden retrievers, views of Mount Everest, all kinds of particulars. Anyhow, it's cool."

"Sounds cool. Sure, I'll come meet her today. I'll come first thing."

"As long as she's not asleep," Gaby said.

Sonja was not asleep when Gaby peeked in at her door, Mikhail's head over her shoulder. Sonja was sitting up in bed, propped on about five, fluffy, bleached and shining white pillows, buried under two sheets of the same shining white, a couple hospital blankets with the scratchy, loose knit, and an old patchwork quilt that she retained from home. Sonja was watching *As the World Turns*, her wrinkled hand and bone-thin arm extended with a remote held in mid-air. She looked transfixed, her blue eyes intense under blue-white coiffed hair.

"Sonja?" Gaby interrupted.

"Gaby!" The woman's face spread into a slow smile, her gaze wandering over the room before it landed on the open door. "Gaby," again. "Come here, dear." Gaby held out her hands for Sonja to squeeze, in lieu of a hug.

"And who's this?" Sonja asked, looking around Gaby at the tall, handsome, young man shadowing the doorway. "A beau? For me or for you?" Sonja's smile spread again.

"This is my friend, Mikhail," Gaby waved Mikhail into the room, across the five braided rugs that littered the commercial-grade Berber. He walked over to her bedside, allowed his hands to be held in the same manner.

"Well!" Sonja waved for Mikhail to come in closer, he bent toward her, and she lifted her hand and placed it under Mikhail's chin. "Handsome!" Sonja exclaimed, then ran her tremoring hand very lightly along both his cheeks, looking him in the face. "And a good soul, I think."

C8   80

As Sonja sat in her bed-cloud absentmindedly twiddling round and round a ring with quite a sizable gem set in it, she dictated this letter to her granddaughter, Betsy, in Tucson, Arizona. Spring, 1998 (transcribed by Gaby):

"Dearest Little Betsy,

"When going through my collection of cards today, I came across this one: a photograph of a small, china tea set, pink, with rosebuds. I thought of you. I remember you very vividly, in my sunroom on Jenkins Street in Carmel, the sun in your hair, the white chiffon curtains ruffling behind you, and you with all your little dolls about in a circle, playing tea time. The old tea set I had to offer you was not quite so pretty, but I'm sure in your imagination it was filigreed in gold and held the nectar of the gods. You were such a sweet child! Buttercup face, rose lips, eyes of cornflower blue. And so sweet.

"By-the-by, if you do not recognize this handwriting (which I am sure you do not), I have found myself a new friend here. Her name is Gaby, and she writes my letters out for me. She has promised not to reveal my deep, dark, secrets, nor my folly. I believe, as well, that I keep her entertained. She helps out here at Safe Places (what a disastrous name!), and so does her friend [which was dictated as "beau," but changed without democracy], Mikhail. She is good to me, so no one in Arizona or anywhere else need worry about me. Gaby will take care. She is a very serious young lady, attending college for sociology, whatever good that is going to do her.

"I have heard from your mother that you are now working at the Tucson Museum of Art, as curator. Good girl! I have always been very fond of museums of all sorts. I remember taking you to the city once, with your brother, and we went to all the museums downtown: the Detroit Institute of Arts Museum, the Detroit Historical Museum... You were so taken with Seurat. You loved all those little dots that made such a beautiful, colorful picture. "View of Le Crotoy," I believe, was the one. If I ever come across a box of Seurat cards, I will send you another letter. You can hang it in your office at the museum and remember your humble beginnings, holding your Grandma's hand, looking at Seurat for the first time with such wonderment in your eyes.

"Well, I must give Gaby a rest from my tiresome rambling and breakneck speed. So you take care of yourself.

"With Much Love,

"XOXOXO

"Grandma Sonja"

 ❧☙

Betsy read the note card slowly, down to the wobbly signature. The rest of the mail—bills and credit card offers, she was sure—lay in a messy pile on the kitchen table where Betsy sat in the low light of a bulb-missing overhead fixture. She wasn't thinking about Seurat, or the DIA, or even too much about Grandma Sonja. She was thinking about the ring. About her crazy mother and about that stupid, obnoxious ring!

Because she knew, even if no one would confirm it, that the ring was behind everything. Behind all of it. Dr. Krantz didn't believe her. She could tell by his patronizing smile that he thought she was the crazy one. She should really get a new psychiatrist. Bob didn't believe her. Nor was he going to hang on much longer, with her waffling in this dual-income-no-kids/dual-income-with-kids no man's land where she kept insisting she was averse to motherhood and any path that might lead there. She blamed it on her own crazy mother and that blasted ring.

It was her thirteenth birthday when several of the pieces of the puzzle came flying at her through the haze of pink-frosted cake and donkey piñata and a sea of flipped-out bobs. Grandma Sonja was there, bearing an arm-load of giant, beribboned packages. She pulled from her purse and donned a floral apron over her neat, button-fronted dress and disappeared behind the swinging door into the kitchen to help plate potato salad and sprinkle paprika on the devilled eggs. Over the shouts and exclamations of her party guests Betsy did not hear the yells muffled by the swinging door until she pushed her way through it and was startled.

Betsy's stomach sank. The door swung back behind her and she pushed back quickly on it to help it settle flat. Then she stood there with her palms and back pressed against it, blocking it for anyone else. She shrunk upwards, shrugging her shoulders and moving onto her toes. They seemed not to notice her.

"You're not giving her that *thing!*" her mother spat at Grandma Sonja.

"Of course I am." Sonja's voice was comparatively calm and cool. "Why not? She's thirteen. And I think she would like it."

"It's *evil!* That's why. It's not getting anywhere near Betsy! I don't know why you've even kept it all these years! Why you wallow in all those lies! That's all they can possible be; lies!"

Sonja's voice took on a controlled crispness. "We've always disagreed about what the ring may be. I don't agree that just because people may turn a thing to evil it becomes evil. Nor do I believe that the world is simply atoms and energy bashing into one another. I may have honored your demand to keep the truth from Betsy all these years, but I cannot be expected to honor that demand forever."

"Oh yes you can! Or you get out of my house, and you never darken my doorstep again!" Izolda's eyes sparkled, her voice had reached hysteria.

"Now, Iz."

"*I am most in earnest, mother!*"

"Calm down, please. I have never understood your manic hatred of this ring."

Izolda's anger focused into a seething, low whisper. "I mean it. If you ever so much as mention that ring to Betsy, I will have *it* destroyed and you will be most unwelcome in my home and in our family."

"Fine," Sonja's mouth was drawn into a straight line. "Luckily, it would be impossible to destroy this ring..."

"You really believe all that?"

"I do. And you certainly do, just in a different way."

"NEVER infer such a thing." Izolda slumped in on herself and the dishtowel hung limply in her hand. She said flatly, "I think its powers of division are power enough to hate."

"If you think so. But I will not be parted from Betsy."

"No, mother. Then behave."

Ↄ ⁊

Adam loved Stellar the moment he saw her, sitting on the wheel well in the back of a pick-up truck, skidding to a stop in his front yard. She was surrounded by friends who were laughing, falling into one another, a halo of smoke around her head, a large-toothed grin on her face. Her straw-blonde hair was long and wild, her hands thin and elegant. She never even looked over at him as he jumped in the bed of the truck and they went bouncing down the road. His eyes never left her for more than thirty seconds.

Adam and Stellar went to the same college, met each other with friends for meals for awhile until suddenly and magically Stellar fell head over heels for Adam, all waxy black curls and brown doe's eyes and alabaster complexion and nine years her junior. They had a tumultuous love, violent in its positive and negative passion, in its youthfulness. Stellar threw a lamp at Adam, Adam sketched Stellar in charcoals while she slept on his tiny dorm room bed. Stellar coaxed Adam into a water fight in a public fountain, on a winter day. Adam plastered a wall of his senior art exhibit with photos of Stellar's curves: her spine, her hips, her jaw line.

As history repeats itself, Stellar was gravid before she was properly hitched. As angels foretold in conversations with one another, Adam loved Stellar, fell even more in love with her as she blossomed with the glow of new life. He insisted they follow the pregnancy through, get married afterwards. They discussed the future in his room, ELO trebling loudly through the wall next door.

"You have to promise me," Stellar was saying.

"Sure, yeah."

"No. I mean *really, really* promise me. That you are going to marry me after. You won't freak out after you see her, after you have to change a shitty diaper."

"Yeah, I won't freak out after I have to change a shitty diaper. I love you, Stellar. Let's do this." Adam smiled disarmingly at Stellar, and she returned his smile.

"You have a Bible in here?" Stellar asked, getting up and shuffling around the room.

"Um. I think maybe. On that shelf." He pointed. "Why?"

"We're going to make this as ceremonious as possible before we have this baby."

She found the Bible under an incense burner, dusted it off, sat cross-legged in front of Adam. "All right," she held out the Bible on her upturned palms. "Lay your right hand here."

Adam placed his hand solemnly on the Bible. "Look Stellar," he said, meeting her with his eyes. "I completely promise to marry you after Ethel is born."

"Ethel!" shrieked Stellar, hitting him in the upper arm with the flat of the Bible. "Yuck. Now you have to try that again."

"All right. I absolutely, positively *will* marry you and spend all my days with you from now until forever, no matter what. I do."

Stellar looked at him. "I do too."

Then she threw the Bible down, scooted her belly toward him, and grabbed his hand, placed his hand on her stomach. "Now promise her. Promise on her."

"What makes you think it's going to be a girl?" Adam asked.

"She just is. Now promise."

"Okay then." He looked down at the stomach he loved, for two reasons, with both his hands placed on it. "I promise to love you more than life itself, to raise you right, to marry your mother and make an honest woman of her." Stellar punched Adam on the shoulder, where a bruise was beginning to form. Then he looked at Stellar and said, "We'll buy a little house, before Ethel is even born. We'll be a great little family; the three of us." And inside Stellar, the two little ones swirled around with glee.

Adam reached over to the handkerchief bedecked crate that served as a bedside table and switched on his radio. It crooned:

"And The Queen and her lover
    Ran for cover
Holding each other tight.
While the tall story man

And his evil war band
Chased down the beautiful knight.
Where have all the heroes gone?
I want a stately red-headed queen
     to make love to angels
     and wield a sure sword
And Jaden to save the day,
Oh-oh Jaden to save the day."

CHAPTER 9
LESSONS

ഗ൭   ൫൭

Gaby propped a clipboard on her lap, poised a pen over a card with a picture of a Yorkshire terrier on the front, ready to fill the blankness inside. She waited for Sonja to gather her thoughts, to begin with the addressee. Gaby looked out the window at a landscape of grays, wetness, chill, skeletal trees on whites, her eyes vacant. Sonja was buried under her quilts, rattling the ice in her cup and looking over at Gaby.

"You better not let that one get away," Sonja remarked.

"What?" Gaby shook her head and looked down at the card, wrinkled her brow.

"You better not let that one get away; Mikhail," she said.

Gaby snapped to. "Sonja," she laughed airily. "I don't *have* him to begin with."

"Mmm," is all Sonja replied, with a slight nod of the head and a narrowing of the eyes. "Well," she said much louder and just as airily, "I don't really feel like writing a letter today. How are you?"

Gaby shifted in her chair, dropped the clipboard and card to her side, dangling against the armrest in her left hand. She brought her right hand to her face, placed the tip of the pen it held on her bottom lip. "Fine, I guess. Annie's long gone," she frowned briefly.

"She left for school?"

"Yeah, a couple months ago. And I'm not sure I like it," the shadow of a frown again.

"You have been together for a long time."

Gaby adjusted herself, squirmed around and then settled. "Still, we've never been the wear-the-same-outfit kind of twins, or anything."

"No, but you're still twins, and sisters. I think that counts for a lot."

"I don't know what it's like *not* to be a twin. Or a sister."

Sonja leaned over to set her cup on the side table. "Don't you have a connection with her that you don't have with anyone else? Something special?"

"I suppose so. Of course, I love her more than anyone. And sometimes we 'have a connection' that I wouldn't be able to explain to you, verbally. It even gets really strange."

"Like when you both fell on the night of graduation?"

"Like that, and a thousand other little things. But enough about me…"

"I'm fine," Sonja apprehended. "This home is still as good as I can expect. I like writing letters with you, I enjoy your visits. I'm just biding my time, really."

"No," Gaby said. "I've seen people around here 'just biding their time.' That's not you. You still get dressed, still comment on TV shows, still *write people*. I'm sure people enjoy getting your letters. I would."

"Maybe. But no one wants the burden of me anymore. I won't mind passing on. When you end up here—even if you haven't given up—you're overdue."

Gaby sat forward in her chair, her eyes earnest. "Don't say that, Sonja! I can't believe anyone's overdue. There's got to be things anyone can do. Love people, vote, send their money to charities."

"And what about when they can no longer think? Can no longer reason? Can no longer even wish charity on anyone?"

"But you're not there…" Gaby trailed off.

"You've seen them around here, Gaby. Breathing vegetables. *Are* they alive? Life is not all about what you can *do*, Gaby. It's about who you are, and sometimes it's just about walking about breathing and being, no matter how much pain is endured." Sonja seemed to catch on the last phrase, as if she just realized the topic on which she spoke was a personal one. She leapt back from the brink, her eyes betraying a little confusion and fear.

"Well, you've got more years on me," answered Gaby.

"But you have it all figured out," smiled Sonja.

Ↄ ⁊

When Sonja was forty-two and a curvy, breasty woman with cascades of russet hair and almond-shaped baby blues, she decided—in the stillness of the uneventful nights beside her permanently placid husband—that a life-long restlessness would be vented in a solo vacation, somewhere warm and somewhere she had never been. She had no aspirations for overseas travel; some exotic American locale would suffice for the single hiccup in an entire life spent in the Midwest and in fact, Florida would do just fine. She smiled up at the ceiling in the dark.

This resolve was a secret, which made it alluring to her and also was the best way to bring it to fruition, a way to bypass the familial and friendly protestations that would face a shoes-always-tied housewife traveling alone five states away. She did her research at the travel agency on the sly, charming her husband, a grown Izolda, and her sisters as best she could manage without giving a breath of her intentions, without inviting tag-alongs. Two years she planned and connived and then she announced departure and disappeared.

She stayed in a rented house on the shore of a broad river near the marshes of Florida's tip. She could walk to the shore of the Gulf in ten minutes, where she spent whole days with dime novels and thermoses of iced tea. She lived quietly and meagerly, thoroughly enjoying all the details of being alone—standing in a shaft of light in a local shop, perusing shell earrings, with no one waiting outside, no one to ask about the purchase, if she should so choose. She ordered meals without any consultation and very little deliberation, kept the little kitchen spic-and-span while throwing her clothing dramatically around the bedroom whenever she de-robed. She sat out on her deck, watched the manatee and porpoises and osprey and heron and likewise enjoyed the reality of love and security back at home.

She rented a car for driving to movie theaters and nearby fishing villages. One morning, she decided to drive a few hours up the shore to seek surprises. She landed in a very wealthy town, newly developed, elite in its flood of eternal sunshine, low-sunk on the Gulf shore. She sat and watched the boats passing and walked down the impressive streets in the infernal heat, perspiring through the back of her blouse. She bought a collector's spoon of Florida for her husband and a box of Florida cards for her collection. She walked into the first restaurant she spotted for lunch and hydration.

The restaurant's lunch menu was heavy on delicate specialties. The dining room featured abundant windows and a domed, frescoed ceiling, open and airy and filled with Florida sunshine, light breezes, the freshness of air wafting around ample potted trees. The tables, the chairs, the floors, walls, ceilings, were white and yellowed-tan, very structural, architectural with the tang of a pseudo-relaxed Southern fiefdom. The seats were padded, plush, the kitchen emitted intoxicating smells, fresh smells, high-quality smells. Sonja asked for a table for one as the host eyed her quickly.

Sonja ordered a crispy noodle cake with prawns, steamed vegetables, and a red-orange wine sauce (which heavenly taste she could remember to her dying day). The water quenched her parched throat, an excellent mint iced tea followed, floating prettily with strawberries and mint leaves, perfectly-sculpted ice cubes. After she drank and ate her fill, she leaned back in her chair, crumpling her linen napkin into a ball on the table beside her plate.

She was so absorbed in the process of de-parching and consuming good food that she was surprised when she reposed into—not a comfortable company—but a subtly hostile environment. Amidst the light clinking of china and silver, amidst the hushed whispers, plastered smiles, glinting of earrings, airy laughter of lunch dates, business rendezvous, and family outings, she allowed herself to feel the tightness in the room; the fear and rejection that all the tilted bodies were sending out toward her in perverted tendrils. She was not even sure what exactly marked her so obviously, so readily, as an interloper. She assumed she had decent table manners, she had money to pay for the moderately-priced meal. But there was something in a crease in her blouse, in the stitch of her skirt, in the last-years-ness of the flip in her hair, that marked her. The hostility scorched the beauty of the place and she shifted uncomfortably in her seat under the glances thrown over shoulders. Then she slouched, on purpose, and smiled at the full spot in her stomach, tilted back her head and shut her eyes.

She paid for her meal, left the required tip on the table, and engaged the host in a conversation on her way out. He asked how her meal was. In a moment of inspiration, she turned her head over her shoulder and remarked rather loudly, "Excellent food, but I found the company rather low. I suppose I won't have my brother the Duke here next week, after all."

CR BO

Gaby bit into a beef jerky strip, ripped at it with her teeth, looking into the low, fluttering, foliage at the side of the road. White cumulus puffs floated listlessly through an enormous expanse of shocking blue. The world shone as if scrubbed with golden soap.

"When are you going to go vegan?" Mikhail asked from his cross-legged position on the hood of the station wagon.

"Just hold on," Gaby responded. "You should really start by pressuring me to just be *vegetarian*, I think. Or give up red meat, or something. Maybe just bacon."

"You'll break down one of these days; on your quest for the meaning of life and death and all. Vegetarianism and veganism are all about the sanctity of life. Respect for life."

"You're just a softie," Gaby teased.

Mikhail did not respond for awhile. "Well you're just mean. Look at you ripping away at the flesh of some poor animal that was probably abused during its whole pathetic factory life and then slaughtered in the cruelest possible way. You ever read *The Jungle*?"

"Not exactly the facts of today."

"Whatever," he said. "These are different days with the same evil in men's hearts."

"Plus," Gaby interrupted him, "I'm not on a quest for the meaning of life and death anymore."

"Oh?" he asked looking down at her.

Gaby looked away from watching his hair blowing in the breeze, golden in the sun (having returned his hair to its natural blonde after a few unnatural shades). She liked Mikhail's fly-away hair, liked anybody's fly-away hair, she mused to herself, not just his. He watched her gaze shift quickly from him, a habit she had that confused and discouraged him. They were on the way to see Melodie during the warmth of her first spring in Marquette. No Doubt started to play on Gaby's sad excuse for a car radio, she turned it up loud and pulled over on the endlessly straight and flat two-lane highway flanked with corn fields pocked with green stubble. She jumped out to dance around the car with the door thrown open, like a wild banshee. It wasn't the first time Mikhail witnessed such uninhibited behavior—which of course, made him love her more—so he let himself be coaxed from the car where he danced around with her until the song ended and they sat exhausted on the front hood, watching the occasional car pass.

"Yeah," Gaby smiled mischievously at Mikhail. "I'm more concerned with the plight of the elderly."

"Oh no." He smiled as he threw back his head.

"Oh, yes. Do you realize that old age is one of the few existing totally acceptable—even institutionalized—things you can be prejudiced against without social consequences in this country?"

"Sounds about right," was all Mikhail ventured.

"I love Sonja, you know. And I love my grandparents and my other elderly relatives. It bothers me to see them victimized, that's all." But looking at her sideways, Mikhail knew that wasn't all, that there never would be a "that's all" with her, and he wanted to say, "Gaby, I love you," or even, "Gabrielle, I love you," because he was in earnest. But he couldn't make up his mind and something hard grew in the pit of his stomach and he said instead, "You're a special girl."

He dodged her suspicious gaze, abruptly sliding off the hood and making for his open door. "Someone's going to think we need help and stop. Or a cop is going to pull over and arrest us for noise disturbance and unnecessary stopping at the side of the road."

"You think they could ticket you for that?"

"If he made it up, we wouldn't know the difference." He turned to lean against the hood, again.

Both of them took in the breezy brightness for awhile and then lay back into the hot metal and tempered glass, absorbing sleepiness like lizards. After awhile, Mikhail asked, "You know how that lady used to tell me stories? That lady in the woods?"

"You mean Mercedes?"

"Oh. Yeah. I didn't know you would remember."

"Mm-hmm." Gaby flicked her wadded plastic wrapper up into the sun and then tried to catch it, but it lifted on the wind and sailed down beside the car.

"She told me this story, once. Another story about The Queen and The Angel. I guess they were all really love stories, but I don't know too much about romantic love." He let the pause eat at Gaby, hoping recklessly for an intervention. When she did not stir, he continued. "I've been thinking about it lately. Maybe because you're so obsessed with aging and death. But in the story The Angel has to go to The Queen's castle to deliver a message into her dreams. A vision. And it's been a long time since they have crossed paths. They have stopped trying to create ways to see each other and accepted their star-crossed fate. Unlike Romeo and Juliet. Very *un*romantic, really. And The Queen is probably middle-aged and I remember Mercedes saying her red hair was becoming streaked with brilliant gray. I imagined silver. That sounds beautiful. Anyhow, it turns out that The Queen wakes as soon as she feels The Angel in the room and they defy the world and spend one fleeting night together, just holding on to the darkness as long as they can. Inevitably, dawn breaks and so do their hearts: that's another phrase from Mercedes."

"I got it. It's wonderful. Keep going."

"Oh. Okay. So in the morning The Angel lulls The Queen to sleep, kisses her on her cheek and leaves a note for her on her war strategy table-thing. But before he can fly out the window, the dark leader of the Demonis, the one who has stolen all the stories, stands there darkening the room and cutting off the red sunlight. The Queen wakes again and she

and The Angel stand holding each other once again as the
Demoni guy reveals his use of powerful magic to separate them
forever. He is hoping that The Queen will join forces with the
Demonis or succumb to them and leave her throne empty. Of
course, he wants the girl, but that's just stupid. Like she would
ever marry the crazy Evil Storyteller. Oh, well.

"So the Evil Storyteller completely botches their
wonderful, heart-rending farewell and he manages to send The
Angel off without another word between the couple, except for
the heart-breaking look in both their eyes as they accept that
this will be all history wrote for them. Then, with a violent
blow to The Queen's face, the Storyteller leaves, promising to
return in a week.

"But The Queen picks herself up off the floor and wipes
the blood from her cheek and spits out the window in the
direction of the Storyteller before she notices the note there
among the carved warhorses and armored men and miniature
flags. She picks it up in trembling hands and reads it. It says
what she had long feared: that though she was a mere mortal,
The Angel is immortal. That he does not age, and she would.
Of course, he cares nothing of her age because he truly loves
her and always will, but The Angel says their mortality and
immortality are illustrations for the bigger picture: their lives
are not congruent. They cannot be together. And now, beyond
the note, the Storyteller has made it real. The note urges The
Queen to continue on with her life without hope of ever seeing
The Angel again.

"Fearing the Storyteller's return in a week, The Queen
gathers one of her most noble and loyal land-holders, Jaden the
Hero. She discloses her story and offers him both her hand in
marriage and the bonus of ruling the kingdom in return for his
warriors and his valiant protection of the kingdom. He accepts.
He falls just as in love with her as everyone else does—maybe
even more—and they are married by the weekend. All right, in

the real story it wasn't 'the weekend' but it had something to do with fortnights or whatever."

"Go on, doofus."

"That's it. Jaden saves the kingdom, or The Queen does, depending on how you look at it. She sacrifices herself for the people and has some sort of spectacular scene where she uses magic to end the war and Jaden does the manly thing and even though she is rent from her true love forever, she and Jaden are well-matched and they are really happy together and have babies who grow to rule a peaceful kingdom where the Storyteller has perished and their mom and dad go down in great ruler history. The end."

"Huh." They lay side-by-side in the heat and the silence.

"I thought we were going to get arrested if we stay here much longer."

CHAPTER 10
NAMES

Nadine kept a spiral-bound notebook in which she recorded the major—and sometimes minor—events of Mikhail's life. On page one, the story of his birth. On page twelve, his first word. On page twenty, his first step. On page sixty-four, it is written:

"It is a snowy day in Michigan. I hated to have Mikhail wait out in the cold for the school bus, but he must go to school. As Mikhail stood at the door with his little backpack, his boots pulled snugly on, his coat zipped up to his chin, I wrapped a scarf around his little neck (his face all the while screwed up in disapproval), and told him to put on his mittens. As I reached for his stocking hat and made to put it on his head, he quickly placed his mittened hands over his head and said, "No, mom.' 'Why not?' I asked. His face implored me, 'Because it gives me eidetic energy!' he triumphantly argued. For a few seconds I just stared down at him with the hat hugged to my chest and question marks on my face, wondering where he got those words and what he thought they meant. Then I realized, 'You mean static electricity?' 'Yes,' he said."

When Nadine was ripe with her first pregnancy, she made a time-biding trip to the five and dime to perhaps buy a baby journal. Upon discovering wire-bound notebooks on sale, she considered inflation and bought not one, not two, but six notebooks, each in a different color. She told herself surely there would be brothers and sisters, and surely this was the best deal she would get on their notebooks. Plus, they would all look the same; same size, same thickness, same paper weight, same veiny blue lines perfectly aligned and faint, all filled with different stories.

When Nadine got home, she placed the red notebook on the office desk at a perfect forty-five degree angle and wrote inside the front cover, "The Life of Mikhail Aleksandr, child of Nadine Julianne and Alexy Aleksandr." In the event that the child was a girl, they had already decided the name would be Mikhaila Aleksandra, and would simply necessitate the adding of two "a"s to the notebook. The remaining five notebooks; blue, green, yellow, orange, purple, Nadine wrapped carefully in a plastic bag and set on the top shelf in the nursery closet.

The five colored notebooks lay in the bottom of a box at the back of a storage closet twenty years later, covered with dust, the pages yellowing.

Nadine's life was rent with Alexy's abrupt death. The violence happened when she was still honeymooning over both her handsome, capable husband and healthy baby boy. Alexy was in Wisconsin helping to oversee the construction of a bridge when an unfortunate series of events culminated in him being pushed by machinery into one of the long, broad legs of the bridge as the workers were filling the mold with wet cement. There was nothing to be done. Nadine's dreams dissolved and a plaque was put up on the pylon, a flesh-and-blood messenger sent to Detroit with the sad news that would fill Nadine's nights with flashes of terror as she dreamed the horrible facts into allegorical nightmares again and again.

It was dusk when the messenger arrived, handed over a sealed letter and verbally revealed its contents. It was dusk when Nadine slunk to the floor in the doorway, her left hand grasping for the doorknob, her left arm giving out, her left hand giving up and slinking down after her. It was dusk when the messenger left Nadine like that, in a ball on the floor with the sealed envelope laying disconnectedly in front of her, Nadine unwilling to respond to his questions, his timid concerns. It was night when the baby woke up crying, when Nadine left her spot in the open door, shivering in the cool summer air. Not a tear had fallen, just a shock had washed over her. She moved around the house in mental confusion, on auto-pilot with some synapses misfiring here and there. She could not decide what she was supposed to do now. She slept in the bed, making sure not to fall over the middle line. She stayed inside the next two days and took care of Mikhail in a detached, obvious way. It was Nadine's sister, Ruth, who came to visit after Nadine missed church. Ruth knocked, she rang the doorbell, then she let herself in the house. Nadine said, "Alexy is dead," in a way that Ruth's first impression was that something had slipped in Nadine's reality.

Ruth temporarily placed baby Mikhail with a cousin, escorted Nadine through funeral plans and proceedings, making sure there was food in the house, casseroles for dinner, warding off indiscreet bringers-of-condolences. She put Nadine to bed at night, brought her breakfast in the morning, and was by her side when she visited the funeral home without a body, first saw what awaited her in a sickening flash of realization—the first of many successive realizations that someone is permanently and irrevocably removed from your space-time continuum in its forward, linear motion.

It was the permanence that rattled Nadine the most, the inability to do anything to change Alexy's being ripped from her. His death was unalterable, unchangeable. It would take years heaped up on years for her to accept this one last thing.

As she struggled with it, she vowed never again to wed, to fall in love; a commitment tattoo on her life. There was the Nadine that answered the door, and there was the Nadine who lay on the warm, cement doorstep of a house in a summer dusk, curled on the ground, mortally wounded.

It was during that turbulent time of dissociation that Alexy's mother approached Nadine with a poor excuse for an explanation and the breathtaking locket with its cockamamie tale. The locket was beautiful, something special. She had *not* taken it to be appraised, as strictly directed, but assumed it was very old. Possibly worth something, but she doubted it. Would she sell it if it were? It meant something to Nadine, Alexy's mother approaching her in the wake of his death, talking with her about something, even a locket. And the locket had a magnetism all its own.

Alexy's mother—Tania—said that the locket was a family heirloom, very old, very special. Originally, a wealthy ancestor had it crafted to house a seed. Yes, a seed, she said. A magical seed. Magic given from the gods on a somewhat rare occasion to us humans. Like Prometheus, but a seed. That would explain the lock on the locket. Never seen anything quite like that before. The locket may or may not be empty, Tania explained, because the powerful locket—powerful because of its magic seed—was stolen hundreds of years ago and since it was finally recovered (through a few generations of striving, loss, poverty, and even murder), it had never been opened.

But there were promises, Tania continued. If the seed were there, it would find its way to the lost half. The magic would return to the Aleksandrs. Poppycock. What business did American Russians have with a mystical locket steeped in ancient Middle Eastern legend, anyhow?

Nadine cherished the locket. Kept it put away and ready for Mikhail. Ready to grace the carved collarbones of Mikhail's future wife. Soon. Very soon. And her grandchildren could fill her life with a noise that was never to be hers as a mother.

ⅭⅤ ℥

To celebrate Annie's summer homecoming returning from State, Stellar planned a family picnic, complete with Bill and Julia and Stellar's half-siblings and their families, Adam's parents Tony and Gia, Aunt Celia, Uncle Cal, Aunt Susanna, cousin James, and all their families, Mikhail, Melodie (who was also returning to Butter for the summer thaw), and Sonja, among other neighborhood and school friend additions. A tent was rented, rows of mostaccioli, ambrosia, and baked beans lined on two adjoining picnic tables, white paper tablecloths flapping against masking tape in the breeze.

A hose stretched from the house to a kiddie pool filled with freezing water, in which floated bags of ice and pop cans. It was a nippy summer day, so not too many people donned bathing suits and hopped in the pool. Instead, the hose, curving and taut in the grass, promised "water sports" in the afternoon sun. More than one person grabbed it up, turned the spigot, and aimed a cold spray at a group of people. Gaby and Annie sat at a picnic table with Sonja in a wheelchair pulled up to the end, Gaby and Annie nursing a plate of potato chips, long strands of wet, matted, hair, and Sonja looking at them from her wheelchair perch with but a little envy in her eyes.

"Look at Maddy," Gaby remarked, pointing loosely at a baby cousin sitting in the grass with the end of the hose in her uncoordinated hands, water splashing out slowly, her diapers soaked in a large puddle of water, grass, mud.

"She's cute," said Annie.

"Now, whose is she again?" Sonja asked.

"She's Mom's youngest sibling's, Gloria, and her husband, Randy. They have, like, at least twenty other kids. Not really. I don't know."

"She's the youngest cousin," added Annie.

"Hopefully the last, jeez. Do you think we could populate the earth more?"

Annie rolled her eyes and Sonja narrowed hers against new-fangled ideas. Seeing the response of her audience, Gaby added, "But where would the world be without Maddy? She could be the next Einstein, the next president of the United States."

"In that case, maybe we better take a picture of her now," Annie said as Maddy stood up and wobbled around pulling at her sodden diaper in an attempt to remove it. She had half-succeeded already. "I'm going to go get my camera. I'll be back."

With the hose abandoned by Madeline, Mikhail tripped on it and then turned it on a group of pre-teen cousins who were chasing after him over the lawn. He stuck his thumb over the mouth of the hose and showered them with cold rain; they scattered. He looked down at the hose and around at the groupings of people. Melodie happened to be walking casually by with a pop to her lips, on her way to the swing set. Mikhail turned the hose on her with a large grin on his face. Melodie screamed, threw her left arm up to shield her face, and then ran toward Mikhail, throwing her pop to the ground in an arch of orange liquid. The two engaged in a wrestle for the hose, both managing to become sopping wet in the alternating aim of the spray.

A ripple of mutters went up from the people watching the action, and one obnoxious uncle yelled, "You two lovebirds cut that out!" The match ended in a truce and Mikhail jogged over to turn off the hose. Then Mikhail and Melodie walked off in the direction of the park.

"What does that mean to you?" Sonja asked Gaby.

Gaby shrugged and frowned, "Nothing."

"Are they dating?"

"No. But so what if they did? It'd be the first time Melodie dated a decent guy."

"What about you? You ever think about dating Mikhail?"

"He'd have to ask me out for that to happen. Plus, I'm not interested. Guys are jerks," Gaby threw her glance anywhere but at Sonja's face, and took a sip of pop from a can that was already empty.

"Mikhail's a nice boy."

"Yeah, Mikhail's not really a jerk. I know. But I'm not interested. I have so many things to do. I don't have time..." Gaby trailed off as Annie approached the table. She was suddenly thinking about theories of probability and how logic holds even in the particulars.

Sonja would not relent. "I've told you before, and I'll tell you again. You better not let that one get away."

Annie slid onto the bench next to Gaby. "Who, Mikhail? God, don't I know. Wish I could find a guy at State like him."

"So why don't you take him?" Gaby shot back and then in sing-song. "Before Melodie does?"

"Whatever. He doesn't like anybody but you. Never has. He follows you around like an adoring puppy."

Gaby's face was stormy. "I didn't ask for that. I don't want it."

Annie retorted, "Well then here's the big question, Gaby." Sonja's gaze volleyed back and forth between the sisters. "Why the hell not? What's wrong with Mikhail? Or are you just too good for him? You a closet lesbian? Or do you know about that third green, alien, arm that he hides from the rest of us? What gives?"

"Shut up, Annie."

"Come on, we all want to know."

"We all, who?"

"Everybody wonders. But *me. I* want to know."

"Well, I don't know, Annie. A lot of things. He's never actually asked me out or shown any interest in me, *that way*. And who wants to ruin a good friendship with a bad relationship? I'm not ready to settle down. Plus, I've got plans."

Gaby's eyes brightened. "I'm going to travel around, finish college, maybe go to graduate school. I'm going to solve the hunger equation in the world, I'm going to adopt a greyhound, a couple kids, see the Northern Lights, write a novel..."

"Hey," Annie interrupted her. "This isn't the dark ages. Relationships don't hold women back anymore. At least not relationships with men like Mikhail. Mikhail wouldn't be a hindrance, he'd be a *partner*, a best friend to do all those things with you."

"I'd rather not try it out and end up losing, thanks."

ᘒ   ᘓ

Gaby started spending her time at the nursing home bouncing between writing with Sonja and interviewing community members that were coherent enough for an interview. Her senior thesis—which in her excitement she was already starting her sophomore year—was tentatively titled *The Last Two Acceptable American Prejudices: Obesity and Senectitude*. In order to continue spending time with Sonja in addition to conducting the interviews, Gaby increased her hours at the nursing home. She saw less of Stellar and Adam, Mikhail, Annie and Melodie, slept rarely and at odd hours, got thinner— was it possible?—from forgetting to eat half her meals for days at a time.

The interviews spanned the whole winter, and in the spring she picked up with two local Overeaters Anonymous groups. She promised to use false names in her paper, and kept a crate next to her bed filled with page after page of interviews (on napkins, in notebooks, on lined paper), ideas, and research notes (mostly on color-coded index cards). She breathed research, lived it. She turned into a waif of the cause.

One Saturday morning in the spring, Gaby woke up in the small hour's with an idea about the paper, threw her word processor, a stack of library books, and the crate in the passenger seat of the car, told Stellar she'd be back sometime the next day, and drove off down the road. She stopped at a Tubbys' Submarines where she bought three sandwiches, three bags of chips, and a large lemonade, and drove to the nearest camp grounds. She paid for an overnight sticker and bought a bundle of firewood (just in case she decided to use it, since, they informed her, the office closed in the early afternoon and there would be no turning back at that point.)

She felt woodsy, one of the only campers on the grounds. She felt left alone and productive. She climbed in to the back seat of the car, propped the full-batteried word processor on her lap, and after an hour, the back seat was strewn with papers and Tubby's wrappers. The windows were all open to a warm spring day, the breeze occasionally lifting the edges of the papers, throwing a whole corner of the back seat into disarray. Around two in the afternoon, the gray sky dropped rain—a warm rain—and Gaby, who was too intent on her progress to see it coming, threw the back seat into a flurry of paper and limbs as she struggled to quickly shut all the windows. The sodden papers were then laid out on the dashboard and in the rear window, and she sunk back into her work.

The narrow beam of a head lamp kept her working into the night (the word processor dead by now), the firewood abandoned on the passenger seat floor and more discarded Tubby's wrappers. When her head began to hurt with the strain of turning papers and making notes in the dim, she clicked off the light, stacked everything back in the crate on the front seat, shoved all wrappers in a plastic bag, and rummaged in the trunk for a blanket, a pillow, an old flannel coat, a pair of mittens and a stocking cap. She lit her emergency "heater"—a candle set in an empty coffee can—and snuggled it up next to her stomach, embracing it with her arms, her knees drawn up under it. Like this, she fell asleep, curled on the back seat, an orange glow dancing on the ceiling in a wobbling circle, the rain pattering on the metal roof and on all the windows.

CHAPTER 11
CROSSED WIRES
1.5 YEARS LATER

ᔥ   ᔥ

Outside the Tinbro Toy Company Toy Factory, Gaby stood on a makeshift wood platform, behind a makeshift wood podium draped with a "STOP CHILD LABOR!" banner, her voice ringing out over a small crowd, churning with placards and energy.

"We *must* do something to stop child labor," her voice finished with a feedback squeak from the rented speakers, "And we must do something *now!*" A small cheer went up from the audience, a few, "Hey!"'s, and a wave of signs being lifted up. Adam clapped at the back of the crowd, where he stood uncomfortably; support a person, not a cause. He could understand; children were being forced to work in terrible conditions somewhere in some foreign country, and some companies in richer countries were prospering because of this cheap labor. It took jobs away from Americans, he was told, and as Gaby said, it was cruel (a "sin of omission" she had called it) not to defend the defenseless.

The few workers who agreed to picket and the other protestors (mostly conscripted from other causes around the area), hoisted their signs up to their shoulders and humped them back and forth in front of the platform and along a chain-link fence that separated them from the parking lot of the factory. To their left, the fence was interrupted by the entry gate, a trickle of cars in and out of it. The cars drove wide to the far side of the drive, made apprehensive by the restrained picketers.

"Stop child labor *now!*" was the first chant they took up and they were still chanting it when Gaby spotted the local news van approaching. She walked slowly down the two or three stairs, her hand shielding her eyes from the glaring, fall sunrise.

"You see that?" Tricia—the thirty-something organizer of the event—approached her as Gaby descended the platform. Tricia sounded excited, kept glancing from the news van to the clipboard she had propped against her stomach, and sidled up next to Gaby.

"I see it. It's great."

"It's just what we wanted."

"Maybe you should go introduce yourself?" Gaby offered.

"You too. That was a great speech," Tricia smiled over at Gaby. "You can better articulate some of the concerns."

"But you're the brains behind the operation. The fire. I'm just along for some of the ride."

"Well, you have other things to champion," Tricia offered, as they both slowly approached the van and the side-door slid open.

Gaby hung back a few steps away scanned the crowd, looking for her dad and assessing the turn-out. "We've discovered—have documentation actually—that Tinbro Toy Company is utilizing child labor in at least three different third-world countries, eating up as many as three thousand jobs right here in the Detroit area…" Gaby heard Tricia discussing the story with a news camera pushed in her face.

"And how about you?" the news anchor turned on Gaby. "What is your name and why are you here?"

Gaby was drawn back toward the camera. "My name is Gaby and I believe that no child should have to work in the kind of environment that these children are forced to work in. Twelve hour shifts without breaks, no attempt at temperature control, low light, dampness that breeds disease. They are asked to do repetitive tasks that eventually rob them of the use of limbs or phalanges thanks to carpal tunnel, arthritis, eye strain, and other work-place hazards that would not be tolerated here in the United States."

"I see," responded the newswoman. "So what is the answer?" She placed the mike back in Tricia's face, and Tricia began articulating on "nothing short of the closing of this factory until the matter can be rectified," just as the noise level of the crowd behind them rose. All three of them turned to look at the sudden bustle. In the parking lot on the other side of the fence, a contingent of Tinbro workers approached in a mob, bearing placards that read "DON'T PUT AN AMERICAN BUSINESS OUT OF BUSINESS!" and "WE WORK HERE, TOO." They waved them in the air, chanting "It's a free ec-on-o-my!" as they approached. The people on the outside of the fence responded by gathering in toward the fence, booing and yelling. Tricia quickly jumped into the fray, encouraging the group to chant, "Your jobs are o-ver-seas!"

As the workers reached the fence, a couple from both sides started to tussle through the chain-link, rattling it with their fingers interlaced in it, rattling it with their bodies thrown against it. Both chants went lame as yelling broke out at the fence and two police squad cars pulled up on the fringes, sirens cutting on and off. The newswoman ran into the crowd, her cameraman trailing behind. She was outlining the events as she back-peddled, "There seems to be the beginning of a fray here at the Tinbro Toy Company factory today. Members from both sides of the skirmish have gathered at the chain-link fence that separates the outside world from Tinbro, yelling over each other to be heard…" She disappeared in the crowd.

Gaby watched from the fringes herself, unable to completely decide what she should be doing. She looked to the right and over several heads saw Adam looking toward her. He caught her eye and waded toward her. Gaby continued to scan, watched the faces of the Tinbro contingent rouge with anger and scream things that were wound into a ball of inarticulate shouts and stray exclamations. She read their placards, watched them bob. There, right on the noisy fence, was a woman that Gaby knew as Kelly, a picketing Tinbro assembly line manager with her arm thrust through the fence, her hand tangled in the mass of someone's hair. Likewise, the mass of hair had shoved her arm through the fence and had hold of Kelly's ear, and was twisting it. Kelly's face was contorted as she screamed something at the assailant.

"Hold on, Dad," Gaby yelled to an approaching Adam as she ducked into the crowd and toward the fence.

"Hey!" Gaby yelled, over Kelly's "Fuck you!" Gaby grabbed for the hand on Kelly's ear and pried the fingers loose. Then she yelled, "Kelly, let go!" Kelly released her grip, pulled her hand back through the chain link, took a step back, and looked at Gaby with distaste and anger. "Fuck her. I work here too!" she yelled.

"I don't work here, anyhow! My brother does!" Gaby turned to face a familiar voice. Melodie looked at Kelly through the fence, rage burning in her eyes. Quietly she added as she turned away, "He needs this job, Gaby."

Gaby froze as the world swirled around her. She gaped at Mel walking away from her, as if in slow motion, a stray hair lifting into the wind, her left hand slowly finding its way into the back pocket of her jeans as she navigated the crowd and leaned into someone who put their arm tentatively up onto her shoulders and Gaby knew that arm. She knew its thinness, its paleness, the freckle at the elbow.

Mikhail looked back over that arm, over his shoulder at Gaby as he escorted Melodie away through the throng. He shrugged, raised his eyebrows in apology.

∞ ∞

Gaby was furious. She knew Mel and Mikhail had been hanging out more together without her, felt the tension when the three of them were together. But that was good for Mikhail, right? And good for Melodie? Two good people together, even if the best friend was to become a third wheel? Still, she was furious. Mel was clearly wrong for valuing her brother's crappy salary over the welfare of third world orphans and widows. She was also clearly wrong for not shouting from the rooftops that she would be taking part in the anti-humanity protest *and* dragging Mikhail along. It was a direct betrayal. It couldn't be that jealousy had any footing in Gaby's pure heart. Or could it? She couldn't find it in herself to be mad at Mikhail, much. That would be too lonely a road.

Mel called that night, but when Stellar walked the phone up the stairs and poked her head in Gaby's door, she was surprised to get a "Tell her I'm busy" with such bile (Gaby's face furrowed at the book propped on her knees) that Stellar asked no questions and disappeared down the hall with a muffled, "Sounds like she doesn't want to talk right now. Sorry, Mel."

Mel called the next afternoon and the same scene occurred, although this time in the sunlight, and Stellar mumbled into the receiver, "I think something's wrong," to which she received the cryptic response, "There is something wrong," and a sigh, a click.

After a few more attempts, the calls trailed off to every other day, then every third day or so. Gaby refused to answer the phone at all. She gave herself a smug smile in the mirror when she thought to herself that the calls were tapering off for good. And she kept reading and writing and reading some more, stacks of books over her floor, her bed. Today; in stacks all along the picnic table in the back yard, texts held open with rocks, papers fluttering in the breeze like wounded butterflies, grounded.

From the back porch and over the hum of the pool heater and light splashes, Gaby heard (through the open sliding glass door) a knock at the front door. "I'll get it!" She bounded up, tapping her pencil eraser against an open *Foundations of Philosophy*, pleased with the way her studies were coming and with the warm breeze, the clear skies, and comfort of her home on a summer's day. She thought to herself she might jump in the pool later on, smiled all the way to the front door, bouncing, wagging the pencil in the air.

She swung open the door and her face dropped. Framed in the doorway and edged in close was Mel, her hips off-center, a pleading look in her eyes. "Gaby, I..." was all she got out before she saw Gaby's face turn to a stony frown, and felt the light breeze of the door as it shut solidly against her.

"Fine, Gaby!" she yelled, bitter now. "Fine! I'm not going to beg anymore! What sort of peacemaker are you, anyhow? You're just being a baby! A BIG *FAT BA-BY*!" Mel finished with her head in an open window next to the door. She looked in at the shadows of table, chairs, pillar candles, her hand shielding her eyes. She heard a few thumps in the foyer move closer, then suddenly there was a shadow blocking her view, Gaby's head hovering a few feet above her behind a pane of glass. The window came slamming down. Mel looked up and flicked Gaby off, which Gaby barely saw before she turned abruptly and padded up the stairs.

"Where are you going?" Stellar asked, at the top of the stairs.

"To take a dump," and Gaby disappeared in the bathroom, slammed the door behind her.

Stellar saved the usual admonishments and instead, jogged down the stairs and out the front door with a quizzical look on her face. "Mel, wait!" she called, Mel's head turned toward the rear window, the hum of the car escaping in reverse under the soft, rhythmic thud of her bass.

The following day a cardboard box appeared on the front porch, hugging the door jamb. Adam lifted it in and set it on the kitchen table. He peeked under a top flap and then left the box where it was. The box sat there for days, untouched, and finally he asked. Stellar didn't know what it was. Gaby would not answer him. A thorough investigation would have told him the box was full of Gaby's belongings; things accumulated at Mel's over the years. Curious now, Stellar rummaged through and set it in the middle of the floor of Gaby's room. From there, it mysteriously transported to the hallway, right outside Gaby's door, and from there, to a random shelf in the laundry room.

There the box stayed, collected dust as the sun tilted farther from the earth, as swimming pools floated with leaves, then worms, then froze over, as the moon waxed and waned a handful of times. Melodie took the long trip north again, and Annie and Mikhail went to see her off, both of them accustomed by then to not asking Gaby if she was going. Nor did they mention Gaby's name to Mel. They were thankful enough that they were allowed to move freely between the two, neither one resisting their relationships or delivering ultimatums. In fact, it would be fair to say that Mikhail often wished that Gaby resented his friendship more. Only once or twice did jealousy flicker over Gaby's face when Mikhail turned down an invitation because of prior plans made with Mel. Most of the time Gaby was locked away in her tower with her books, in the library, at the nursing home writing what had turned into hundreds and hundreds of letters for Sonja.

On a cold day in December—the air crisp and the sky blue as fresh paint—Sonja was watching a soap opera, dozed off, and never woke up. Gaby was called, as was Sonja's out-of-state granddaughter, Betsy. Stellar took the call and rushed to the library, where Gaby left a stack of books on the table—some of them her own—and drove like a maniac, dodged around cars in the parking lot, pulled onto the sidewalk and rushed into the nursing home only to find things running as usual and Sonja's bed vacant. She broke into sobs that wracked her body in violence and screamed into the controlled hush. Gaby hit the bed with her fists, kicked at the bed frame and Mikhail came rushing in behind her in his aide scrubs, throwing aside a clipboard as he lurched for her. He grabbed around her waist, fought her flailing arms until she was still and then he held her for a very long time, and he breathed warmth through her curls and onto her scalp.

She didn't fight.

Sonja hadn't cared to leave a will except what the nursing home had made her fill out in forms. In neat script, near the end of the form, Sonja had made Gaby write, "I don't care who gets it, I'll be gone by then. Just don't fight over anything." There wasn't much to fight over, and Betsy gathered most of it up in her Jeep before heading back to Arizona, bequeathing the entire card collection, one rug and one quilt to Gaby.

Back in the summer when Gaby's relational drama erupted into WWIII, Gaby reported day after day to Safe Places, and Mikhail wore her down with his endearing smiles and his unwillingness to make explanations for his being with Mel, for his dating her. He was in the room when Gaby told Sonja the story of the Picket Line and the Betrayal. Mikhail was in the corner folding sheets and Gaby paused over a card, sitting next to the bed. She outed with it, and occasionally Mikhail tempered a fact or strategically cleared his throat. Sonja listened, then tried to talk to Gaby in her own language. She called it "an iconoclastic clash of idealism and pragmatism that only immaturity would let flare into a passion which could destroy old loves and maybe even petrify sins." She told Gaby that she believed in her, ultimately, and even in Mel. Somewhere in them were the warm, recessive pools of compassion and generosity that would hopefully unfold into something where love would usurp philosophy, where even wisdom would develop into—not dominate—faith and hope.

It would not be an easy progression. Gaby wrenched the Ellis Island card shut and Mikhail snapped his white sheet, loosening the smell of chemical lavender and the glare of reflected sunshine on them all.

CZ &O

The funeral was a small affair, not representative of one-quarter of the people Gaby wrote to for Sonja. Adam, Stellar and Annie came in noiselessly for the service, slid into seats in the back. Gaby and Mikhail sat in the second row, Gaby's face still stony yet bereft, but a little more tired than that. Mikhail wore a black suit and tie with a freshly pressed and starched white, button-down shirt, his hair cut for the occasion. (Nadine handed him the cash, ordered him to run down to the barber, and when he returned, had his suit and shirt hanging neatly for him in his room.) He cut a handsome figure next to Gaby, in a knee-length, fitted black dress with a full skirt, her hair pulled up and off her face in a messy knot. She wore a black lace bracelet with a single, black rose, black Mary Jane pumps, her eyes bluer than usual with the washing of tears, her cheeks flushed red with grief.

At the viewing, Betsy moved up to Gaby. She wore a black dress cut in postmodern lines, asymmetrically. A velvet hat perched on her short hair and sported a tiny black net which she wore down over her mascara-streaked eyes. Dark on dark on light. She told Gaby thanks for everything.

"Did she say anything? Anything about… the ring?"

"No. I'm sorry."

Betsy looked disappointed, and turned away, then seemed to think twice about it and turned back apologetically. "I would have believed her, you know."

"I'm sure you would have." Gaby didn't know what else to say.

Gaby leaned into Mikhail as they fell in line to view the body, her arm through his, the rough feel of suit coat on her hands and arms. Gaby looked down at Sonja with her eyes, her chin kept level and Mikhail led her away quickly. They read the names on the flower bouquets and baskets, stared without talking at the young photos of Sonja around the room, had some bitter coffee laced with refined sugar packets and oily pseudo-cream, then left together. Mikhail placed Gaby in the front seat of her own car, noticing how thin she had grown, how fragile, then rummaged in her purse for the keys, climbed in the driver's seat and queued into the funeral procession.

"You hungry?" he asked as they neared the cemetery.

Gaby was hugging herself, staring blankly at the dashboard. "Yeah, I guess I really am."

"What do you want? Any processed food product you can think of. All available right here," as they drove down the main stretch of some town, their orange funeral procession flag slapping lamely against Mikhail's window.

"But what about the burial?" She looked at him, partly worried, but with a glimmer of hope flickering in the recesses, pleading.

"I'll pull the flag out of the window and jump the line. You're not holding up too well," and he pulled into a Subway, jumped out of the car, and came back with two sandwiches, two drinks.

When he returned, he handed her one of the glasses, "Drink this."

As he again turned the keys in the ignition, his eyes caught on the keychain: one he gave her years ago, facetiously, a red heart-shaped frame with a photo of himself in it.

They walked up and over the snowy hill as the casket was being lowered, heard the priest say a few, clear words that were lifted up and away from the huddled crowd of people. They were the last two to throw dirt in the grave and then they wandered off back to the car in silence. There in the cemetery in Gaby's car they ate their sandwiches and started talking about a few things that weren't Sonja, that weren't old age, and weren't life and death co-mingled.

Gaby let Mikhail carry her up the stairs on his back when they got home, since she was beat; half out of exhaustion, half because who wouldn't like to be carried up the stairs? He flopped her over on her bed, pulled off her shoes, and she cuddled down into the blankets. "I really need to change out of this dress," she said, looking at him.

"I'll leave," he replied, not moving from the foot of the bed, where he was sitting.

"No, I'm too tired, anyhow."

Mikhail took his suit coat off, threw it on her chair, Gaby watching the wideness of his shoulders. When he turned back to her, her face was red again, tears running down over her lips. "Mikhail, I've really messed up," she halted along the proclamation. He was there by her side in a moment, his arms around her, her arms thrown thinly around him. She sobbed into his neck for a long time, wetting his shirt, his T-shirt. When the sobbing turned into a tired stillness of the body, she backed away from him and they looked at each other.

"I... I miss Mel," she said, although she could have said much more. She could have said things about the direction of her life, about her failure as a social writer (which, actually, would not have been true and some modest publications and awards would have refuted), about all the wisdom that slipped through her fingers like sand, about all the good that she *wasn't* doing, about all the people she wasn't saving from hunger, persecution, grief, death. At the moment, she felt unmoored. And she looked into Mikhail and knew that she loved him—for one flicker of a moment—then she felt like she was falling, the room started spinning, she started to cry again and held onto Mikhail, smelled him, pushed hard with her cheek against his chest. In the silence, she fell asleep this way.

Soon after, he placed her back on her pillow, rolled over next to her, pulling a throw over himself, and slept there with his back against the wall, one hand resting palm-down on her left shoulder blade.

CHAPTER 12
ANOTHER TRAGIC END TO A CAUSE
ℰ◯   ◯ℛ

Somewhere in a mesh of sweeping dirt roads and straight, long, sparsely populated highways, an understated train trestle spanned a dramatic dip in a low-traffic road. The train came seldom and the cars just a little more often. Betsy liked to come here to be alone. What was her stupid mother thinking, anyhow, moving them here to the middle of nowhere with a bunch of hick kids in the little school. She worried that the motive was to insert a distance between Betsy and Grandma Sonja. Her mother was so crazy.

She kicked at the ties nestled down in the gravel and dust, spraying tiny pebbles up over the rails. She scuffed the toes of her sneakers at the rails, making sure to clear them of debris with all the nonchalance she could muster. She plopped down in the middle of the bridge, her feet dangling over the side, and swung them hard as she looked out over the road, the bush foliage and encroaching trees suffering, whispering together, through the long summer. She looked up at the blue sky, so enormous and plain that it hurt her to see it. She would swear the sky was less blue here. Clearly washed out, bleached by a relentless sun.

She didn't do much of anything, just sat and looked and thought, kicked and occasionally threw a rock down the road in a high curve, especially when she remembered certain things. When she remembered that her mom had screamed at her as she stomped out the door to go grocery shopping, Betsy threw a rock at an oak tree, as hard as she could muster. The momentum made her wobble a little forward and she steadied herself, a little chastened.

No! She would not be scared! Her mom was scared! A complete coward; afraid of everything! Afraid even of her own mother. Of sharing Betsy with anyone. Of that stupid ring, still, she just knew it!

Betsy held a small rock in her right hand, rolled it around in her dusty palm, and leaned back against the ties and the rail, feeling for a vibration in her tail bone, the distant approach of a train. Everything was still and the cicadas that chirruped made not a move. She wondered if she would survive a jump from the bridge unscathed, or at all, and she decided to whip this rock at the next car that went under the bridge. She'd probably miss it anyhow.

Only seconds later, she saw dust at the far end of the road, rising between the trees, an offering to the pale sky. Then she heard the hum of the motor and the crunch of the tires on the road growing from inaudible to louder. The car was coming fast, its tires hardly touching down into the potholes, the car a brown shape as it moved into shadows, a glint in the sun as it cleared them. And lots of dust.

As it zoomed toward the trestle the sun took over and the shine made Betsy look away. But it was coming close, fast, and Betsy squinted as she zinged the rock right at the car. She heard it crack as it hit the windshield, hard, and heard the tires slide in the dirt as the driver braked strongly. Betsy jumped up, and ran off the trestle into the foliage. Running down the tracks, hidden in the grass and trees. The brush caught on her, hit at her face, and she kept running until she was far away, panting and sweating.

Her mother made no attempt to chase her down the tracks in high heels and a pencil skirt. She had already seen her, legs dangling on the bridge, slinging rocks down at her windshield.

Cৰষ   ৰও

On Betsy's wedding day—that first wedding day that seemed so far away, now—she wore cream crepe, her hair swept up by the local beautician that morning, a veil skimming her face, gently tugging at her eyelashes when she blinked. The church, like everything else around, was alone in a field dotted by trees. Betsy was worried about getting ticks in the layers of dress and slip that trailed down through the tricky weeds. She was worried about getting married. She was so young. But she loved James. He was a real country steal. Heck, she was a real country steal.

She leaned into the bathroom mirror, re-adjusted her train so that it would not trail in the toilet, or anywhere near the toilet, for that matter. She ran the tube of plummy lipstick across her lips, mooshed her lips together on themselves, then puckered.

"Betsy?" Her maid of honor, a fake-blonde so skinny she was barely there, slipped in around the cracked door and let it shut behind her. Faith asked, "You about ready, sweetheart?"

"Yeah, in a second." Betsy used a finger to pull at the corner of her eye and she stared inspecting in the mirror. "Where's Mom?"

"She's in the kitchen, of course. We can't get her out of there. But she said she'd come out when you did and take her place at the front. She looks great."

"Well, it's her kind of day. Looking good and serving guests; always was good at that."

"Yeah." Faith sighed, whether at Betsy in her wedding gown or the hospitality of Izolda, Betsy was not sure. Faith had a habit of sighing. "Well, come on, pumpkin."

"Oh, all right." Betsy threw up her hands in surrender. Just then the door behind Faith swung open, hitting Faith in the derriere and sending her flying. "Whoa there, cowboy!" she called out, dusting herself off and wobbling a little on her be-flowered stilettos. James stood in the doorway. "Take a hike, Faith. I need to talk to Betsy."

"But you're not supposed to even see her! What, you couldn't wait five more minutes?"

"Well, I see her now. So get out."

Faith slunk back out the door with a "Sheesh. See you in a sec, Betsy," and it closed.

James moved toward Betsy but she held him off with two out-turned palms. "You can*not* kiss this face yet. I just finished lacquering up."

"Oh, yeah. I didn't think of that. Sorry."

"It's all right." She eyed him suspiciously. "You know it's bad luck to be in here. Plus, I'm pretty sure we're supposed to be out *there* by now." She pointed at the door. "Honey, why *are* you in here?"

James clasped his hands behind his back and looked down at his feet, one of which was tracing a pattern on the tiles. "Um, Betsy. You're grandma's flight was delayed. She won't be here in time."

"What?" Betsy went pale and her eyes widened at him. "No!" She looked for something and grasped on to the sink attached to the wall.

"It'll be okay, hon. She'll be here later, I promise. And she gave me something to read to you."

"Gave you...? What?"

"Well, she told me over the phone and I wrote it all down. It took like half an hour and now I have a cramp in my hand, but... Well, here." James dug into his pocket and retrieved a crumply piece of lined notebook paper, unfolded it, and brought it up to his face, clearing his throat.

"No! Wait!" Betsy snatched the paper from him with one well-manicured hand. "I'll read it. You go."

"You sure? It's kinda weird."

"Yeah. Positive. It's always weird: it's *magic*. I'll be right out."

"All right. See you in a minute." James extant.

The paper, except for the spelling errors and minus the smudges and manly scrawl, read:

"The Evil Storyteller was once a child, just like any other child, in that he was a child. Only rarely are children truly extraordinary, and most of the time children are let be mediocre for awhile. Bless them.

"This boy, whose name at one time was Keir, or so I have been told, lived in a small village in Russia. Clearly, he was not from there, but his parents were traveling merchants and had wandered very far from home before coming to rest, for a brutal winter, in the town. That is all that is known about him. Perhaps his parents were loving and supportive. Perhaps his father was cruel or his mother was angry. Perhaps he was doted on. Or neglected. Or just a child, like any other child. He was, after all, just a child.

"The horizon over the town was dominated by the estate of a wealthy family. Their house was a mess of fanciful turrets and imposing walls, doors, windows, gates, and a bustling lot of servants. This was the House of Aleksandr. The boy looked up at the house every day and he wanted what the Aleksandrs had. It is an age-old feeling.

"Now, traveling merchants are often adept at things that you and I consider wrong, or dark, or just plain rude. Keir could pick a lock, could quiet a horse to lead it away, could slide a bag away from a man on the street without him noticing, what have you. One day, he saw the wife of Aleksandr in the town, in all her fine clothing and dimpled skin. He walked close behind her and then walked away, in his pocket the locket that she was wearing only moments before. When he got home, he ferreted it away under the floorboards, only briefly noticing how beautiful the working of gold and silver and copper filigree, how fancy the encrusted gems of reddest red and bluest blue and goldest yellow, and also the tactile hum that was coming from within.

"That's all there was to it. He stole the locket—and the magic seed therein—as an afterthought. By the time the Aleksandrs had the locket back, two hundred years later, Keir had turned into the Evil Storyteller, died; the locket tarnished and rusted a bit; then hidden away in obscurity."

Betsy let the paper fall with her hand down to the bodice of her shimmering dress. She thought of James laboring over all that writing, of James with the phone receiver cradled on his shoulder and the dumbfounded look he must have had on his face. Then she thought of Sonja, still hundreds of miles away, even though Betsy wanted her to be right here. Could she go on with the ceremony without Grandma? In some ways, all this Indiana life had nothing to do with Sonja, but in others ways, Betsy still needed that primal connection. Sonja always was Betsy's best cheerleader.

So why, in lieu of her own bodily arrival, did Sonja send *this* story? Betsy imagined the actual storyline held very little importance compared to the gesture of sending Betsy a Northwythan story for her wedding, the kind of story Sonja was always telling her while Betsy was in her formative years. She hadn't sent a story about the ring; maybe she meant to keep the peace during this special time, leave Izolda alone. The Northwyth stories weren't always about the ring, and the magic echoed in all of them; they fit together like pieces of a puzzle when half the pieces were missing.

That's how Betsy felt now, standing looking in the cracked, church restroom mirror in her white, princess gown; like she was putting pieces together but they weren't all there. She let her mind slide lightly over her memories of the stories, over the tales of princes and princesses and angels and sages and paupers and hags. The stories were everywhere, all around. She heard them in songs, read them in books, studied abstract art with pretentious critiques snorting "the Northwythan references are post-modern in their constructive fabrications." Which came first, the world or the legend?

Faith poked her head around the door. "You ready or what?"

Betsy folded the paper neatly in half, then in quarters, and then in eighths. She slipped it neatly down the front of her dress and with a little difficulty secured it against her stomach, where no one would ever detect it through the rigid brocade. She turned from the mirror, "Ready as I'll ever be."

☙ ❧

Gaby volunteered the night shift at the nursing home, when they needed her. It was so peaceful in the home at night; the play of rare light and plentiful shadows easy on the eye, silent except for the hum of computers, the whir of the dishwasher, the heavy breathing of the community members. In the dark and the quiet, Gaby could distract herself from missing Sonja, which she did valiantly, instead of having to avoid the old room, the new tenant, whenever she walked down that hall on busy days. In the daylight, in the bustle, she superstitiously skirted around the door, facing the wall, giving herself and those around her reasons to think she needed to turn that way to get a tray by a member, or that she suddenly saw a crack there in the wall that enthralled her.

In the evening, Gaby pulled to the front of the nursing home, dropped off a crate or a duffle bag straining under the weight of books, then parked in the lot. She walked back to the front with her laptop over her shoulder and hefted the books into the home. Then she'd set up shop in the front office or in the staff lounge, depending on whether she was hungry or not, had food to prepare or not. Her co-workers threw glances at each other, muttered as they followed her approach routine out the front window, "Looks like Einstein's on the night shift."

It was one such night in the spring, near the end of Gaby's thesis, and she was on night duty despite the fact that the deadline was drawing near. In her optimism, Gaby envisioned a long, quiet night spent synthesizing research and finalizing details. She could turn it in tomorrow tired, fall asleep in a desk until the obligatory lecture was over.

Gaby greeted her co-workers, threw her books on the table in the lounge, and then went to check the nurse's station for the night nurse on duty. She returned to the lounge as the workers were one-by-one trickling out the door. "Bye Sue, have a nice night." "See you, Larry." The lights in the hallway were dimmed as she stepped into the square of light on linoleum that marked her all-night vigil in the lounge.

After a couple hours of bent head over books and occasional tapping at the laptop keys, Gaby sighed over her almost-complete work and decided to treat herself. She rummaged in the freezer, found a pizza with "Gaby, March 2" scrawled on it in Sharpie, and popped it in the oven. She rubbed her eyes, stretched her jaw and then threw her arms over her head, sauntered down the hall to the staff restroom.

When Gaby emerged from the fluorescent brilliance of the restroom, she looked both ways down the hall at the circles cast orderly by the dim, round lights, listened to the little creaks, the squeaks and clicks of people turning over in insomnia. She could hear the rhythmic clapping of one of the dementia patients, who must have been awake, but soft, muffled behind his solid door.

Gaby turned to her right and leisurely walked the hall, put her ear up against the clapping man's door, where she let it rest for several minutes. Then she continued down the hall, slowly, and then down another, and another. She looked closely at doors, listened to whatever small noises she heard, took a long time walking and walking, swaying back and forth, lifting to her toes, whatever. At Sonja's door she paused, stood directly facing it and placed her palm flat against it, her wrist bent back at a right angle and her face close enough that her warm breath came back at her. She sighed. Then she took three deep breaths.

She returned to the main hall with more speed, walking steadily in and out of the light pools, when she simultaneously smelled something amiss and noticed a smokiness in the air exacerbated by the light-and-shadows outside the lounge. Alarms sounded at points all down the hallway and she pulled her hands up over her ears. Community members made the noises of not only waking, but panicking. There was banging, yelling, screaming, and a few doors already thrown open by the time Gaby ran down the hall toward the lounge. She reached it as the sprinklers came on in the lounge and main hallway. She looked around and saw that the oven was engulfed in flames, the ceiling already beginning to char black above it, the counter top ablaze and blistering. She saw her books in the water, her laptop. She had a moment of hesitation during which the bottom fell out of her abdomen and her brain experienced vertigo. The she turned and ran down the hallway, yelling, "All right! Come on! Everybody outside! Everybody follow your fire plan!"

The nurse, Phyllis, came running toward her, shielding her head from the sprinklers, her scrubs already speckled with water. "Is there really a fire?" she yelled to Gaby.

"Yes, in the employee lounge."

"Holy Lord," Phyllis muttered.

"The fire department should be on their way."

Phyllis's face turned from surprise to realization, her muscles suddenly tightened and she sprung into action. "Let's get everyone out of here," she said as she sprang at the door nearest her. She ran in, coaxing Mrs. Peller to wake up, we're going to have to go outside, and quickly.

Gaby, Phyllis, and the security guard who had arrived in the hallway made their way from room to room, ushering people in walkers and on their own, unsteady feet down the hallway, shuffling zombie-style. They wheeled wheelchairs down the hall at haphazard speeds, came back and wheeled cots out, trailing IV bags. They ran in and out until two fire trucks, a few ambulances, a few squad cars arrived and numerous firemen and policemen joined in the chaos, Phyllis, Gaby and the security man soaked and yelling orders to them about which patients were cleared, who needed help, which way to evacuate.

By the time the night was over, hours later, Gaby propped her back against the main hallway wall, her hair dripping water over her sooty face, and sunk to the floor. It was quiet again, but with a buzz of sleepless community members, worried sounds coming from nightmares, things dripping from the heavy spray of the fire hoses (now curled up and gone home), things splashing down in black puddles in the front part of the building. The front office was now exposed to the cool, night-cum-morning breeze: there would be a herd of workers here soon (even at 4am) to stop up the gaping hole in the roof and wall with plastic tarp. There were sounds of voices in the rubbled rooms, a few people—nursing home manager, owner, lawyer—stepping over things as they assessed the damage.

When they emerged from space that was once the office, the manager with a sodden, charred book in her hand, Gaby was already gone, driving down the road with the windows rolled down, getting as far from the place as quickly as possible.

She had started by just standing up and walking to the car and flopping into the driver's seat. But after Mikhail showed up with a spare key and was conscripted to help with clean up, she started the ignition and realized she couldn't get moving fast enough. She broke her usual speed as she flew down the forested roads, which faded into straight roads between plowed fields, which faded back to forest.

When she pulled into the driveway, she realized she had nothing, not even a driver's license. If her new cell phone hadn't been melted into a plastic blob, she would have gotten a message (which she would have found odd, since the phone was only for emergencies). The message was Annie, calling to say she had almost burnt herself and her whole house of fellow students to a crisp. She was baking banana bread, reached in the oven to take it out, and caught a towel on fire. She threw the towel in the sink, yelping, and turned on the tap, but somehow that didn't work the way she wanted it to and a housemate named Mandy burst in brandishing a fire extinguisher and put out the fire. It had been a nightmare to clean up and the rest of the housemates caught a faint whiff of burning as they nodded off to sleep. "Don't worry, Gaby. I'm okay."

The nursing home community members all made it out and then back in the building, alive. The stress clung to some of them for a while; two members were pulled from the community and placed elsewhere; there were a half-dozen threats of lawsuits; but most of the family and caregivers of the members came calling and left satisfied with the competent emergency response. Considering the physical state of many of them, this had been no small feat. Part of the convincing began unseen, when all staff had been immediately summoned and sent to changing sheets and diapers, mopping up sooty footprints and halls and wet floors. By the end of the next day, the place—all except the disaster that was the front entrance, the office, and the lounge—was returned to normal. Within a few months, the disaster area was demolished, fund-raising and book-balancing done, and the offices re-built and re-supplied.

After Gaby's night flight from the scene of the disaster, she fell asleep in the car, her head on the steering wheel, exhausted, ash-streaked pale lines standing out on her cheeks where tears passed by. Stellar found her there the next morning, already alarmed that Gaby's bed was vacant, then alarmed that Gaby was slouched over in her front seat, then further alarmed when she knocked on the window and Gaby stirred: looking an absolute fright of sleepiness and sooty disarray.

Gaby did not attend classes that day, did not turn in a paper that had been obliterated by the flames. Her professor allowed her a few weeks to gather everything back in, and Gaby dutifully locked herself away from the questions and re-pieced the paper which was never to return to quite its height of glory as the destroyed original. She also dutifully paid off her rather large library bill amassed from destroyed property, and even borrowed from her parents to purchase a new laptop, carefully selecting an extended warranty.

Then without many words, she drove to the school, turned in the paper, and drove away again, having passed all her classes. By the time a graduation ceremony was in order, she had met Sara and was gone.

CHAPTER 13
ZION

ഇ   ര

John Robinson was never a big boy and he didn't become a big man. His dad, Robert, hadn't been a big man, either. But the Robinsons—besides being storytellers—were back-woods men, were northerners, were survivors, and—as the legal restrictions allowed—huntsmen.

Robert took John on his first hunting trip when John was ten. John had a hand-me-down gun which he practiced with in their wooded yard until they drove in the pickup a few hours up the mitten of Michigan to Kawanachee. Deer season was in early December, and year after year Robert traveled to the same boarding cabin next to the same pond, which was half the time already frozen over, or at least disastrously icy. Other men came, sometimes they changed. Robert had been rooming with an old college buddy, but now he would room with John.

They woke the first morning at the cabin when it was still deep dark, as if morning had no intention of coming. John had to will himself to slide out from under the blankets, warmed by his body heat, and set his thick-stockinged feet on the cold floor. He bounced around to keep the cold out of his toes, smacked his hands on his body here and there, rubbing at his upper arms. He hated to go from his pajamas to clothes, and was glad to see—by the light of a lantern on the table—that Robert was slipping into his jeans and button-down flannel and sweater with his long johns still on.

In the dining room downstairs, the host and hostess already had breakfast on the table and men sat on all sides, grunting down at their plates and looking blank. John found it hard to eat so early but Robert forced bacon and sausage and fried eggs on his plate; told him he better eat. John sort of wanted a steaming cup of black coffee, just for the heat. He didn't think he was ready for coffee, yet.

John and Robert layered coats and gloves and hats and pulled on their boots—Robert's seemed impossibly large and heavy to John—and followed a trail where the snow was stamped by several pairs of boots before them. Eventually Robert turned off to the side, plowing into the snow that still glittered in the moonlight, snow that looked soft under the stark slicing of black, bare trees into a starry sky. John's cheeks were icy cold and his fingers were beginning to chill where he held on to his rifle with an intense grip. His heart pounded out against his ribs.

They settled into a deer blind, one which Robert must have planned coming to, maybe came to every year. Robert settled down with a sign and set up what he had toted. And then he became determinedly silent, his storytelling heart set on being undetectable in the hushed woods, the snowy woods where the contradicting blanket of white dampens all sound and the cold clarifies each twig snap, each joint pop.

John was able to take a hint. He sat, frozen to the bones, silent and waiting, trying not to move or breathe too heavily, his breath coming out in tentative puffs on the air. They sat like this for the morning, John scanning his gaze over the wooded terrain, across the sweeping snow drifts and the sculptural trees, tiny twigs reaching out of the downy drifts between the sparkles.

The sky washed from black to navy to a limpid mix of white and blue and pearl, purply pink before the sun broke over the tops of the trees and clarified everything with harsh light. The sharp shadows stretched long on the ground were as imposing as the branches reaching high. And then the day softened, the hours went by. Sometimes there was a small noise and Robert would poise his gun. Once or twice he jutted a finger out into the woods, pointing at a Chickadee or an erratic track where a Cardinal had passed, throwing snow with its tiny toes and wing tips.

John's stomach was rumbling, was turning in on itself. He thought about this for a long time before he finally whispered hoarsely into the still, "Dad. I'm hungry."

Robert, lost in squinting reverie, startled a little. "Oh!" He looked at his son before he undid his jacket, rummaged around in the shirt pocket over his heart, and produced a packet of beef jerky. "Here." He mumbled as he handed the jerky out to John.

"You want some?" John asked, well-versed in politeness by an attentive mother.

"No, No." Robert looked over the woods, up in the sky, searching for something. "We should be headed in. Get warm. No deer. Didn't even get to see one. Tomorrow."

"We don't have to go in." John was freezing and bored and starved, but he was determined to show his patience. And the mystery of the wood, the quiet camaraderie with his dad, was calling him to stay, too.

"Sure we do." Robert winked at John, who was shivering and tearing with his teeth at the tough meat, made tougher by the cold. "Come on, son."

They trudged back to the boarding cabin, just as a light snow of large flakes began to fall from a clouding sky. They banged around as they came in the entryway, stomping their boots on the rug and reaching down to pull them off. John fumbled with his laces, his fingers a bit numb and painfully thawing. Then he straightened up to deal with his coat.

A girl stood before him, scrawny and with waist-long curling brown hair the same color as the pine trunks, as were her large eyes. She was bundled in a flannel dress, a sweater, cable knit stockings and wool socks in sturdy shoes. She held the handle of a basket in crossed arms on her chest. The basket looked too big for her, too heavy, so she arched her back a bit against it. The basket was brimming with foil pouches, some with traces of char, in which were interlaced little things like pinecones and pine needles and twigs and acorns. The girl was looking John squarely in the face. "Pastie?" she asked, clear and loud.

John looked to Robert. Robert reached out a hand, still gloved. "Yes, please."

They each took a meat- and potato-filled turnover from her basket, wrapped in foil and hot to the touch. Heat against thaw sent a sharp, aching pain up through John's fingertips, into his palm, up into the wrist, but John made sure to hold on tight. The girl stood unmoving, staring still at John. John stared at her.

"Whuddya want?" John tried.

Robert cleared his throat.

"I mean, what's your name? Mine is John."

"Mercedes."

ᘓ   ᘔ

John and Robert returned annually to the boarding cabin. At first, it was just a place Robert had always gone, and a nice boarding place besides. But then, as John's and Mercedes' chasing games of hide and seek turned to long talks sitting side by side on the porch swing, the frozen chains groaning under their weight and their breath thick on the air between them mingled into one cloud, Robert made sure that they kept returning. For "John's friend."

John married his friend. She walked up the aisle in a flowing gown, flowers in her hair, and carrying a basket by the handle, overflowing with forest flowers. How she managed to find so many little blue blossoms on the day of her wedding, John never knew. She looked wonderful and she stared down John with a smile as she came up between the few pews. He whispered, "I thought you brought me pasties," which made her smile wider.

They moved far from Mercedes' secluded life (which was burst in on only during certain hunting seasons) and to another cabin—much smaller—in the woods not too far from a small town consisting of one avenue of shops, called Butter. John and Mercedes were the only people in the wood who stayed for all the seasons, all the years. Most other cabins, secreted away from them by the leaves and woods and animals and fresh air, huddled around lakes, so close they nearly fell in. The cabins teemed with people for the summer, mostly on weekends. John drove to his day-job in town, at the auto repair. Mercedes walked to her work at the convenience store on a lake, making a small fortune off popsicles and candy.

Then Mercedes' belly swelled, she took long walks in the summer afternoons looping around the cabin, waited. Then they had a boy, Jamie. Even as the city encroached, even as Butter turned into a township and wove streets of prefabricated houses into the leveled woods, the usurped farmland, Jamie grew up largely the way Mercedes had: at home, nestled by his mom and free to roam the woods and chase the robins up into the trees, to shoot at raccoons, and to wait expectantly for the holiday seasons to interrupt the peaceful, exciting flow of his life.

Jamie knew when John would crunch his tires over the dirt track up to the cabin every weekday evening. He grew with it set in his biological clock. He also knew that after dinner John would take Jamie up onto his knee and tell him stories. Mercedes told Jamie that John had begun with the storytelling when Jamie was too young to have a memory, just an infant too small to even smile. She also said that John started telling *her* stories the first day they met. Told them all along. For some time she thought they were lovely, then cute. But she hadn't counted on the ferocity with which he included Jamie, the driving need to tell all of the stories, over and over, to a sick Jamie and a bouncing Jamie and an uninterested Jamie.

John said Jamie would be the next storyteller.

Mercedes said so what if he didn't want to be?

John said he would, as if that ended the conversation. It didn't.

"You know these are just stories?"

"No, Mercedes. They're not. I've made it clear I believe they are much more than just stories."

"What would that make you, then?"

"A believer. But also someone who passes on the truth and protects it."

"I think you might have some grandiose delusions."

"You can stop throwing big words at me. I know what I know, and I am insistent that I teach that to Jamie. I never hid this from you."

"I never really thought it would last past your own childhood."

"So why did you pretend to believe?"

"I didn't pretend..." Mercedes had, in fact, been lost in John's stories, caught up in their magic and their wonder. She could sit for hours and listen to him tell stories of Northwyth and of so many other things. Like any child, she was the center of any story she heard; a princess, a queen, a little orphan girl. *That's the way stories are supposed to work.* And John agreed with her, but he said the stories were something more. He said they were old and honest and were his responsibility.

It was summer again, ten years after Jamie was born and fourteen years knocking around the same, little cabin, watching the world grow from afar, sweeping the same floors, filling the same bird feeders, polishing the same kettle. It was tornado season, Jamie home from school after his lone walk from the bus stop, and the gray sky brewed above gusts of wind that lifted the many leaves and sapling branches up and into a swaying frenzy. It didn't come as a very big surprise when the civil defense siren broke above the whishing of the foliage and the creak of the branches, telling Mercedes and Jamie to take cover in the cabin and huddle under the lower rafters with the wireless radio and a flashlight.

They waited there, curled up on the couch, Jamie with his homework draped over his knees and Mercedes with her knitting trailing to a basket of yarn. The rubbing of pencil eraser and clacking of needles did nothing to distract from the low hum-squawk of the weather report and the tension that built up in their stomachs, wondering if John was safe and if a tornado would plow up what little they held dear.

It was, as always, both exciting and terrifying for Jamie, and when the clock hands passed over the face of the clock to remind them that normally John would be home, Jamie looked up from his homework, his body stiffened. Mercedes watched Jamie, knew that John might not be home for hours or even all night, staying cocooned in the shop while the siren wailed. The siren still came strong on a deathly stillness and then disappeared in a gust of wind, back and forth.

"Jamie, it might be awhile. Dad is safe at the shop; you can bet on it." She reached out to lay a hand on his upper arm.

Jamie was ten. He would not tell his mother he was scared. "He isn't here to tell the stories."

"The stories?" Mercedes looked like she'd never heard of them. Jamie let his homework fall to the side as he drew his knees up into his chest and looked at the weather radio. Mercedes leaned forward and turned it off with a pop. Then it was so silent—only the noise of things scraping against the cabin walls, brush and branches and mice and the distant, insistent wail of the siren—that it was worse. So Mercedes took a deep breath, and began:

"Sand sprayed across The Queen's body like thousands of needles...."

C3 80

The chances of Gaby meeting anyone during the weeks after the fire was very slim, to say the least. She moved between secluded places (her room, her car) and neutral places (the library, the office supply store, her professor's office). She did no real interacting, kept her feelings to herself and far away from what she needed to accomplish. Sonja. Disaster. The meaning of her life.

She had been on her way to turn in the paper when she saw a small commotion on the stairs of the student building which she avoided by circumnavigating around. On her way back, she was so distracted by the alien hint of a good feeling resulting from the deposited paper, that she cut dangerously close to the little crowd of commoters.

A sprightly bolt of energy burst out and quickly caught on to her arm and introduced itself.

"HiI'mSaraandwhereareyougoinginsuchahurry?" Sara was back-pedaling just inches ahead of Gaby, keeping up as Gaby returned from oblivion and quickened her pace.

"I'm not interested." Gaby moved her gaze out to the horizon over Sara's shoulder.

"Not interested? Well, are you interested in ending the torture and exploitation of over 143 million displaced children?"

Gaby couldn't help an almost imperceptible side-glance, but pulled back out to focus again at the horizon.

"Are you interested in doing what you can—which wouldn't have to be much; just stuffing envelopes, handing out fliers—doing what only *you* can do to end the suffering of disenfranchised babies? Are you interested in…"

Gaby could hear her own voice, but she was thinking that she could hear something else; the voice of duty calling. She could hear the voice of guilt, but she thought that she could hear the voice of fulfillment. Sara was the wind that had blown at just the right moment, catching Gaby freshly unattached. Hers was a rebound cause. And Sara had no idea the force that she was summoning in such a work-a-day way.

Gaby stopped suddenly in the midst of Sara's speech. She looked her in the eye. "In fact, I might be interested."

"Well, great."

"Do you have any literature that I could look at?"

"Come with me."

Sara led her back to a fort of crates that were serving as table, podium, and library of information, where she fished out a half-dozen leaflets of various sizes and colors. She kept talking to the bent ear, meanwhile, and Gaby didn't really end up needing the leaflets to make a decision. Before she left Sara and the group of other excited world-savers, Gaby had committed to spear-heading a banquet for the developing world's orphans. The banquet would lead to making connections among the helpers, which would lead to Gaby's new life's purpose of loving on abandoned children, which would lead to a mission that involved air travel and around sixty-three meals of falafel.

And she was off.

ɔ﹩ ﻭﻭ

Gaby gathered her closest together for a meeting. They assumed she was going to present another cause to them, maybe with a Power Point presentation and plenty of slides of the Rwandan genocide or Burmese rebels. They were all nestled into couches in the living room at the LeFevres' house. From left to right, Annie, Mikhail, then Stellar and Adam.

There were no appetizers. No hand-outs visible, no computer propped in front of them. Gaby held no video, no book. They were nervous.

To tell you the truth, Gaby looked a little nervous herself, which was cause for red-level alarm. Mikhail's heart fluttered.

She stood there, not saying anything, with her hands clasped behind her. She was wearing a keffiyeh as a bandana— these were differences that gave them pause, clues.

They knew this: when Gaby returned from turning in her thesis, she had flipped into a different set of behaviors. She delved into the internet. She had some new do-gooder friends, interested in child welfare. True, she still disappeared for afternoons and evenings, but not to the library or school. The circles faded from under her eyes. She was eating, maybe even gaining weight.

And now she said, "I have a plane to catch tomorrow. To Israel. Well, via JFK and Switzerland, but…" she was starting to relay details about a one-way ticket nonchalantly, but her audience would not have it.

"What?" Stellar was on her feet and grabbing Gaby by the shoulders to steady the room. Adam was saucer-eyed. Annie's mouth hung a little open. Mikhail had gone white as a ghost, although it was hard to imagine him getting any whiter. He swallowed at the lump in his throat, tried to will the fast thrumming in his chest to stop.

"Are you crazy?!" Stellar yelled now. "Are you crazy?!"

"Stellar!" Adam worked at prying Stellar's white knuckles out of the red pits they were forming in Gaby's upper arms.

Gaby, in her sort of myopic-needs-based view of the world, had not calculated for this possibility. If she succinctly articulated a need, wouldn't anyone understand her great lengths, her urgency? Release her with their blessing? She looked shocked and sheepish together, not an attractive look. Her arms were down straight by her side and she refused to look away from Stellar and Adam at what the other two might be doing in response to her announcement; her eyes moved between her parents without any other movement of her face or head.

"Stellar!" Adam managed to loose Stellar's grip on Gaby but Gaby's rigidity didn't change. Stellar's clenched fists stayed at her side, pulsing up and down. Adam looked helplessly back and forth between Stellar and Gaby.

Stellar yelled into Gaby's face. "What were you thinking!? How could you do this to us?!"

And then Adam said, "Stellar! You're yelling in Gaby's face!"

So Stellar turned her fiery gaze to Adam. "I know I'm yelling in her face! She doesn't seem to notice me any other way!"

"Now you're yelling in my face!"

"That's because you're yelling in *my* face for yelling in her face! And anyhow I can yell in any damn person's face I want to!"

"All right with the cussing, already!"

"ALL I SAID WAS DAMN!"

"WELL, I THINK YOU SHOULDN'T HAVE!"

The two stood huffing at each other, locked into silences and into each other's eyes. There was anger evident, but that was just further proof of fear and even concern. Gaby made a reluctant beginning.

"I… I am leaving tomorrow, like I said. I just bought the ticket, but I felt I needed to go now. I will be meeting a friend-of-a-friend when I get there. I… I could be very useful to our people over there."

Stellar's body convulsed at the last sentence. "What people!? What are you talking about that would make you run into a war zone?!"

"It's not exactly a war zone, Mom." Gaby became defensive, articulate again. "I'll be based in Jerusalem, and more people die of violent crime in Chicago than die of bombings in Israel. And," she picked up her pace at the reaction to the word "bombings." "There is little to no violent crime there. It's just a different culture. I'll be *fine*. Plus, like I said, I could be useful over there. Did you know there are more than 13 million orphans, worldwide? There are places where sick or special needs babies are left to die, and the child mortality rate in some orphanages is as high as twenty per cent. And some of those babies, all they need is antibiotics or even *just someone to hold them*."

"Reality check, Gaby! WE HAVE ORPHANS HERE!"

"I know that, Mom." Gaby was now visibly shivering, facing down her mom like this. "But *this* team has been formed, *this* team has plans, and they asked for people to fund their own plane tickets and go on to a hostel in Jerusalem."

Stellar's arms were crossed lop-sided in front of her. She exhaled deeply at Gaby's words, flatly said, "Only three thousand years of war but no war zone, huh?" and whirled around, stormed out of the room and up the stairs.

Adam looked defeated. "Gaby. I know you care about a lot of things, but how could you do this to your mother?" He too went up the stairs.

Gaby stared after them until someone on the couch said something.

"Gaby, I..." was all Annie could muster at first. She wagged her head for a while. "Fine. Then tell us something more."

Mikhail sat very, very still. They could both see the blood had gone from his face. He said not a word while Gaby and Annie volleyed information and feelings back and forth to one another. He said not a word until Gaby walked him down the driveway two hours later. He lingered and then looked right at Gaby to breathe out a quiet "No," before turning to go. Gaby was speechless. She stood out under the stars and a little smudge of Milky Way, staring up. If she lay down on the cement to star-gaze, she wouldn't go inside and pack. She should have been packing all week, but the official news just arrived from Children Global today. She was going to be so tired tomorrow.

What did Mikhail mean with his little "No?" Wasn't he always going around with the traitor? She-who-was-not-to-be-spoken-of, but who went around crashing perfectly legitimate pro-human rallies? Did that make him a traitor, too? Fraternizing with the enemy. Maybe she shouldn't have even invited him! But she knew they were still best friends and that for all the fun he might be having with Mel, he was still enjoying Gaby, too. The darkness of past-midnight had revealed to her that her forgiveness of Mikhail blossomed largely from her need of him. She didn't want to go through long, lonely days without him. It was already mysteriously bleak without Melodie. The Sonja-shaped hole hurt. The Safe Places fire stung. Annie was gone so often to school.

Even after her bags were stuffed to bursting and half-zipped by the front door, Gaby lay awake in her bed well into the night. Her thoughts had been circuitous and rambling for hours: The only way she could escape her confusion was to go. She needed to go.

She narrowed her thoughts down and repeated them in a mantra: I'm an adult. The orphans need me. I already have a fairly expensive ticket.

Mikhail is not in love with me.

As the blackness around the stars lightened outside her window, she fell asleep.

Across town, Mikhail also spent the night awake and lying sleepless in his bed. He began the night with the assumption that he would not fall asleep, so the local alternative rock station played quietly from his stereo, the lights in his room dimmed down to a single lamp covered with an Indian wrap that Gaby had given him a few birthdays ago. It was made in a small village. Fair trade.

His chest ached. But that he could deal with. He had been dealing with the ache for several years, on-and-off, as Gaby moved in and out of interests, disasters, and even school-girl crushes. Tonight, as well, his head was spinning so that he could not find his bearings. Pulsing through all the confusion was the renewed realization that he loved her. But he was just now learning that he might have to do something about it.

He felt that he had nothing to offer.

What could motivate a poor kid like Mikhail? Just love? If only. It was, in the end, his love mixed with a song on the radio, which suddenly crept into his conscious thought. It was the "Just Like Heaven" cover by Dinosaur Jr. It asked him why he was so far away. And Mikhail answered. (While the workings of his heart were largely foreign to him, music he could understand.)

He answered, *I'm right here!*

∞   ∞

It was more than the insistent crack in Mikhail's voice or the sudden sprouting of a few odd facial hairs that told Nadine and John and Mercedes that the thirteen-year-old Mikhail was growing into a young man.

Mikhail was not at a stage where he rode his bike a whole lot anymore. When he got around, it was on his own two legs or on a skateboard. But he still yanked the bike out of its garage entanglements (of lawnmower, weed whacker) a couple times a month to ride to the end of the street and off onto the trail that led back to the Robinson's woods. He found that when he came knocking it often startled John and Mercedes, as unaccustomed to visitors without cars as they were. He liked best to catch them at something in their "yard," which is what they called the wood immediately surrounding their cabin.

It wasn't hard to catch them outside.

One particular day, John asked Mikhail to help him and Mercedes with weeding the shady garden. Of course he said okay, thinking of neglected chores at home. Then again, the Aleksandrs didn't have a garden. Maybe it would be fun to weed? Beat making the bed or emptying the trash?

The three of them slumped over the loose dirt, muddy hands and sore backs. Mikhail was on his knees, dirt stains the length of his shins. John asked, "You want to hear another story?"

Mikhail was silent for a bit. "John?"

"Yes?" he straightened up with a groan under his breath.

"Why do you tell me the stories"

"Why do you ask?"

Mikhail kept pulling at little green tufts at the base of a head of lettuce. He narrowed his eyes at them as if they were the focal point of his thoughts. "Well, I just hear things. I hear some of your stories other places. Sometimes they are different. And... There's this girl in my geometry class. She says she goes to the Church of North. Says she prays to The Queen."

"Really? They have one of those around here? Huh." John wiped the back of his sleeved arm up over his brow and then started rubbing his hand in his beard.

"That's what Lisa says."

"Well, people will say all sorts of different things. Unfortunately, they can't *all* be right." John walked the length of the garden as Mikhail and Mercedes tracked him. He sat down on a stump. "You want to know what I believe?"

"Yeah, I guess I do." Mercedes busied herself with collecting the uprooted weeds to throw out into the roomy trees.

John just sat and cleared his throat, looking hard at Mikhail, until Mikhail thought he should ask a question. "You think there are remains of a Northwyth castle?" He quickly caught his stride in an accumulation of pent-up thoughts. "A Wood of Branderby? You think The Queen's and Quicklander's bones lay moldering under a real accumulation of Earth's crust somewhere? You think there's a *ring* and a *locket*? And other things! Do *you* pray to The Queen?" Mikhail was almost yelling now. Irritatingly, Mercedes laughed quietly from the brush.

"No, I don't pray to The Queen," John answered him. Then he caught his own steam. "Sometimes I see someone who shouldn't be there, have a dream that tells the future. Sometimes I hear what someone has thought as if I've caught it on the wind. Not everything can be explained simply, or perhaps at all. Sometimes unexplainable things happen to me. Don't they to you? Or hasn't anything special ever happened to you? The moment your heart started to beat? When you first noticed the depth of the night sky? When you hold the woman you love in your arms? Well, I suppose not yet on that one."

Mikhail was blushing, so he didn't feel like he could say anything.

"I suppose that's enough to think about tonight as you fall asleep."

Mikhail smiled lightly. "I do most of my thinking in the shower."

"Yeah, you would be showering every day, you suburban knucklehead." Mikhail had grown to love John's friendly teasing and it eased his awkwardness.

"John, do you think all of it is true, then?"

"Well, I have my suspicions about some things. You know, the stories were entrusted to some of us, but then they disseminate out into the world at large. What happens to them, then? For example, I don't really think the bracelet of Gaston exists, on any level. Just a rabbit trail away from the most authentic of the stories. A hunch, maybe, but that's what I think."

The zagging hum of bumblebees and the chirp of birds hung between them. "Now let's go have a cookie. I can smell them here all the way from the cookie jar."

CHAPTER 14
INTERMISSION
ℬ   ℭ

At ten, Adam won the county-wide spelling bee. At thirteen, he was in the aeronautics club. At sixteen, he ran track, joined Math Club, and was a very handsome, painfully shy, boy. Always, he was sketching, drawing comics, studying drawing books.

The girls in his catechism class were sweet on him. He was oblivious, wrapped his broken glasses in tape and stashed his sketchbook under his hoodie. The jock girls got all excited as he ran by on the track, on the cross country trail. He felt he was embarrassing himself snapping shoelaces and tripping over tree roots.

Elizabeth, too, thought he was handsome, if not inconsequential. Elizabeth's mother was charmed by him. Elizabeth's brother eyed him sideways, noticing the continued absence of a smoke behind his ear, or greasy fingernails. Elizabeth's family lived in the kind of house that was straight up, white, and maintained up to the minute. They had a dog with its own house, a neatly kept cleaning closet with a new Hoover Constellation. There was a successful lawyer at the helm, funding all the Betty Crocker delights and Neiman

Marcus three-pieces. This lawyer had friendly crinkles around his eyes when he smiled, a square jaw, and a very attractive, high-waisted secretary.

Adam's house was long and brown brick, hugged the earth between mossy bushes and cracked sidewalks. There were children under every rock, pedaling furiously at bikes all hours of the day. The nights were still and full of cicadas, which sounded like an electric thrum in the summer air. Each house was nearly a cookie cutter of the one next door. All the fathers worked in "the" auto factory, which was true in similar neighborhoods all across the metro-city, just that the "the" in "the auto factory" changed. Ford. General Motors. Chrysler. Ford. General Motors. Chrysler. Adam's carpet was a little dingy. His dog was rarely bathed, but was petted and coddled and run around the neighborhood daily.

For Elizabeth, Adam began as a challenge. She heard someone say, "He's so cute!" And then someone else, "He's so weird." And that set off a chain reaction in Elizabeth that ended in her focused interest. She cast a side-long glance and then many more over a few weeks, a few months, as she moved in and out of attachments.

It was during the track season that Elizabeth had her opportunity.

She was dating Frank, who was a blonde, square-jawed, spike-haired, grin-boy. He won a lot of medals, but ran track mainly to stay in shape in the off-season for basketball and football. Frank was well-suited for Elizabeth, but she was bored with him. He requested that she wait for him daily at the track so that they could go out and get a burger afterward. When Elizabeth realized that she could watch Adam as well, she hung around a little more; a little earlier, a little longer. Frank was thrilled.

Adam had no expectations. Elizabeth sat in the pew in front of him at Saint Joseph's. As he moved through puberty, he watched a steady progression of necklines, hairdos, skirt lengths, stockings. He followed her through the seasons of her scents. He stammered a "H-Hello," and turned pink, but she never seemed to notice him.

He actually did a face-plant into the dust the day that Elizabeth—mini-skirted and go-go-booted —said his name from the dust of a fence full of spectators. He knew she frequented the sideline and knew she was there to see Frank. He held his breath as he passed her, every race, every round. But when she exhaled his name! He glanced, or more like flicked the front of his face at her to make sure that he understood, then he caught the top of his left foot under the bottom of his right, and he fell like something between a tree and a noodle, and splayed out on the ground.

Elizabeth blushed.

She blushed! Giggled. Turned her face behind her hand. Even he could see that. And he apologized.

Things moved forward in a brisk progression of flirtations and apologies. Elizabeth invited herself further into Adam's life, found that she was actually falling for him. But as hard as she tried, he just didn't ask her out. She said to her friends, "I could just *scream!*" and the ever-popular, "What is wrong with me?"

Adam, on the other hand, played mind-games with himself. To be honest, there were several more obvious ways to go about snagging Adam than Elizabeth was trying. She fluttered her eyelashes, bumped into him in the hall, giggled and whispered with her friends as she glanced over her shoulder. She even sent messages to him on the breeze of high school gossip in attempts to get him to ask her to homecoming, spring fling, prom.

To no avail.

Her little thing with Frank ended in a spat, a throwing of a class ring and some name-calling. She was romantically-focused for an entire eight months of her teenage years. Eight months! What more did Adam want from her?

Prom came and went. (Adam did not attend.) Graduation came and went. Adam and Elizabeth were busy packing bags at two ends of town. Elizabeth came across a photo in the yearbook: a track team photo. She looked at Frank. She looked at Adam. And a fire of growing feminism lit under her. She touched herself up with just a pinch of rouge and huffed out and down, to the family car, across town.

Adam's mother was surprised. Elizabeth asked for Adam, her face flushed, and Adam came in a hurry, not knowing what to think.

"Adam! You're just a dummy!" she breathed, at last. "I've tried everything I could for the past year to tell you that I like you! I decorated your locker, I sent you cookies, I set my schedule so that we'd cross paths in the hallway, I…" She wagged her head at the ground, then looked him square in the eyes. "I leave soon, so do you. It's too late for us and that's your loss. But I feel like I've wasted this year, and we both really oughta learn something from it. Personally, I'm going to try to shoot it straight. But you—you just need to get a *clue!*"

Elizabeth wheeled around on her heels, and in a moment there was just her sweet scent and a whiff of her fury.

C03 &O

Adam tried to comfort Stellar, but Stellar would have none of it. She was a wounded animal, retreated to a corner to lick a wound. He followed her in, she wouldn't even respond to him. What was a guy to do?

After a couple hours in the garage, tinkering with what— even he did not know—and Adam made another attempt at the stormily silent, stuffy, dark bedroom. Stellar was lying face down on a bed. There was this, that made Adam feel like she was a teenage girl, but Adam had never known Stellar in this way. There were other things: the wide hips and sloped shoulders, the absolute still and heavy quiet, the steady breathing that somehow did not signal sleeping, that made him realize she was no teenage girl.

He approached her cautiously, his hand hovering, about to rest on her shoulder blades when she pulled a mom trick: "Don't. Just don't, okay?"

"Stellar, honey, I…"

Stellar wheeled around and up into a cross-legged position. Her face was smooshed on the side (he could see this even in the faint moon- and street-light) and she smelled like closeness and salt. Her eyes were bright and swollen.

"There is no comforting. There is no peace anywhere. I don't want my baby going into a dangerous country and I am going to stop her." She glared at him like he was the enemy.

"Honey, I…" he tried again.

"You can't stop me. And don't take her side. This is all your fault…"

"Whoa, whoa, whoa!" He put one hand up and the other on his forehead, as if it were shielding him from the sun. "I don't know where that statement is going and I don't care. I have absolutely no blame in Gaby deciding to go to Israel."

"Tomorrow! Don't forget that part! She packed right under our noses! She's a sneaky, devious…"

"Wait a second! We don't even know the first thing about this whole situation. You can't just…"

"See!" Stellar was fully engaged with Adam, swinging her arms around her head and taking him on with wild eyes and a face jutted forward. "You are going to defend her! I knew that you would! You *always* defend her!"

"What?!? You've always coddled them! From the day they were born you…"

"You're kidding me! You've GOT to be kidding me! *I* coddled them? *I* coddled them?!" She thrust a finger into Adam's face. "You indulge them in everything. Why didn't you just buy them tickets to Rwanda long ago and be done with it?!"

"You've lost your mind," Adam offered.

"What?! What did you say to me?!"

"Nothing," he mumbled as he quickly slid in and out of the bedroom door.

She pursued him down the stairs, escalating her voice with his increasing distance. "Yeah, just run away, like you always do! What are you going to do about this situation? Run away from it, too? Just pretend like it isn't happening? Until what? Until tomorrow? Because that's when she's leaving, Adam!" He slammed the outside door, here, and she ran up against it. She banged her fist on it and yelled into it. "And that might be the last time you see her, Adam. The last time! What if it is? You know what kind of stupid, stupid things she would do to 'make the world a better place?' It doesn't stop at the caution tape, at the mine field! Do you hear me?! Do any of you hear me?!" She turned to yell at the cavernous expanse of the house, the dark, the breath-held silence. "Are you all just going to ignore this situation until we get a casket home?!"

ভ ৪০

It was not actually silent at the other end of the house. Annie could not even hear the yelling, except when it flitted past her door on the way downstairs. She rolled her eyes, and then fell backwards into the golden glow of her own life; the soft play of pop rock from sub-woofers, the pulsing glow of an overhead light with a fan on low and a fuchsia lava lamp, the modernly bombardment of electromagnetic waves and a hum of machinery and electronics: alarm clock, TV, VHS player, computer.

Not as crazy about academia as Gaby, Annie settled for a good deal on a PC about halfway through her college education. A friend assembled it for her and it worked just great for class papers, email, instant messaging, and surfing the internet.

Which is what she was doing on the night Gaby dropped her bomb. She stuck around for the rest of the Gaby Show and heard what little plans and thoughts Gaby already had about going to Israel. She felt that it was inevitable, and that she always half-expected something like it, wheedling away in her heart. Annie had been applying to jobs around the country, in expectation of her upcoming graduation. She was going to have a business degree and would go where the good opportunities took her. Separation was going to be hard, but it was a long time in coming.

Their starting blocks had been erected over twenty-two years, aimed to send them in two different directions.

Annie spent the evening between muted tears and hours of research into the history of Israel, the modern Middle East, and safety abroad. She printed out safety checklists and took note of the things she wanted to make sure Gaby had with her. She ordered Lewis's *The Middle East* from Amazon.com and even checked into flights to visit Gaby, with a layover in Italy.

Dreams of layovers in Italy helped to soothe the pain, enormously.

During the twins' elementary school years, they both loved to play school with their myriad stuffed animals or imaginary people. On one such day, Annie stood at the front of her neatly made bed. The bed was lined meticulously with (at each place) a notepad, a pencil, and an assigned reading book (which consisted largely of the *Little House on the Prairie* and *Babysitters Club* books). Each notepad and book were stickied with a different student's name: Ashley, Brandon, Samantha, Ryan, etc. A prominent place at the head of the bed was reserved for James, Annie's current (and pretty consistent) schoolgirl crush. His name was finished off with a heart.

Annie wore a pencil skirt, a mom-sized button-down shirt and jacket, lense-less glasses, and a pair of rather large high-heels. Her hair was in the closest approximation of a bun that she could come by on her own. She cradled a notepad in her right arm, her left arm checking off columns of cast-off company steno with red ink.

"Ashley?" Check. "Victoria?" Check. "Austin?" She looked around the bedside. "Austin?" She made a notation on the clipboard. "No Austin today," she mumbled to herself.

"All right then, class. We'll pick up right where we left off yesterday, with Mad Math. Samantha... excuse me, Sam, would you please hand out the addition sheets?"

Since the last class, Annie had taken an extra addition quiz from her fourth-grade classroom and copied it over by hand the necessary twelve times to fit her class. "Make sure you leave one at Austin's desk for a take-home packet. What? Oh, that's right; you can't get up because you sprained your ankle. It's fine. I'll just hand them out."

With just a little huff Mrs. Cameron (which was James's last name) picked up the math quizzes and distributed them with instructions: "Keep the quiz turned over until I have handed them all out. Then I will say 'Go,' and after five minutes I will say 'Stop.' You *must* stop right when I say 'Stop.' Any more pencils moving and you will receive a zero on the test."

The test proceeded without incident. In the quietness of a summer's day outside Annie's open windows; a distant lawn-mower, a clang of something shutting, the soft slide of light curtains and a test paper in the breeze.

"All right. Time's up. Stop."

She surveyed the room.

"Brian? Is your pencil still moving? Brian? Brian! Put your pencil down?!" He stuck his tongue out at her, very deliberately. "All right, then. That's a zero for you! Now, give me your test." She marched over to him and held out her hand, flat palm up. Just then, a breeze caught Brian's paper and it settled to the floor. Somehow, his notepad, book and pen also managed their way off the bed.

"Brian Boitano! I cannot believe you!" Shocked gasp. "You march right up to that blackboard and write your name."

The whiteboard marker remained still on the ledge of the board.

"That's it. You are done at this school, Brian. I have had enough of you in this classroom. You can just take your things and go home!"

She slammed the door behind him and then saw that his things were still laying on the floor. She picked up his assigned reading and stomped over to the window. She fiddled with the screen latch, pulled it out amidst a little puff of pollen and dust, and pitched his assigned reading book (*Logan Likes Mary Anne!*) right out the window and into a high trajectory over the yard and down two stories.

Stellar stood up from weeding the strawberries and brought her work gloves out in front of her to examine them where they were ratty. As she did so, *Logan Likes Mary Anne!* plopped right into her arms.

She startled, stepping back, and looked up at the sky, then the house. Annie was framed from the waist up in the window, leaning on ram-rod straight arms and making an O with her mouth and more Os with her eyes.

"Un-be-lieve-able!" she breathed. "Now take that book and go home!" And she threw her finger out to the horizon, slammed the window, and she was gone.

CHAPTER 15
STILL ZION

Gaby arranged to meet Mikhail in the parking garage so he could walk her into the airport. She arrived with her family and let Adam lug her trunk into the ticketing wing while she loitered at a pre-decided cement column at the head of the B level of the garage. Her stomach dropped as a familiar vehicle squealed around the end of the closest row of cars and swerved toward her. Gaby assumed Mikhail would get Nadine's car for today, since she couldn't drive him. She hadn't counted on this.

"Hey, Gab," Mikhail said out the open window as the car hugged the curb. Melodie stared away out the windshield with a set jaw. Gaby lowered her posture enough to peek in past Mikhail.

"Thanks for bringing him."

"Mmm-hmm." Mel still stared out the windshield.

"Look, Mel."

"What?" Her face was stony as she stared pointedly at Gaby.

"Nothing."

"What?!"

"I said nothing. This is a big day for me. I don't think we need to do this now."

"Do what when?" Mel opened her car door and was standing so that her arms rested high on the roof of the car. She spit out her words over the warm, taupe surface. Mikhail exited the vehicle. "*Do what when?*"

Gaby gaped at Mel. "Make a scene. Like what you're apparently hell-bent on doing, anyhow."

"Look. I tried to talk to you. I tried to apologize. And…"

Gaby broke into her string of sentences. "You had *just* crashed my protest…"

"Hup!" Mel flung her arm out in the air to gather attention. "I was talking! And what I was saying was that I have had to *share my* friends—my boyfriend—with your stubborn ass for the past *year*. How selfish can you be, Gaby? *How selfish?!*"

"Look, if he's your boyfriend, then you take him!"

Mikhail's gaze volleyed between the two and now rested, eyes wide, on Gaby and on the last sentence she had said, caught in the air around him. The girls turned to him. He did not move.

"That's an argument you won a long time ago, Gaby." Melodie slid down into her seat. She shifted into drive and pealed out before squealing around another corner of parked cars. Gaby and Mikhail stood listening to her driving erratic in the distance, until the sound of it disappeared.

ɞ   ʚ

After the outward explosions and the inner fireworks that marked the LeFevre's Saturday, Sunday was remarkably unified. Stellar gathered a rather representative remnant of the family, impromptu. There was a smattering of aunts, and even an uncle (since most of them had begged off, saying they had "things to do. I can't help it that she decided to leave *today*.") There was a grandma, a couple great-aunts, and quite a gaggle of the youngest cousins. Stellar was there, and Adam, front and center, looking a little worn from the night and Stellar threatening with wet eyes.

Annie served as director: informing people where they could and could not go in the airport to see Gaby off; which tickets and identifications Gaby would need most handy; what things were accounted for in her carry-on; where Gaby could change currency and how much she should expect to pay for a sherut from Tel Aviv to Jerusalem. She looked through Gaby's luggage more than once, added a folder full of print-outs, spoke for her at the ticket counter, shuffling ID like a travel agent on speed. She made sure that photos were being snapped, stationary and envelopes tucked into Gaby's rather small suitcase. Even at the exorbitant airport prices, she coaxed some money out of Adam to secure a few rolls of film for Gaby's camera. All hugs were accounted for.

Uncle Cal made friends with an oddly-dressed man who seemed too ancient to be standing so tall. He introduced him to Adam.

"He said his name is The Sage." Cal shrugged.

Adam responded, "Oh, like that song: 'The longeviteee of the Saaaage...'"

"Yes, exactly."

Aunt Susanna piped up. "I thought it was 'the Jenny bean was-a sayin'," she finished singing.

Cal looked askance at her. "What are you, crazy?"

Adam joked at the old man, "Aren't you long-dead, Sage? I mean, weren't you around in the times of knights and castles?"

The Sage explained patiently, "I have the gift of longevity."

"And where are your friends, The Queen? And Jaden the Great?"

A sigh. "The Angel is immortal, but were he here you probably would not see him, anyhow. The Queen and Jaden were mortal. They *are* dead."

"Huh." Cal looked at the old man like he wished he had chosen his airport acquaintances more carefully.

Mikhail—usually attached to Gaby at the hip—lingered at the back of the pulsating, morphing crowd, his hands thrust deep in his back pockets. He held polite conversation with Aunt Susie, and Aunt Joy noted to herself how handsome Mikhail was looking. He was still wearing the usual almost-fitted black zip-up hoodie, then jeans and Chucks, and a blue T-shirt that made his steel-blue eyes so bright. His hair, that same unmanageable fluff as always, currently an impermanent jet black. Dimples, check.

He was a little nervous. Or maybe a lot nervous. At any rate, he hadn't expected such a large turnout today. He decided he would say something, give Gaby at least enough of a sentence fragment that she would understand that he loved her. Only as he was standing there for a half-hour of parting rituals did it occur to him that he should have written it down in case, that he should have brought her flowers, a gift! He should have brought her a ring? A pair of earrings. Anything would have been better than this empty-handed feeling that he had, that he had nothing to offer her and nothing with which to communicate to her; a distinct aching in his palms.

He second-guessed himself so many times that he was rocking back and forth on his feet, going, and then not going. Moving toward her, and then not. Looking around people as they politely conversed with him.

Gaby bounced about from the arms and hands of one person to the next. She looked confident and ready, but Mikhail could sense a fluttering of uncertainty below the surface. There was a falseness to her smile that made him wish he was going with her to help with luggage and with fjording a country where everyone else speaks another language. Whose shoulder would she fall asleep on in the airplane?

Plus, there was something that felt so wrong about her leaving him. How could he possibly *be* without her, after all this time? His silence made it inevitable.

He felt a soreness on the insides of his arms, in the palms of his hands.

And he kept resolving to approach her and to say something. Why hadn't he planned it out better? What was he going to say? And how could he manage a private moment in front of all of these people? Honestly, what if she laughed? If her face gave it away and everyone knew that it was a one-sided affair? He felt himself a coward for even caring, but his stomach was churning in a very unpleasant way that would not stop for all his shifting. And what about Mel? Sure, their relationship had been dissolving into a mere friendship, but they hadn't really discussed it. Would Mikhail make a very good two-timer? His intent wasn't to hurt anyone.

Gaby's goodbyes began to look final. Her luggage was checked and she was standing with her ticket and passport in hand, her backpack slung over her shoulder, and the people closest to her had moved in to hug her again, grab her at the shoulders to say one last important thing. His stomach churned harder, there was a frantic flutter in his chest. He was dizzy, light-headed.

Annie caught his eye, waved him toward her. "Mikhail, come *here!*" she mouthed.

He moved into responsive action, his hands at last falling out of his back pockets. He loped toward Gaby, waited in line for what was both a very long and a very short time.

He held her in his arms harder and longer than he had anticipated. She buried her face in his shoulder. When he pulled back, he very quickly wiped a tear from his cheek. "Gaby, I…"

She smiled weakly at him. "I'm sorry this is so sudden…" like she said it a hundred times. Then her eyes swung around at all the other people surrounding them and caught back at his. "Come visit me," she offered. And then more honestly, "I'll give you a call as soon as I get settled." She touched his hand and it caught on fire. She backed away and he was left with his mouth half-open. It took several moments of her retreat before his brain lit up. *HE HADN'T SAID ANYTHING!*

He was drowning in self-loathing, and spinning in his head, his insides, trying to come up with some way to still make this happen. He would have to do something drastic, it seemed, pull a Hollywood ending.

Everyone gave one last wave and turned as a herd to mope away, as Gaby disappeared through the security checkpoint. But Mikhail saw that she would be making one last loop back past them, where they could still see her through a glass wall, although she would be confined to a path about thirty feet away. He pressed himself against the glass, hoping he was not breaking any security regulations.

There she was! He tapped on the glass. Tapped just a little harder, just a little louder. She looked!

He grinned at her, waved frantically. Her face brightened a little, she waved back through a sadness. And then he did it: He actually mouthed the words.

And his emphatic, momentous "I—LOVE—YOU" disappeared behind a glare in the glass. And Gaby continued to wave and smile bitter-sweetly at him as she disappeared in the flow of the crowd around her and was whisked around the bend.

ಚಃ ಇಂ

It had been less than a month since Gaby got her driver's license, but already there was something stirring in her, as usual. She and Mikhail drove somewhere for the twenty-eighth straight day in a row, this time to a Butter high school hang-out, The Junk Field.

The Junk Field—not a regular for Mikhail and Gaby—was part junk-yard, part make-out point, part drinking get-a-way. Gaby and Mikhail came just for a place to hang out on a Tuesday afternoon. Cars parked helter-skelter across the field, some of them abandoned and permanent, others still idling or still warm to the touch, littered with teenagers. Occasionally a beer or soda can took flight in an arch through the sun, or a hot cigarette butt zinged a clean trajectory near someone's head. Muffled conversation and an occasional outburst lost energy in the palpable heat.

Swamp frogs droned their low, guttural pulse, the sun intense and bodies glistened, the waist-high grass sounded dry. The field was surrounded by woods, and somewhere in the distance: a trailer. It may have been uninhabited, for all anyone knew, but clearly had been inhabited at one time. For there, all around the drinkers and the cars, were monument upon monument of cast-off detritus: tilting piles of old tires; rusted out cash register teetering on the frame of an old baby buggy, one wheel missing; a half-de-robed spring mattress stood on end against an old trash can, decorated macabrely with doll heads, arms, and legs, a lot of the facial features missing or run-through.

Gaby cut the engine and she and Mikhail got out of the car. Mikhail bent down to pick something up off the ground. He handed it to Gaby as they seated themselves on the hood of the car, reclining on the windshield and sunning.

"What's this? Junk? Oh *thank you*, Mikhail."

"Look at it. I thought you would appreciate it."

Gaby looked down at her hands and found there, beneath the cakey dirt and the scratches and chips, a small figurine of The Queen. At her hip was a broken piece of metal. At one point, she might have been a keychain. "Well, what d'ya know."

Mikhail lay silent for a long time, Gaby sighing occasionally, thinking about something and turning The Queen over in her right hand. "You have something on your mind?" he offered sarcastically.

Another sigh. "Do you ever want to just *go*?"

"Meaning what? Where?"

"Just *anywhere*. Sometimes I just think about backpacking across the United States, or even Europe. I really want to go to England. See some castles, sheer some sheep, drink lager and fall asleep under the stars. Carry everything I would need on my back."

"You mean you want to go now?"

"Well, I don't know. I do, but I guess I could wait until I graduated. But, I don't know. You know, my mom traveled around the U.S. with a bunch of hippies, and then she stowed away to Canada and just walked back over the Ambassador Bridge. I think I could just do that forever. It sounds so great."

Mikhail shifted uncomfortably. "Yeah, it sounds like fun."

"Where would you go, if you could go anywhere?"

Mikhail lay there for a long time, his eyes closed to the sun. His mind passed over the vague and commercialized ideas he had of a handful of random countries. "Peru." He said decisively.

"Peru? Why Peru?"

"I want to see Machu Picchu, I guess. Lake Titicaca? I found this great catalog for adventure vacationing once, and you could hike the Amazon up to Machu Picchu and boat the lake and spend some time in Lima. I think it would be great. Plus, my mom sponsors a kid, and he lives in Lima, so I could visit him."

"Your mom sponsors a kid?"

"Yeah," he drew a circle in the sky with his outstretched arm, squinting into the sun. "She sponsored kids for, like, forever. She started doing it when I was little when I saw a commercial about Compassion International on the 700 Club or something. I convinced her to do it, and then I wrote the kid letters. He's actually older now, but then my mom got another kid, and she mostly writes to him. He's a cute little kid. Jorge."

Gaby took a moment to process his line of conversation back into her own. "See, but that's what I mean. If you wanted to go visit him, then you would have to have a passport, you see?"

"Sure, but…"

"I'm going to get one. I'm sixteen now, which means that they last longer. I had one when I was little, but it's expired. I'm going to get one now, and it will be good until I'm twenty-six, I think." A pause. "And then I'm going to always keep it renewed. I mean, what if I got offered a free trip to Australia like tomorrow?"

"Yeah, 'cause I was going to offer you one." Gaby punched Mikhail lightly in the shoulder and he smiled at her as he held the offended shoulder.

"Seriously, you think you're going anywhere soon?"

Gaby looked wistfully up into the sky, a small line of concern crossing her forehead, her upper teeth lightly biting at her lower lip. "I don't know."

№ ☙

She did get the passport, and even convinced Mikhail to get one with her. He turned his over in his hands, now, covered with a dust pattern and completely un-stamped. Any trips to Mexico or Canada he made with a birth certificate, and he forgot where he was even keeping the passport. He looked all night for it after Gaby left for Israel, not even conscious of why he might be looking. He told himself that its whereabouts had crossed his mind over the years and being in an international terminal of an airport brought it to the front of his mind again.

He found it in the back of his sock drawer, in a musty heap of socks whose matches were long ago destroyed or went to sock heaven, some of them a few sizes too small for his feet or holed enough that they felt annoying inside his shoes as his toe poked out and was strangled by fabric. Those were the kinds of socks that Mikhail kept telling himself not to put on, then his fingers would go groping in a sleepy fog in the half-dark of his early-morning room and he'd be stuck all day with an annoying pair of socks. Eventually, they disappeared in the back of the drawer and Mikhail was relieved of the offending socks, only to work a hole into another pair and start all over again.

He sat on the floor next to his un-made bed, turning the passport over in his hands and flipping through the nothingness. Maybe he would go to Peru.

Then he played the scene in the airport back over in his head, for the thirtieth, fiftieth, four-hundredth time. It was pretty apparent that Gaby did not see Mikhail tell her he loved her, but he could not be sure. Perhaps she feigned not seeing, stunned by his ridiculous way of telling her? Or she understood "I love you" as the platonic statement of long-time best friends, even though he never verbally went there. Or she did not have time to respond to him, her mind playing catch-up with what she just saw as she innocently traipsed down the corridor toward her Boeing 747 and Israel. And now he felt he needed to explain and needed to know the answers to his own questions.

She had not seen. He was too far away? She was distracted? She thought he was saying "elephant shoes," like in a child's game?

She did not call from Switzerland. She did not call from Tel Aviv. She did not call upon arrival in Jerusalem, but he was sure that she would call very soon to say she was settling in, had arrived safely.

What if she had not arrived safely? The thought sucked the air out of his chest and sent his mind into a sudden nose-dive. He lost his bearings. He focused back in on the passport, gaining clarity, going fuzzy, regaining clarity. What if he was thinking of her right now as she floated in the great expanse of dark Atlantic Ocean, a pretty piece of flotsam?

These thoughts were his own illusions of grandeur, perhaps, because he had not told her things that were life-supporting for him. It was possible that she considered his love of no real consequence. Was it even a possibility that she loved him, back?

Mikhail violently shoved the passport into a deep corner of his mostly-empty backpack, threw it over his shoulder and bumped his way through the house and into the garage. He mounted his bike and pedaled hard and jerky into the driveway, reeled dazedly down the road and out into the dark world. He was looking for some dead thing to scrape from the pavement and cradle in the ground, under a soft covering of fresh dirt. He had not buried roadkill in years, but somewhere out there was himself, and he would have to find it, now that what was left here was only the part of a man that had been ripped from its attachments, floundering in its own cowardice.

CHAPTER 16
HOLY LAND
ℰ೧   ೧ℛ

Gaby bit her nails through security check point after security check point all the way to Israel and even once she was inside it. She was proud of herself for insisting that she only pay eleven American dollars for the sherut ride from Tel Aviv to Jerusalem. She kept her weary eyes alert, because she was concerned about her things (her satchel held white-knuckled in her lap) and about herself. She sat squashed shoulder-to-shoulder with another passenger, the sherut (like a very tall mini-van equipped to seat ten or more) stuffed to capacity with a hodgepodge of people, languages, and luggage. She also kept her eyes alert because it was a country exotic, and there were many things to see.

She felt excited, and yet everything seemed so dirty and run-down to her. She had never been in a desert land, and the Midwest, in comparison, was a verdant, manicured, eternity of clean corners and clipped shrubberies. Everything in Israel looked magical and mystical, but it also looked dry and very, very dusty; simply overflowing with rocks.

It was hot. The sun was a white everywhere that she had only seen concentrated on the pavement in Michigan through a magnifying glass or a pair of reading glasses. She was choking on the grit and melting in the sun, but somehow her sweat seemed only a physiological reaction: she felt toasty, comfortable, and she could already tell that her hair was calmer (which Annie warned her about). The arid climate was both irritating and pleasant to Gaby on her first day, like an oasis paradise and like a whole country of dirty dens and studies, caked with dust.

The sherut lurched through Tel Aviv, causing a little less alarm in Gaby each time it came within centimeters of another collision. Then it pulled swiftly out into the desert, where it was all tan and white, from the empty sky to the glaring shoulders of the white-brown hills. Gaby nodded in and out of sleep, despite her best efforts, as the hum of the vehicle, the occasional conversation that she did not understand, and the lilting cadence of Arabic pop music soothed her for the couple hours that she was plastered against the window.

In Jerusalem, the sherut began lurching again through the city, driving in the surprisingly modern-looking and yet ancient streets with little regard for traffic lanes. Gaby recognized coffee shops, McDonalds, modern European buildings, just sort of plopped down in the middle of cobblestone streets, two-thousand-year-old walls, three-thousand-year-old walls, and worn-down fifty-year-old shops with colorful awnings splashed with advertisements in Hebrew and Arabic. She recognized her own language some places, and this made her breathe a sigh of relief. Sara told her many people would speak at least halting English.

She found herself dropped at a corner near the citadel of the Old City, abandoned with her few belongings where she could hear the commotion of bartering and smell the wafting of cumin and coriander frying, and pickles. She was studying a nearby cart-with-umbrella and its beverage menu complete with illustrations—realizing that she was very hungry—when she noticed a young woman walking toward her in a T-shirt, sarong, and tennis shoes. The woman held a piece of paper, which flexed in the breeze so that it was only occasionally legible, with "Gaby" scrolled on it. She had very straight, sleek, light brown hair, cut bluntly at her chin and again into short bangs, interrupting the heart shape of her face. Her hazel eyes were big and slanted, her smile broad and toothy. She caught Gaby's eyes and Gaby smiled at her.

"Gaby?" she asked over the din as she approached.

"It's me. I'm here." She tucked a stray hair behind her ear a few times.

"I'm Afentra," she offered her hand out to be shook. "We've got a little bit of a hike before we get to the hostel, and we're going through there." She pointed from the tip of her nose to the opening in the citadel wall, where people oozed in and out and bare, fluorescent bulbs could be seen helping out the bit of sun, lighting stall after stall of olive wood knickknacks and T-shirts.

"I'm glad you have on jeans, because you'll want to be properly covered in some of these alleys." Afentra winked at Gaby as she hoisted her suitcase up and started roll-bouncing it over the slick bricking. Gaby followed, mute and observant, pulling in close so as not to lose Afentra in the crowded, loud, narrow alleyways that were this section of the Old City.

They wove through the heart of an intricate jumble of alleyways, through appetizing smells and foul, through the dry heat and the dampness of old mildew, ducking around the incessant call of shopkeepers and sometimes walking alone in a quiet alley. They went up stone stairs, down sloping stone roads, always surrounded by stone except where the white of the sky—crossed by wires, TV antennae, and clothing lines hung with clothes and blankets stretching and snapping indifferently—peeked out far above their heads.

Eventually they emerged into a courtyard—just old, worn stone building fronts and old, worn, stone grounds, potted with a few palms and surrounded by a few shops and a café that spilled out into a patio of chairs and tables. The alley continued in two different directions across the courtyard, but Afentra curved to one side and sighed, "Home sweet home!" She leaned back on the suitcase and observed the face of the hostel with Gaby.

"You'll like it. It's nice," she offered. "Let's go get you checked in and throw this stuff under your bed."

They started inside. "Are you hungry? Tired? How do you think you will manage the jet-lag thing?"

"I actually have to make some calls."

"All right. Well, first I'll have to take you to an ATM. You can get some shekel there. Then I'll take you to a phone card machine and you can snag one or two of those. *Then* we'll head to a public phone—there's one here in the building, in a semi-secluded stairwell—and we can stand around for awhile arguing what time it is in your city of origin. Only then can you can make your call. It will be hairy, with the delay. But it'll be loads of fun."

By now, they were standing next to a bunk bed in a sizable room sparsely furnished with bunk beds and a dozen lockers. The bottom bunk was freshly made and appeared to be unclaimed.

"Home sweet home," said Afentra. When Gaby just stared at the bed and the wall behind it, Afentra offered, "Welcome?" and plunked down her luggage into the shimmy and sudden sag of the stressed mattress.

"It's just those. I mean, what are those?" Gaby referred to the chipping mural that was on the wall behind her bed and extended out to a couple nearby beds.

"Oh, that. Well aren't you the curious one, already. That's just a mural someone painted like a billion years ago. You get used to relics like that, around here. Walking in the footsteps of Jesus, and all that. It's kind of an interesting case, though. It seems that people have been *re*painting the thing for nearly as long as it's been there. There's talk of having it redone, soon.

Some artist in the hostel would like to restore it, again. Or reinterpret it, more like. It's more evolving folk art than a museum piece, by the look of it."

"But, but, what is it?"

"You don't know the Avengers of Northwyth stories? I thought everyone knew those stories."

"I do. I just didn't know I would find them... *here*."

"Yeah. Here, there, everywhere. You know that one, too? Dr. Seuss?"

"Shoosh!" Gaby found herself already growing comfortable with Afentra and they smiled at each other as Gaby wagged a loose hand at her.

ɔ෨   ෨ɔ

They decided to postpone the phone calls until evening, Afentra threw a granola bar at Gaby and left her laying out on the bed, exhausted. It wasn't long before she was snoozing.

Afentra came back as evening fell, ready to take Gaby down into the New City to make the calls and check things out. Gaby was waiting for her, freshly showered and dressed in clean and wrinkled clothes. Afentra handed a pamphlet to Gaby as she approached, and then stood leaning against the bedpost. The pamphlet was titled, *The Northwyth Mural at the Moshe House*.

"Creative title."

"Some say the ghost of the mural artist haunts the hostel."

"Who says?"

"Westerners staying at the hostel. People who went to summer camp. I mention it because it is obligatory. And amusing." Gaby opened the pamphlet and read,

".... The mural is a creative interpretation of the *lack* of a story surrounding the disappearance of the magical seed. The seed is an integral ingredient in early stories of The Queen of

Northwyth and in the romance of The Queen and The Angel. But where did the seed go? Why does it disappear when the lovers part and The Queen marries Jaden the Great? Some interpret the seed as purely symbolic, standing in for either The Queen's power, or for love, or for the marriage of the two. With The Angel, the 'power of love' disappears, and we need no explanation. More die-hard adherents of Northwyth have spent millennia looking for the seed and hypothesizing about its whereabouts.

"The mural artist (unknown) used a combination of Northwyth dogma and a little-known speculative story coming out of the USSR to paint the scene which is now the prize of The Moshe House. If one studies the mural, they might notice an epic incorporation of various seed stories: when The Queen procures the family seed from a mysterious hag; when The Queen takes the seed to The Angel to find answers, and instead finds love; when The Queen and The Angel join together and use the seed to overcome the evil Demonis and eventually Keir the Evil.

"Central to the mural is the speculative story, which suggests that there were not five children of King Jaden and The Queen that made it to adulthood, but six. The painting depicts a sixth child standing off to the side, embraced by The Queen's left arm, with the seed painted at his heart. The other five children are depicted as they were at their death; be-headed, poisoned, old, etc. But the sixth child stands alone and whole, however with a caged bird in one hand and a knife in the other. This is most chilling, indeed."

Gaby shivered. She wondered about the sixth child, and what it would take for a person to be depicted, after they were dead and gone, with a seed in their heart, holding a caged bird and a knife, and separated from their siblings by their mother. Did this mystery child have the seed? Or did he have internal strength? Was he a caged bird? Or an animal torturer? That would explain the knife, unless that was his death; he was murdered? And was he estranged from his siblings or hidden away from them; the typical literary orphan-type?

The text continued, "The painting seems to suggest to the observer that the seed has not died and, moreover, it exists in a sixth line of ancestry, if not as an actual seed, then at the heart of these great-great-grandchildren."

CB   BD

Gaby cozied up to a full bookshelf. The bookstore smelled like spices and fried foods drifting in off the street and also like worn carpeting and new books. It sounded like passersby and traffic, but was also filled with hush. She balanced a couple of books on the edge of the shelf in front of her, and perused another book while she kept her left hand hung casually over her satchel, still very much a visitor here.

Her eyes scanned the pages of the new copy of *Poems of Jerusalem and Love Poems*—Yehuda Amichai—that she held in her hands. It spoke of trees with roots in two lands. She looked again at her stack of books; she sighed. She had no idea what she was doing, yet. And it was harder to figure things out with a language barrier. But she would start with this stack, although she was pretty sure the authors were all Israeli and might not be sympathetic to the Territories. Or maybe they would be.

She sighed again, looked at the stack: *Mr. Mani*, *A Book That Was Lost (And Other Stories)*, *A Perfect Peace*. A. B. Yehoshua, S. Y. Agnon, Amoz Oz. She had never even heard of them before, but she had a sort of guilt feeling that she should have, just like she had a guilt feeling about every country's authors and artists, politicians, music, cuisine… She could never have paid enough attention to everything. But here were these four books to begin.

She already had a few casual friends at the hostel. She had slept for hours and hours. She had already worn herself out walking up and down and up and down and up and down all around the city in the dry heat. She had already tried falafel pitas from no less than three vendors—all claimed by someone in the hostel to be the best in the city. And she had already started to play a game with herself.

In the game, she stayed mute in public, moving about the unfamiliar city with a false air of intimacy. She wanted to see how many people would offhandedly say something to her in Hebrew or even Arabic. So far, she had amassed four comments, and once even maintained a mini-conversation as she read a passerby's body-language with his clipped request for her to step to the side. She stepped, and he thanked her and moved on, giving her a smile and never being made any the wiser about her embarrassing American status.

She thought that looking Israeli or Palestinian meant dressing European: in tight, black clothes. Ethnically speaking, there were even blondes here, though tan from the constant sun. This was the land in between everything—between continents and countries and people groups, between time, between religions—and while there may be some ethnic traits here or there, there seemed to always be someone popping out to surprise her: a Russian Jew with blue eyes or curling, blonde sidelocks. She felt the thing that made her most foreign to the land—since it was filled with pilgrims and curiosities from around the whole holy world—was that she had never served in the Israeli army. How long was she going to live here? Should she enlist, fulfill a duty? Would she even be allowed to, or required?

The truth was that she had joined a bandwagon this time and wasn't leading one. Uncomfortable. She was listening and learning, doing as much outside research as in, as always, in her constant mission to save the world. In this land of extremes and of deeply drawn lines, she was beginning to feel that she didn't quite agree with anyone.

What Gaby could agree with was the presence of suffering and pain. Whose was it? Everyone's. She saw it on both sides of the myriad checkpoints. She saw it in the eyes of those who stood outside the places they revered and prayed for year after year for ownership. She observed it in the constant stream of news from the region: innocents' houses steam-rolled, civilian busses bombed. She heard it in the baby's cry as she walked along the road to the market. As she passed, seated beggar-women pinched their babies to draw Gaby's pity and her U.S. dollars.

The world was full of so many festering wounds.

It only took a couple days, and Gaby abandoned the brochure-shoving tactics of her friends, and was assigned to an orphanage in Bethlehem; such a quiet oasis. She met someone who volunteered there and networked her way right into their immediate trust. She set up a plan with them to volunteer daily, which was a welcome anomaly: they usually grabbed volunteers for a couple weeks at a time, an hour here and an hour there.

She would hold babies by day and hopefully serve coffees by night. In Palestine by day and in Israel by night. She thought she would like the dichotomy, the life, crossing countries over a twenty-minute drive and a flip of a passport, not unlike many other Holy Land dwellers. This was—she knew it as well as everyone else—everybody's sacred land, even hers and it had drawn her, helpless, to its soured bosom.

CHAPTER 17
WHERE WE COME FROM
ℬ   ℭ

Melodie was not a green thumb. But neither was anyone in her family. She came by her gardening ignorance honestly.

When Gaby accosted Melodie in the parking garage and flew for Israel, she had left Mel freshly graduated from college and about to launch out into a world of work and responsibility. Except that she hadn't yet secured a job and had no means of getting her own place. She moved back in with her parents, insisting that it would only be for a minimal amount of time, although they pacified her with warm welcome. And she took up gardening between interviews and resumé strengthening.

There was a plot of abused, overturned soil at a sunny corner of the family yard. Her mom, her dad, and a brother had all tried their hand at growing their own vegetables at different times. But even tomatoes and bell peppers proved too much for any of them. Accident after pitiful accident and eventually abandonment took residence of the plot.

Melodie contemplated gardening herself for a long time, but unlike the previous family gardeners, she did not deck herself out in a bandana, gloves, and gardening clogs and acquire hundreds of dollars in Lowe's debt before she "started it right." Instead, she came home from the airport, and simply decided to sit out on the back deck. Then she decided to walk over to the abused ground. Then she decided to bend over and rake her hand through the dirt. Then she decided to fetch a hoe out of the shed. And then.

She plowed in her Sunday's best, although she did don a pair of old gardening gloves when she realized she was getting blisters. She attacked the earth, beat it and cut it until it smelled earthy and it looked dark and fresh. She raked the weeds off to the side in a pile she was already thinking of as compost and furrowed her brows at her task. She perspired and she grunted and she showered before falling into bed exhausted, the hoe stuck abandoned, standing straight up out of the terrain.

In the morning, she drove to the only nursery that she knew of, having gone there years before to order flowers for her prom corsage, which she arranged herself. She talked rapid-fire with the employees, finding out not only what vegetables were the most cost-effective and hearty, but also taking note which wore the prettiest greens, which donned the loveliest flower. She asked "What won't I kill?" and she asked "Which are the hottest peppers?" And she drove home with flats of little sproutlings of tomatoes and pumpkins and watermelons and cucumbers, and chilies and strawberries and a bag of soil, some plant food.

She hefted the plants around to the backyard and set them to the side of the dirt patch. When they were all set haphazardly there, their stalks at odd angles, she went right to work again, without breakfast and without lunch. She dug and she patted and she filled and she watered. She stapled veggie names to old paint stirring sticks and marked her veggies. She came in for dinner, with dirt under her nails, a burn on her nose, and her hair smelling like fresh air. Otherwise, she stank of sweat.

On the third day, she came home from an interview to water the garden in her suit. As she sprayed the plants and sniffed the cold wetness in the air, she decided that she needed another plant. She drove back to the nursery and spent an hour meandering through the outdoor aisles of wet and soil-streaked cement ground, tables upon tables of cramped flowers and shrubs, herbs and trees, fruits and vegetables. She chose a small, potted shamrock and she took it home seat-belted next to her. At stoplights she admired its greenness, its cute heart-shaped and tented leaves. She set it on an outdoor table and doused it with water before going to bed.

A week later, the garden was showing signs of productivity. She continued to water it and watch for signs of other things—like disease, insects, or critter munching—which didn't seem to be happening. But the shamrock was barely even there anymore. Its leaves browned and wilted back to shriveled vines. She despaired. It looked as if she were probably going to get a great job as a mechanical engineer with a great company, and she sat there at the table outside with her chin in her hands, a frown on her face. She watched the water soak into the earth around the sad shamrock. She watched as soiled water dribbled out of the bottom of the pot and pooled in the saucer. She touched the few remaining green leaves—tiny and sad—with her fingertips and let out a little whimper.

She felt like a failure. She was alone. Where was she headed? What was she going to do? Was she going to get cats and eat TV dinners every night? Go clubbing with her co-workers and do Jell-o shots on the weekends? Where was this going? Why hadn't she thought more about this before, and where was the person who was supposed to be there with her?

Mel felt these uncertainties in her chest like a gaping hole. How had all the good times come to this, she wondered. Did anyone even notice that she started a garden? Would they notice when she left bushels of beefsteak tomatoes on the counter, gallons of fresh pico di gallo in the fridge? Everyone was doing their own swirling dance around her, moving in the tides of life and she somehow disappeared, drowned without a single sound, slipped under the surface.

She blinked a couple times to come back to herself. She focused in on the shamrock plant. She took a long breath and picked up the plant. She walked it across the yard, set it carefully on a table on the far side of the shed. There was shade there during the day, there was cool.

"Maybe this will help," she said softly. And she went to bed without writing any poetry, without even brushing her teeth.

A week later and at a final interview, Mel accepted the job and came home with a bottle of wine and a bag of groceries that would amount to a nice spaghetti dinner for whoever in her family happened to be home. She deposited them on the kitchen counter and she walked outside, trekking through the yard in her pumps, dragging the garden hose behind her. She watered the garden, enjoying the happy routine that had formed into a pattern.

When she finished with the garden, she pulled the hose toward the shed and around the back side. She had not watered in almost a week, since it rained every day. As she aimed the hose toward her little shamrock, she saw him: verdant and full, topped with new, petite, white flowers; the old, brown things discarded at his feet.

C> <O

Afentra was in love with her swing set, with her porch swing, with her hammock, but most of all with her tree house.

Her father had built her that tree house. He was that sort of dad. Or at least he was, and then later he wasn't. And then he was gone. What began as innocent Midwest childhood games became a refuge and a place for becoming, and for avoiding. In the tree house she read her way through every single *Sweet Valley High* that was released while she was still young enough to enjoy them and then kept reading L. M. Montgomery long past the prime of her young adult reading category. In the tree house she became someone's blood sister, studied for Sunbeam and Girl Guard badges, made science fair projects. And as clichéd as it was, she had her first kiss in the tree house; Bobby Ford, fifth grade. She stashed cigarettes, she changed into short skirts before dances, she cried over spilled milk, she cried over being the only kid in her class with separated parents. She had a short-term obsession with crossword and logic puzzles and another with macramé potholders during which she sat for hours after school and during long summer days, lounged back against pillows stolen from beds and sofas, working with a serious face, a worriless face.

Afentra made curtains for the windows in Home Ec; the wind breezed in the windows, tossing the sun-bleached material, playing with the edges and snapping them delicately. When the sun shone in the windows it made golden geometric pools on the floor and she could smell heat on wood, a memory of the newness of the tree house combining with the oldness of it. When the fireflies came in the windows, they began as a neon streak in an opaque blackness, as falsely colored as Mountain Dew, and then transformed in the artificial light of the lantern into a gray-brown bug, just nothing special at all.

Afentra rubbed the soles of her bare feet on the boards, laid her back flat against the hard surface, feeling the smoothness that was also so many bumps and evenly spaced cracks and thought of the empty space beneath her and gravity and her feeling so solid there, hanging above the world. She had hidey holes, places for treasures like an expired best friend pendant, a Polaroid of her and her father, a piece of fool's gold. She had boxes and cupboards, places for rock collections and journals, sketch pads and pastels in every vibrant color of the rainbow.

She was allowed to have sleepovers in the tree house, occasionally, and on the weekends. It was awhile since her last, but she and her sort-of-long-time best friend Amber decided to have another, during the long stretch of summer vacation between seventh and eighth grades, when Afentra was still a dad-still-there Afenta. They planned for popcorn, soda, candy, sleeping bags, their coolest pajamas, make-up, board games, flashlights. They let the word get out *just in case* some of the boys might want to stop by or prank them or (they secretly wished and would remain wishing for a lifetime) serenade them or recite Shakespeare up through the vines that clung to the tree.

The boys didn't serenade, but the word-of-mouth worked just as well as they wanted it to. B.J. and Dan arrived during a waning game of *Life* and started pelting the tree house with pebbles. After being scared, then mad, Afentra and Amber flushed with warmth and excitement. "Get up here, quick!" Afentra hissed. "Before my mom sees you!" B.J. and Dan scrambled up and everyone stared awkwardly, tucked limbs underneath them, and painfully made a little conversation until the boys produced a backpack, unzipped, and flashed what looked like a lot of alcohol to all of them. They boys had raided a secret supply of an older brother and did the girls want to have some fun? Sure, sure they did. Nobody really seemed confident, but they all took a beer, opened them hesitantly, sipped, made fun of the taste, and continued to drink through that and the liquor until they were prematurely inebriated, laughing too loud, too long, too easy.

They became reckless somehow, daring and cool. (If only they could have been sober flies on the wall, all their drinking illusions would have vanished that night.) Amber suggested Truth or Dare, or how about Spin the Bottle? Strip Poker? Stiff as a Board? Anything that she could think of that she would never have otherwise suggested but that she—and everyone else—always found alluring, titillating and secretly wanted to do. Was there a Ouija board?

One of them threw an empty rum bottle on the floor and so it was Spin the Bottle.

It began as innocently as any Spin the Bottle game played in a tree house in the middle of the night during a sleepover where some of the participants were not invited and there was illegal booze and junior highers involved. There was a kiss here and a kiss there; at first like an electric shock through them and a burning at the point of contact. Then those kisses became commonplace and adjustments had to be made: kiss longer, open mouth, tongue, and finally put your hand on her boob. With only four people (and never the creativity of pairing like-genders), there weren't too many combinations between them, so the game eventually dissolved into a make-out party, a first for all four of them, though none would admit it.

This is the way that it went, nobody able to find a foothold to stop themselves from doing things that hid a moral nagging. There was heat, and spit, and the squishiness of tongues and hard-sliminess of teeth, the intuition of evolution, the awkwardness of virginity. They stumbled, their eyes glazed over with steam, their eyes closed in on their own selfishness in desire for what made them feel tickly and tingly and warm. Liked? Relaxed? Safe?

Eventually B.J. vomited out the tree house window and Amber begged off that she was about to fall asleep (which was not only inevitable, but a really great idea). The boys stumbled down the ladder, all the contraband materials stuffed in their backpack, and giggled in zigzags across the lawn, their outlines fading into the black. Afentra watched them and then turned around to find Amber already asleep and snoring loudly on top of her sleeping bag. Afentra crawled across the floor to her own bag, climbed in, pulled the top over her head and—despite the foggy thoughts swirling there—was fast asleep before she could catch one of them.

In the morning the girls had an awfully hard time keeping their last night a secret, discreetly cleaning up B.J.s vomit while holding heavy heads and making secret trips to the lavatory. They did everything quietly and really didn't say more than a few words between them. Perhaps they didn't keep their secret from Afentra's mom at all. Either way, the girls moped around in Afentra's room until Amber's mom arrived to pick her up and she went home.

That week Afentra walked up to Amber in the school hall and Amber asked where she had been the day previous. "My dad left." "Oh," Amber said, and turned and walked away. The pain was excruciating at first, and then there was just a hint of something dark and stinging in the air, then a wind blew through and revealed an empty place.

A year later and Afentra realized she could not remember being in the tree house even once since the bacchanal night the year prior. She wandered out to the yard where the fall was turning cold and gray, colors being traded out for bareness and life rotting in slick piles on the ground. She stood there in the dirt, where the grass had worn away with repeated use of the tree house ladder, one foot on the bottom rung and her hands weakly grasping a rung at eye-level. She looked at the tree and the ladder, thinking how just looking could make her taste and make her feel, even feel with the soft skin of her cheeks or the softer still skin of her lips. She felt too tired to climb and realized that she didn't want to go up. She was feeling too old for a tree house.

Afentra's mother stood framed in the kitchen window, hidden behind the edge of the draperies and the cloudiness around the edges of the pane. She watched Afentra stay there digging the toe of her sneaker into the patch of hard earth and thought desperately, *This has actually happened. She is nearly away from me.*

ଓଃ ଓ

A couple of idealistic bums in their senior year at a prestigious university in Boston were talking one night (with the light persuasion of some cheap beer), got up from the couch, grabbed any camp-like amenities they might have had, some food and a couple pair of socks, and walked off campus. Afentra was a student in psychology when—after trudging and hitchhiking across four states—they showed up on her doorstep in Chicago. They had on light backpacks and smelled like the road, their hair in greasy, tangled ropes. They asked for a place to sleep.

Of all the millions of people they could have asked, she was the one they did (or at least the first in a string that said "Yes"). She tossed and turned all night and when they woke in the morning, she set the table with fried eggs, bacon, toast, orange juice, and her own packed backpack, complete with aspirin, bedroll, mess tin, and a roll of twenties. She cleared out her cupboard as she shouldered her pack and left with the idealistic bums, toting ramen noodles, granola bars, and powdered drink mix. A Discman was her contribution to their traveling company.

According to the original Boston plan, they mostly walked, and walked, and walked. But they also hitched, maybe a ride in the back of a truck or even on the rails. But this felt dangerous to Afentra, so she enjoyed the walking, and the sitting, and the laying out under the blue sky and settling under picnic shelters in a rainstorm. They relied on the kindness of others for shelter and food most of the time, kept largely to populated areas so they could meet people and find things to do and to observe. Networking worked well for them, and sometimes people knew they were coming before they even arrived.

After a month, Afentra realized she would have to return to Chicago to empty out her apartment, since conversations with her parents via phone made her realize that there were responsibilities to be, at the very least, severed. Then, despite their worry, she could wander around and find herself, check in with them every once in a while, and live like a vagabond with no admitted regrets.

She made the trip from Wyoming to Chicago on her own, mostly with an elderly couple in an RV bound for Niagara Falls. She put everything she had up for sale at a poorly-attended yard (or really stoop) sale and dumped the remainder at a thrift store. She said goodbye to a couple friends and spent a large part of her savings on a ticket to England.

In England, she got a gig with a small, family farm that employed her to be a sort of shepherdess. They trained her briefly, fed her meals, furnished her with a modest room, and even a small allowance. She started saving up again, avoiding pubs and towns where she might spend the little she was ferreting away. Her only friends happened to be a nearby settlement of Gypsies, who very quickly wheedled their way into her social worker's heart and her American sense of both justice and intrigue.

A year later, she landed herself in Sighisoara, Romania, where she linked up with a group that was dedicated to the education of the Eastern European Gypsies. She volunteered herself to fill any capacity, including cleaning, manual labor, food delivery, driving (which was more than scary going from the Midwest to a year not driving to the wild streets of Romania), and mostly doing day camps and week-long camps with Gypsy children.

In Romania, the Roma (Gypsies) were largely considered second-class citizens. While Afentra had a hard time even distinguishing who were Gypsy and who were ethnic Romanians while walking the curvy streets of Sighisoara, Romanians had an innate ability to tell who was who and to discriminate in that direction. Roma could be tow-headed, with enormous blue eyes. Romanians could have the tawny skin of a Gypsy and dark, curly hair—obviously from some inter-marrying—but they were treated better. Unfortunately, part of the differentiation between the two was the Romas' lack of hygiene, blossoming from generations of second-class citizenship. They often smelled of days without showers, defecated in their dirt yards, were confined to living in villages of shacks, literally "on the other side of the tracks."

So Afentra did what she could to educate the families about cleanliness and health and about the rest of the world, where the educated—in her experience—had at least a theoretical belief that everyone was equal and equally entitled. She scrubbed children, scrubbed shacks, helped bring clean water sources and define safe places to poop. She helped send Roma students on to higher education and helped, helped, helped at the grass-roots level, avoiding a corrupt government which was mired in a post-communism sink-hole.

She loved the Gypsies of Soard, especially a little boy, Ourielle. He was a runt, and was one of the Gypsies that confused her: his family lived in the town, not the Gypsy village. Ourielle dressed decently, and he looked to her just like an Eastern European with his ruddy cheeks, pale skin, sandy, straight hair and blue eyes. But he was an outcast. And he came from a desperate home situation, which was not uncommon among her Romanian acquaintances. He was beautiful.

He was vulnerable, but as she watched his innocence scuffed on the detritus of struggle, she was surprised to see that he was still hopeful, still a child, through and through.

Ourielle went with her when she took thirty elementary-school-aged Gypsy children on a four-day camp up in the foothills of the Transylvanian Alps. They spent their days on boating expeditions, a horse-cart ride to a castle (the horse-cart not being anything special for the kids, whose bus-trip out to the mountains was far more novel), having water fight after water fight, finger-painting in a barn, making up dances to Euro-pop, everything they normally might not get to do. Afentra watched Ourielle flourish. He ate three square meals a day (if milk-soup and bread with butter could be called square,) and his smile was broader each morning.

The camp took place in a ring of miniature cabins huddled around a common area, all owned and operated by a tiny Romanian orphanage. It housed only a handful of young orphans, who occasionally wandered out to play with the Gypsies, all blonde-headed, blue-eyed, and thin as toothpicks. Like the other children (and many children), they were love-starved, and would line up (not in any orderly way, mind you) to sit on a lap and have their toenails painted or their Polaroid snapped. Half of them, boy or girl, were named Florine.

Afentra fell asleep hard from hard work and mountain air, and dreamed pipe-dreams of whisking Ourielle away from his love-less and hard-knocks life. She dreamed of being a mother. In the morning, she shook off the dreams as they clung hard, reminding herself she was on very little income, only rented an apartment, and was currently squatting in a country on an extended visa.

Ourielle and his family contracted tuberculosis. His two younger siblings succumbed quickly, and Afentra secured Ourielle a bed in a local clinic. She found out sooner than later that both Ourielle's parents—unable to find sympathy or medical treatment anywhere—died alone, in their shack. Afentra poured her energy into Ourielle and he was quickly back on his feet.

There was no place for him to go. There were no orphanages to take him, and the paper trail was getting out of hand and finally ground to a halt. Ourielle went back to his hut, and one day he was gone. Probably gone to beg in the streets, lost in addiction to huffing and brain damage and early death. That's where the Gypsy orphans went. He could have been stolen, sold into slavery. She would never find him, here or in Bucharest.

While shut in her rented room with the shades drawn and both an empty stomach and heart, Afentra saw on a random English TV channel that Romania was closing its borders to adoption. She felt sickened, helpless, angry. Sour. She didn't leave time for numbness to creep in, but cut her time in Romania short, saddled her backpack once again, and crossed the Hungarian border on foot. She continued to walk helter-skelter through Europe, until she worked her way half-blind with despair into Greece and then into the Middle East and Israel. She wandered into the hostel in the Old City as an accident of fate: she wanted a bed and a meal for her last few bucks. She fell asleep and slept right through her rent and into the next day. One sleuth resident connected with a humanitarian organization paid the next weeks' rent and stealthily stocked her pack with peanut butter, dried apricots, and pita, fruit nectars and bottles of water.

After days of sleep and another several hours in a stupor, Afentra found her way to a foot-long schawarma and a cup of Turkish coffee. It took no time for her to discover that she still had a few nights in the hostel, a little food, and a debt to repay just one compassionate person.

⚬⚬ ⚬⚬

Gaby felt an affinity toward Afentra on her first day, although the sadness that bubbled under Afentra's serene surface was foreign to Gaby. Not for a lack of wanting: Gaby felt keenly that she needed to know some sort of sadness, some sort of wrench that would force her deeper and throw more variation of color across her life. Afentra insisted this was unnecessary, and that keenness of feeling came not with pain, but with joy and peace, a tranquil mindset that was outside of circumstances. Afentra was not living *more*. In fact, she thoroughly enjoyed Gaby's hope and youthfulness. Afentra thought it might save her, pull her up inch-by-inch from the well that she was in.

Gaby said, "Well, I'm here to save someone," which was always the way she felt.

"Maybe you could relax a little bit." Afentra was picking at a pile of French fries, eating chunks out of their sides like a bird would.

"Like you're one to talk," Gaby smiled at her, crookedly and out of the tops of her eyes. The two of them became confidential quickly, taking a crash course in each others' lives in such close quarters. They shared a bunk in a common room at the hostel and also an arms-length-away status with the hostel's resident organization. Gaby and Afentra volunteered at the same orphanage, hunted down meals together, walked around the mellower, orange city well into the night together, wandered to bed at the same time.

Gaby continued, "Do you *do* anything but wander around the world and help other people? Do you do anything *now* but volunteer?"

"Mooch," Afentra offered with a dry laugh.

"Yeah, I thought so." Afentra was looking for a job, and Gaby currently floated Afentra's rent and her meals and nagged the café manager to hire Afentra. "No more Americans," he kept saying. "You'll change your mind," Gaby kept telling him.

"Oh, I keep meaning to ask you something," Gaby's face turned serious, she leaned in and finished chewing, washed it down with drink. "What do you think about Alistair?"

Afentra choked back on her minute bite of fry. "Why?"

"Because,"—a sly smile—"I think he likes you."

"No." Afentra shook her head, her gaze suddenly buried in her plate of fries and her cheeks rouged. A quick smile flitted across her face and then disappeared.

"C'mon, I think he throws himself at you."

"What parallel universe have you been in?" Afentra raised her eyebrows and shifted her gaze through passersby, her tone suddenly too muted for her question.

"He's cute," Gaby teased. She started to tick off her fingers. "He's funny and nice and *British*!" she held out the last word and her fingers flashed all ten, palms forward.

"So why don't *you* date him?"

"Afentra, I'm just teasing you, except that I think it's true. What's wrong? You look like your mother's just died."

"I just don't know if I'm ready for something good to happen, yet."

"What do you mean? Like you're still in mourning..." tenuously, "for Ourielle?"

"Well, maybe. Yeah? I don't know..." her voice cracked off.

"Afentra, really I..." Gaby covered her hand with her own. "I didn't mean to."

Afentra retracted her hand and gave a smile, though a tear was sitting at the corner of her eye. "It's fine, Gaby."

"Just maybe you could use something like this. You're a good person and you deserve some love."

"What about you?" Afentra quickly changed. "You're a good person who deserves a relationship. Do you have one?"

"No..." Gaby trailed off and it was her turn to look at her dinner plate. "Plus what are you? Chopped liver? You're something good in my life." she forced a smile.

"You're avoiding the subject. I know something's going on with this Mikhail fellow." Gaby turned pale and flinched, but Afentra didn't notice. "Long distance romance?"

"Mikhail..." she trailed off in a whisper.

Afentra just sipped at her juice, watched Gaby over the rim of her cup and waited for a while. Gaby was zoned, her eyes unblinking, looking into a nonexistent distance. Then, "Gaby?"

Gaby shook her head and let her chin fall to her chest. "No, nothing. Mikhail has never liked me. We're just really great friends. Maybe he'll come over and see me. We'll see. Then you could meet him."

"And then *I* could date him. You make him sound like…"

"No!" Gaby's face turned dead serious and she swung her eyes into Afentra's.

"C'mon. I was just kidding. But what about it anyway? You like him?"

"No," she said as she leaned forward and buried her forehead in the palms of her hands. She started to rub her forehead. "Mikhail's dating Mel. Or at least sorta. That's sucked for a long time. I mostly just don't think about it. I mean, do I like Mikhail? Are they really dating? Do I really hate Mel anymore? Yes? No? No. I burned a lot of bridges back there." What she said lost momentum even as she said it. "When I was leaving the states, he was there at the airport with everyone else. He was acting really odd, really jittery or something. And he stayed at the window to wave goodbye to me. Afentra, I think he might have said something to me, but I couldn't quite tell. What did he say? What could he have said? It was such the wrong moment; so obscured or… or," she put her mouth in her hands, searching for the right word with a shaking head and narrowed eyes. "So late?" She combed her hands through the air and clapped them loosely together. "I don't know. There were just so many ways and so many times he could have said *anything* before then. But I can't ignore that we were always so close to each other and nothing ever really *happened*. Why not?"

"Blighted love," sighed Afentra. "Maybe you were too busy?"

"When he hugged me goodbye," Gaby continued, "he smelled too wonderful and it felt so nice just to sink into him. I keep thinking it was like we were just one body—like he was the rest of me that I was missing—and we just molded right into each other and it was warm and pleasant and, whatever.

I'm just getting silly. Absence makes the heart grow fonder, or sentimental, or something."

The girls climbed up onto the roof of the hostel later that night, by way of a ladder leaning down into a balcony outside their window. The roof was flat stone all the way out to its downward walls, and was situated high enough that they could see around the maze of the Old City, and over the distant wall into the bowl of lights and noise that was the New City. They spent the night drinking pop, complaining, and giving each other inexpert advice. Gaby spat into the night about Mel, and Afentra soothed her with a story about The Woodsboy and His Son, a story of forgiveness.

"You're right. I don't hate her. I still love her. But I am really hurt by her being a traitor, still."

"And by her stealing your boyfriend?"

"He's not my boyfriend!" Gaby took a long swing of Fanta looking out over the city. "But I guess I have been jealous. He's my B-F-F. Always has been."

"Now I think we're getting somewhere."

They left the roof, found the common area of the hostel deserted and walked downhill to the video rental store, uphill back to the ancient TV and video cassette player. Gaby tossed the video to Afentra and she read front and back. "*Russian Filigree?*"

"Yeah, it's based on a Northwythan story."

"Like the mural by our bed? By the way, were you awake the other day when that freak had a flashlight on us, *supposedly* studying the mural?"

Gaby laughed. "I was only half-asleep, but I'm pretty sure the beam stayed mostly on the wall."

Afentra opened a flap on the back of the cassette box and read out loud from the inside:

"The Evil Storyteller had the seed. It made him powerful and brought him wealth. With its magical power he drained the stories from the Story Keeper and left him—the last of his line—senile and confused and empty-headed." Afentra said aside, "*I don't know, Gaby. Sounds like a real winner to me.* The Evil Storyteller's power was later stolen from him by the woodsboy along with the cupboard of distilled stories. As the woodsboy disappeared around a grassy bend in the road away from Kerr's fortress, a shifty (or thrifty) maid was busy sliding her hands between her deceased master's neatly folded undergarments— *whoa-ho, Gaby! What kind of movie did we get?*—until her finger snagged on the chain of a locket—*That's not all it snagged on*— and when she felt the thrum from inside, she stole it, and the seed within. Thus, the stories went one way and the totem of the stories went another." Afentra bobbed her eyebrows up and down at Gaby, in a fruitless attempt at heightening the suspense.

"She had children, who had children, who had more children. Her line thrived, but none of her grandchildren knew just how to use the magical seed in the locket. They intuited that they should keep it, protect it; that its story was older than theirs, would go on long after theirs.

"During these long generations of the maid's family, the Aleksandrs were looking, always looking, for the locket with their magical seed. Would they find it?"

CHAPTER 18
FORTUNE COOKIE
ɛๆ   ૮ঽ

It didn't take long for Mikhail to realize that another attempt at telling Gaby he loved her was in order. He saw a movie and made a plan. He was going to print the message in reddish pink on a piece of fortune cookie paper, enclose it in a letter he had been meaning to write anyway, and send it on. She would see it and she would immediately understand that their fate, their predestined fortune, was to be together. Well, at least she would know that he loved her. She might even think that he was being romantic or creative.

He went through a number of printed messages, and he sat with the un-sealed letter among a litter of fortune cookie papers in 360 degrees around him on the floor, sighing over each one. "I love you"? That was simple and truthful. "Gaby, I love you. Mikhail." That was less likely to be misconstrued. "You are the love of my life. Come home." Would she even recognize him? And yet the agonizing raw emotion in that message struck him as least veiled. "Mikhail loves Gaby." "I have always loved you." "Marry me." A bit much? "I can make you happy." What was he? A delusional stalker?

He put one paper in, and then another, took the second one out, took the first one out. He was on his knees; in one fist the letter, in the other, a fan of fortune cookie papers, the finalists. And that was when his mother gave a quick, quiet knock and walked in.

He dropped what was in his hands in a flurry, reaching out in a panic to cover some of the papers on the floor with his arms. He didn't have enough arms, so he swung around wildly, grabbing up papers as he saw them. "Mom! Get out!"

Nadine looked startled for a moment, her mind catching up to the scene in front of her as she passed through the mental candidates. She believed she might have caught him in some kinky sex habit, or some Satan worship or some drug abuse. When she saw that it was papers with writing and the dropped letter fell against her foot, she read the addressee, crossed her arms against her chest, and leaned against the door-frame. She ignored Mikhail as he continued to shout and then plead for her to leave, watched him scramble around the room and stuff most of the papers under the edge of the bed before he flopped face-first down on the bed.

"Mom!?" came the muffled, final exclamation.

After a dramatic pause and with an amused smile, Nadine queried, "What is this?"

"Nothing." Muffled again.

"Hmm. And yet..." she bent over and picked up the letter, turned it over in her hands. She stood there ruminating long enough, and he lifted just his head and just enough to look sideways at her. "Mom! What are you doing?" He jumped up to snatch the letter, but Nadine slid it around her back. When he grabbed for it there, she slid it around front and down the front of her shirt, which solicited another disgusted "Mom!"

She stood there, looking him in the eye with a pleased smirk on her face. After ten seconds, she twisted her mouth in thought and then let out a big breath. "It's not as if I didn't suspect that you love her," she began.

Mikhail caught his mother's eyes, his own flickering between fear and confusion. Had he been found out long ago? Did everyone know? Did Gaby know?

"I'm your mother, Mikhail," she interrupted his process. "Gaby is a pretty girl, if you like bobble heads," Mikhail rolled his eyes "and you have always just adored her. But Mikhail…" She looked concerned as she trailed off.

"What?"

"Nothing."

"What, Mom?"

"What were all those papers you were hiding, anyhow?" Nadine walked over to his bed and fished her hand underneath where Mikhail shoved the papers, as she turned around and seated herself on the bed. Mikhail grabbed for them, but Nadine threatened to slide them as well down the front of her shirt. He relented easily and sat down next to her on the bed, just after she reached over and patted the spot to welcome him.

Nadine un-crumpled papers enough to read them. An amused smile slowly evolved into a sadness behind the eyes, a tired look. When she finished reading all the papers, she went through and smoothed each one into her lap. She rested her hands on top of them and directed her gaze at Mikhail, who was looking wistfully out the window.

"Mikhail—" His name broke off in her throat in a painful knot. Her heart sat like a stone and her ribs ached around it. "Mikhail, sweetheart. I—I'm not even sure what to say. Do you mean all of this?" she gestured lamely at the pile in her lap.

"I guess so. I mean, I do. But some of it is just silly. But I do love her, if that's what you mean. And I can't…" his throat was suddenly so dry he couldn't speak. His eyes pleaded with Nadine for respite.

"Mikhail, sweetheart, there are many things that you just don't understand. Women, for example. They are basically like another species. And while I am bound to stick with you no matter what kinks your maturity takes, well, your best friend

can't be expected to wait around for you forever, unless,"
Nadine cleared her throat and spoke now very precisely,
"unless you tell her in plain English."

Mikhail looked a little hurt. "Honey, I know that you have
it in you. I have invested all my love in you already. Gaby needs
you to have courage and romance. She needs someone that will
defend his love for her, in front of his mother and in front of
an airport full of people." Mikhail started again and Nadine
caught his eyes as she excused herself from the room. "I
believe I've said enough."

CB BD

The white legal envelope had "AIR MAIL" written in
royal blue marker on both sides, and the address printed in a
forcibly neatened male scrawl: "Gaby LeFevre, c/o The Moshe
House, #5 Rue de Baptistes, Mt Zion, 91012 Jerusalem
ISRAEL." There was a handful of thirty-two-cent stamps in
the corner with portraits of Elvis, a return address sticker in the
other corner, with the watercolor picture of a red robin and
"Nadine Aleksandr, 43115 Battle of Antietam, Butter MI
48116."

Inside lay folded a piece of lined notebook paper. On the
notebook paper, in a boyish scrawl, a letter of painfully stated
facts about life, interspersed with some leftover adolescent,
emotional reflection about life. Mikhail's mother was well. The
convenience store at the corner was changing to a 7-Eleven
with a gas station. Slurpies were awesome. Annie was missing
Gaby very much.

Tucked between the letter and the sealed side of the
envelope, a slip of white paper cut to the exact size of a piece
of fortune cookie paper that Mikhail had sitting on his desk,
leftover from a trip to Golden China. On the paper—in a
reddish-pink computer print—"Gaby, I love you. –Mikhail."

The letter traveled in darkness, an occasional watery, diffused illumination coming from the walls of the envelope. It moved from one leg of its journey to the next, in and out of pitch blackness and dizzying brilliance of sudden sunshine, in cold and heat, passing lightly between hands, pressed firmly through machinery, crushed under a magnificent amount of mail.

It was weeks later that it finally caught a mail plane for Israel, then shipping truck for Jerusalem and then a mail truck into the Old City. The truck parked outside the Damascus Gate and the mailman—an elderly, balding, Israeli with owl-round spectacles and soft hands—walked an army-green, heavy, canvas bag of mail into the winding maze of people, noises, and smells. The letter was lost in the middle of the bag, bound with a rubber band to a dozen other letters headed for the Moshe House. It was on the top of this packet, its corner bent under another packet on its way to a residence on The Via Della Rosa.

At the Moshe House, the mailman's hand fished around a little, a burst of fresh air entered the bag as he inspected the contents, and the letter with its packet was lifted up and out, several pieces of other mail dropping to the side. It was midday when the letter was thrust into a wooden box attached to the outer stone wall of the Moshe House. Gaby breezed by it on her way out for lunch, and it was mid-afternoon before the letter found its way into the cramped, hot and dry, maybe a little dusty and disorganized (as is seemingly everything in Israel) office of the Moshe House.

Gaby returned after an unexpected ramble through the New City and a cup of tea at The Second Cup as the sun set. She asked for mail and messages at the desk, and was handed the letter. She glanced at the address, her heart skipped a beat, she stuffed the letter with feigned nonchalance into her own side-pack, of a black-nylon variety checked with various cool traveling patches, all Israeli, crudely hand-sewn on with embroidery floss in primary colors.

The letter then waited, each new draft of light and air renewing a hope around the world and across the Atlantic, in a dense vastness of forest, field, and cement known to geographer Gottmann as the megalopolis of Chipitts. First, a wallet was retrieved from beside the letter, then thrown back on top of it. The letter was jostled on Gaby's bony hip for hours. And only under the cover of night was it suddenly picked from the bag and cradled in two warm palms.

Gaby's eyes rested on the address sticker and she snickered a little. She turned it over, started to tear very slowly at the corner, picking more than tearing. She turned it back over; the scrawl of her name on the front sent her stomach flitting, but almost imperceptibly. She paused a long while over the envelope, studying it without a word or a movement more than the necessary movement of a finger or a hand to turn it, to perforate it.

Gaby was sitting by herself at a round table meant for four at The Second Cup when a baby-faced, heavy-lashed young man seated himself across from her. He wasn't even looking at her, and when she looked up from her book, she thought he had mistaken her table for an empty one.

"Can I help you?" she offered, aiming at scaring him away with her English.

"Ah, yes." His accent mirrored hers, not European or Hebrew, as she expected. He smelled like freshly-applied deodorant and donned a worn, gray T-shirt almost fitted to his rather fit chest, and a pair of ratty khakis, the usual Birkenstock sandals. He glanced away again.

"Yes?" Gaby lowered one eyebrow at him and surveyed the shop. It was now obvious that he was with friends; a table of giggling twenty-somethings prodding him with glances over their shoulders and around their textbooks to go ahead and do it.

"Oh," he said, when he saw her look at the boys, and then at him. "The jig is up, then?" He hesitated while she waited, never looking away from him while he squirmed and produced a very charming smile. "I just wanted to ask you to come with me."

"Where?" Gaby was teasing him with her eyes and she sat back in her chair, crossed her arms across her chest.

"Just out around town, tonight. We're meeting out front of the King David Hotel. I just ask because you are so beautiful." He said the last as if it were an undisputed statement, and one he was not used to saying. He had a boyish awkwardness that pleased her, and a bookishness (disheveled, black hair, a worn paperback classic crumpled in his grasp) that pleased, as well.

Gaby narrowed her eyes in reservation, in thought. "Maybe I would. Could I bring someone?" The time was given, directions ("You know the hotel?" "Yes, of course."), and names exchanged. He was from the Eastern seaboard. His name was Andrew. She dropped everything in her satchel and left the shop before it got awkward.

‹§ ›§

Gaby returned to the Moshe House, breezed into her room long enough to find out from a cat-napping contemporary that she just missed Afentra outside in the courtyard. She gave her teeth a brush and her hair a quick tease in the cloudy, cracked bathroom mirror before thumping down in the chair next to Afentra with raised eyebrows, a look like "I dare you to ask me what."

Afentra—contrary to what Gaby thought she would do— insisted that Gaby and she go on the outing. She was feeling restless, and needed some "fresh air." Besides, Gaby agreed, they could always duck out early. Nothing to fear.

They got just a little dolled up (in night-life black, not quite as tight-fitting as the locals) and splurged on a cab that weaved through the city like a spastic drunkard. They exited the cab at the King David nervously, hands tucked under arms, and stood shuffling their feet in the orange glow of a night in Jerusalem, their furtive glances belying their casual conversation and misplaced snickers. When the boys came noisily up the walk there was a sudden burst of energy and muffled comments and one of the guys was projected toward them with a shove from the shadows. Andrew managed introductions while most stood with their hands shoved in their pockets, and in silence.

Afentra gravitated toward a guy Andrew introduced as having spent the summer touring Eastern Europe. He was studying archaeology in the area and spoke to her in a Texas accent that did not exactly match his architecturally structured glasses, fitted black T-shirt, and combat boots.

Andrew sidled up to Gaby and they edged away from the crowd as it started to move down the walk, carrying Gaby and Andrew with it. They talked, found they had a compatible sense of humor, a common love of academia and philosophy and were both currently reading *Les Misérables*. The group headed to a café where they lingered awhile and involved themselves in typical young people revels, then moved on to an industrial building which advertised out front for free dance classes. Gaby and Afentra found themselves on the third floor, buzzing on more coffee (free from the Thermos on the finger food table), crashing a room full of ardent Israeli-dancing students, whirling in rhythmic circles, laughing, clutching at stitches in their sides. Andrew met Gaby's eyes, then whirled away, did it again. His hand brushed hers. Their shoulders were touching.

During a break between songs, Gaby escaped out the side door. She lay her arms on the edge of the shadows, looking out over the orange, be-craned, nighttime Jerusalem, ignoring the few people who were decorating the balcony, a couple in quiet conversation. The night wind felt refreshingly the slightest bit cool, and Gaby let it blow her straight in the face, taking a few stray hairs away from her flushed cheeks.

Suddenly, she remembered the letter in her satchel and her stomach dropped out from under her.

Gaby repositioned herself to catch some escaping light, spraying out on the page in a soft glow of creamy yellow light; modern bulbs glancing off timeless stones. She felt alone, even though she clearly was not, and ripped the edge of the envelope off with appetite. She slid her hand into the cool, whiteness of the envelope, wrapped the tips of her fingers around the letter inside. As she lifted it out, she felt a wrist slide over her left shoulder, a warmth that spread to the right shoulder, where Andrew suddenly appeared, smelling of coffee and soap.

She glanced from the assaulted shoulder up into his eyes. "Hello there," he said after a gulp of water from a paper cup. He pulled his arm back to his side. "Sorry. Too much?" Gaby slid the letter back into the envelope, smiled at Andrew, and failed to notice the fortune-cookie paper caught dangling, clinging, and then floating in the wind, across the roofs of Jerusalem, and into its gutters.

CHAPTER 19
L'AMOUR
℘   ℘

Suddenly, Andrew. And suddenly, Israel's romance and intrigue were multiplied and multiplied and multiplied again. Where once there was an ever-more-likable dustiness and rockiness, there was now the goldenness and the sunnyness. Where once there was the sacredness of all, there was now a particular and personal religiosity. Where once there was a quirky and heavy history, woven from ancient threads coming from all different directions, there was now a oneness with the place, a feeling of the soul's home, and destiny for Gaby right there. This was the place to be. Because Andrew.

She loved Israel, even more than before (because, truthfully, Israel feels to many like a coming home, and we all leave with heavy hearts). She loved her dirty hostel room and her grungy hostel bed. She loved her friends (although she wasn't seeing *much* of them, these days), she loved the quaintness of the stones in the courtyard, the curve of a mango nectar bottle, the way the woman in the courtyard frowned as she painted.

Gaby didn't love having a fuzzy headspace. She was uncomfortable with it. She wasn't sure why she kept showing up late to work, why she kept sloughing off her duties at the orphanage, where her resolve had fled to, where the driving attitude of responsibility, the intricate philosophies that sustained her world view. Whose spastic endocrine system was she now burdened with?

A surprise for Gaby, Andrew asked her if she wouldn't like to spend a week with him up on the Sea of Galilee, away from their friends and away from their responsibilities. Andrew was studying in Israel at an ostensibly religious school, tramping all over that blessed country (the size of New Jersey) while learning about the politics of the Middle East, the history of the Middle East, and the religions of the Middle East. The students in his History of Christianity class spent a few weeks touring the Sea of Galilee early in the semester (which included some time on Cyprus and in Greece, following the ministry of Paul). Andrew remembered—besides the café life in Tiberias— a quaint "kibbutz" on the more remote eastern edge of the sea and also a couple of backpackers who suggested to a friend a hike down a riverbed in the Golan Heights.

Andrew's friends had made the exact trip the weekend before and so he felt it was something he could handle and found himself looking forward to it. *I am a camping god*, he told himself. And he spent an afternoon shifting from dorm room to dorm room, begging and sometimes pillaging the familiar bunks for a full regalia of camping supplies. This would be such a special week. He was thankful and flabbergasted that Gaby agreed to go with him.

And there were, of course, other things on his mind as well. Such as privacy.

They set off on a Saturday, Friday being impossible because Shabbat closed down a lot of the country. After an urban hike about a mile from the hostel with their gear, they caught a bus on a corner in mid-town. Their conversation was holding up very nicely. The bus took them as far as Tiberias, where they stopped for lunch at a piano bar built on a dock that jutted out into the sea. At the mouth of the dock was a shop where Gaby and Andrew picked up a medallion with The Queen's image. The inscription etched underneath: "Patron Saint of Lovers." *Since when is The Queen the patron saint of anything?* they wondered. They had a good laugh and Gaby pocketed the medallion before they caught a taxi to a campground deep inside the Golan Heights.

They were already tired from traveling, and from some nasty haggling with the taxi driver, when they dumped their gear at the foot of a picnic table. The table was on a long, cement slab, covered with a wooden pavilion. There was a water fountain, a water spigot, remedial restrooms, and a wall of large, rusty lockers. Adjacent to the pavilion, a field, fenced in on four long sides with a slatted wood fence, designed to keep in cows, not keep out anything else. It was in the field that Gaby and Andrew understood they were to sleep the night.

Field was a nice word for it. It was really an *old* field, now just hard-crusted ex-mud and manure. It rolled in hard bumps, and still smelled mostly of cattle dung, in a removed way; like the ghost of poop was visiting them. There were two tents set up on the dirt, set at odds with each other across the expanse of it. One tent was meant for one seriously intense hiker, the other a rather large tent, not meant for hikers at all. It was around this tent that a group already gathered in the waning daylight.

Gaby and Andrew ate a snack of pita with peanut butter at the picnic table, drawing it out as they glanced sideways at their accommodations. The sky darkened in an undeniable way and they saw that the field was not lighted, nor the pavilion. They wandered into the field, plopped their gear down again in the middle of it, and threw out their sleeping bags in the dust, wrestled into their pajamas while prone inside the bags.

They forgot about the manure and grew accustomed to the smell. Above them hung a night abundant with stars, a clear sky unlike Gaby's suburban one or her urban Jerusalem one.

Andrew and Gaby both tried out their amateur astronomy on each other, but did not talk long before they were too exhausted to continue. They lay silent, waiting for sleep, both battling insomnia due to the loud, drunken revelries of the non-hiking campers across the field. Gaby woke up a few times in the night, shivering in the cold, and feeling desperately lonely, yet so close to something else; drawn inexplicably to the warmth beside her but unwilling to reach out and touch it.

೦೩ ౭౦

In the morning they woke up with the sunlight, surprised to look at their watches and see that it was hours earlier than their normal wake-time. Andrew welcomed Gaby to the day with a soft kiss and a "Good morning, beautiful." Gaby blushed for maybe the second time in her life, feeling suddenly very sleepy, very crusty, very vulnerable. She realized she must have the day's dirt and debris smeared across her face, her hair must be a disheveled mess. At once, she felt that camping in a manure field was both the stupidest and most wonderful thing that she could ever have done.

They dressed in their sleeping bags and splashed their faces with water. Gaby pulled her hair up and they used the restrooms, they ate of their provisions for breakfast: bananas and granola bars. Then they dubiously locked away their possessions in the rusty lockers and shouldered their day-packs, full of water, food, cameras, sandals, etc. They were layered in bathing suits and cargo shorts, because a fall hike in the riverbed promised getting wet throughout the day. There was still a nip in the air, but the relentless, white sun meant that the water—no matter how cold—would be welcome.

First they hiked a short distance across a flat and open land to the head of one of the gorge trails. Then they came to a sudden greenness, where the sandy vastness of tan gave way to a slit in the earth that flowed with verdant lushness. Bamboo, oak, and feathery conifers filled the deep crevasse that was the riverbed, and they lowered themselves into it, down a steep, rocky slope.

At the bottom, the trail followed the river and meandered at a low grade toward the Sea of Galilee, which they could not yet see. In fact, all they could see from the valley was their present bend of the river. At times, they wound through shrubs and trees, noting obvious nature bedding locations, perhaps for the temperamental, wild boar that they were hoping to avoid. They made their way through giant, waxy-leaved bushes, shaded from the heat by the thin, pale green, shivering and swaying up by the sun. They clung to rock walls when the riverbed grew slim, and saddled their packs on their heads to swim across the river, gratefully sliding into the wet coolness.

Around one bend of the river, the bed grew slim and seemed to rise up insurmountably. The river disappeared in light rapids into the thick bush, and a wall of rock rose up from it. Metal stakes were bored into the rock, meant for Gaby and Andrew to climb them and mount the edge. They did, still at a level below the rising valley wall, and looked out over a steep drop and more metal pegs. They lowered themselves and their packs carefully, one peg at a time. And then they were in a hollow, which featured a round, deep, rock pool, a waterfall spraying into it, and an open cave behind the waterfall. The pool looked out to the south-west over another drop and into a widening of the river bed that panoramaed the continuing, green valley, its parched, brown, stony abutting lands, and the shimmering dark blue of the Sea of Galilee.

Tired by a long morning of hiking and sweaty from the climb over the rock wall, Gaby and Andrew decided to lunch and take a dip in the pool. They dined on hummus sandwiches, more granola bars, lots of water from their canteens. And after sunning on a large rock like lazy lizards, Gaby and Andrew stripped down to their swimsuits and slipped into the waters.

They swam to the waterfall, played under it. They found a rock just under the surface of the water at the entrance to the cave, sat on it, and then dropped into the cave, which encircled a churning pool the size of a Jacuzzi, and filled with warm water, swirling around them, in a wild torrent.

The air in the cave sparkled with sunshine and with a mist from the swirling waters. It was warm and wet and raucous. Gaby and Andrew were buffeted by the rapids, awed by the view: looking out of the cave, there was the vast blue of the sky, looking out over the next waterfall, and then the distant Sea glinting in the sunshine. Closer up, there was the bigger pool, bright at midday, a curl of foam sliding into the calm of it. And even closer, the torrent of water obscuring the cave view, occasionally becoming only mist in the breeze. A rainbow arched across the entrance, made of mists and sunlight.

And then there was the kiss. Because Andrew could think of nothing else, and realized that if there were an opportune time, this was it. So this was the king of all kisses, a pure kiss, fiery enough, and if the girl had a lick of sense, she would take it and never look back. Trysts like these were not meant for complications.

And then there was what he said.

"Do you think we're dating?"

There was something in that, somewhere. "We *are* dating," and she inched away a little.

"We are dating?"

"Yes. What we're doing: hanging out all the time, kissing under waterfalls on weekend getaways, this qualifies as dating." Mistiness came crashing down around her.

"Mm."

Gaby could not believe that there it was; a buzzing in her head and a sudden fuzziness and heat. She was not going to get in a fight when she was so in love, so enamored and so… Well, normally she was cloudy around Andrew, but her judgment always gave him the benefit of the doubt. Suddenly, it was as if the water around her suspended, as if the sounds had ceased vibrating mid-air, and the sunlight crystallized; then everything reversed. With the imperceptible scratch of a supernatural phonograph needle on a record, everything jumped and shimmied and flipped on Gaby. From in love to fuzzy and hot and a buzzing in the brain. She felt herself trapped in her own anger and regretting what was not yet said. Without another word happening, life was now on fast forward and on an inevitable kamikaze collision course.

"Mm? *Mmm?* What is mmmmm?"

"Nothing. I just wondered what you thought."

"You're kidding me, right? I mean, you do know what a fatal blunder you just made."

"Me? You're the one getting all bent out of shape."

"No. You did not just say that. What is wrong with you? You just..."

"What is wrong with me? You're so super-sensitive."

"...Did you just say 'so super-sensitive?'" she did her best cheerleader. "So! Super! Sensitive!"

"I don't even know what that is."

"Yeah, Mister New Jersey. Like you don't watch *Baywatch* like everyone else in the world. Don't even superior culture me. Superior culture, my ass!"

"Point proven."

"Point proven that you're a snotty dick." She made a sudden look of disgust when the graphic picture born of her own crassness reached her consciousness. She looked sideways at Andrew. He was not looking at her. He was staring in the space that turned to sky above pool. He had no expression on his face, except a slightly furrowed brow and a darkness behind the eyes. Gaby felt static between them and nothing else. She had a theory about moments like this, when something died between you and another person. This was just one of many schisms that would begin to define them, she thought morosely. Eventually, the shape of their love would be defined by all of the times that they disappointed, by all of the times they felt unreached, all of the times they felt a cold chill coming from one another. Would—in the winter of their love—they be assured that there was a warm trickle of compassion running deep under the iciness of these moments? The same fights over and over? The things about yourself that you know your lover despises, when all you need is some little affirmation in a language you can understand?

Sitting in the numb haze that was before the pool, Gaby realized she barely knew Andrew, and she was unprepared for a moment like this: their history of love, their level of commitment, was unable to stand up to the doubts in her mind. But she also realized—right before Andrew swam out of the cave in icy disregard—that they would probably keep going when the cold electricity beneath their skin gave way to a comforting nothingness and then more moments of hot electricity and swelling nervousness in the chest. All these things would build up and build up and build up and someday, the momentum would take them into the oblivion of the future, or the haltingness would prevent them.

Thinking about all these things calmed her. She forgave him in the silence, but still wanted love. She wanted many, many things from him, and she wondered what he would give. Of course they were dating, but what the hell did he mean?

☙ ❧

Gaby made it through another afternoon at the orphanage and through a wild sherut ride through the back streets from Bethlehem to Jerusalem which cleverly—or not so cleverly—evaded the checkpoints at rush hour. Involved were requests not made, Arabic shouted from the open window, streets too bumpy and narrow to be considered passable in the States, and the occasional pedestrian actually leaping from the psychotic, reeling path of the vehicle, sometimes crashing into a wall. She thought about completely disappearing into her bunk when she and it intersected, but a hostel bed was not always as peaceful and relaxing in the early evening as one might want. So she instead gathered up some things and walked down the hill, past carnage-displaying delis, garbage-strewn alleyways, and thumping discotheques and into one of her favorite Europeanesque cafés in the New City which sold mostly giant crepes filled with fruits, cheeses, sweets, and even cured meats and eggs.

Gaby thought about Andrew, which was all her mind felt good for, lately. She sighed at herself. What did she know about him? He smelled good and was relatively handsome. He was mostly a nice guy. He was goofy. He was really intelligent; academic. She found herself wondering what parts of that list would stay with a person as they aged. Would he grow out of the habit of applying cologne? Decide showers wasted too much water and relegate himself to a cue-ball shave and sponge-baths? What did his dad look like? Loose waist? Saggy chin? Bulbous nose? What did he act like under pressure; after four hours of a traffic jam on a bad day in a town he didn't really want to live in? Would the goofy become that thing people always said you might fall in love with now and grow to hate later? Who were these harbingers of disaster, anyway? What if Andrew were hit by a drunk driver and lost a large part of his brain function? Or all of it?

In that case, what was it that drew two people together, was strong enough to hold them together from vows to oh yeah, *those vows?*

Andrew grew up traveling the long, straight roads of the Sonoran desert. He told Gaby about the relentless sun with its dry, white heat, picking oranges from the burdened trees in his yard, and those long, straight lines through near-empty Pima territory, fringed for miles and miles with the glitter of broken, glass bottles ground to sparkling shards as endless as a shore of sand.

Phoenix didn't remind Gaby of the type of people Andrew's parents must be, but they didn't live there anymore, anyhow. And Phoenix didn't seem like the place Andrew would have spent his formative years. Alas, Andrew was full of stories of his time in Phoenix. When a high schooler, he had a laughable run-in with the law. What began as a boat of an old, stinking car full of rowdy boys drinking Cokes became boys hanging out of car windows dragging trashcans down the road, laughing and crooning and scraping plastic on cement, the backfire of the engine into the otherwise quiet darkness. It didn't end there, and before long a hefty baseball bat was produced and now boys were leaning long out of the car window, slicing the bat through the night and destroying mailboxes; watching pieces sail through the dim light of porches and taillights.

Then there was a different kind of light, a flashing, multicolored light and for a brief moment the driver thought of taking off. They pulled over, they acted humble and yes-sirred and all that, and were taken into the police station, their parents called, all of them properly chastised and grounded and one even enrolled in an anger management program.

This was all after the powers-that-be identified Andrew as a genius, or at least a near-genius. In elementary school, he was shuffled into testing and then into a magnet program that pulled Phoenix's most potential brightest-and-best and stuck them by grades into neat little classrooms with caring, conscientious, and well-credentialed teachers. The credentialed teachers encouraged him to learn in ways that would most benefit him. He formed strong memories of singing out his science homework, presenting his countries of the world project as an original play in three parts, and also of creating an art project learning limericks. He got so absorbed in the creation of penguin characters out of decoupage (to illustrate the limericks) that the teacher facilitated "penguin day," where parents and students provided everything penguin, and the day was topped off by a penguin wedding (between his decoupage penguin and another student's,) officiated by yet another penguin, attended by penguins and a weepy mother-of-the-bride penguin, performed completely in limerick and ended with a two-tiered, sugary, wedding cake.

Andrew's eyes sort of glistened as he told about those days. "Fourth grade. The best year of my life." *Was* he being facetious?

By the time he got to college, which he attended in the Northeast, he was free to be academic again. His friends were nerds and artists and had weekly meetings for things like beer and fantasy lit night and outings to symphony performances. Among nerds and artists, Andrew was a real playboy, trailing girls behind him along the classroom building corridors. He didn't want for a date, but he was also distracted by all the fun he was having at the Tolkien Convention and at mixed media workshops.

The student union was a small-enough space, with ultra-low ceilings and a warm glow. Most nights it was crowded with informal student meetings, loose study sessions, snackers and coffee drinkers, a handful of loiterers, and chronically that one loud laugher who shot through your concentration at regular intervals. Often, some sort of small-scale entertainment took place on a square of hard floor off in one corner, where students would pause to glance from their booths and tables or even gather around on the low, cushioned seats to listen to a garage band, watch improv comedy, or scrutinize a poetry reading for clues to meaning.

It was winter, a bitter cold night, a Friday. Andrew didn't have plans until late, so he wandered to the Student Union with friends, crammed himself into a booth and joined in goofing off playing paper football. Coats were smashed into the booth behind him so that he could barely sit and he wore a broad smile, a gleam in the eyes.

Andrew's schedule was heavy on liberal arts classes, and this semester he was more often than not in the Literary Arts building, toying around with the Life section of the newspaper, in a poetry workshop, or at one of his seminars on C.S. Lewis and Alfred Hitchcock. No matter where he went, there Clara was. Who knew how he even knew her name? He usually stuck to a tight knot of friends or to himself and his ultra-focus, but she was there in the workshop (nose to paper as she mumbled sanguine lines about periods or boy bands), she was there in both seminars (her Lewis boxed set thunked down on the table top or her hand waving frantically to mumble about Hitchcock's approach to the mental sex of Jeff Jeffries in *Rear Window*), was there in the newspaper room (on general staff, cranking out cross word puzzles and anonymous answers to the Dear Wolverine column). She was there, leaning up against the water fountain as he passed, staring at him. She was there, squeezing out the classroom door, close enough to smell her: tuna fish sandwiches and cats? She had cats at school? She must live off-campus. Or maybe the tuna was *for* the cats.

Andrew took a paper football in the forehead and the simple sensation dominated his current existence. The guys at the table burst out with a groan-laugh at Andrew and the paper football to the head. He slapped his hand there and turned around to fish the football out of the pile of coats. And then he heard a line of song waft out over the union crowd; "I-yi-yiy will be yours-oh-yours until I die-yi-yiy!" Something in his stomach clenched and a chill thrilled through him. But he grinned as he threw the paper football back and someone said—looking at the stage area—"Hey! I know that girl. She's a fuckin' freak."

That was putting it a bit strong. And now all the guys at the table were ogling her, rudely, and listening. Clara perched on a tall stool, her Mary Janes sitting on a higher rung, and an old, cheap guitar balanced on a knee, blocking the world from seeing up her tweed, pleated skirt. She strummed and picked at a remedial melody as she sang with a voice that was surprisingly clear and strong and pretty. Her eyes closed under heavy bangs.

"I should be saying these things in metaphor:
I'm feeling blue and seeing glaciers,
But that doesn't seem right, does it?
Not with your heat in the classroom.
Oh, Andrew! Oh, Andrew!
I-yi-yiy will be yours-oh-yours until I die-yi-yiy!"

Action at the paper football table ceased while they watched Clara and waited for something in her singing to make fun of. But this? Their heads swiveled toward Andrew, eyebrows raised, mouths broke into broad grins. "Oh, Andrew!"

"I-yi-yiy will be yours until I die-yi-yi-yi-yi-yiy!" one guy clutching at his heart and falling dramatically back into the booth.

"No, guys, seriously. *Is* she singing about *our* Andrew?"

Andrew reddened at the ears and he shook his head furiously. "No. Nope. Not me. I don't even know her."

"Of course you do. She's in like every Literature class this school has to offer. And she's on newspaper staff with us."

"Oooh! Andrew!"

"You are hers! Until she *dies!*" More swooning.

A chorus of rough, unharmonious voices rose raucously; "Oh, Andrew! Oh, Andrew! I-yi-yiy will be yours-oh-yours until I die-yi-yiy!" Everyone in the union now looked over at them, some giggled, some gave them nasty looks. Andrew sunk down into the collar of his sweater and he turned and looked over his shoulder at Clara. She, too, stopped playing and singing to look at the gruff chorus and scanned them while holding the guitar out to her side, by the neck. Her eyes met Andrew's and hers went wide and terrified, then glassy. She breathed a quiet "Oh no," then dropped the guitar to the ground with a clatter as she ran off stage right and slammed into the exit door, disappearing into a whirl of snow and darkness.

CHAPTER 20
THE BETTER HALF
℘   ℭ

Annie took off from college with great force and speed. While her colleagues floundered waking up from their drunken stupors and went to therapy to deal with their promiscuities and parental cleaving, Annie focused and applied feverishly to a number of nonprofits until she landed a job as a fund-raiser/grants director for Bioethical Farming U.S.A., based in California, but offering a position in the Big Apple. It was a long way from home (more culturally than geographically), but her ambitions were sterilized, fresh, and in a zip-locked compartment of the procession of her life. Then, as Gaby moved in circles so far in the subterranean of Annie's life (or maybe in the outer space of that world), Annie moved fast and faster. While Gaby drew small shapes with the pattern of her life: questions and answers, relationships in all their gore, beginnings and endings; Annie's time arched in a brilliant blaze up into the clear blueness of oblivion.

She wore many hats: from fund-raising/grants directing (a lot of thankless work and late nights, not to mention coffee brewing and sandwich fetching, plus squeezing one person into two positions when funds were limited and staff skeletal) to technical writing and—her favorite—online, "green" columnist. Running with this thankless job crowd, hob-knobbing with the lobbyists for the International Land Conservation, her life became crowded with soirees, flashed smiles and highly intelligent conversations.

She wasn't leaving a trail of money or Gucci handbags—in fact, she was able to stay in New York because of the existence of nearly half-a-dozen roommates and a sense of destination which was yet to be assailed. She left here and there a trail of dazzled important people and approvingly nodding others. She was conscientious, sure, but she could also spot a valuable suit from across the thrift store, could weed through the flea market and the classifieds with hound dog precision, trailing the good stuff (good chocolate, good shoes, good art). She was young and beautiful, could manage her makeup and an aura of power.

Her destination? While it seemed clear, it was also fuzzy. None of her moves were goal-oriented, exactly, and yet they seemed to further the forward blaze. Straight through the wilderness, machete flashing and debris flying and... Could it be she would return to an old path? Or look back at a field of angles? Never! On toward *bigger* and *better* and *more* and *happy* and *someone*.

❧ ☙

Annie spent a lot of time in her apartment, often spending the weekdays pounding only the pavement between her apartment and the library, the newsstand, the grocer underneath and the Thai restaurant on the corner. Most days her roommates came home to her snuggled in the corner, in sweats, with Thai food containers in a precarious tower and chopsticks sticking out like very modern art, the palor of her skin precisely the hue of the computer screen glowing back at her. The curtain might be bunched up behind her chair, the blinds hunched into a skewed mess, the cat (belonging to someone who actually liked cats) meowing and pawing at the cupboard with its food inside. She was turning into her sister. Or she was her sister.

Either way, one of her roommates—Caroline to be exact, a waitress at Blue Danube (the per-capita waitress ratio in New York being higher than most)—pulled her out of her seat one evening, got her drunk on mint Schnapps and homemade chocolate chip cookies, and convinced her to go to her next free yoga in the park.

Saturday morning, Annie and Caroline slung bags over their shoulders, brimming with the tops of yoga mats (Annie's brand new) and bumpy with water bottles, wallets, other yoga implements (like belts, blocks). Annie wore tennis shoes, tennis socks, stretch pants (which were making their way back into fashion), a T-shirt, and a headband with a pony tail. She walked along with a bounce, blending in with the breathing of the city on a clear morning. Honk, swoosh, eternal ebb and flow of voice and babble, machine, mechanism, bang, crash, buzz, and the cool air getting cooler down by the pavement, far away from the sun that burns away impurities, down in the blue.

They walked, descended into the grit and otherworldliness of the subway. Screeched along until they came to Central Park, emerged, walked along jostling with so many other people who never looked into their faces and whose eyes they never met. Crossed a street. Crossed a street. Waited for lights to blink and things to chirp and cars to move. Cars, but never people.

In the park, Caroline chattered with Annie while she didn't even think about the way they were headed. Caroline guided them there without a word of instruction, toward an opening between the trees, a grassy spot with a slight slope and not perfectly smooth ground. Still chatting, she un-rolled her mat and Annie followed suit. She removed her sandals, Annie removed her shoes. She sat down and began gently stretching out, got quiet. Annie wondered what she was doing here, looked around at the other people gathering. Mostly young women, even a few people with only beach towels laid out instead of yoga mats. In T-shirts and yoga pants and tank tops, and even the occasional peasant shirt. There, a man in running pants that swished when he moved, no shirt, just a chest full of curly hair. He was contorting himself into the most unreal positions, balancing in ways that defied gravity, and keeping his hands always perfectly o'd between the forefinger and thumb, his eyes closed.

Show off, Annie thought, but found it difficult to look away.

After signing a release form that went around the group for the newbies, Annie joined the instruction, already in session, but so far the instruction consisted of telling them to sit in any ol' comfortable position (although Annie noticed most people sitting the same way and did what they did) to meditate on the nature around them and the connection to her body. And then her body, and all its harmonious parts, and the beating of her heart, the moving of her blood, and lots more things personified.

She found that burning through a series of at home Pilates videos had readied her enough to keep up with the instructor as she called out both familiar and completely unintelligible Indian words and zipped through series after series of poses. Not that Annie could actually manage a Lord of the Dance Pose, Side Crane, or a Wild Thing the first time, but she could manage a Downward Dog into a Lunge and then back into a Plank over and over. Excuse me; a Sun Salute.

It felt good to be moving around, to be in a little knot of people, and to be outside. She took a break to drink some water and looked around at everyone, in the middle of a pose called the Warrior. She could feel the water moving down the back of her throat and into her stomach. She was winded a little, and wondering how she could jump back into the cadence of the class. She watched Caroline, who seemed poised and experienced, but who lacked the perfection that must have taken years and a wall mirror—or natural affinity—for a few of the other students to master.

Near the end of the session, the teacher got everyone into the Savasana, lying supine on the ground with their arms and legs out straight and relaxed. Annie could feel the bumps of the lawn through her soft yoga mat and against her back and her tailbone. Blades of grass itched and tickled at her wrists and hands, off the mats to the sides. She felt the breeze, its relative clean-ness, listened to the birds, the sounds of city traffic, slightly muffled, to the people around her sighing and groaning and breathing, and finally, to the sounds of the leaves popping together: a noise not heard when there is only one, but that becomes pregnant and sweet and wonderful when in a chorus. Alternately, she closed her eyes, opened them, closed her eyes, opened them: no matter which she did her lids seemed to want to naturally fall the other way.

When the teacher led everyone in the chant, "Ommmmmmmmmmmm. Ommmmmmmmmmm," Annie tilted back her head and sighed. She really didn't feel like "ohm-ing." What on earth did that mean, anyway? Instead, she let her body sink into the ground, imagined each limb and part of her body filled with the suggested sand, visualized each muscle relaxing with her exhale. She stared up at the trees, at the complicated lacing of branches against the washed out sky. She noticed how the trunk turned into branches turned into twigs turned into buds. It would be impossible to paint each one so that the painter caught the three-dimensionality of it, the overlay. It reminded Annie of soap bubble paintings, where you blew bubbles in paint-swirled water and then pressed a paper on top, reducing the pearlescent mountain to a sheet of curving lines.

She decided not to reach for the throw-away camera that she usually carried when she saw it: between all the intricate, dark webbing against dazzling white, a clearing in a perfect circle and in its center, a single leaf.

C3   80

Gaby spent a few hours of a day off from the orphanage wandering the Old City with Afentra, weaving through the heady aromas and tangled alleys until they were lost except for a distinct and intuitive sense of compass direction. Being just two American girls, they were asked the time twice, the way to the market, if they would marry someone ("...You love me, I love you. It's good, no?"), and watched two men and one girl urinate in the street (but not all at once), on top of the usual shouting of "Fluffy!" (which inexplicably meant big-chested) and the usual stalking and hawking of wares. On their way back, a man approached them and spoke quickly in commercial Hebrew and Gaby yelled out "Oh, jeez!" to Afentra's laughing and the man turned and walked away.

Therefore, Gaby asked some guy—any guy—from the hostel to accompany her to work that night. Afentra walked her there, too, and then said goodbye to the two guys who chaperoned them, the guys promising to return at the end of shift. Afentra nestled herself into a corner table at the café and spread out her coffee and napkins and bag and a book. She bent her head over it in the gold and brown glow and looked aloof, absorbed.

Gaby continued in to the back, tied on her apron, waved to the manager pulling shots down the counter to let him know she was there. The smell of coffee pervaded; it was on Gaby's apron (but with that day-old, singed undertone) and would be well in her hair before she left for the night. The light in the café shone diffused and understated, but altogether bright and yellowed. The front of the café was open to the night, and the light spilled out of it over thin-legged tables and chairs which made Gaby think of VanGogh's *Café Terrace at Night*, but this was a long way from France.

After a rush of students, Gaby's manager let her break during a lull. She slumped into the chair across from Afentra, taking her unawares. "What are you doing? Quitting?"

"Nope, on break." Gaby picked up a book off the tabletop without really looking at it, then set it back down. "So, what are you up to over here? You been reading all night?"

"Mostly. I talked to some neighbors, but they left."

"Right. So what are you reading, then, that's so interesting?"

"Oh, the usual: Trashy romance novels, weaponry magazines, mail-order bride catalogues…"

Gaby poker-faced it. "Can you get me one, then? I need a new wife and I prefer that she's Persian."

"*Or* I'm reading one of those Northwyth books you lent me. You choose."

"Mm." Gaby sat forward and took a sip of Afentra's latte, looking down at the book in front of Afentra. "I didn't know you had started it. You like it?'

"Yeah, it's entertaining and all. How did you start reading them?"

"Well, they're really popular back in the States, now. And some old sort-of-boyfriend gave me the first one when I had a broken leg; a really romantic parting gift. Anyhow, *The Maid's Ancestors* came out the winter before I left Michigan, so I grabbed a copy to read on the way here. I think the series is almost done? I dunno. What does it say?" She was looking at the back of it, now.

Afentra yawned, stretched out her arms into the air and looked around at the café over Gaby's head. Gaby continued, "Yeah, this one was pretty good. I mean, obviously the guy didn't come up with the stories, but they sort of come to life with all his earthiness and grit. Let's see…" She opened up the book to the spot where Afentra nestled a bookmark, and started to read,

"With Olivier's blood still fresh on his coat, Gaston took the damaged locket, spilled the seed out on to his palm—you think *that's* an innuendo—and dropped the encrusted piece of jewelry into the fountain, where it shimmered as it sank to the bottom. He did not care if it was hidden, it did not matter. The locket was now inconsequential. Only he and the seed were important now.

"It took only a moment, standing there in the shimmering, low light at the side of the fountain, Olivier's soul still hovering around the hovel in which he had lived, which now stood at Gaston's back. It took only a moment for Gaston to reach into his deep pocket, pull out the substantial bracelet and open the miniature door hidden among the metal's folds and the gems' luster, took only a moment for him to drop the seed inside the door, close the door, and hear a solid popping noise that sealed it forever. *It was very finely made*, he thought. *Well worth it.*

"No one would recognize the seed now." Gaby snapped the book shut and did her best evil laugh, "Mwah-hah-hah-hah-hah!" making everyone look over at her.

Her manager yelled from behind the counter, "Gaby! That's how you choose to use your break? Come back here and work!"

Afentra took the book from Gaby. Gaby made to stand up but leaned in conspiratorially to Afentra. "You know, the crazy French ancestors retrieve the locket from the water and the stupid fools don't realize anything's wrong with it and even after Alyosha rips it from Olivier' great-great-grandson's neck (whom she has just seduced and rufied), the present day Aleksandrs don't have a clue." She bobbed her eyebrows at Afentra.

"You idiot. Stop giving stuff away and go make a cappuccino."

Adam and Stellar remembered a day when weddings and baby showers were a monthly occurrence. They remembered when they were sent away by their church on mission trips and asked to sing with the band. They remembered playing volleyball in the yard and not walking away crippled, sinking helplessly into the pool to cope with the neck tension. They sort of resented aging in an *almost*-accept-the-things-that-can-not-be-changed way.

"I guess we're really middle-aged then?" Stellar sighed as she sunk back against the side of the pool, her arms resting out and behind her on the ledge.

"No. That isn't right."

"How isn't it right? You mean *you're* not middle aged? We're not that far apart in age, you know."

"I just mean, well, isn't ninety the new eighty and all that? Like middle age is moving up since people live longer."

"I don't know." Stellar leaned her head back and stared into the brazenly blue sky, little wisps of white fringing the horizon. "We're empty nesters."

"That's a terrible phrase."

"It is." She closed her eyes and let her body sink down under the water, her hair lifting up toward the surface and the coolness and softness touching all her skin. A bubble tickled her nose as it passed by with the exhale of her breath. The world was a little pink and a little blue through her eyelids, rippling with sun through water. When she surfaced, Adam was talking.

"…for sure. We just about killed ourselves with yard work."

"You know I was underwater, right?" Stellar rubbed her hands up past her eyes and over her scalp to remove water drops that were running toward her face. She opened her eyes and saw Adam at the pool's edge, looking up at Mikhail. "Oh, Mikhail! I didn't see you there!"

"Hi, Mrs. LeFevre."

"Hi, Mikhail. You want to go for a swim?"

"No thanks. I haven't got my suit anyhow."

"Oh. Well, we don't usually see you here with the girls gone."

"No. Well, I just, I just sent a letter to Gaby awhile ago but I hadn't heard anything... so I was in the neighborhood," he indicated the neighborhood with a sweep of his arm and then his arm slid behind his head, his long fingers scratching at the opposite side of his neck, "and I thought I would stop and see if you had heard anything from her, recently."

"Well no. Not really. I think she must have fallen a little behind on her letter writing. Annie said she hasn't gotten anything, either. But we did talk to her briefly this past weekend. Just working at the café and the orphanage and having crazy adventures with that Afentra friend of hers. We try to talk to her every weekend on the phone. Come to think of it, she seemed distracted. But I think she's doing all right. Did she seem distracted to you, honey?"

Adam shrugged his shoulders, the only part of his torso that remained out of the water. "I guess. It might have been late, or something. I can hardly keep track of the time difference. But we didn't talk long, no."

"Well, Mikhail. We're not much help. Next time we chat we'll ask her if she got your letter."

"You don't have to do that." Mikhail swayed on his feet and wrung his hands together.

"It's no problem. We'll tell her you dropped by. Sure you don't want to go for a swim?"

Mikhail slouched around the corner of the house in sun-dappled shadows that moved with the breeze on the lilac bushes and oak trees. He stared at the ground, chiding himself for happening by Gaby's house, catching the LeFevres in their pool and muttering about who-knows-what. Now that he was out of their line of sight he did a little punch in the air and grimaced at himself. He murmured, "Stupid!"

It was weird to be here anyhow, like visiting the house you grew up in after you moved away to another town. He'd swam in that pool hundreds of times. He walked through those lilac bushes as they grew from waist-high to towering foliage that scented the whole neighborhood for a short time in the spring. Lilac was so overwhelming to him, but it was Gaby's favorite. She told him this dozens of times as she walked him through it to the gate. She never stopped at the gate; she stayed with him out to his car, even if she were just in her bathing suit. Gaby in her bathing suit; *let's not think about that right now.* Too late.

His new, old car was already stifling in the Indian summer heat, heady with deteriorating plastic and ghosts of second-hand smoke and Lord knows what else. He was surprised the pool was open this late in the year, but it really was perfect weather, today. He cranked the driver's window down and turned the key. A flood of heavy music blasted out of the old, car speakers. These days he actually drove his own car. Gaby used to be the one with the car. She liked to drive, anyhow.

As he turned at 35 mph into a curve on a wooded road, he realized he had been lost in thought since Gaby's house and didn't remember driving, at all, since then. That always swooped his stomach out from under him and made him a bit unsure of himself. But this curve... it sent him into more deep thought. This was the curve—right here under the filtered sunlight and the reddening leaves—where Mikhail picked up his first ever roadkill and took it into the woods to bury. Those woods secreted dozens of roadkill graves, and was the beginning—on that day when some house on the lake had a fatal gas explosion—of a strange and incremental relationship with John and Mercedes. For years (or maybe that's just the way it seemed?) Mikhail buried an animal and then walked through the dappled foliage to John's house and to Mercedes' cinnamon doughnuts and spiced cider and stories. Mikhail imagined there wasn't a story Mercedes didn't know.

Sometimes John told stories instead. Mercedes said he was the real storyteller, that she learned everything from him. Mikhail loved to hear both of them; their voices rising and falling in a lulling rhythm, inflecting like an understated actor, making him fall into a trance where he felt alternately sad or mad or happy or appalled or scared or surprised or even in love.

"You know, that's how dreams are," John said one afternoon, as a much smaller Mikhail sat in a heavily cushioned chair, swinging his legs and holding a plate of oatmeal-raisin cookies in his lap.

"Dreams?" asked Mikhail.

"Yes, yes, child." Mercedes swept the cabin floor, even the oversized, braided rug. Mikhail's gaze went from John to Mercedes. "He means when you have a dream that is so real that when you wake up you stay in the entanglements all day. You *feel* like you are still a part of the dream, even when you realize it was not real."

"I once had this dream," said John, "that I was dating Farrah Fawcett. It took me days to shake that one. I felt like a right jerk, seeing as I was married to Mercedes already, and all."

Mercedes propped the broom against a wooden support beam and settled into another squashy chair. Her eyes focused somewhere outside the windows, as if she hardly heard what John said. "Once, I had a dream which seemed to last for weeks.

"First, I was chosen from among all my high school classmates to join an archeological trip to somewhere deep in the South American rain forest. Then we flew and arrived in a town with rocky cliffs that jutted out of the cool forest, huts built right into shallow caves. I made friends, entrenched old enemies, and had my suspicions about others.

"The whole place was saturated in an eerie feeling, and I remember seeing things here and there that were like clues to a puzzle. Odd things started happening. At one point, I was in a cave-converted-room with a shifty European man with very round, wire spectacles and when the sun filtered into the room in a narrow beam, it hit him in the eyes. He screamed, lifted into the air with his arms outstretched and feet dangling. He stayed caught staring and screaming in the amplified beam of light until it disappeared.

"Another odd thing I can barely recall now: I was hiking down a stepped piece of somewhat cleared jungle—our excavation, right behind the building I was staying in—and when the sun hit the valley below me, it changed, and it was suddenly full of mud buildings and tribal peoples and the dancing flames of cooking fires. Then the sun shifted, and it, too, was gone.

"I was now very suspicious and scared, so I felt glad when our last night at the dig arrived. However, that night was a full moon, and as a bright moon rose over the dark horizon, I was sitting at the back of our building and once again the valley filled up with ghostly buildings and people. The moon was in a cloudless sky, and the ghost village was not going away, nor were the people. Drums rose from the ghost village, echoing in my head, and I ran. The drums beat, repetitively the same rhythm, all night, bouncing off the valley walls and off the rocks jutting out of the jungle and over the tops of the forest.

"I was captured, with the other Americans and other dig employees, and we were dragged, kicking and screaming, down into the valley and to a large bonfire in a town square of sorts. Turns out, we were about to be sacrificed by ghosts to their ghost god for our crimes against their holy land, as an astrological appeasement.

"It was then that I woke. But I lay awake, terrified, all night. And for weeks, I had this creepy, suspicious feeling, and even my feelings toward the people in my dream were changed and I couldn't help it. There was one girl whom in the dream I had come to understand better and know her past, and in my life I found it hard not to think that all she told me was true, and that we had become great friends."

Mercedes refocused her eyes with a stern look at John. "I also once had a dream where I was married to a charming Chinese Canadian and he had a small son and it took me days of lethargy to mourn the loss I sustained upon waking from the endless snow and the little boy and my new husband."

CHAPTER 21
HE TRIED NOT TRYING
ℰꙨ   Ꙙℛ

There was no response. At first, Mikhail was anxious. And then angry. And then he found he would have to blame himself or no one at all: he had sent Gaby a piece of paper in an otherwise unexciting letter and expected that there would be no glitches. Had the letter gotten there? Had it gotten there intact? Had she taken the paper for a joke? Or had she rejected him? And not even called? And then he was angry again. Why was love so many things?

He played with all the other fortune cookie papers that he left in a loose wad on his desk. He paced the floor of his room evening after evening. Then he threw the papers away. Then he fished them out of the trash. Then he threw them in an outside bin. Then he decided that he needed to get out.

Then came the problem of where to go or who to call. He was temporarily working as an assistant editor for a Detroit publishing house, while waiting for the right time to continue his education and become something else more prolific and profitable. He became friendly with some other newbies on and around his cubicle neighborhood. They sometimes went out for lunch or ate all together at a table in the office cafeteria. On

Fridays, sometimes, they went from work to a bar for drinks. There had been talk of an evening of bowling or a concert. But socially speaking, Mikhail was more the twig in the river type, and the thought of organizing was not going to cross his mind. If it did, it would make him feel tired before he even began.

Gaby always came up with the brilliant ideas. Or Melodie. Or even Annie. Melodie. Maybe Mel would want to hang out. Maybe she would have a brilliant idea. What was she doing now? Would she be around on a Saturday afternoon? Where would he even have her number? It had been a long time since he had called her, and his previous phone—with all its speed-dials programmed in—went in the trash last month. Mikhail went sifting through the debris on his desk, a little aimlessly. Like where would he have Mel's number scrolled on a random piece of paper?

After Melodie had squealed away in the airport parking garage, she didn't bother to call Mikhail. She told herself it was a long time in coming, that she should have stopped calling him long before. She tried to remember a time *he* had ever called *her*. Then she shook off that depressing thought and fantasized about him appearing through the fog outside her window with a handful of pebbles and a song. She fantasized about him leaving notes that would lead her on a hunt of clues to a flowery field and a tethered hot air balloon, him grinning at her from inside. She imagined Mikhail and Gaby saying goodbye at the airport, embracing each other at last... And then she shuddered and decided again to *never* call him again.

Mikhail picked up the receiver of the cordless phone and stared at it. Hit the talk button to turn it on. Listened to the dial tone, remotely, until that fast-busy signal sounded. This startled him a little and he hit the talk button again. Off. He thought of getting the phone book from the shelf below the hall table, but then thought of calling someone who knew Melodie. He had a sudden rush of panic and loneliness. He dialed Gaby's house and got Adam on the line. Adam hummed absentmindedly while he rifled through the junk drawer in the kitchen for the address book. Flipped pages. Recited the number, three numbers followed by three numbers followed by four. Ringing.

"Hello?"

He almost hung up. He didn't know why the receiver was trembling in his hand.

"Hello?"

"Who is this?"

"Umm…"

"Mikhail?"

"How could you tell it was me when I 'ummed,' but not when I said 'Hello?'"

A dry laugh, but sort of warm underneath. "I guess I just needed a few seconds?" Then a pause. "You still there?"

"Yeah. Um… Sorry. I called you? Yeah. I'm just… I mean, do you want to go do something?"

Melodie sunk into the counter by the phone, with her hip. She inclined her head, twirled the phone cord around a finger and grinned. "What do you mean? Are you finally significantly bored enough to call me and ask me out?"

"I'm just—I mean— I was hoping we could hang out."

"Sure, Mikhail. Whatever." Neither one of them were sure what that meant. "Okay then, what?"

"I don't know. I mean, how about I pick you up and we brainstorm." *Brainstorm?!*

"Brainstorm? Okay. Fine. I can be ready in a half hour."

"Sure. Okay. Yeah. See you."

With her eyebrows raised in a tired expression, "Bye."

CŽ   ΒᎠ

They drove away from Melodie's house and Mikhail noticed that she smelled like soapy flowers or France and her nails were long and neat. Gaby's were always cut down so far that there were no whites. Too much upkeep, she said. And not very sanitary. Melodie's nails looked very sanitary and like little pearls.

They decided on a Saturday matinee of *The Triplets of Belleville* and were the only ones in the stadium seating, put their feet on the backs of the seats in front of them and ate contraband Nerds from Melodie's purse. They threw a few at the screen while looking over their shoulders at the light streaming from the mysterious, square window. They giggled.

Afterward, blinking into the sun, they drove a few towns over to visit the nearest Whole Foods, where Mikhail needed to pick up some vegan provisions. After shopping and trying on the funky scarves and jewelry at the Help Desk kiosk, they sat in the car and ate Paul Newman's chocolates (Melodie) and tofurkey jerky (Mikhail), watched the dying leaves skitter across the windshield. They shared a Jamaican Lemonade.

For a while, they people-watched in silence, chewing. A girl came out carrying a few items: a bag of apples, a bag of rice cakes, a box of rice milk. Then she paused just outside the door, rummaged in her purse with half a free hand, stuck a cigarette in her mouth and lit it. She took a drag and then continued on down the sidewalk, dropping her lighter in her purse with the rice milk. A mid-twenties boy came out of the store with a one pound box of mixed spring greens tucked under his right arm casually like a Trapper Keeper. From his other arm and in one fluid movement he threw down a skateboard, jumped onto it with both feet, and slid away with the tell-tale, diminishing click-clack, click-clack, click-clack. An unkempt man went from the exit door to the car parked next to Mikhail's, but the farthest side, the passenger side. He reached in the window and through the disaster that was years of junk piled on all the seats and the dashboard, he rummaged through a Whole Foods bag for a while, pulled out an organic chocolate hand-pie. He turned from the car and then turned back to the bag, reached in and fished out two more pies. He walked away a few paces, turned around and came back, put two of the pies back. He did this a few more times, ending up with two chocolate pies, one in each hand. As he finally rounded the front of the car, an elderly man shuffled stooped toward him and reached out to take the pies. He was very grateful, and said so, and smiled. Then he put the pies in a plastic bag and shuffled away and down the sidewalk, saying familiar hellos to everyone he passed. They all had warm greetings in return and things to say, like "How has the cat been?"

Mikhail told Melodie about sitting in front of a Butter gas station when they were high schoolers, and Gaby and he started talking about how one would know if someone else's blue might be your brown, but how could you know if you couldn't actually perceive through someone else's brain. Just that day, Mikhail's history teacher had off-handedly mentioned the Subjective versus Dispositional Theories of Color, which stated that colors are either subjective or perceiver-dependent. Gaby had been eating Doritos, that night, and a Coke, and Mikhail thought she must be some sort of philosophical genius.

Mel stiffened at this, then shifted in her seat and set the lemonade aside like it was bottled sulfuric acid. Suddenly, she said, "I'm holding on for a hero."

"Isn't that a song?"

"And a truism."

"I don't think that's the word you're looking for." Mikhail picked up the lemonade and took a swig.

"You love her, still?"

Mikhail choked on the lemonade that was just being swallowed. "Sorry. I think I just spit on the mouth of the lemonade."

"Have it." He offered it to her anyway and she pushed it away with a gesture. "Eeew... I'm serious, Mikhail. I don't know if this was supposed to be a date, but it's a little hard to assume that you don't still love her. And since she used to be my best friend, and since I have been a part of your history for so long..." She trailed off. "Look, don't just think you can randomly call up old girlfriends and then take them to cool movies and grocery shopping—okay, so a little lame there—and have a great time and expect them to just be your *friend*, like Gaby. I'm not saying this to be a douche because really, underneath it all, I still love her, but she's sort of a freak. I mean, you are a *catch*, Mikhail, and don't go turning all rosy on me there because you do have your faults and I think one of them is that you still love Gaby and you won't just find closure there. Do you know what I mean?"

What? Instead, "Closure?"

"Yes, *closure*. It's a little overused and somewhat psychobabble, but all I mean is that you need to find out if you stand a chance or not and then either swoop in and claim the princess, or move on with your life. Or do you already know? I don't think that you do."

"I don't. I don't know. I don't know how I can talk about this with you."

"Sure. We have our history. I think it IS history. You ever discussed this with *anyone*?"

"Just my mom."

"Wow. And you love her?"

He winced and squirmed. "Ergh. Do I really have to...?"

"You could just nod or something." He nodded slowly, looking out over the steering wheel. "Then this wasn't a date?" He paused, then shook his head no.

"Just so you don't feel too guilty, I figured it wasn't. I know you pretty well, Mikhail, and I've always known that to deal with you meant to deal with the spider web of your relationship with Gaby. You two are so knotted up together it would be nearly impossible to extricate either one in one piece. The thing is, one of you is way too timid to confront the other, and one of you is way too idealistic to see the other. I guess you deserve each other."

"I guess we do."

"I'm sorry. I didn't really mean it like that. You just have to change. Or move on."

"Wait. Wait a second. A second ago you just said that Gaby was too idealistic to see me. You mean she would inevitably fall in love with me if she had more, more... more clarity? Or did you really mean that she already... well," he couldn't really say what felt too powerful, "likes me but doesn't know her own self?"

Melodie sighed and shrunk back into her seat. "To be honest, Mikhail, I don't know and never did. Furthermore, I don't think that anyone can answer that question. Perhaps she doesn't love you at all, after all."

"That is the assumption that I have been working with, yes."

CB   BO

When Gabrielle and Annibel were not yet in grade school, Stellar stayed home with them, keeping house, managing the family affairs, taking them to parks, friends' houses, the mall, library class on Tuesdays (where the librarian read to them the most animated books and sang songs with exaggerated hand gestures), the science museum on Wednesdays. The neighborhood kids were invited over on Fridays to swim in the in-ground pool. One summer, after a family vacation out West, the pre-K twins returned to domestic serenity and a promise that they would go back to the museum to see the newly minted dinosaur trail, which was much anticipated by the tots and opened while they were away.

On the day of the usual visit, the weatherman predicted in the wee hours of the morning to Stellar and through coffee steam, that it would be storming most of the day, but scattered. Stellar informed the girls they would still try the fifteen minute drive, but if it was storming, the Dino Trail would have to wait until another day and they could spend a little time wandering through the kinetic energy and Kappla block displays inside, instead. With this in mind, she did not pack the usual water bottles and lunch boxes, nor did she grab even the usual bag of spare undies and clothes, sunscreen, bug spray, and other various childhood accoutrements. Such was the setup due to the weatherman's prediction.

In lieu of storming, the heavy clouds kept the summer day hot and humid, and when the sun shone, it shone with unmatched ferocity. The Dino Trail was indeed open; what was usually a peaceful meander through the various exhibits that made up the folded two-mile long indoor and outdoor museum was instead a hectic bustle of humans, shoulder-to-shoulder and stroller-wheel to stroller-wheel in a mad stream from the parking lot (or overflow parking lot, if you were so unlucky), through the indoor museum with its admission desk and winding queue, to the Trail, about a mile away.

By the time Stellar had pushed two thirty-pound four-year-olds in a double stroller up around the paved walkway, ooh-ing and aah-ing at the loudly painted, life-size, and sometimes animated dinosaurs, then interacting with the various outdoor activities (like fossil digs and talking headsets) while diplomatically dealing with other rogue toddlers and screaming infants, they were all very hot and tired and thirsty. Stellar promised them drinks at the café, just outside the Dino Trail. They pulled up to the café, left the stroller in the stroller parking, purchased orange juices, water, and a muffin for all to share. Fifteen minutes later, they exited the café and all stopped suddenly back at the stroller parking. There was no stroller. Not one. Just a rectangle of smooth, gray pavement and a few flecks of water from the rain that was just beginning to fall. Stellar acted fast, grabbing the girl's by the hands and charging into the café and up to the counter, ignoring the other customers in line.

"Hey," with a mandatory smile. "My stroller has been stolen."

The teenager behind the cash register simply gaped, as if not comprehending. Then he turned and disappeared into the kitchen. Returned. "Are you sure?"

"Yes. I'm sure. There is not one stroller outside this café."

"Okay." And then back in the kitchen. A manager appeared, walked Stellar to a table, and took a description of the stroller. He said that this was highly unusual. "Just wait a moment." He too disappeared into the kitchen, but returned while talking into a walkie talkie and informed Stellar that all employees were on the lookout for the black double stroller with two pink umbrellas and one yellow cloth Better Maid bag folded neatly in the bottom. He headed *back* to the kitchen, Stellar drummed her fingers a bit, stared out at the few drops of rain that had stuck to the hand-print smudged window, then jumped up. Her newly minted plan was to sit by the exit at the front of the museum and watch for the stroller. It was a long shot.

Her long-legged, angry pace was a little much for the girls, who demanded to be carried part of the way. Stellar introduced herself to the museum manager (who breathed that this had never happened before and *didn't* have to say there was indeed no protocol for them to use), sat the girls down on the window sill of the gift shop, and stood cross-armed in front of them, making conversation with a grandmother about the missing stroller. All the while she chatted, she worried that she was tipping off this grandma, who would stealthily tell her thieving daughter the whereabouts of the stroller's owner and the two of them would slip out some side door. She eyed everyone suspiciously. While she chatted, Gabrielle and Annibel kicked their legs back and forth, slumped on the sill, looked stricken by the very thought that someone would just take something of theirs.

Stellar had pity and came up with a new plan. She dragged Gabrielle and Annibel to the minivan, buckled them in the back seat and threw coloring books and crayons at them. Then she persuaded a very passive parking attendant (with the story of the missing stroller) to let her sit right at the entrance to the museum, windshield pointed right at the doors. She waited. She had an hour and a half until the museum closed. It was also a long shot, but if she managed to spot the stroller, the price of replacing it would be more than enough to justify the couple hours' worth of work. So she sat. And with her eyes glued to the doors, her mind went over and over the possibilities of what had happened to the stroller, how unlikely it was to still be around, and exactly what would happen if she saw someone with the same stroller. She imagined herself questioning anyone with the same stroller, but discovering mostly innocent mothers with babies sleeping under the canopy, abashed by the idea that they would steal a stroller, but also so sympathetic. She looked for the pink umbrellas, the flash of yellow in the netting underneath.

After about forty-five minutes, a stroller like hers came barreling out the doors, pushed by a skinny, young mother, flanked by an also-young grandma, and loaded with four or maybe five kids and just tons of stuff: raincoats, baby bottles, sandals, a soft cooler, etc. etc. (At the moment they exited, Stellar discovered neither of the girls were coloring at all, when they both yelled out "Mom! There is our stroller!") The group moved as a cohesive knot, bee-lining it from the doors to the left side of the parking lot. They were moving so fast that Stellar didn't have time to move, but had to use the car instead. She deftly pulled up alongside the woman, gently yet forcibly stopping her in her tracks.

Stellar leaned a little out of the open window. "Ma'am, I hate to ask this, but is that your stroller?"

Startled, "Why, yes."

"Well, someone has stolen my stroller; it is the same kind as yours and I just had to ask." Her eyes were roving the whole time she spoke, and just as the woman was gushing her sympathy about the stolen stroller, Stellar's eyes fell on a thin line of sunshine yellow at the very bottom of the stroller's under-basket. Stellar leapt out of the car, the car door flying open as if by itself. "Ma'am, may I look under your stroller? I just need to check something." She was already crouched and reaching—although still expecting nothing—and barely heard the woman give her unswerving cooperation. She lifted the mass of stuff off of the yellow fabric.

When she saw the Better Maid logo, blood rushed to her head, she began to shake. In fact, it felt like fuzzy electricity hit her from inside, somewhere. She stood up, almost too fast, and looked the woman in the face. Pointing at the stroller, she said crisply, "Ma'am. This. Is. My. Stroller."

After that, things moved in fast forward to the rhythm of the woman's verbal diarrhea. No story really unfolded, as the excuses morphed from one end of the incident to the other. The stroller was quickly vacated, the grandma and the children never said a word, and the manager and two security guards appeared magically in haste. The Better Maid bag was produced, the story morphed and morphed some more, the woman was escorted inside to file a report, or something else. Stellar gave her name and phone number, folded up the stroller and opened up the trunk. She fairly slammed it into the back; it seemed more solid than usual, a little heavier. The hatch went down with a muscular swing. She slid into the driver's seat and pulled away. It felt like flying, like they were lead carried on the wind.

To Gabrielle and Annibel, Stellar was a hero. She was like steel, hard and strong and beautiful.

Stellar remained confused with herself.

Cʒ ɞ

Gaby lingered in Betsy's mind, long after Sonja's funeral. Gaby was so young, so sad. And ultimately, it was Gaby who was so selfless and so loving, when Sonja had been a nuisance to a granddaughter trying to make her own way out in the competitive world. Betsy had looked over many times during the services, at Gaby's wiry frame and smooth skin, the circles under her eyes and the tears caught on her dark lashes, at the thinness of her small hands and the fullness of her thick, curly hair. *Like a bird*, she had thought. *Like a funny, little bird.* And yet she was the one who had stepped into a river no one else had wanted to cross. When she stood, all the wiriness and big hair became a flower which you would think would bend in the wind, all the way to the ground. But no. She was a poppy with a core of iron.

When the image of her iron poppy buried itself under the joys and cares and memories of more and more living, Betsy cleaned out a closet and came upon a large, unmarked, cardboard box. Inside were some of Sonja's things, things Betsy had not wanted to part with but had found no practical use for. She left the box where it lay, and went immediately to the store. At the store she found a beautiful, cedar box with stained wood inlay and took it home. She ceremoniously transferred some of Sonja's things there; things that she thought Sonja would want Betsy to keep, and objects that Betsy had memories which lit up when she encountered them. She placed the new, smaller box on the bureau in her room, stood there in her pajamas and in a pool of lamplight, turning the objects over in her hands. She held a quite-old, velvet jewelry box in her hand, turned it over questioning. Was this? Could it be? And she hadn't noticed?

She popped open the box and found there only a grimy necklace with discoloration on every link of the gold chain. The pendant was a large opal, surrounded with filigree and encrusted stones in intricate patterns, nearly lost in tarnish and dirt. Why had Betsy even held on to this? But when she went to set it aside, the box stuck in her palm with the magnetism of an unanswered question. Still, could it be?

With sudden inspiration, Betsy took the box and yanked the necklace up, which caught on the backing in the box, where it was fastened into neat little metal loops. The backing lifted up and out of the box, revealing a bed of yellowed tissue paper packed tight and there—in the middle—a ring.

Betsy's mind swam. All those years and all that dissension and separation and here was the ring, with Betsy, just as Grandma Sonja had wanted. If only Izolda had lived long enough to see her wearing this! No, she would never wear it. It was too ridiculous, the whole thing. Too crazy.

Betsy lifted the ring out of the tissue paper, felt a heat and a thrum in the tips of her fingers as she held it, a pounding of her pulse outward at it. She dismissed the feeling. It was quite a ring; fashioned from metals of gold, silver, and copper, a dark metal, an almost white metal. And how well all of them had stood up to time. The ring was simply covered with small stones weaving in and out of the metal; what looked like diamonds, topaz, amethyst, rubies, emeralds, peridots, and other colors besides. In the center was a giant, red stone, paler than any ruby Betsy had ever seen. And in the center of the gem, buried deep at its heart—Betsy squinted down at it—was a seed. *The gem must be glass*, she thought. She pushed aside the nagging thought, *No, it's magic*.

Betsy set the ring back in the tissue paper, wedging it tight, put the false face with the pendant back, and snapped the jewelry box closed. She cradled the small box down inside the wooden chest and set everything—her thoughts, her memories—aside for now.

The ring lay hidden in the cedar box for more months, hardly being noticed or thought of, until Betsy was informed that she would be taking a business trip to the Detroit Institute of Art. That night, as she flopped about in the hour before sleep, she saw the box on the bedroom bureau top and remembered the ring and that she thought once or twice about giving it to Gaby. It was a long shot, right? Would she still live there? Did she want it? It didn't matter, yet. She meant it as an expression of gratitude, as well as a guilt that would not abate over the years. She also meant it as a sort of penance to her grandmother. Maybe she didn't realize it, but it was a way of paying for a forgiveness that had already been given freely.

☙ ❧

Sonja's house was generally old-fashioned, even for the 60s, and was usually filled with the smells of groaning buffet tables laden with casseroles and spiral-cut ham, low-burning candles, cigarette smoke, all of which were homey to Betsy. Most people who passed in and out on Sunday afternoons were older, friends of Grandma and Grandpa, and some of Izolda's, too. There were people from the church, sometimes a minister, and once in awhile, another kid.

Betsy didn't always enjoy it when another kid visited. She liked retreating to the sun room—the one with three walls full of tall windows, like the room itself was being thrust out into the yard and sky—with the neat, low shelves stacked with toys and interspersed with flourishing, potted plants and mislaid books and ashtrays. She liked to play with the dolls, especially, in their lacy christening gowns (or that's how they looked, anyways) and their frilled bonnets. She placed them in and out of their wee beds, covering them up, giving them a diaper change, feeding them from bottles where the milky contents magically disappeared when she tipped the bottle up into the baby's pursed lips.

This was a quiet Sunday afternoon, and as far as Betsy knew, there was no one else about except for Grandpa puttering in the basement, since Izolda had run to the store. Sonja perched in a straight-back chair in the sun room, leaning forward over Betsy, her face full of expression. Natural light sifted through sheer, white curtains as she moved paper puppets on popsicles sticks in between them, telling Betsy another of her wonderful, magical stories.

"When The Queen died," began Sonja, turning the paper cutout of The Queen so that she was laying flat on her back. "When The Queen died, she was, of course, wearing the special ruby ring; the ring of love. King Jaden, a bit younger than The Queen and still very much alive, grieved for his lost love, even though he had a sneaking suspicion, every time his gaze fell to The Queen's lovely hand and the imposing ring, that The Queen's love was not as uncomplicated as his own." Now, the paper cutout of Jaden the Great was leaning down over the prone queen.

"He allowed for the ring to be buried with her, so you see, Jaden was a very decent man, and his clear conscience allowed him deep sleep at nights. But there were others whose dreams were haunted by the ring; others, who stood in the general assemblies or sat at the council meetings, or kneeled at the roadside as The Queen's entourage passed, seeing the blazing red glint of light as a ray of sun caught on The Queen's most prized possession. All of them were afraid of The Queen while she lived, for both her kindness and power protected her, and the ring—by what power no one knew—only magnified her grandeur and imposition.

"But as soon as The Queen was encased in her family tomb, a dozen citizens across the kingdom hatched secret plans to pilfer the ring. Before The Queen's children were out of mourning, a dozen meetings took place where heads bent together and hushed voices discussed how best to enter the castle and the tomb. There were ears everywhere in Jaden's kingdom—not his spies, mind you, just scavengers and gossips—and before long a meeting was held in a rented room where what had now become more than thirty conspirators of various positions and genders and social statuses argued about how they might—as one—manage the impossible.

"Now, it is obvious to you and I what was going to happen to some extent, for how could one piece of very valuable booty assuage a few dozen crooks? Most of them knew it, too, which is why each of them, while going along with the plan superficially, had secret plans full of trickery and deceit in which they ended up the sole possessor of the ring. Some of them knew that others must have their own secret plans, and they had *especially* tricky and deceitful plans, hoping to outsmart or out-brute all the others before the Night of Thieves was over.

"The plan was complicated and brilliant and I won't go into it too much here, because, well, we just don't have enough paper puppets. Jobs were given based on special abilities and places in society. Those who had early involvement—like luring a gate guard away from their post—were impatient and ended up walking the moat of the castle, converging very conspicuously at the gate where Lykus the Cupbearer was to emerge with the ring hidden deep within a sack of rice. But Lykus never emerged, the watchers turned on each other and mutiny, suspicion, and violence ended their snooping outside the castle.

"Inside the castle, Lykus never got the ring. Instead, Hilary the Concubine, after leaving an inner door ajar for Berenice the Healer to slip in and poison the tomb guard's wine, crouched behind the door in the dark. When Berenice entered, Hilary struck him with a heavy candelabra, heaved his body out of sight, and continued with the poisoning and then the slipping down into the tomb herself, before the proper time. She found the tomb already open, as had been arranged for Lykus, and slunk out of the tomb in shadow and darkness, hardly breathing and with the ring in her tiny, smooth fist. She wound her way where Lykus was sure not to be waiting, back to her shared rooms.

"She kept hidden in the concubines' quarters, knowing that she was not safe even so, and after a few days she simply disappeared, light as a shadow, over the horizon. (And that is why Hilary is sometimes called "The Shadow.") Somewhere very far away and extremely cold, we are told, Hilary made her fortune with her beauty and the allure of the ring. But Hilary married for money and lived a suspicious and loveless life, and eventually the ring overpowered her and guilt and remorse flooded her heart. Love was too strong a force for Hilary, and she died fighting the ring.

"The ring was passed from generation to generation until a line would run thin or especially poor or greedy, and the ring was sold and then bought, traded and stolen and lost and found. Its history grew murky; its future as well. For we know that the two halves of the seed belong together, that they are seeking one another, but the ring is deeply lost, steeped in legend, a mystery.

"Or, at least, that's how the story goes. But *we* know where the ring is, don't we?"

Betsy's eyes widened as she looked up at Sonja, Sonja's arms slack and her elbows leaning on her thighs where her floral skirt skidded to a halt at her stockinged knees. The paper cutouts on popsicle sticks stuck out at odd angles from her fists, forgotten. "*We* know where the ring is?" Betsy breathed.

"Yes, we most certainly do." Sonja set one half of the paper cut outs on her lap before smoothing out her skirt with the free hand and then displaying the hand in front of Betsy's wide eyes. There, amazingly ornate and giant in proportion to the other rings she wore, was a ring with an enormous, red gemstone nestled in the curling metal and swirling detail and glinting brightly in the sunroom sun. Sonja leaned in to Betsy and whispered loudly, "Now, make sure you don't tell your mom I had it out, or she's likely to throw a fit. You don't want Grandma in trouble, do you?"

Betsy shook her head no, still staring at the ring with saucers for eyes. She reached out, slowly, laid a finger on the ring and left it there. It felt warm, and she could just feel the magic rising up into her.

CHAPTER 22
ANOTHER GO

Mel was the new kid in school. After a few years, her parents had become convinced that the Butter public school system was a fine place for Mel to be educated, and pulled her from Saint Thomas'. What they may not have realized was that this Detroit suburb was not the easiest town in which to be the new kid. She started at the socioeconomically-polarized elementary school in the middle of the year, right after their winter break. It was daunting to enter that cold, glue-smelling classroom at the back of the school and have her mom guide her, reassuring her with a hand at Mel's shoulder blade, and then talk over Mel's head to the teacher while Mel looked at all the curious, quiet faces. Then be left alone with them.

Mel was a bright kid. She noticed right away what happened. Within a couple days of coming to fifth grade at Hawthorn Elementary, she made three friends. One was an inconsequential boy. One was a bookish girl. One was a tall, abrasive, blonde girl who had somehow, miraculously, already sprouted boobs and was wearing an impressive bra that the boys liked to snap when the teacher wasn't looking. The boy, she could keep. But it was unspoken and powerful, a rule of the social games, that Mel would have to choose between the other two; one was popular, one was not, and she was a social chameleon. Her future in junior high and then high school depended on it.

She didn't really like the blonde girl as much as the other, but what could she do? A lifetime of popularity (or at least a fair shot at it) or being ousted now, never to return? Just to hang out with the bookish girl, and to do what she, Mel, felt she wanted to do, which was playing games on the swings like kicking off shoes and jumping to see who could get the farthest, and not skulking at the fence, flirting and talking about bras and nail polish colors?

She was stalling for time and that wouldn't last long. Eventually, maybe today, the outcome of stalling would be the blonde girl—Teresa—refusing to hang with her anymore. She would uneventfully slip into being a target for Teresa's sticky ridicule and simpering cruelty. This would continue seamlessly as they moved on to Hobart Middle School, where Mel would be scorned if she got the coolest new shoes before anyone else had them, pestered if she dared cross the wrong person in class, in the halls, at the lunch tables; even accidents were punishable.

Week two, Mel was near the last in line as the class headed from the classroom, through an adjoined corridor (only thirty feet long; not long to decide), and out into the diffused light of a gray day. She stood still at the doorway, surveying the playground with its puddles and dry spots, its clusters of kids running and yelling and hanging upside down from monkey bars. Mel saw Teresa and a couple other tall kids standing under a lone tree, isolated from the gleeful throngs. Then she saw Gaby, already in a swing, soaring up and back down, her dark curls trailing behind her and circling her face.

"Mel! Come swing!" she yelled.

This would be on her terms. Mel ran over to Gaby, where she settled into a swing, pushed off and pumped furiously into the sky, skimming over the gravelly puddle underneath and yelling for Bobby to mark the ground because she was going to break the record.

CB BO

Mikhail called Mel one more time, tried to apologize, get a friend back.

"You like her."

"Mel. We were having such a great time."

"That's it! I don't want to be a great time. I want to be the lifetime sweetheart. My parents went through hell together. Drugs. Infidelity. Like a billion kids. And they are lifetime sweethearts. I have a distinct feeling I'm just the inevitable rough patch on your way to true love."

Mikhail's loss for words was hardly extraordinary.

"Plus I've decided I miss Gaby. I can't have both her and you."

"That doesn't make any sense."

"It does to me."

Another pause where Mikhail's mind and lips wouldn't meet. This conversation was not going as he wanted it to. Something was shoving his intentions off-track.

"Goodbye, Mikhail. I really hope we can be friends because I'd like to be in the wedding."

He ignored the last bit of what she said. "Yeah, friends! Can't we be friends again?"

"Sorta."

"You're confusing me."

"Yeah, sorry. Goodbye."

This was it, then. He, Mikhail, would take life by the balls and he would look Gaby in her eyeballs and say to her something that could not be mistaken or misconstrued: "I love you. And not like a friend. Gaby. Look at me. I mean I love you like I want to spend the rest of my life with you and always be with you and I want you to have my babies." Well, maybe not just like that. But he was definitely going to tell her face to face what he had been meaning to tell her. And despite his resolve, she remained thousands of miles away, in a foreign country.

Where to come up with the money and the vacation time? Should he tell her he was coming? No. That might lead to unpleasant pre-conversation conversations and why give away the punch line now when he was so close to the end of this dreadfully long joke? These were all after-thoughts, anyhow. He would go and he would do it as soon as possible. Like ripping off a Band-Aid.

Like one especially long Band-Aid which takes approximately a month to extricate.

03 80

Stellar was having a bummer of a day. Or was she? Something about it was just ticking her off. She was at home with Gabrielle and Annibel and they were four years old and being rambunctious. Or were they? Something about their play today was driving Stellar crazy, making her want to smack something or punch something or throw something. Plus her throat was hurting since yesterday, and while it wasn't getting worse, it wasn't getting any better (despite a constant flow of warm apple juice with honey).

Stellar caved to the soreness in her stressed neck muscles and curled up on the papasan in the play room, a blanket pulled up to her ears, and her eyes closed in the warm, afternoon sun. She could hear the girls, hear them "reading" aloud to themselves and flipping the pages of about thirty-two library books. She could see them in her mind's eye, sitting perpendicular to each other, legs straight out in front of them and backs bolt upright. She wondered why it was that she could not sit that way anymore; even with aerobics her hamstrings were too tight or her posture was so poor it had pulled her deltoids tight or something.

Gaby seemed to be having a lousy day, as well. She also was complaining of a sore throat and of an upset stomach. She was told to rest, have some warm apple juice, and had a hot water bottle that she was nursing on her tummy. Stellar could hear the pad of little feet toward her just as her mind began to blur; it snapped back to attention.

"Mommy, can I go in the office?"

"No, Gabrielle. There are papers every..."

Her body simply melted into a pile on the floor, limbs splayed out and then convulsing in turn. "But Mmmooooooooooommmm!" And then the whining, which was immediately unbearable. "I *have* to go in the offfffffiiiiiiice!" Etc.

"Gaby. Gaby. Gaby!" with the whining simmering on and on. "I know that you want to make me a card, but..."

"But that's a SURPRISE! I just *need* to go in the office!" Etc.

"Well, Gab, I know how *thoughtful* you are and that you *always* make me cards with the least bit of provocation, I mean, every time I am sick. But. Right. Now. The. Office. Is. Just. Too Crazy. So. You. Can't. Just. This. Time. Now Sweetie, please let Mommy rest," and she sunk her head back into the cushion, the room almost quiet, and drifted...

It had been what, fifteen minutes? Gaby was suddenly back before Stellar and she realized she had lost track of reality, maybe even fallen asleep, for a little bit. She focused her eyes, blinking them repeatedly, and there was Gabrielle, *right* in front of her, smiling as broad as was possible, her eyes shining and staring into her face. She extended out to Stellar a bright orange plastic bowl and a blue plastic spoon. Stellar didn't have to look to know.

"Gabrielle! Applesauce! That is just so kind of you. Sweetheart!"

As Stellar propped herself up on an elbow and awkwardly took the applesauce, she felt a pang of guilt; not just for not letting Gabrielle go in the office and contribute to the mess while making a card, but for a lifetime of not doing the right thing, for sometimes considering motherhood an inconvenience. She forced herself to eat every last bite of the sauce, the tang and coldness surprisingly wonderful. Mothering, and mothering well, was the stuff of life. She struggled to wrap her mind around the act of staying at home and could never articulate exactly what it was and what it meant. There was no job more satisfying and no job that demanded as much endurance and sustained commitment. But there it was, if you just let yourself focus in on it every once in awhile; from their time in the womb, each girl was every day the reward for all the years of labor.

ᘓ   ᘔ

The sun shone. The dust rose. The sherut swayed until Gaby jabbed into the passenger sitting next to her. The passenger didn't even acknowledge the intrusion, such was the way they were all intruding on each other's personal space all the time in Jerusalem, in a metropolis this teeming with the wealthy and the impoverished. Hell, Gaby might right now be being silently robbed by the stout woman beside her with the serious stare (into the back of the seat in front of them), the scarf wound around her head, the armload of typical Jerusalem wares: fabrics and bread, a Turkish tea pot, shoes. She seemed to be past a graceless middle age, tight-skinned from the sun, cracked from some sort of labor. Making pita? Washing clothes? Shouldering an automatic rifle? One could never tell.

And then they were pulling up to the corner where Gaby got out of the sherut, day after day, wondering when the heat would abate and marveling at the comfort of the dessert, of the Arabic lilt wafting, of the fragrance of cumin and parsley and yeast mixed with the smell of urbanization. She still panicked a little when the stop was coming, wondering what would happen if she were abandoned in the territories in an area she did not know: alone with not even a language. So she jumped up when the sherut was still slowing and made her way over the woman (who did not budge from her posture) and out the door. Then she waited for the sherut to clear and negotiated across the bustle of the intersection: boys kicking around a soccer ball, the call of vendors, the constant noise of cars laying on horns and cars struggling to survive, held together with will and duct tape, hung with ornamentation that Westerners might find gaudy but which had a beauty anyhow. Angels. The hand of the prophet's wife. The all-seeing eye. Flowers; some foreign to her, some familiar but nonetheless with an exotic beauty, here in the sand. Cross and crucifix. Air fresheners. Beads. One over another in an assertion of clutter, bright and swaying, glinting and sagging and gathering dust.

As she carefully picked her way across the street, she could feel the usual eyes on her but could never determine if they were meant to be merely curious or hostile. How could she just assume that they were hostile? Because they felt hostile, or because she was just a little bit scared to be vulnerable? She held herself erect and stepped lightly, looking like she did this every day. She did do this every day. And she was starting to pick up bits and pieces of the language. *Anna. Leh. Na'am. Assalam alaykum. Asif. La-assam.*

She made her way down the street, not looking men in the eyes, but catching the back side of one of them as he urinated into a cubicle in the stone façade of yet another tan stone building. She stepped even lighter. She made her way a couple of blocks uphill (everything here seemed uphill, or upstairs; just *up* until your calves burned by day and cramped at night). She turned left into an alleyway and through an open metal gate, painted a lively green several years before, and down a still, relatively cool, quiet road abutted by tall, tan, stone buildings, windowless, on either side. Near the dead end of this short alley, she turned into a capacious doorway, and squeezed through the cracked opening of the metal gateway and an open corridor which felt like just another alleyway, but with a more solid roof. It would be hard for her later to define exactly where in this cool maze the netherspace ended and the orphanage began.

The orphanage was like every other building, with foundations and structures thousands of years old. Stone floors and stone walls with new things where new things were warranted. She often wondered how they managed to create modern lavatories and small bedrooms from all this colossal stone. Just wood and plaster? The diversion of pipes and ducts? Cleverness? But overall, airy spaces and open windows and doors, as if people in other countries did not feel the need to carve the distinction between outdoors and indoors so deeply. There were rooms that were long and held lots of neatly-kept beds, as if this were the scene of a pleasant movie about orphan babies. The babies were sometimes in them, although nappers would face afternoon brightness, sifting white through the fluttering curtains, fine as thin linen. Or were they lace? The effect would have been about the same.

Wood cribs stretched in neat rows and Gaby wound her way among them, looking for something; for little eyes looking up, for the stir of a body, sweaty from naptime, or for arms outstretched, imploring her to meet a need that she could do in the simplest of ways and for the shortest passage of time. She reached down into the crib, took the baby under the arms, and lifted. So light. And so like a monkey, wrapping itself around her by instinct, fitting into her bony curves as if this were comfortable. Sliding arms around her, like a comfortable lover.

In fine weather she would take the infant or child out into the courtyard where likely many other children were playing. (When was it not fine weather in an Israeli winter? If it hit a low of the 70s Gaby spotted snow suits.) She cooed to the baby, hummed, asked questions in a language that sounded even more like babble to them than whatever they heard daily from the French nuns. Against the walls were rose bushes, in a rainbow of manicured beauty: reds and oranges, pinks and yellows, white. Their perfume was heady and wonderful, combining sweetness and spiciness, depth and musk into one complex aroma that became part of the courtyard and part of whatever happened there. It was a green, grassy square full of luxurious, thick turf, surrounded on three sides by high, stone walls. The fourth side simply was nothingness, where the ground fell away into a complex maze of gardens and stairs and terraced walls which met the street down below with buffeted wall and gate. What you saw from the courtyard was the "little town of Bethlehem," white and gold, solid and loud, a chorus of lives and urbanity. And mostly, sky, blueness except for where the sun-drenched statue of whom she supposed was The Angel, with his arms outstretched over the yard and, presumably, the orphans. The Angel's wings faced out over the drop-off to the city, suspended in stone amidst a backdrop of endless blue and openness. His back to the city.

Gaby would do whatever came to mind, which seemed appropriate and loving. She would set down a toddler, sit down in the grass, and be swarmed by children. She would sing to them, make exaggerated motions to songs which usually had no motions—"Koombiyah," "Hey Jude," "Where the Streets Have No Name," "Elderly Woman Behind a Counter in a Small Town," "Jesus Loves the Little Children"—and they gathered around, leaning into one another, and watching her. Just watching. They stole her things and shrieked away to be chased. They ran their grubby hands through her hair until it hurt. They fought over their turn on the tire swing and indicated over and over and over that they wanted to go again, they wanted to go higher, they wanted her to stay.

Sometimes there was a sick child. Sometimes there was a distressed baby. She held these babies, slipped away with them into a corridor with a white statue of a woman holding a baby. (Was it a *pieta*?) She let them bury their snotty faces in her shirt and set her face against them where they could feel her breathing, feel her low humming as a vibration. There were real names that she learned during play: Amir and Lourd and Natalie and Deyanna, but she had made names for the neediest and the smallest of babies: Dribbles, and Bubbles, and Fever. Tears. Nothing clever; they were like Care Bear names that just tripped out of her mouth as she talked and talked to them, needing a handle for the things that she said over them; the prayers that she imagined for them to accompany them through the rest of a life without her.

There were also times when one of the children would suddenly be taken from her by a nun that smelled of the offices, like a receptionist. They were going to spend time— often a holiday which Gaby had never heard of—with their family. Maybe an hour with neatly-dressed half-siblings in the courtyard. Or maybe even a weekend or week when a religious step-father might feel temporarily obligated to his orphaned step-child. It broke her heart to watch those little children go. She would come and go, and mom would come and go, and even nuns would come and go.

There were times when Gaby left and she felt calm and victorious. She sighed wistfully to herself as she drank Bethlehem in on the way out of town, at peace with herself and full in her chest, as if loving someone else and giving without reward had filled her there. Sometimes she left disturbed and brooding, reaching out for the nighttime when she sat in the glow of a city night in a courtyard café, oblivious to the mutterings, and smoke, the sound of mugs on saucers, while she craned her neck into book after book and devoured line after line of philosophy and poetry and story. Maybe she thought these things would salve the ache she housed, when children were obnoxious and even giving returned with thanklessness and loneliness. Loss. And above all, confusion.

For isn't that what Gaby wanted most of all? *Clear answers.* Clear answers. For an equation, a philosophy, that stated if A, then B. If you do A, Gaby, if you are a good girl, then B. You will be happy. You will be loved. You will have found redemption. But really, that wasn't all, because despite her searching for the truth and for the right thing, the right way to do things, she also felt to the tips of her little, dusty toes that she just wanted to give and give and give. She wanted, then, a philanthropic statement of the world that was not only straightforward but actually true.

If only she had known that she was expecting too much of humanitarian achievements and all the libraries of books in the world.

And then Lourd shot by her, like a flash of color and giggles and smell, and a projectile came out of the cloud that was Lourd. The rock hit Gaby in the forehead as she sat on the grass, braiding Deyanna's hair. It shocked her in a wave down her limbs and briefly short-circuited her brain. She felt the pain and her hand moved up to her head. *Ow!* She was mad, but this registered only slightly on her face since she was not mad enough to forget that this was not a place to be mad. It had not been a great day at the orphanage, rather one where she felt the kids were disobedient and ganging up together in their common language against her, and had sorely abused her both body and spirit. She had found refuge in the quiet Deyanna heaped in her lap, in the shade, and then this! She really just wanted to curl up and cry, to set Deyanna on the ground and walk out of the orphanage and all the way back to her bed. No more clamoring. No more spitting. No more teasing and yelling and running and climbing up her.

Lourd saw her face scrunched, saw her hand to her head. She was nearly across the green by then and twirling in lopsided circles. She stopped. Her own brow showed curiosity, then registered concern. She ran across the green, flung herself between Deyanna and Gaby and enveloped Gaby's head in a full-body embrace. "Oh!" she said. "Ooooooh!"

She pulled Gaby's face back from her own and looked into her eyes. Lourd scrunched up her lips and furrowed her brow at Gaby, held the look of concern for a moment and then broke into a full smile, the smile of the penitent who are self-serving, who want to be adored, before engulfing her head once again and shouting with glee, "Momma! Mama!"

CHAPTER 23
LOVE, LOVE, LOVE
ℰℬ   ℭℛ

There were the statistics that said that Jerusalem was about as safe as Chicago. In Chicago, statistics linked you closer with rape, armed robbery, or murder. In Jerusalem, rapists, armed robbers, and murderers were largely deterred by the Uzi-toting soldiers meandering the city streets. That said, tourists (especially the young Americans who loved to flaunt their sexual liberation even when warned not to because it could prove dangerous) often encountered sexual crimes of the garden variety: stolen kisses, flashing, frottaging, loud taunting of a sexual nature, etc.

Gaby and Afentra wandered the Old City for an afternoon. Gaby needed something from a shopkeeper, Afentra said she would go along if they stopped by Noah's book shop. So through the alleyways they went, among the winding streets filled with Jews or Arabs and cats and bad smells and people yelling out and calling them in. "I will give it to you for ten shekels because you have pretty eyes, beautiful eyes!" "This is hand-made. I sewed this with my hand!" A shopkeeper would lower a price from forty-five shekels to fifteen, but couldn't go down to fourteen.

Bartering became a game, fun even in and of itself. "I know a good price for that, and it's fifteen dollars U.S." "Do I have beautiful eyes?" "No you didn't!"

As they walked a tunnel deep inside the winding alleyways, the tunnel crowded. They clogged almost to a stop, and squeezed along with carts stacked with cheap olive wood merchandise (the kind where you can see the clear glue crystallized along the cracks, yellowing with the years as it sits on your mantle), donkeys led despite stubbornness, men in yarmulke, women in burkas, and the smell of urine and coriander, body odor and roses.

A man worked his way through the crowd via a few BYU students (proudly displaying their BYU T-shirts and clean, shining faces). He was stooped, hobbling along in a cloud of stench and with a crazy look in his eye. Afentra looked over Gaby's shoulder as he neared the BYU students, leaned in, and kissed one of them smack on the lips as the student's innocent, starflower eyes popped open into saucers. He leaned into the next girl, and she managed to turn her head so that he planted one on her cheek.

Gaby saw nothing, and Afentra didn't do the math right: as she was watching the man so intently he suddenly turned and saw her and was to her in no time at all. He leaned toward her face without any hesitation. Afentra froze, her lips slightly parted as she stared right into his face.

A cart hit a deep rut in the tunnel floor, it hitched to the side, some trinkets fell, a large woman bent to pick some of them up, her ample bottom shoved into a few nearby people, a young man included, and the young man, looking out over the crowd at the entrance to the tunnel, pitched forward, threw his arms out, and ran right into Afentra, nearly knocking her over. Afentra steadied herself and looked around. The old man was gone (she could still sense him hovering right in front of her, his smell, the anticipation of his moisture on hers). The BYU girls exclaimed to each other and giggled through rouged cheeks. The cart owner argued with the woman for his wares. And there was this young guy who had knocked the man away, rambling on at Afentra. What was he saying?

Afentra tuned in to him, grasping for straws in his fast and furious, unknown-accented exposition. He waved his arms around, nearly taking people out in the small space, with his clear whiteness and enthusiasm. He was tall, lanky, and pasty. Unkempt brown hair shot out from under his high-fronted, white baseball cap. He beamed at her and looked around at the crowd, gesturing to the cart, in the direction the old man had moved along. "I'm your hero!" He finished, out of breath.

"Yeah, my hero." Afentra was weary.

Gaby was obviously not tracking. "What the heck just happened?" she asked.

"Well..." Afentra began. She didn't think she spoke quietly, until the young man burst in over her.

"That old man was about to lay a big one on Your Majesty here, and I, Jaden the Great, intercepted and saved the fair maiden from certain defilement!"

"Come again?" Gaby asked, one eyebrow now arched at him.

"I, Jaden the Great, have saved The Queen from the kiss of death!" The man threw his arms wide at the last.

Afentra dropped her hand in front of her face and indulged in a giggle. Gaby got sassy. "Hey buddy. First off, you are *no* Jaden the Great. Second, Afentra here is no Queen." Afentra shot Gaby a look when she said her name. "And third, *no* kisses of death. *Capiche?*"

"Oh, humble peasant!" The man was clearly addressing Gaby but now kept his gaze and his wide smile only on Afentra. "You are mistaken! Do not mistake *me*, for I will make you pay for your heresy! For I *am* Jaden the Great, and this amazing flame of beauty before you *is* The Queen!"

Afentra just balked at the two, going back and forth. Gaby continued, "Look, Romeo. Me and your un-red-headed *Queen*

have to be going. We'll see you around like donuts, Crazy."
Gaby pinched Afentra's elbow between her fingers and shoved
her ahead of herself out of the crowd and down a tiny alley,
barely escaping the slighted lover.

☙ ❧

Several of the young people at the hostel formed varied
friendships. They wandered around Jerusalem together, and
over the abutting countryside. They looked for the cool places
to hang, shared their favorite places, and forayed into touristy
spots. A Saturday, they headed down to Hezekiah's Tunnel, at
the south end of the Old City. It was a hot fall day, and they
thought it was the right day to escape into the darkness and the
water that was a little piece of history.

Whoever forgot flashlights purchased candles at the
entrance and they all descended the steep, stone stairs to the
gated tunnel. Right as Gaby and Afentra disappeared into the
tunnel, Afentra looked over her shoulder to catch one last
glimpse of white daylight and the crazy man who claimed he
was Jaden pushing through the line behind her and calling out,
"Queen! Queen! Wait!"

Afentra pushed on Gaby. "Move it, quick," she
whispered. "That weird Jaden guy from the alley the other day
just spotted me. ETA: *now!*" The two surged ahead of their
friends. It was narrow and winding, cool and dark. They all
tripped over stones and splashed through the underground
stream, their noisy talking and laughter echoing before and
behind them. Sometimes they fell silent as the walls pressed in
on them and they all felt the horror movies they had seen
suffocating them. They wound further and further into the
depths, wondering how far they were in the earth and what
would happen in an earthquake.

Afentra and Gaby, in their anti-crazy-guy urgency, shot off ahead of the others early on. They spent much of the time whispering and giggling together, and turning their flashlights off to wander speedily in the pitch black and bump body parts against the stone walls. After awhile, they were so far ahead they could no longer hear their friends or see their lights bouncing up the corridor to them. They enjoyed the covertness, the complicity. And nobody yelling to them that he was Jaden.

They had their flashlights on and were whispering to each other when they came over a rock and into some deeper water. Up over their heads, the top of the tunnel gave way into a small cave. They looked up into it as they wandered under and kept moving and conversing. In an instant, they saw feet and then feet-and-a-face fall down on them from above. Gaby gasped as a strong blow landed on her shoulder and a weight pushed her to the ground in a fumbling confusion of glancing light and darkness. Afentra let out an abbreviated scream.

Jaden-the-Lesser had spotted Afentra as she stood in line for Hezekiah's Tunnel, but when she slipped into the dark and the quiet and the damp cool several people ahead of him, she was whisked away by Gaby and the two disappeared in a tornado of chatter and flashing smiles. He, on the other hand, was detained by commoners who insisted he hand over some shekels and take his place in line. After that, he pushed ahead in the tunnel, but couldn't quite catch up, in more ways than one. He thought of The Queen, in the dark, of maybe glancing off her hand with his or brushing against her... He pushed forward, banged his toes against several rocks.

Jaden-the-Lesser was now ahead of most everyone else, wondering how those two girls could go so fast through this crazy tunnel, when he heard a scream. He was sure it was The Queen, and she didn't sound like she was having fun. She sounded scared? Or hurt? His heart rate quickened, he felt blood rush to his limbs and his mind electrified. He jolted into a sort of hopping run, splashed through the stream and over rocks. He smacked his head into an invisible rock, but he didn't feel pain. He kept moving.

He came up over a rock and splashed down into some deeper water and he was on top of a ball of movement, limbs flailing and muffled grunts. He could not tell how many people were involved, but he quickly figured that The Queen was among them and that she was being attacked. Then he saw her friend struggling valiantly, and could see pieces of what must be a man: a solid leg, a little muddy; a care-worn hand with hair on the back. How these were the things he saw in the brief flashes of light in the dark, he could hardly tell, but his mind kicked into automatic. Before he thought, he was attacking the faceless man.

Amidst all the struggle and confusion and in such a small place, the story never was completely sorted out, even between Gaby and Afentra, try as they might, much later. Jaden-the-Lesser threw fists at the man, grabbed him, wrestled with him. Jaden-the-Lesser had never thrown a punch before the incident (at least not one that really happened), but his loose fist met with flesh and bone and he was amazed by how much it hurt his hand and how the solid body gave way under the force. Jaden-the-Lesser grabbed the man around the thickest part of him, some of his limbs also caught in the embrace, and fell with him to the ground. There was more rolling, more knocking about on the stones and against the close walls. He had a feeling that he just wanted to keep the man on the ground, to still him, so Jaden-the-Lesser continued to scramble and hit and to subdue him with gravity and weight and with the element of surprise in the dark. The man eventually flailed himself loose of Jaden-the-Lesser's hold and scrambled up the tunnel in haste, crawling away and then finding his feet in the dark.

There were several seconds of quiet in the tunnel, then the scampering was long gone and all that remained in the world was the sound of heavy breathing, gasping, and the trickle of water. No movement for one moment. Then, a shaft of light came bouncing from the opposite way up the tunnel and they heard voices breaking in. All three of them shuffled in the dark and a flashlight went on, inspecting started, simple questions.

"Queen?" Jaden-the-Lesser swept with his hands through the beam of light. "Queen?"

"I'm fine. I'm fine." She reached out and grabbed his hand very lightly, mid-sweep. They found each other's faces as Gaby pointed the light. "Thanks, Crazy," she breathed, as the rest of their group came up over the rock and upon them. "Hey guys! Move it!" smiling. And then as they shone light in their faces, "Hey! Whuh? Gaby! What happened to you? Afentra!"

Afentra was badly bruised and swollen on the side of her face where she had been thrown down and into the wall. The mysterious Jaden-the-Lesser had a cut on his cheek from the scuffling. And out in the light of day, there were other things: bloodied knuckles, a gashed knee, Gaby's skirt nearly ripped off and someone offered a jacket to wrap around her waist. In the end, it turned out that Afentra fared the worst, since the man managed more of his intended grabbing and prodding, with her. Jaden-the-Lesser's wounds were physical, and the incident had given him a rush of adrenaline and testosterone which was beguiling. Afentra's wounds were emotional and spiritual in nature, and it would take longer for the burning sensation where the man's hands had touched to subside.

Gaby and Afentra were back up on the Moshe House roof, feet dangling over the people below, who sat around circular, wrought iron tables with coffees, dinner, books open with corners fluttering in the hot breeze. Gaby and Afentra talked the incident to death. They joked and looked uncomfortable about Jaden-the-Lesser.

"Maybe we shouldn't call him 'Crazy.'" Afentra's conscience was getting the better of her.

"It's not like he's given us another option. I mean, what *is* his name?"

"Jaden the Great?" Afentra winked over at Gaby, but Gaby was looking down to the people below.

"Har har. He *is* crazy."

"Well that's not too very PC of you. What if your next save-the-world cause is mentally handicapped people? What sort of penance will you have to do then?"

"Har har, again. You know, you really should go into comedy." Gaby held a paper from her gum out over the people's heads, watched it flutter, held in between her finger and thumb, and then brought it back in, stuck it in her pocket. "You know *anything* about the real Jaden the Great?"

Afentra shrugged. "A bit, I guess. Here and there I hear things."

"There is a storyteller in Butter. His name is John. He and his wife are sort of friends with Mikhail. Anyhow, they tell lots of stories about The Queen and Jaden and other Northwyth stuff, not to mention just all sorts of stories about everything. Mikhail retold their stories and I always liked the stories about Jaden the best."

"Well that's because he's sort of down-to-earth, isn't it? He's not all steeped in magic; just doing his thing and being good at it."

Gaby hesitated and seemed shut off. "I guess so. I never really thought about it."

"All right then, tell me one."

"Tell you a Jaden story?" Gaby looked sideways at Afentra and found she was nodding. "Okay. Let's see. You know I'm really not going to do this justice?" Afentra nodded again.

"Okay; vote of confidence from Afentra. Lemme think.

"So once upon a time there was a soldier in The Queen's army. Of course, he wasn't just any soldier because first, he had once been a poor, lonely, street-roving orphan who had superpowers of strength and amazing reflexes and sonic speed and would one day become so famous it would make you puke, and second, because he was the head of all the guard. As head of the guard, he stood right beside The Queen during all the important ceremonies and things and even sat next to her at the council table and helped to make decisions about the kingdom and sometimes the wider world. This soldier, of course, was named Jaden. No one seems to know his last name.

"So, um… one day The Queen appeared before a courtyard full of people, and high up on the dais she waved her alabaster hand, her waist-length red hair lifting in the breeze and reflecting coppery in the sun, her face impassible, and maybe a little tired for her age, but still legendarily beautiful. Beside her, of course, stood Jaden, alert and still as a hunter on a trail."

"Not good at story-telling then?"

"Bits and phrases are coming back to me. So shut up. All right, so Jaden is alert and still as a hunter on a trail and The Queen is standing there all strong and pretty when she sees, out standing statuesque in the churning throng, an imposing man in a pale cloak, the hood falling down over his forehead and almost over his eyes, shadowing his rugged face. The Queen gave a start, almost imperceptibly, but then she turns to look because Jaden—swifter than a hare—had already drawn his bow, laced it with his arrow, and was standing at the ready with it aimed at the crowd. The Queen's eyebrows raise, and she says, 'Please, Jaden. It is nothing,' and the light tears in her eyes have betrayed her.

"But before The Queen even knows what is happening, the arrow zings from the bow and The Queen turns horrified to the crowd, her heart very nearly on her sleeve where she sees The Angel first, but he is still standing immovable, impassable, and then to a disturbance much closer to the dais, where a man with a throwing hatchet at the ready is falling forward, in slow motion it seems, into the crowd, an arrow piercing his heart.

"'Jaden!' she breathed. All right, enough about The Queen. Anyhow, Jaden—keen as a fox—has watched The Queen all this time and he secretly seeks out The Angel, takes him for questioning, and then arranges to have him appointed to a position close to The Queen. As an advisor, he is allowed certain liberties like walks through the gardens with The Queen, and deliberating. But being that close and yet so far away, after a year The Angel can stand it no longer and leaves The Queen's service. But The Queen never forgot Jaden's keen perception and his sensitivity, nor that he saved her life.

"I always liked the bit where The Queen turns and Jaden already has his bow pulled. It seems like such a vivid mind-picture to me; her blue eyes enlarging, her red eyebrows arched, her hair trailing behind and her brow adorned with a crown that is glinting in the sun. The throng of blurred colors below, and a whisper of a noise as Jaden moves so fast and sure, you could never catch him at it. But there he is, standing with his five-o'-clock-shadowed, sandpapery face pressed to the hand holding the arrow back, one eye closed and crinkled at the temple with the other focused intensely on first the man whom The Queen noticed and then the assassin. I can practically smell the two of them there, like I'm standing right between them, feeling their breath on my cheek."

"Really, Gaby! I didn't know you had it in you. You have a thing for Jaden?"

"Oh, shoosh. You'd make anything crude."

"Well, I do get your point that Jaden-the-Lesser couldn't possibly be the real Jaden. If he were, by now you would have snogged 'im."

CB BD

"Let's go to Egypt." Andrew knelt beside Gaby's bed in the gloom of the hostel room, not so early in the morning.

Gaby felt crusty again, tried muttering so that perhaps her morning breath wouldn't go far.

"What? Andrew." Her eyebrows knit just a bit and she propped herself up on an elbow. Their trip in the Golan Heights had been a little tense after the rainbow pool conversation, both of them lost in their own thoughts about their relationship and neither one sure how to extricate themselves from the fog on the other side of love. But they had seen more beautiful and interesting things as well, had some stimulating conversation interspersed with silence. Touching almost ceased, but there was an affectionate nudge here and there.

Gaby's eyes adjusted to the very low light and she saw Andrew's face, charming and ardent, both sweet and serious. There was apology in his eyes, and there was apology in the bouquet of flowers that he held in front of him like a bride. She couldn't help soften a little at the flowers.

When her gaze paused on them, Andrew offered them.

"Andrew."

"Gaby," he nearly interrupted her with his seriousness. "I'm so sorry. I know that trip didn't go the way we planned. But I think that it's okay. I didn't mean what I said, and I didn't know how to act after that. I'm ashamed, Gaby. I'm sorry."

"Andrew, can you let me get dressed?"

"Let's go to Egypt. Yeah? We were talking about doing as much as we could while we were abroad. I think we should."

"But Andrew…"

"All right. Get dressed. And then come say 'Yes.' I'll be outside."

Someone called out from a near bunk. "Enough already! There are people trying to sleep in here!"

Andrew slipped out the door and Gaby sat hunched and sleepy and holding the flowers in her lap, a familiar voice said from the dark, "Go with him." Gaby just sniffed and ran a hand over her face. Then she fished around in her duffel bag under her bed and came out with a suitable outfit. She sort of lingered in the yellow bulb of the bathroom, splashing water on her face, brushing her teeth, pulling her hair back, inspected a freckle or two. Then she looked herself in the reflected face. *Egypt? What do I say to that? Do I want to save this relationship?* She knew that she did. She still really liked Andrew and missed their warmth. *What would Egypt do to it? And how crazy is it to just go to Egypt?* She also knew she really wanted to go. She was full of wanderlust, adventure. She wanted to go everywhere, and Egypt called to her. It was right there over the border, full of all sorts of famous and intriguing things, so many really, really old things. The Nile! The Pyramids! King Tut! And beneath it all, she was just dying to go to Egypt *with* Andrew. That just sounded too good to be true. *Was it?*

Once she faced him and his imploring eyes, she was powerless against whatever logic said she should not go. They spent some time scraping finances together and making plans; getting travel visas, coordinating bus and train schedules, procuring guide books and Cairo Museum of Egyptian Antiquities brochures. They left early in the morning from a misty, cool, city street corner sandwiched between the Old and New City. That bus swayed along the desert roads to Beersheba where they caught another bus (a "caravan" of a few buses) that waited a few hours before leaving much later than promised. At Rafah, they were delayed another couple hours as everyone on board went through Israeli and then Egyptian customs. Off across the Sinai in the heat of the day. There was nothing out there except bright tan and intense sun, romance. They slid along on the straight roads with nothing to look at after they had their fill of sameness and romance, and they went from chatting to each other about their knowledge of the Sinai Peninsula and Ancient Egypt, to discussing their childhoods and their adventures in Israel. Then they retrieved books from their packs. Gaby nestled into Andrew's side to read *The Tao of Pooh* while Andrew devoured the *Oxford Book of Prayer*.

"Exciting reading?" Gaby taunted after a long time in the same position, stretched out her arms. But just as she did, the bus slowed considerably and pulled into a parking lot. Gaby and Andrew craned their necks over the seat backs and there they were: the Suez Canal crossing. This was it. They were allowed to exit the bus once it was on the barge, and they moved to the front of the floating parking garage to watch as the land approached across the canal. There were a few other people standing with their toes at the edge, and Gaby yelled to Andrew, "This is it! Africa! I've never been to Africa!"

And Andrew yelled back through their giant smiles, "I know! This is so exciting!"

When the barge touched the shore, they ran off into the dust and more of the same bright tan and land that dissolved into sky.

They stopped briefly at a hotel on the Mediterranean—a hotel which was, as far as they could tell, as "in the middle of nowhere" as they had ever seen—for lunch. Then they continued to Cairo. Being from the Midwest, the topography of Egypt was so foreign to Gaby: there was nothing but sand and sun and sand and sun and then suddenly buildings, foliage, animals, palms, bustling life shot up at a delineation which was almost cartoonish, and continued in denseness right up to the Nile. As they travelled down the country, there were times when civilization swept out into towering buildings and messes of spires, blaring horns, yelling vendors, bleating animals, as far as the smog would let you see. Such was Cairo. Then there were places where you could see from the river all the way until the green stopped abruptly at the desert wilderness and the desert wilderness picked up forever. Life was almost completely gathered in a thin line down the Nile. An emerald ribbon snaking through shimmering tan, mile after long mile.

They entered the Delta basin and found their way to their hotel in Cairo. They were there only a couple days before they caught a sleeper train down the Nile. They giggled like little kids when they entered their compartment. "It's like James Bond," Andrew pulled a knob and a piece of the wall came open to reveal a sink and mirror, a little soap dish and toothbrush holder. Their beds also folded down from their daytime seats and in the dark they looked out the tiny windows at the heads of their beds to the moving of dark palm shadows against the black that separated from dark blue above in a straight horizon, the stars so numerous they made fuzzy masses in the sky. It was magical to slide across the desert this way, in the night, with the clacking of the rails. Gaby slid down off her bunk and snuggled in next to Andrew, where she fell asleep listening to the rhythm of the train and Andrew's breathing, the occasional knock of someone making their way down the train corridor.

Aswan was their southernmost destination, and they spent time wandering the sugarcane fields, the alabaster shops, the hotel gift shop with their ever-recognizable Coca Colas and perfume bottles that looked too fragile to touch, so thin and fluted and colored with pastel, transparent glass. They found information on an island garden, Kitchener's Island. They went there late in the day and meandered through the plants and trees on twisting paths, pointing out things both recognizable and utterly new. There were plants that they recognized from Israel, and Andrew picked Gaby one of her favorite flowers from the hostel grounds—or rather picked a fallen one up off the ground, since neither would pick flowers from a park. Gaby tucked it behind her ear and then took the cardigan she wore against the morning cool (which had become obscene in the desert afternoon) and wrapped it into a pretty impressive turban on her head. The garden path led them to a high spot over the Nile and a bench. They sat down when they realized the sun was setting over the desert, which was pristine and vast out beyond the placid waters of the Nile.

Andrew took Gaby's hand on the bench and looked over at her. She did not refuse it. She gazed out over the sand and water. Monkeys squawked in the palms overhead. Lush, saturated green and violent splashes of vibrant color surrounded them and framed Gaby's head. They were alone, sitting in the solace of a carved-out garden and perched on the edge of the burnished, rippled water and the alluring, sparkling sands (which is a lot like looking at the ocean, where you feel the imposition of the vastness which translates as both danger and theology creeping in on your own assumed importance). The sky shone a watery run of red and then pink and then purple and then an almost complete dissolving into white before the blue, blue, blue. A crescent moon rose as the sun set, or was the moon sinking into the sunset?

Andrew kept looking at Gaby, who kept drinking in the scene. She was nearly orange in the dying attempts of the sun to relieve itself of all its fire before setting, but it looked good on her. She looked like a copper statue. Her eyes were also affected by the sunset: the gold was mined to the top and shone under all her thick lashes. Her straight nose reminded Andrew of a foreign queen with the turban swathed on her brow, a few tendrils of dark curl falling from the edges and across her ears to her shoulders. Her lips were held together, her cheekbones outlined by the dramatic shadows, as in a spotlight. Her neck was slender and long above her slim shoulders.

He snapped a photo. She started reciting poetry. They snuggled in closer to each other.

Andrew sighed. "You know, Gaby. I said I was sorry about everything that happened at the Golan Heights. But what I really meant was that I am sorry about what I said at the waterfall. Or what I asked."

"What do you mean?"

"You know." Gaby said nothing in response. "When I asked if we were dating. And right after we kissed. That must have given you the wrong idea. I know that we are dating, I just happen to be cowardly about commitment, as well and bumbling and oft-confused. The point is, there is no one I would want to be with more than you. You are just... awesome. You're... you're funny, and smart, and pretty. You have such a passion for helping. You're so very helpful."

She arched an eyebrow at him, an amused threat.

"Okay, I'll stop. Maybe I could write them better to you in a poem?" That was one of his many positive features. Love of poetry.

"The point is, we *are* dating. That is, if you'll have me."

"What sort of girl goes with a guy all the way into the heart of Egypt with no intention of keeping him hanging around awhile?"

"A hired assassin?"

"Oh, but aren't I 'so very helpful?' Not very '*et tu, Brute*,' I'm assuming." They could hear a breeze pick up in the leaves and the monkey stopped his shouting. She said carefully, "I don't think that what you said was the thing that bothered me most. Sure, it hurt to imagine you didn't have the intentions of a high school girl and hadn't already picked out our china patterns; I wouldn't object if you were totally crazy about me. But that feeling like everything between us just *fell away* so *suddenly* and left a completely black, cold, void..." she shuddered. "Logically, I just can't see how my emotions could hijack all the empirical evidence that I had to contradict what I felt."

"Which was?"

"ALL ALONE! And devoid of a future: hopeless. And like you HATED me and maybe even like I hated you. How do people survive these things? And how do you stop them from happening?"

"Well I imagine that you don't stop them, and you weather them the same way we are: you apologize, you touch each other, you look back at your past and keep dreaming toward the future." He put his arm around her and drew her close in a hug that was more familiar than it had been, he squashed her face into his chest and looked out over the Sahara. She said, "Oomph."

"Gaby, I really, really, really like you. I don't know just where we are headed, but I'd like to keep heading there with you. If I lost you, I would always wonder. I think we have a great fit and I enjoy every minute we have together."

"Except that one by the waterfall?"

"Well, maybe I don't enjoy every minute, but I wouldn't take it back: not even that one."

Gaby turned her face into his chest, breathed in his eternal soapiness, nuzzled her nose against cotton T-shirt over young man chest. "Mmmm," she released a long breath. "I would like to stay around, too."

That night at the hotel, Gaby slipped out of the room, Andrew's arm lying limp on the bulbous, scarlet-bedecked bed. She slid sideways out the door, closed it slowly until it clicked, and tripped down to the spacious entrance atrium. She walked along the tiled mural walls and paused at the window of the gift shop, where small spotlights illuminated a few forward objects. There in the front, standing in the light-in-the-dark on a transparent book stand, was a copy of *The Flight of The Queen*. Here, even? Gaby hadn't read that since ninth grade English.

She stood in the half-light of the atrium and gift shop, bent over to read the back of the second copy that lay beneath the first:

"Illuminated in a way we have never before seen, told in a voice of breath-taking beauty and confidence, Marja I. Stone retells for us the story of The Queen, during the quiet moments of her life, imagining into them the answers we do not find elsewhere. Is it fact? Is it fiction? It does not matter, for *The Flight of The Queen* is an instant classic.

"The story opens with the celebrated marriage of The Queen to the strong and noble Jaden, shortly after which she disappears for many months. Where has she gone? Stone reveals The Queen to us in new and exciting ways, as we follow her to a secret cave where she gives birth to a never-before-imagined love child, croons over the child with a magical midwife, and ultimately slips away back to her life as the ruler, the new wife of Jaden, and a woman who would continue to lead and conquer. But at what cost?

"Where did the child and his nursemaid go? What became of the baby Alexander? And what was in the locket that she hung around his tiny neck and tucked into his swaddling clothes before kissing him goodbye?"

Gaby turned and walked down to the poolside, where Bob Marley was singing his *Best*, yet again, and the pool was still lighted up in startling bluish turquoise. There was not one other person on the deck, the floating minibar abandoned for the winter. She found a suitable lounge chair and sidled up to what light she could get in order to write a letter that seemed suddenly to be urgently necessary. Sure, she owed Mikhail a letter, but there was something urging her to say certain things. She didn't let herself identify the whys and wherefores.

The letter began: *There is this guy. His name is Andrew.*

CHAPTER 24
LOVE LOST
   ℬ   ℭ

This time, Mikhail brought—not words through glass, not fortune cookie paper—but flowers. He even did a little internet research to figure out what *sort* of flower bouquet was most appropriate to accompany what he wanted to say. Of course, it occurred to him that Gaby was not likely sitting over at a computer in Israel, awake at nights doing her own research on the traditional meaning of various flower bouquets, but she was a girl, wasn't she? Weren't other people much more versed in this sort of thing than he was? It did seem people from the ticketing agent to the airline hostess were giving him important looks. Or was it just the idea of any bouquet of flowers sticking out of the top of his carry-on backpack?

Perhaps it was how pale his face had gone. Perhaps they weren't thinking he was loving someone or participating in one of the most adventurous, risky, and important scenes of his life, but that he was actually ill? He was ill, he thought. How would he do it? He just would. He had to. Everything else failed and Gaby had to know or else he was going to lose her forever.

What if he were too late?

Could that really happen?

He felt sicker still.

As the flight attendant came by checking seatbelts, she asked Mikhail, sir, to kindly pry the backpack from his trembling arms and store it under the seat in front of him. Did he think he was going to need a vomit bag? The people on either side of Mikhail looked alarmed.

"No, thanks, I'm fine." He retrieved a Discman from the bag as he stored it, did up his seatbelt, inspected the emergency procedure card from the pocket in front of him. He wondered what the vegan entrée would be at five miles above the earth and halfway between the United States and Germany. His connecting flight was in Munich. This was all so new to him. He had no real idea what he was doing. It was a little exciting. He enjoyed all the foreign languages he heard, all those airline things he had only seen in movies: keeping your bags with you at all times! Boarding by assigned seat number and cut-throat jostling for position in line anyhow! Flight attendants with plastered-on smiles who repeated greetings ceaselessly even though there might only be one person making their way up the aisle! And how much more awaited him in a brief layover in Germany and in Israel.

Israel. His mind tripped on the word and he pulled through a vortex and into a restrictive pit on the inside of his body. He was going. He was doing it.

"You all right?" The middle-aged woman next to him seemed compelled to ask the question.

"Yeah. No, I'm fine."

"You seem sort of *antsy*." Airline bombings and hijackings were just enough on her radar that his apparent squeamishness was beginning to undo her. His obvious clean, suburban-urban American look was not lost on her. She ventured on. "Your first time flying?"

"Well, unless you count the plane I took this morning…"

"So you're not from New York?"

"No, the Midwest. Michigan. Detroit area. You?"

Thank goodness. The conversation went on like this for quite some time. And then there were free movies and funny radio stations to flip through and nasty food to dissect and trips to the lavatory (which was a very new thing, indeed). They sort of kept you hopping on those international flights, what with pilot updates and the beverage cart, dimming lights and flickering seatbelt signs. The flight seemed both painfully long—what a way to spend several hours of your limited life—and alarmingly abbreviated, divided up until it hardly existed.

Then they landed. Mikhail longed to stretch his long legs. They taxied. They arrived at the gate. They waited for something-or-other. Mikhail addressed the middle-aged woman, "Hey, thanks so much for talking to me. I'm sort of nervous about something I have to do once I get to Israel."

"Oh, the flowers." She nodded at Mikhail's feet.

"Oh! Yeah, yeah, the flowers. I..."

A stewardess interrupted him on the intercom: "We need to see the following Lufthansa passenger at the terminal kiosk upon exiting the plane: Mikhail Aleksandr. Again, Mikhail Aleksandr, we need to see you immediately at the terminal kiosk."

"Oh. Oh! What does that mean?"

"Oh, nothing. They probably just have a message about a connecting flight. Why? That's not you, is it?"

"Yeah, it is."

And as soon as the pilot turned off the pesky seatbelt light, Mikhail shot up and squeezed forward with the other passengers. Normally, he would have lolled in his seat, waiting for the aisle to clear and everyone trapped behind him to get sufficiently annoyed, but he was worried. He was in a strange country in—from what he gathered—an enormous airport trying to make a connecting flight on a life-or-death mission, and now Lufthansa had it out for him, just him. Had his luggage been lost? Had...

And he was swept in a sea of bodies out the tiny door, down the aerobridge, and into the airport. The kiosk? The kiosk? The kiosk? Ah, was that it? He made his way to the nearest counter, already manned with a marked, female Lufthansa employee.

"Mikhail Aleksandr. I'm the passenger you called."

"Ah, yes, Mr... Aleksandr, is it?" in a heavy German accent. "You have a message here." She handed him a piece of white printer paper with typing under the Lufthansa logo.

"From who?"

"Um. I believe it should say..." she started to scan the message from upside down, with her finger.

"That's okay. Sorry. I'll just read it."

He read the writing: "Emergency Message for Mikhail Aleksandr, passenger on Lufthansa flight #452, LaGuardia International to Konzern-Internetauftritte. Mother is in hospital. Needs to return home immediately."

"What?!" he gasped. There was no more air. "Where did this come from?"

"I don't know, sir. Can I?" she took the paper and read it. "Oh. Is there someone you can call? May I help you with a return flight? We will have to re-direct your luggage." She started tapping at the keyboard in front of her.

"Yeah. Yeah." He did all three, sort of slowly (like in a dream), but he also felt whisked away. Someone mashed a giant rewind button. He boarded another flight to the U.S. faster than he could have imagined possible. He was in New York. He was at Detroit Metro and waiting for a relative to pick him up. He was talking to someone in the hospital about visiting hours. He was at Nadine's bedside.

ᘓ ᘔ

"Mikhail, sweetheart. I didn't want anyone to call you. I thought it could wait. I know this was so important to you."

"Mom! No way! I would've been upset if no one called. Mom,"

"But Mikhail, what about Gaby?"

"Let's talk about what's going on with you, Mom. I worried about you all the way home from Germany. The message was cryptic."

"You were in Germany?!"

"Yeah, they called me to the kiosk when we touched down on the runway." Already an airport lingo expert, her little boy.

"It happened so soon after I dropped you. I guess if I had just told them to call you, it would have saved you the hassle of an international flight. Will they give you your money back?"

"Mom! Who cares?"

"Well, I'd like to think…"

Mikhail became more subdued. "Plus, you didn't know when you crashed. What *did* you think?"

"I guess I just thought it was stress or old age or something."

"You're not that old!"

"But the doctors knew better. Maybe they thought epilepsy, I don't know. Don't you black out during seizures? Anyway, then they found it…" She choked back a little.

"Mom, no." He reached out and took the hand from its place on her stomach, on top of a snow-white mound of stiff and bleach-reeking sheets layered like filo dough. She was a little Russian pirozhki. "You don't have to talk about it now. I'm sure you're tired."

"No, I'm sure *you're* tired. Why don't you go home and sleep?"

"I'm staying here. They said I can stay on the chair there," gesturing to the window side of the room. "It reclines. It's made of antibacterial plastic, I'm sure. They're going to bring blankets and pillows which will haunt my sleep with dreams of chlorinated sand paper." She opened her mouth to protest. "Stop! I'm staying. I'm staying, Mom. I'm staying." The repetition seemed to soothe her.

"Maybe I won't be staying long. Don't most cancer patients go in and *out* of the hospital?"

"I don't know, Mom." He didn't want to point out that most cancer patients seemed to find out long before they blacked out and crashed into a tree. He wanted to ask if there was anything that she had kept from him. She could see something there, but her normal resolve failed her.

"Go on, go get some food at least. I'm going to rest."

"Yeah, okay."

Lost staring up at the menu in the hospital cafeteria, Mikhail rerouted and took a cab home, a shower, found some decent leftovers in the fridge and plenty of granola bars and toaster pastries to fill a bag, a couple books that were waiting around on shelves to be read, and then a toothbrush still in the package: Lufthansa said his current toothbrush (and everything else he had packed previously) would not be back in the states for a couple days. He discarded his carry-on next to the bed and re-set the thermostat, closed all the blinds, turned on the porch light and took his own car back to the hospital. The bag sat there in the dark of night and in the gloom of a shuttered room in the winter sun, as the days ticked by. The dozen red roses curled around the edges, the petals darkened, they wrinkled, the heads sagged on their stems, limp at the top. They smelled musky and swampy and heady as they rotted. Then they grew dry and dusty: the room was stale and dark and smelled of potpourri.

೦೩ ೮೦

Nadine was a hard worker and a saver, so even though she was a single mom, she had used her education to cobble together a legitimate career, and on top of the settlement from Alexy's death, the Aleksandrs had quite a nest egg. Nadine's company was now taking care of her, after all those years of service. She was grateful for the novel occurrence.

A few corners of Nadine's hospital room blossomed Hallmark, thanks to her sister Ruth and other relatives and co-workers, neighbors, and the LeFevres. There were flower arrangements, cards, balloons, and even small gifts, and so many that every once in awhile the hospital personnel approached Mikhail with the polite demand that he take some things back to the house. Nadine spent days and days in this Hallmark, floating in and out of boredom, visiting hours, books, TV specials which she really didn't want to be watching, and journaling. With her journal on her lap, she looked around the room and out the window, searching her mind and her immediate environment for inspiration. She spent hours studying the flowers and memorizing Ruth's children's colored drawings taped on the wall.

She remembered being a pre-teen when her Grand-Papa had died. Her mother picked her up from school along with her sister and brothers. It happened to be Halloween, and all of them misbehaved in the back seat, buzzing on sugar and wearing all sorts of irregular outfits. They assumed from such a strange occurrence that Mother had an unexpected surprise for them. They could barely contain their exuberance, their grins, their excitement. The anticipation. The not-knowing-how-to-break-the-news-at-this-point. The blurting out at any old moment. The sinking in. The awkwardness and guilt. The crying. No one would look anyone else in the face.

They went to the hospital, but Grand-Papa was already gone and no one saw his body until a few days later, at the funeral home. They loitered at the funeral home for days, on and off. The siblings and cousins spent hours in the kitchen of the home, mixing coffee with hot chocolate powder and sucking it through coffee stirrers, sitting around a Formica circle table and talking very little, not quite sure what talking was allowed to be respectful. Certainly they were not to smile, let alone laugh together, but sometimes they couldn't help it.

Nadine did not remember the funeral service too well. She remembered going to Hudson's with her mother the day before, to buy mourning for the family. She remembered her selection, not drab enough for her mom but she was too tired to argue: a smart black jacket, a pleated, knee-length black skirt, black tights, black shoes, and oh, how she had wanted a black hat with a built-in veil, but Mother insisted on a simpler, black beret. The only color in the outfit was a gold brocade embellishment up the lapels of the jacket and the gold cross she wore on a chain around her neck. She felt so proud of that little outfit, so fashionable. She also felt a little guilty, since she couldn't help walk around the home, strutting like a peacock and shamefaced for it.

Nadine remembered filing past the casket, looking at Grand-Papa's heavily closed eyes under the stark white of his forehead, taking her last look at him. It seemed like so much makeup, and he looked sort of different and very handsome. He had always been handsome, she supposed. And then after filing past the casket, moving slowly around the room all the way back to the doors. Was it meant for them to take a good look at the sympathy gifts? Or was it just the way a couple hundred people exited a funeral when there were so many things to see and so much sadness to carry?

She remembered thinking that there were so many flowers and so many different arrangements, there must be books and books of options at the florist. You could get dyed carnations with a stuffed bear in it. There was one there. There were vases of crystal, vases of glass with decorations painted on them, vases of opaque plastic which hardly stood upright under the weight of the blooms. There were plants in dirt, meant to last several years in the right, sunny spot. There were arrangements full of dried and dead things and topped with a couple lackluster blossoms of carnation, rose, daisy. The room was full of the scent of them, a scent that was nothing like a luscious garden or a field of flowers, but more like the fresh flower section of a grocery store: noxious and astringent, flower ghosts and chemical food, plastic, cheap woven baskets and refrigeration, nutrient-deficient soil. Lots of flower ghosts. There were other smells in the room: old, industrial carpeting, crowded bodies, funeral home scents that Nadine could not place. Maybe preserving fluids? Nadine imagined a room behind the wall of this one, like the lab of a mad scientist, bubbling potions on Bunsen burners and a cadaver or two or three on stretchers placed at slants in the dark room. It would smell odd in there, acrid, perhaps like the smell of the photo processing lab at the high school where Ruth processed yearbook photos mixed with the science lab when they dissected worms: formaldehyde and plastic-y flesh.

There were cards and cards sticking in the flowers. They were propped up among the stems, tied to the vases, woven into the prongs of those clear, plastic pitchforks staked in the nutrient-deficient dirt. Nadine read them.

Nadine pulled back from the memory, looked at her own flowers around the room. She too had cards sticking into most of them and triangulated in front of them on the room's surfaces, so that she could read the fronts. Get Well Soon. Missing You. Hope You Feel Better. Hang in There. Photographs of puppies and peaceful valleys; sketches of balloons and comic characters with dialogue above their heads: "And this is Glurg, your anesthesiologist." "The wallet. It has to come out." Drawings stuck to the wall, balloons floated just below the ceiling in shapes like ice cream cones with four and five and half-a-dozen bright-colored scoops.

Mikhail sat in the spot that had become "his," in the recliner where he spent hours of his days lounging and most nights sleeping. Nadine could not manage to chase Mikhail back home and back to his own life. He had taken time off work to go to Israel, and once that time was up, he just commuted from the hospital to work. He shuttled family members, ran errands for Nadine, fetched her meals outside the hospital: the absence of their usual diet could really get a person down. As far as she could tell, he would stop by the house to collect the mail and never walk in the front door unless she contrived a compelling task for him. He did not like to go in the house.

C3   80

Mikhail had just returned from a trip by the house, and he sat, leaned back, with a sizable pile of mail on his lap. He sorted out bills, flicked junk mail to the floor, his eyebrows furrowed as he scrutinized return addresses. He had all but taken over the household finances; Nadine weakened by her treatments and incapacitated from the side effects of its aggressiveness. She thought to herself just how capable he was becoming now. And if she died, who would he have to take care of? He would be like a floating particle, no strings attached anywhere. How could it be he had no close family or family-like friends? Would Ruth take him in? Would Stellar or Mercedes become the maternal figure he would need? And how had she never thought of this before?

She was watching him closely as his eyes fell on a certain envelope, his hands paused, his face relaxed into simplicity of feeling. He looked up at Nadine, and she smiled weakly at him. He managed a faint smile and then stood up quickly, placing the rest of the mail pile on his seat, crossed the room and exited in a few firm strides.

In the hallway, he ripped the letter open, careful but so fast it was alarming to an aid passing in the hall. The envelope fell to the ground as he stared at the first line.

He came back into the room hours later, his sweatshirt holding the smell of outdoors and the cold of a snowless winter night. He slumped into the chair, looked out the window to steel himself to say what must be said quickly and definitively. "It's over, Mom." He meant that to be the end.

"What happened?"

"No, Mom. I can't."

"I just... How could she say no to you?"

"She didn't. She just..."

"Then are you sure?"

"Yeah, Mom. For now. Forever, I don't know. I have no way to know now."

"Did she disappear?"

"Mom!"

"Just tell me. Please."

Mikhail leaned forward, rested his elbows on his knees. He sighed and set his forehead firmly in the palms of his hands. "There is someone else. She is dating this, this Andrew. He is wonderful. They are having a wonderful time. They will have a wonderful life together like in the Bahamas and make 50 babies together."

"Oh. But it's just one guy, you know. I mean, how long has she even known him? It's just a fling."

"Mom!"

"He's got nothing on you. Gaby's a numbskull."

"Mom!"

"Sorry, honey. I love Gaby, but this is painful."

"You think I haven't noticed?" They sat in silence for a while.

"Mikhail... Sweetie, perhaps it would be healthy for you to move on for awhile, too."

"What do you suggest? A dating service? Or should I just hop on over to the nearest brothel?"

Nadine cringed. "I don't mean that you should date, exactly, just that maybe you could make some friends, some good friends. You could reconnect with old friends, join a club, pick up a hobby. What about people at work?"

"No, Mom."

"Just think about it. Spend some time away from here; it would be good for you. And for me. I don't want to see you waste away here as I…"

"Not again, Mom. I'm here. I don't want to be anywhere else. They're just waiting for your white blood cell count to return to normal."

"Fine. If you don't start finding friends of your own, I'm going to start setting you up with people. Starting now. If you don't have a date for Friday night, I'll make one for you."

"Great."

Nadine was lost in her own thoughts while Mikhail sat staring into space and occasionally squirming. It started to snow and large flakes melted after they struck the tinted window, but still the cold from the window seemed to push back against the heat of the room.

"You know," Nadine said softly, not sure she should be saying it, "I thought she would be the one."

"Yeah, Mom. Me too. Thanks for clearing that up."

"No, no… I just meant…" She slipped into reverie again and Mikhail searched her face. He thought, for a moment, that something was seeping into her brain, something bad.

"Mom?"

"Oh. Sorry. I just. Mikhail, let me tell you something, in case…"

"There's no in case, Mom."

"Okay, fine, whatever." She pounded a fist down onto her leg under the white sheets, but it was a feeble punch. "Just listen to what I have to say, and don't forget it. All right?"

"Okay. Sure." Mikhail pouted as he sunk back into the chair.

"When your Dedushka, Alexy's dad, died, he left something to me in his will. I never expected anything from him, not after Alexy was gone, but he was always a generous man and he left us money, and money for you, too. I used much of that money to pay for your college."

"But Mom…"

"No interruptions. Let me finish. He also left something else that seemed so strange to me; we had not seen him in a long time, but when he and Babushka sent gifts, they were always new toys and household items. Anyway, he left an envelope to us in the will. It was the manila kind and I slipped it beneath my jacket without looking because I thought it would have been rude to look. And when I opened it at home, well, it's weird, but there was a story, Mikhail. The postscript claimed the story explained the locket your Babushka gave me when Alexy died; the one so heavy and ornate it would sit heavy on the breast of any person. Honestly, I was confused. It seemed ridiculous, preposterous. I had never heard your Dedushka say anything about it, anything like it.

"And that, with Babushka's hints of ancient magic! I know, I know…" she waved Mikhail back. "Now, I thought they were crazy. But the more I was around that locket, the more I was magicked, myself. I knew it must be a fake; something bought for a joke or made to trick unsuspecting buyers a few generations back. But how could it be so weighty and so beautiful?

"I went to Tania—your Babushka—with questions, but I was given no answers. Either she didn't know about the story, or she was unwilling to tell me. Really, where she had seemed mysterious about the locket, she now seemed uninterested in the story. She said that Dedushka probably meant it as a fairytale for you."

"Over the years, I stumbled upon the Northwyth Legends here and there and upon tales of a missing locket of the famed Aleksandrs. But to leap to the conclusion that the locket was real and that our family was *the* Aleksandrs; that just seemed silly! So I stopped paying attention. I put the locket away, and it's hidden with the story, and I wanted to let you know just in case... in case. It's behind" she had to wave him back, again "my jewelry box. There's a secret panel on the back; it won't take a rocket scientist to figure out how to get at it and I'm sure you'll manage if you have to."

Mikhail sat for a few moments and then decided to ignore the story for what might be hidden behind it. "Mom, what have they been saying about the leukemia?"

"It's coming along fine, they said. My blood count is rising."

"Have they said anything about how much time there is? We don't know how much time you have, Mom... time until anything."

"None of us knows how much time we have, son."

"Yeah, but you know: I just mean your time might be... limited."

"Mikhail. *Your* time is limited. You get a certain amount. You don't know what that is. You play your cards accordingly."

⚃ ⚄

The things Nadine told Mikhail about a mysterious locket and story haunted his dreams until he made his next trip home to check the mail and fetch Nadine a sweater. He stood in the doorway to her room, noticing the chill, the stuffiness, the dark of it shut for so long against the sun. He wondered how long ago he had last come in here, before the cancer. It used to seem private, but now he came in here often to find things for

Nadine, to dig through her sock drawer and pull shampoo from the shower ledge. He never felt right about it.

This time she didn't know he was here, hadn't given permission for the intrusion. He didn't want her to think he thought she was dying, he just wanted to see the story. After all, Babushka said it was for him.

He straightened his shoulders and strode across the room to the lower of the two dressers. Her jewelry box dominated the top, set on a doily which was surrounded by a dust which had never been there before. Mikhail wondered if he shouldn't be vacuuming and dusting in here. He ran a finger through the film before reaching up to turn the jewelry box around. Nadine was right; it was not difficult to locate the secret compartment and push against it, setting a spring to launch a little drawer out at him. He removed it and tilted the contents out on the dresser top.

First he opened the box and inspected the locket. It really was amazing, even in the dim light that came from the hallway. He put it back. Then he took the paper and unfolded it, walking drawn by the hall light as he read.

"When the tailor came to sew The Queen into her wedding dress, he gave her a sideways look before he thought about it. She held her chin even higher, but her hand fell reflexively to her stomach and its new, taught roundness. She said suddenly to him, 'Make sure that no one can tell.'

"'Yes, your majesty.'

"'Thank you, Philin.' She relaxed the creases in her forehead to smile at him in the mirror.

"Philin kept his word. Not only did The Queen float down the aisle looking slender, virginal, and majestic in embroidery and gathers, but he did not tell even his wife or his best friends, making him the sole secret keeper of a mystery that would endure for ages. It was a chambermaid who slunk through The Queen's room one night, changing out a basin, and caught a glimpse of The Queen undressing and holding the naked, growing mound with the flat of her hand. She spoke of it indiscriminately, but her word was not immediately effective. The story turned into a rumor which turned into an alternative story that would buzz about, also for ages.

"After the wedding, The Queen knew it was essential she disappear very quickly. She kissed her new, good husband goodbye and left a momentarily peaceful kingdom, saying she needed to seek The Sage and his council. She did not go looking for The Sage, but for a midwife, whom she procured in a destitute situation in a rural village in a distant land. Together, the midwife and The Queen sought refuge in a cave, deep in the Northern Mountains and high on a ledge. The cave was spacious, secreted from the wind, and complete with a small tunnel for directing the smoke through and a clear stream that trickled among the rocks.

"When they began their vigil, The Queen was unable to hide her heavy stomach, although she was not yet at a waddle. She released herself to the ministrations of the midwife, who hunted and gathered by day and cooked stews, brewed teas and did laundry by night. The midwife made a large nest of straw and moss in a secluded corner of the cave and unpacked her linen cloths, laid out her basins and tools.

"Months later, The Queen was sitting out on the ledge letting the wind brush through her copper hair and staring out at the wide, lonely forest spread below with a look of longing when her abdomen tightened into a spasm and she withdrew to the cave, and the nest.

"Alexander came screaming into the world in the solitary glow of a beeswax candle, the firstborn of one of the most notable royal leaders of all time, and in complete secrecy. The Queen would nurse him, would hold him long, bittersweet hours, and then would wean him to goats' milk and leave him in the cave, with the midwife. As he grew, the midwife would take him—a healthy, young boy—down to the hills and find him a life, a family, a livelihood. He was released to the fate in which he was conceived, allowing it to take him where it would and to protect him.

He was wise and noble and kind and shrewd, and he made his fortune beginning with only the mountain-boy clothes on his back and the locket his mother left lying on his chest wrapped inside his swaddling. He never parted with the locket, sometimes laying in bed beside his wife stroking the golden A and the gemstones, humming a song that seemed to come to him from another world."

CHAPTER 25
CONSPIRACY
ℰꙄ   ℭꙎ

Gaby was in Israel one year to the day from her meeting Sara outside Alford, and it was one of *those* days.

It begins with little hints; things that would typically be absorbed into the normalcy of the rest of the day, the rest of all days flowing by in a river which almost never ends and never begins. Hint one: she woke up in the drawn-curtain gloom of the hostel room, swung her feet to the floor and right into the neck of a half-full bottle of beer, spraying it in hundreds of alcoholic droplets across bedding and belongings, sloshing it out onto the floor, and covering her legs and feet in the sticky, fragrant mess. When the owner proved nowhere to be found, the beer had to be cleaned up before Gaby could then wait in line for a shower she hadn't intended to take. Hint two: She was already running behind on her own idea of the day, and still needed to sit and wait for the public computer that the hostel offered. For a long time. She settled herself into the hard chair in front of the computer—all hollow metal legs and lacquered, unidentifiable plastic, like melamine—started opening email, and *zap!* the screen went black. Gaby could not get it back, the other people in line could not get it back, the hostel owner could not get it back, and now it was practically lunch time. Hint three: When Gaby finally gave up on the whole computer situation and turned on her heels to huff away, her cardigan snagged on the back of that plastic-metal chair and stayed fast while she moved on. It was wrenched right up the side, and not along any seam, either. Her favorite sweater! How much did she wear that thing?

Then it became a little more serious. Gaby returned to her room to change her shirt and as she fumbled around under her bunk she felt a sudden pain on her hand. It started as "Ow." Then it became "Ow!" Then it went, "Ow! Ow-ow! OW! OWOWOW! *OW!* Holy shit!" At first a prick, and then a sting, and then poison, and then a burn. More burn. Unbelievable burn. She flailed around, jumped from foot to foot and cradled her hand in her other arm. She retreated from her bunk, returned to peek tentatively around, study the ground in the vicinity of her previously probing hand. What had stung or bit her? She found her way alone to a doctor she had already visited for incidentals, managed to be seen and reassured, bandaged; the swelling oohed and aahed over. She was a freak.

With her hand in an obtrusive ball of gauze and ACE, she boarded a sherut for Bethlehem for an afternoon shift at the orphanage. From where she was at the doctor, she caught the sherut around Damascus Gate and the driver worked his way around the west side of the Old City before heading south to Bethlehem. Just north of Jaffa Gate he plodded through heavy traffic, traffic lights, and reliably crazy drivers. For a moment. And then he pretty much stopped. The street erupted with honking and yelling and the cars and taxis and sheruts and busses shuddered in place, as if they could move forward. It was gridlocked around a construction truck crossways blocking the intersection. While taking a load of lumber to one of the new million-dollar apartment complexes, something came loose and flung slender, straight beams of wood out in a fan, into traffic. Gaby slid down into her seat, sighed, and waited in the smell of bodies, decaying upholstery, the rustle of scratchy fabric, the murmur of voices around and behind seats which were not towering directly in front of her.

In the time that it took to clear the mess and then extricate vehicles one at a time, Gaby thought about the course of the day. The pattern was clearly entrenched. Fate conspired.

She couldn't have been more right. Right after the sherut of silent, tense people slid over the Palestinian border into Bethlehem, there was a loud, sudden noise coupled with a confusing shift of momentum and a flash of dark stars at the front tips of Gaby's eyes, leaving only a rim of daylight for a second. Her thoughts came to her through a wall of figurative molasses, slow, one at a time, confused. Was everyone all right? They had crashed into something. Some passengers spilled out on the floor or knocked against seats in front of them. Belongings rolled about, thudding to the ground and lolling in the aftermath. But everyone seemed to be okay. The driver was yelling, then he was out in the road and yelling, arms swinging around his head, at someone else who was also yelling and standing out near a dented fender. Was Gaby okay? Yes, she seemed to be fine. Maybe she had whiplash and didn't know it yet. Isn't that how it happens, whiplash?

Everyone more or less gathered their things, settled into their original seats and postures, tucked stray hairs into head wraps, murmured to each other and shook their heads, swinging dangly earrings. Gaby laid her head back, again, waiting again, and thinking too much about whiplash. When the confrontation ended the driver climbed back in the sherut, it shuddered with the slamming of his door, and they drove more, winding into the heart of the city.

Then she was out in the urban, desert air, Middle Eastern in aroma and texture. Sun blazing. Movement. Gaby up the hill again, her calf muscles working against the terrain of the Negev. She was very late, yes, she was sorry. There was an accident. Exclamations. Reassurances. Halting French-Arabic-

English conversation petered out and she was worked into the modified schedule; she could go outside and supervise the children at play for the next half-hour.

A handful of children played outside, even though it was an oppressively bright, warm afternoon. Amir was probably less than two, but it was hard for Gaby to tell since American kids seemed so robust to her, like they were on steroids and hormones. Or were they? He was slight, anyhow, and appeared to Gaby to sit right under two-years-old. His hair was cut close to his head, but not so close you could not tell it was tight-curled like wool. His skin was nut brown and soft, his eyes large, round hazelnuts with lashes and more thick lashes. It was easy for him to be a favorite.

On the green, there were a few pieces of playground equipment built neatly out of two-by-fours and still smelling of pine. Among them, a tower with the top platform standing about shoulder height and hung over with a canvas canopy. It was a beloved place for everyone, and the older kids dominated, spending hours pow-wowing and goofing around. When not in use that way, there was a lone girl, just reaching the awkwardness of pre-puberty, with a chapter book, yellowed and with edges spread out like puff pastry, her face silent and intense.

Today, with only the toddlers and young children out on the grounds, they had default possession, and they swarmed. The workers and volunteers stood at the base of the tower, with children swirling around them and splashing up over them onto the tower. Each worker had their eyes on a couple kids, and Gaby was mostly playing games with Amir. He said little, and nothing in English, so it was peek-a-boo and physical movement and silly faces and gurgles. She wondered if he should be up there, his little legs still so funny and unsure. But his face was plastered with a grin, his eyes flickered with joy. All tiny teeth and big dimples and long lashes.

He climbed up the tower ladder, slid down the slide, up and down and up and down. The monotony calmed Gaby. He climbed up the ladder, one slow and chunky leg at a time, his chubby fingers wrapped around the ladder rungs, oblivious to the other kids flailing their limbs close enough to do damage. He forced his butt in the air and straightened his legs out, then pushed up his top half, and turned in a U at the top of the ladder. He stood at the top of the slide, Gaby standing just below him with her arms outstretched and flanking him in case he should falter. He faltered, catching his heel on some invisible obstacle and took a slanting step backwards. The momentum was too much for him and the other foot followed. And then the other. She thought he would fall onto his bottom, but he just kept moving away from her arms, which were extended out toward him, straight as rails and accented by her earnestness. She thought of the scenarios, she knew with certainty that his fast, choppy route across the tower was much quicker than her circuitous, kid-broken route around the tower, and there was nothing to launch her fast enough over it. Her arms felt cold, hollow, impotent. Her eyes riveted to him. She prayed that some other worker would be there, suddenly, to grab him. He would surely fall on his bottom before he reached the edge!

And then he hit the edge, his eyes registering surprise as he threw his arms out straight to the sides and took a final step into air. The foot came down unexpectedly hard and gravity dragged it down with Amir following. The look on his face was terror; Gaby's stomach dropped out from its usual place, nausea rose immediately into her throat and mouth. He fell back, straight as a board and all four limbs splayed before he disappeared from her vision. She hurdled over some children and pushed around a couple workers, not consciously seeing anything but a fuzzy blackness and her vision of him sliding through the air. She met him on the grass, dazed, and staring up through her face. She mentally thumbed through her brain for the right piece of information. Should she touch him? Not touch him? Should she move him? Not move him? What if his neck were moved but there was spinal damage?

Then Gaby sensed other people gathering above her, she stopped thinking. Her arms shot out from her torso and cradled under Amir's body. She felt the cool grass softly scratching the backs of her hands and forearms, the soft solidity of dirt underneath the weave. Amir's body too was both solid and soft against her, warm, cotton T-shirt fabric and the coarseness of his cropped hair. He kept looking up at her, focused in on her face until she buried it into her chest. She kept him smothered there as she stood, made her way quickly across the grass, walking, and into the orphanage. She found the Mother Superior in the front office and caught her eye, kept her face with a look of panic, questions in her eyes.

Mother Superior moved toward her, gently took the child and enfolded him in her own arms, looking into his face and asking what happened in broken English.

The phrase had been turning and turning in a wide-empty space all the way into the building. "He fell off the playground tower." The nun shot her gaze up at Gaby, alarm in her eyes, in the arches of her eyebrows, like sails loosed to the wind.

 Cʒ ꙮ

Gaby stood at the corner at the bottom of the hill. It was always shady at this time of day, there, and she usually waited in the long, blue shadows to hail a taxi. Today, though, there was no gold outside the articulated blocks of blue; the world had drabbed over, clouded, the sky felt oppressive with rain. Where had it come from? When Gaby was in the orphanage handing over a tattered child to a nun who resignedly told Gaby to "Go," the clouds moved in from a distant Mediterranean, and blue faded to watercolor gray. The day came crashing back in its obvious perversity and the sky opened up on Gaby long before she managed to get a taxi. It had never been hard to get a taxi in downtown Bethlehem before.

As the taxi sidled up to her, she stood in a puddle of sandy foam, dripping wet. The taxi was an old one, patched with duct tape, rattling and clunking down the road, hung with as many Fatima's hands as the driver found necessary to keep his money maker moving forward. Gaby settled into the seat and leaned her head back to negotiate her usual price. She found herself running out of gusto, placed her forefinger and thumb over closed eyes as she settled for a lost shekel. The driver probably thought she was green. She sighed her lazy exasperation, said out loud, "You ever have one of those days?" and then didn't really listen to the answer.

That's when the taxi gave a heave, sputtered, and died. Gaby narrowed her eyebrows and brought her cheeks up. "What the hell?" she muttered. The driver got out, tinkered around under the hood in the rain, cars easing around him and cutting it close, laying on horns, waving arms behind the shelter of their windows, lips moving to indicate annoyance. The tinkering, unbelievably, worked. The driver, hunched under his coat, slunk into the front seat, turned the key, and made a sound of approval as the taxi sputtered to life. They continued on through the storm and back into Jerusalem, as close to the hostel as the taxi would take her, which was a few winding alleyways away.

She was running late, anyhow, and was supposed to be meeting Andrew in a nearby tunnel right about now. Gaby was soaked through and uncomfortable, and sure she looked like something the cat drug in, but was beyond caring and anyhow weren't they getting far enough along that they could start letting things hang out? Hadn't Andrew attempted to actually fart on her leg just last week while watching *The Fiddler on the Roof?* She hadn't supposed he was capable of such a thing, but now she had seen it with her own eyes.

She walked briskly to the stone archway and was disappointed to look around and find that Andrew was not yet there. She had been walking all the way there, head down and unseeing, imagining collapsing into his arms and the story of her day would just melt out into him and he would hold her to his warmth and say such nice things to her, like how it was no big deal that she smelled like mud and taxi and dehydration, she was still wonderful and still looked beautiful and he could hold her all day if she needed. When he wasn't there, something clicked inside of her and—although she had never had an addictive personality—she suddenly wished she had a negative coping behavior; the warmth of it in her chest, the imbibing followed by calm. And was there a dizzying of the consciousness, too? That would be nice.

Andrew arrived five minutes later.

An alarm went on somewhere deep inside her. She was unable to heed it. "I've been standing here fifteen minutes."

Andrew sort of took a hop back from where he was leaning into her, ready to lift her into a hug. His eyebrows heightened, his hands paused at her elbows and settled. His chin dipped so that his eyes could meet hers and attempt to lift her gaze into his. "You look…"—wait, he wasn't born *yesterday*—"water-logged?"

She turned her head up and over as if she had just been slapped and then turned back, narrowing her gaze directly at him. "You did *not* just say that. After the day I've had!"

"Say what?"

"Yeah right. You think I look like shit so just say so."

Andrew looked over a shoulder and then the other while their conversation multiplied exclamation points. Gaby resented this. It brought ripples of static up on the surface of her arms and in the palms of her hands. If she could think through the muffled fuzz of heat that was engulfing her brain, she might have thought that she could throw balls of electricity right at Andrew. That superpower would come in handy just then. He took in a deep breath, closed one eye and let it out slowly.

"Hello?" Andrew tried again, "I don't think you look... bad. I just mean that you don't look... I mean, what happened? is all."

"What happened? Now you just want me to just... to just..."

She sputtered because somehow a fuse had not connected somewhere inside, and he smiled at her. She cooled in waves through her limbs and then they laughed together, just a silly little snickering. It was then it occurred to Gaby everything might be okay at the end of a day even like today, when Andrew said "Actually, I had some really bad news today, so I might as well be out with it."

"Oh?" And now she felt herself reeling in a whole other direction.

"Yeah, not *only* are our tickets to the concert tonight absolutely *no good*—hold it—but my mom got me on the phone this afternoon..." he bit his lip and looked away from her, somehow his face was both deeply saddened and nervously sheepish. "And my grandma has died. A heart attack. Unexpected."

"My God, Andrew!" she reached out for him but found that she could do little more than place a limp hand on him and stare stupidly. There was nothing she could think to say.

Andrew met her gaze only briefly and then spoke looking over her shoulder, his hands wringing the paperback book that he was now holding, had fished out of his waist band. "I'm gonna' go now. I'll be back later? And, you know, the tickets are no good anyhow." She flinched. "So I have to go back home, and I'll be leaving really soon."

"Oh."

"Don't worry. I know." And with that, he turned suddenly and walked briskly off into a swarm of barterers and shopkeepers and was gone. Was it possible that she hadn't even held him just then? She couldn't extricate any individual fibers, the day was so complicated, but she felt heavy and hopeless. So she just moved slowly, found her way to a bus station, and hopped a bus which she took around town and to the other side of the New City, but didn't really see anything besides a blur of city life and the thoughts that wrote themselves out in her mind. They were too many to separate, to isolate. She slid the headphones to her Discman over her ears and listened, instead, to funnel the torrent in one direction, to single out emotions to the rhythm of a coherent composition. She listened to Over the Rhine's *Good Dog Bad Dog*. And by the time she got to the soothing waves of "Etcetera, Whatever" with its insistence that everything was going to be all right, she was thinking that the point of it was not to be in love, but to somehow come by a commitment that has some real chance of sticking. She was absolutely sure she should be feeling grief for Andrew, but she found herself wrapped up in her own paltry concerns. She often wondered why people's own shit smelled the rosiest. She thought her own sins, even the one that she was just now committing in her self-absorption and cruelty, were the most adorable. Was this something she had studied? Illusory superiority, was it? Or the above average effect?

It's not like Andrew was all perfect. His being Romeo to her Juliet had lasted only a couple weeks. Their fight under the waterfall had broken a spell, and since then there were more than a few casual glimpses of a bad mood, a haughty disposition, a predilection for taking the most worn path. She didn't feel completely safe in his affection.

Her heart was being broken. Or was it? Perhaps she was just unimpressed. Or tired. Or about to be *rejected*. Perhaps it was time for her too to go home.

Annie had called the week before, out of breath, said she had been trying to catch Gaby in the hostel all day, but she didn't sound worried. They struggled through the lag on the line.

"Well, what's up, then?" Long pause.

"They want to put us in a book." Long pause.

"What?! What on earth do you mean?" Long pause.

"They're writing a book, there's already a publisher involved," she paused a moment and Gaby started to talk but by then Annie was talking again in the lag and Gaby stopped and then Annie heard her and so she stopped but then Gaby just shut up, she was used to this dilemma by now. "So, as I was saying, they have a publisher involved. It's about twins and strange coincidences, in a nutshell, and obviously we're perfect candidates. In fact, I wouldn't be surprised if this person got the idea from us because they live right here in Butter. But there will be other twins involved, it sounds like they've already written about several different twin-pairs from around the world and they have some sort of deadline pressure, of course. Anyhow, we will need to do extensive interviews about how weird we are."

"Get the heck out of dodge!"

"And guess who the writer is? Total riot. You remember Mercedes?"

"Like Mercedes and John?"

"Yeah, the very same. I mean, it's not like we read each other's minds, but those incidences like when you had that fire—sorry, that's sticky—and I nearly caught fire, or when you fell down the stairs and I fell off the roof—yeah, that's sticky, too. Well, sticky all 'round. Maybe we shouldn't do it?"

"No. Sounds fun. Make us famous." Gaby grinned into the receiver.

"Well, Gaby, you'd have to come back here for the interviews…"

"Oh." Her grin faltered.

"You don't want to come back?" Annie sounded crestfallen but not surprised.

"No. No. I do, it's just that I'm busy."

"All right, then. Once-in-a-lifetime experience. Just thought I'd ask."

"You know, I have the orphanage, and Andrew, and a *job*. I mean, Saleem isn't just going to hold a space for me." Gaby thought for a moment they had lost their connection and then she heard breathing, six thousand miles away, right in her ear. "Well, maybe I can do it. How's Nadine, anyhow? I don't hear too much from Mikhail."

"Well I'm not in Michigan yet, same as you. But I hear she's just plodding forward with the treatment. Turns out she might be okay."

"It would be good to visit."

"It would always be good to visit."

"Fine, I'll see what I can do about the interviews."

"It would be fu-un...."

"Yeah, I know."

❧ ☙

Andrew showed up early—Gaby half-expected it—standing at her bedside when the tiniest sliver of a diffused dawn sky peeked in the hostel windows facing the courtyard. "Come on, Gab. Wake up."

Her voice was muffled by the pillow and her drowsiness. "Don't call me that."

"Gaby, get up."

"All right, all right. Can I put on some clothes?"

"Not if your Js are decent. Just throw on a sweatshirt. I don't have a lot of time." Someone groaned in their bunk and Andrew walked off toward the door with his thumbs in his back pockets, his body silhouetted against the hall light as he opened the door and exited, turned to lean his back against the wall before it swung shut.

Gaby met him in the hall after she brushed her teeth, wrapped a sweater around herself and pulled on wool socks. She hadn't bothered with her hair or the smudge on her left cheek, hadn't cleared the eyeliner from around her puffy eyes. She shuffled past Andrew and out through the lobby into the courtyard, where she shivered as she sat down at one of the small tables and he joined her. The metal chair still held the chill of the night and was beaded lightly with dew.

Gaby yawned.

"Well." Andrew sighed. "I'm leaving today. It's good, because I need to be home before the viewing this weekend." His voice cracked at the word "viewing."

"I'm so sorry."

"Yeah." He wasn't looking at her, but into the distance across the courtyard, at what exactly, neither of them knew.

"I mean, about your grandma." Gaby was tracing tight figure eights in the moisture on the table top with a finger.

"I know. But it's okay. I knew her pretty well, but I'm a guy, ain't I? I'll just suck it up and be fine."

"Maybe you could write about it?"

"Or read. I'm thinking Conrad Aiken, or maybe just Dickenson. You think they'll have a copy at duty free?" He managed a smile at her and their eyes met for the first time. "Look, Gaby…"

Now, still looking at him, her face fell and she registered apprehension.

He faltered, but continued. "I don't really know where we're headed, now that I'm leaving like this. I mean, it's almost time for me to head back for the summer, anyhow, so I, I won't be returning."

"You won't come back?" Of course, that's not nearly all she meant by the question.

"No, Gaby, I don't think so. This might be goodbye."

"But. But." She couldn't help but stutter. Just last night she herself wondered about their future, about just how unsure their relationship seemed at the time, but now this felt hostile and unwanted and surprising, even.

"Oh, come on, Gaby. We had fun and I really like you, but lately it's been kind of…"

"Strained. Yeah, I know."

"…patently *un*romantic."

"But I'm not a romantic, like you! All reciting poetry and whisking me off to exotic destinations for alone time!"

"You're not romantic?! Your whole life is one big romance! Loving. Impractical. Imaginative. Or maybe imaginary."

"Wait a sec. This isn't a psychiatric evaluation."

"Well, maybe it should be. Time for us to be honest and to grow forward; no time like the present. And while we're on it, I *do* think you live in the impractical and the imaginary, anyhow. I mean, you actually think you can save the world, Gaby, can change the world! And all you've gotten for your good intentions is disaster after disaster. You think that's just a coincidence? The world has it out for you, Gaby, trying to be so visionary, so forward-thinking!"

Gaby mumbled into the pause, "I think it's just because I'm not good enough."

"That's it! You're not good enough! None of us are. All our plans go awry at some juncture because we're *not* good enough."

"Like this relationship?" She had meant it to hurt him, but…

"Like this relationship. Our best intentions wouldn't hold up against our physical distance and my present circumstances."

"But they *could*."

"And that's another thing. You mistake stubbornness for a virtue."

"It's not stubbornness. It's drive."

"Sure, yeah. Whatever. You keep using that 'drive' to move you on your relentless path to save everyone around you, especially yourself. It's not success you need. It's faith, hope, and love; in short, mercy."

"You've been reading too much Anne Sexton."

"Yeah, if you only understood that reference."

"What does *that* mean?"

Andrew leaned forward so that his elbows rested on his knees, his face toward the ground. "Forget it. Not what I needed to say to you." He looked at his hands, studied hard the lines on his palms. "I just came to say goodbye. To say I don't have plans for us."

"Can you hear *me* out?"

Now he looked at his watch and then sat back into his cold seat. "Sure. If you can confine it to a few minutes. I don't want to be mean, but..."

"Forget it, then." Her eyes flashed menacingly. "I guess I don't have anything to say if you've already made up your mind. But it doesn't matter, anyhow. I was thinking of ending all this, anyways. Going home, myself."

"Well, maybe you ought to, then." Andrew sighed. "I like you, Gaby. It has nothing to do with that." He took her stony silence and her crossed arms as an opportunity to stand. "I'm going to go. I'll send you a letter, or call you at the hostel."

"I won't be here to take it."

"Fine."

"Please have a safe trip. I hope to see you, again." She shifted in her seat. "Can I... Can I come see you off, later?"

"Sure. Fine. But I doubt it'll help." He turned to go and called over his shoulder, "I hope you find what you're looking for."

CHAPTER 26
WITH AND WITHOUT
ℰᴼ   ᴼᴿ

Annie lay face-up in her bed, an old pain snaking its way up her spine and out into an arm. She hardly noticed it, looking intently instead at the pattern of watermarks on her cubby-small ceiling. She imagined the ceiling as one in a neatly arranged sea of similar ceilings, like a mathematical pattern that went on for thousands of three-dimensional iterations. Up, down, left, right, there were not only ceilings and ceilings and ceilings full of watermarks, but also people underneath them, sandwiched between the ceilings below and the suffocating stack of ceilings above.

Then the sheer largeness of imagining all the people laying in beds, cooking, eating, showering, copulating, arguing, crying, became top-heavy and caved in on itself and Annie started to think about how pleasant her little nook was. True, she complained about it a lot, in the entitled American kind of way, but in the scheme of things—she could hear someone's measured words vibrating against the front of her skull—her little, gritty shoe box in New York City was the life of kings in centuries past, and was beyond imagining for the starving masses. Clean, running water? A clean bathroom and a place to dispose of almost everything? An endless stream of information which took no more than a flip of a switch and a pale movement of the fingertips. It was boggling, imagining a scrawny Nigerian youth sitting on her bed, his dusty legs dangling over the edge and beating against the comforter with the agitation of youth. His fingernails long and dirt-embedded as he exclaimed and pointed, looking through her eyes as her impatient glances took in what she no longer found intriguing or mysterious; rows of clean, fashionable clothing; electrical switches and lamps; bookshelves of books; the computer screen with electronic 000s and 1111s swimming across it in the visage of a goldfish in the bowl of the monitor; a couple pair of shoes casually discarded on a chair; a calendar; a cork board pinned full of band flyers and work memos; several photos peopled with grinners taped to the wall; the suitcase propped against the closet door, packed and ready to leave for Michigan on a red-eye flight.

She closed her eyes and sighed, and was so exhausted that it didn't take long to fall asleep, unintentionally.

ෆ   ඞ

The ground was dry and compacted from the long stretch of heat, but after Mel dug into it and watered the dirt around a new plant and sat on the top of the picnic table, the smell of earth permeated the fiery air and subdued it. Mel took a long breath in, closed her eyes against the blaze of summer sun, let the cold ground water flow limpidly out of the hose and over her bare legs and feet (her clogs barely holding suspended in air on two cute lines of muddy, relaxed toes). Her mind worked against the tendrils of sweat spider-webbing over her shoulders and down her back and tickling her spine, sucking up the sense that water molecules were actually floating into her nose and smelled so wonderful. How was that?

Her garden was, well, verdant. Which was saying something because she hadn't known before that she could have a verdant garden; could create a verdant garden and keep it verdant. She felt a goddess in it, or was it more nymph-like? She felt powerful and at home in it, like she wanted to lie down in the mud and be sucked into it. She picked at bugs, she pruned leaves with her bare fingers and walked among the rows and the clumps-which-weren't rows, feeling the vines grasping at her legs and the stiff hairs of the vines sticking into her skin. Her skin felt green when she closed her eyes like this. Her muscles relaxed.

On the picnic table beside her sat a basket half-full with late-summer vegetables: tomatoes (ever prolific), bell peppers, eggplant, hot peppers. She thought she would take them in and make another pot of ratatouille, even though everyone else who happened to be home sort of ate through it without recognizing the gift of it, transparent in hedonistic eating. She feasted on it with all of her senses.

Mel also had not known she could cook. But the greenery of fresh, dew-covered herbs and rows of bulging, sensual vegetables springing from the earth and smelling of the soil's minerals had inspired her to thumb through a new heap of cookbooks to look for ways of cooking them that favored their sensuality. And when she had perfected baba ghanoush and lamb stew and ratatouille, she suddenly found herself up to her elbows in clouds of whole wheat flour and with the aroma of fresh-baked bread emanating from the oven and surrounding her, even in her remote bedroom. Her family kitchen engulfed the plot of land and then snaked tendrils out in search gardens and farms and mills outside its walls and outside the yard's fences and was pulling them in, devouring them too, using its magic of combination and of heat to bewitch Mel and draw her back and back and back.

The smells went with her everywhere: garlic on her fingers, beef roast (pregnant with sweet onion and caramelized carrot) in her hair, peppermint on the skin and lanugo of her forearms. She took the food with her, too. There was the warm, lemon-cinnamony smell of Moroccan chickpeas and couscous wafting from her lunch pail. There were co-workers' birthday cakes layered with mocha frosting and dripping with homemade caramel. There were potluck entrances where she uncovered trays of neatly-wrapped dolmades glistening with olive oil or blue-cheese stuffed olives garlanded with pansies and rose petals from her own garden. She was a quick learner, her creations emanating from her like the arms of Kali, but where nourishment replaced death.

༄ ༅

Two paths converged. Annie woke up from her impromptu nap just in time to dash out the door and catch a taxi and her flight. Mel went inside and made the ratatouille and ate it with her parents as they made sidelong comments about how much they loved having her around and did she have any long-term housing plans? (She did! She did! How it was not happening yet, she couldn't even say.) Then Mel went up to her room with an arm full of work papers. As she slid her feet into her slippers and simultaneously read the first paragraph in an open binder, she happened to catch a glimpse of the calendar on her desk. She remembered with a start that she was picking Annie up in the middle of the night from the Detroit Metro Airport. Crap. Oh well.

The airport was quiet, the few people who were around and about scattered loosely over the grounds; solitary figures leaning obliquely in dark corners, eyes slanted outward and thoughts slanted inward, a wreath of smoke. Mel crept by the doors outside baggage pickup, listening to the pull of tires on tiny stones chipped from the pavement, from the world, and scanning the sidewalk for Annie. The wind had been pouring in the windows for the forty-five minute drive southward and around the suburbs to the west of Detroit, cool and dry, beating at her face, pulling at her hair, and drowning out the radio. Now, the wind tapped at the car—at the space between the half-opened window and roof—and at her face, an irregular, light drum beat, full of impending dew, the smell of pavement and the day's burnt oil.

Mel saw Annie in a pool of light loaded down with black luggage and nosed the car up toward the curb. They struggled the heavy bags into the trunk and then Annie slid into the passenger seat with a bulging backpack on her lap. She leaned her head back on the seat rest and sighed. "Man, I am *so* tired. I kept nodding off during the flight."

"I bet. I kept the windows open on the way here so I wouldn't fall asleep while driving."

"Yeah, thanks for picking me up. It was such a bad time, but at the time the savings seemed like a good idea."

"Oh. No. It's fine. I didn't mean…"

"Well, I'm sure you would rather be in bed." The wind picked back up in the car as Mel edged onto the freeway, until the wind was a torrent. Annie ended her comment with a shout and Mel let it be ripped away from them in the night.

Mel thought that Annie had fallen asleep when she noticed passing headlights flash across her glistening eyes. She yelled to her, "YOU KNOW, THERE'S THIS BENEFIT BAKE SALE AT MY WORK THIS WEEK! IF YOU WANTED TO COME…!"

"WHAT'S IT FOR?"

"THERE'S A READING PROGRAM, LIKE I READ WITH A LITTLE KID AT A LOCAL SCHOOL ONCE A WEEK! THE BENEFIT IS FOR THE PROGRAM!"

"SURE! MAYBE I'LL COME! I DON'T REALLY HAVE ANY PLANS!" And the yelling over the wind exhausted out.

A few days later Annie made her way to the front desk of Captiv Design Services with a Tupperware container of blondies tucked under her arm and followed the receptionist's directions winding through the hallways and cubicle aisles to Mel's desk. Annie stood in the entrance to the cubicle and scanned the retro unicorn calendar and the Slinky and the stress ball and the photos lined up on the shelf at eye-level. She held the Tupperware neatly at her pelvis and shifted awkwardly while Mel quietly sketched for her the basic form of work at an engineering firm.

Then Mel walked Annie in the mazelike layout of endless, stifling air conditioning and fluorescent lights, halfheartedly pointing out the great ideas and the ergonomic chairs, the cafeteria with its artificially lemony smell and the centrally located, sneeze-guarded salad buffet.

Next to the kitchen was a long, broad room, void of furniture and carpeted with brown, industrial Berber on cement. The few windows were un-curtained and light shafted in, slanting against the commercial-grade dust. Mel conscripted Annie to move tables from a nearby storage closet, unhinging them from tall racks of metal framework. They set them up in neat rows in the long room, peopled the tables with a few chairs a piece, and covered the table tops with bright paper cloths. Kitchen staff wandered in and set out a corner table of ice water pitchers, leaning towers of Styrofoam cups and plastic cups designed for a meager sip of fluid, and monstrous, shining silver coffee carafes, ticking as they worked, and smelling of low-grade burnt coffee. In fact, almost not like coffee, but like burn.

Annie was handed a platter and set out her blondies in blooming concentric circles, little crumbs filling the cracks between. She used the Sharpie thrust in her hand to write a reluctant price on a folded index card. 50 cents. That seemed like a pretty good deal for a benefit bake off. Then she placed herself squarely behind the table with the blondies and waited, her most casual expression gracing her face.

A couple hours later Mel wandered Annie's way and stood over her shoulder. "So? How's it going? It looks good."

"Yeah. Most of the food has sold. My blondies are gone, thank goodness. There was some really awesome food. Like *yours*. And then there was stuff like *that*." Annie pointed a crooked, wagging finger at a plate heaped with clearly burnt chocolate chip cookies and a tray of mystery muffins the color of an orange Easter egg. They were clumped together at the far, front corner of the table, like two nerds clinging together on the fringe of prom in the school gym.

"Perhaps we should move them?" Mel reached over Annie and slid the two trays toward the middle of the table, which was currently uninhabited.

"I don't think it will help." Annie lowered her voice to a whisper and cupped her hand next to her mouth. "I was afraid they might scare people away."

"Well, there's almost no one left." Mel scanned the room, leaned forward with her hands buckled under her straight arms on the low table. Her fingers were turned toward her body, as if they were free-swinging from her arms, slender wrists forming right angles with the table top and sporting thin, black rubber bracelets which delineated the long-lined-thinness and mirrored the quick sleeve cuts of her tight black T-shirt against her shoulders.

"It went well, yeah?"

"Yeah. Yeah. We raised more than we needed. So it's great."

"And you won like eighty-two awards."

Mel's cheeks rouged and she looked out the window. "That was probably unfair since I helped organize everything."

"Except all your food was amazing. Some of it even *looked* unbelievable. And I bought a cream puff from the table here. It was exquisite. And so dainty and *fancy*. When did you learn to cook like that?"

"Whatever. Just recently. I really enjoy it. Really. It's fun."

"Well I'll have to have you over to make us all dinner some night, or do you just do sweets?"

"No way, I'm a full-blown foodie. You mean the whole fam?"

"Well, except Gaby."

"Yeah, I know, except Gaby." Again her focus shifted out the window to a silver stretch of parking lot and the lacquered paint of lines of cars in red, white, black, tan, and gray, glinting back at the sun and a characterless blue-washed sky. A young tree leaned into the frame of the window, hugging the building, and thrashing translucent, lime-green leaves against the window. The leaves twirled in and out of blue shadow and blank white light, occasionally plastering themselves to the glass, revealing their tender skeleton in stained glass against the sunlight, clear and naked and vulnerable. And brief.

Mel stood this way, with her left hand bent against her cocked hip, for a full minute until Annie—rearranging the loose cookies onto one plate and making a "FREE. TAKE ONE" sign complete with ska-inspired checkerboard edging—interrupted her. "Can you believe this is where we are? Working a juvenile reading benefit and hawking cookies for the sake of literacy... And Gaby's not even here twisting our arms?"

"Seriously." They both smiled in on themselves, their eyes shifting in the way they do when recalling someone or something familiar. Remembering. Her lean, generously-maned face and her mischievous eyes, sparkling over massive tureens of steaming soup-kitchen soup.

CHAPTER 27
HOMEWARD BOUND
ℰ   ℭ

Gaby barely slept before Andrew showed up in the courtyard in front of her hostel, a beat-up piece of wheeled luggage fallen in a streak of sludge, a back pack lamely strewn across it, and the tell-tale paperback book rolled in his hand. His other hand was hooked on his back pocket, his hips shifted to one side and his chin and shoulders tipped two different directions. He smiled nervously through the post-rain urban mist and in the outlining, silver light of modern establishment. Tragedy became him. He looked beautiful posturing there; his full lips and straight teeth, his doe eyes and tousled hair. She was afraid of him.

They handled each other like china dolls. Very little was said, especially anything of substance. He was going straight to the airport outside Tel Aviv and would just wait until there was a plane to the states that he could board. Her fingertips touched his temple and traced the length of a lock of hair, she looked intensely at the dip to the outside of his eye. Such soft skin there.

"How will you sleep?"

"Just in the airport. The ground. Or a bench."

"Oh."

And then they walked quietly to the taxi. He wouldn't let her shoulder his backpack or yank the suitcase in spastic lurches along the old stones. He did that himself. He let her walk beside him, holding the rolled book in both hands and swaying. Her beauty was a comfort. Warm like gingerbread cookies. Like patchouli and Turkish tea and honey, all alabaster and ebony and sweet and spicy. But he didn't think of it in those terms, he just walked in near-absence, his mind unsettled.

His goodbye was chilly and hasty, as he kept a leery eye on the taxi driver who loaded up his bag and had already started talking steadily at him about Ameerica. Their kiss was virginal, soft skin pressed against soft skin and then a whisper of it left on the lips as their eyes dropped so low they brushed at their cheekbones.

Andrew lowered himself into the taxi, backing away from Gaby. She stood at the car door as it shut against her, just another *thwap!* in a busy city alleyway. She edged closer to the door; she was almost pressing her stomach against the metal of the car. The window reflected mostly black up at her, with a modernist spatter of bright, clearly delineated circles and dots and rhomboids, distorted in the smooth glass. Her own face looked faintly back up at hers, from behind a rudely disfigured waist and soft mounds of breast. She could see up her nostrils, see her cheekbones slicing toward the darkness cupping under her eyes. But she bobbed her head, looking for Andrew behind all the refraction, a serious panic arresting her.

She found his face, there, looking back at her, but only in pieces through the moving glare. Their eyes caught, but the catching felt weak. She couldn't hold him there as the taxi pulled forward in quick jerks. He was now a movement of shadow in the window and she pressed her left hand on the glass as flat as she could and tried to hold it firm. The slapping sound that the gesture made called his attention and Andrew slapped his hand back against hers. She could sense his solidity beneath the smooth glass. She stared at his hand, there, in silhouette, greedily. And she ran beside the taxi, with her hand still stuck. For several steps she managed to stay like this, tripping over the stones and the urban debris. But the taxi eased into its speed and pulled away from her. Her hand separated from the window but her arm stayed taut, reaching out into the city, out into the chaos of a Jerusalem night.

❧ ☙

Gaby surfaced on a stone wall of a very old cemetery, which was situated on a slight slope near the city wall on a precipice that fell to just one street and the Hinnom Valley before the New City spread itself out in all its modern Middle Eastern glory. She could see a little Old City, but mostly New; million dollar apartments and stores with rack after rack of black clothing and grungy grocers with fading posters on the windows and Arabic music with halting, frenzied beats and wavering voices pumped into the crowds. Lights in the dark. Millions of orange lights and a sickly orange glow. But it felt beautiful, too.

Gaby was trying to think of all those strange moments in her life that gifted her with an unexpected smile, the kind that came all the way up from the toes. The time when she was driving down the road in Nadine's minivan, Mikhail behind the wheel for once, and they looked over to see a magnificent white horse galloping along the side of the road, mane and tail streaming out behind it, and mounted by a handsome and photo-perfect Native-appearing man, dressed in pow-wow worthy garb: feathers, beads, leather. The sun shone on him. His long hair trailed out behind him, too. Gaby and Mikhail looked at each other to make sure they were not losing their sense of reality. They pointed and exclaimed. Their car pulled further and further ahead and the man and horse were gone.

There was another time when Gaby walked through a Wal-Mart (Oh, how she had once loved the cheapness of Wal-Mart, when she was blissfully naive!) and she was suddenly breezed from behind, nudged a little to the side by her sense that something was about to swoop around her from behind. And something did: he swerved around her, just missed her, and kept going; a small, East Asian man (so stereotypical in stature and appearance), with a few items under his arms, and bound for the check-out lines; riding a pink, little girl's bike, the handlebar streamers ruffling in the breeze he was creating in the staleness of this inside world.

And another time, (was she with Mikhail, again?) driving down another freeway. Gaby and Mikhail looked over together to see a station wagon slide by in a lane (of many) to the left. The car was filled with uniform foliage, plastered against every window, both fore and aft, and even protruding from couple-inch cracks at the tops of three of the side windows. "Whuh? What? It looks like a bush has taken over the car!" "Like a bad horror movie," he said. They laughed.

Why did these things bring pleasure? What was it about the different, the unexpected, that made them enjoyable? Was it innocence? Was it possible that not knowing anything but the obvious part of the story gave Gaby immense joy?

She shook her head as if to clear it and then wondered what a strange gesture that was. Did she do it because she had some sort of Hollywood-formed idea that this is what people did to represent clearing their heads? Or was it just so natural to shake your head when it was clogged with swirling thoughts that people just did it, including her, just now. Then despite herself, she shook her head clear again.

Sitting above the city like this, inhaling its majesty and its pungency, she sort of panicked at the thought of leaving. Could she live here forever? Did she want to? How disoriented was she by Andrew leaving? Should she chase him? This appealed to her adventurous nature, surely, but was it true that she was really more logical than adventurous? There was also a part of her that wanted to lean forward into the desert wind, open her arms at her sides, and fall out over the rooftops. Then catch in the wind and be tossed up, master the forces with her body as she kneaded the night air with her limbs. The blackness below and above her, the orange light streaking past her retinas and waiting below in the soft, rushing landscape, the hard lines of the city melting into a dark desert, stretching out and up. She would fly until she was cold and the stars were scraping against her face like so many butterfly wings.

Out in the lonely winds she could feel a heaviness in her chest that threatened to sink her back down to the earth.

ᑫ ᕫ

The Angel had a habit of stealing into The Queen's chambers, when he was in the neighborhood. He never let her know, never so much as left her a note or attempted to wake her with his breath on her exposed neck. He flew in at the balcony, under cover of dark, and walked in at the open doors. For this reason, he came mostly in the summer, when even the palace necessitated a fresh breeze.

The Queen noticed that the men and horses and even trees on the war table would move on their own, in the night. Only once in a long while. She dreamed it might be The Angel, even after all those years. But then she told herself she was playing tricks on herself, deluding herself. How could she, The Queen, want this affirmation after all this time? She slid the errant knight back with a trembling hand.

Her guards pushed the giant doors wide and Jaden came striding in through the doorway behind her, his voluminous robes trailing behind him. He was still very powerful in build, stood unwaveringly tall and straight, just like The Queen, in fact. He walked without hesitation, saw her standing there with her back to him, a hand outstretched toward the war table, her crowned head inclined as if in contemplation, her silver hair falling to her waist, where her purple cloak trailed to the stone floor.

"The Sage is here," he said without preamble.

She didn't even look up. "Oh?"

"You don't seem surprised." She was unable to truly join the conversation, she was so lost in her private memories.

"It has been a long time since we have seen him." The Queen spoke trance-like.

"I almost thought we had never seen him. I was beginning to think he was from our collective imagination."

"Yes, he was mostly from before your time." There was a soft, broken tone given to the last three words. The Queen thought better of herself, lifted her chin, and turned her powerful gaze out onto the room that had almost dissolved around her, toward her old husband.

"That's just part of it. How can he still be alive? Is it an apprentice?" Jaden seemed quizzical and amused.

"No, no apprentice." She allowed herself a smile at him. "He has the gift of longevity. I have a feeling his life is very far from over, very unlike ourselves."

"That again? You want to just hand over the kingdom when you have been such a magnificent ruler—"

"You sound afraid of our children."

"Enough. This is a tired fight. But still, you believe that The Sage really has such a gifting?"

"Why not? Even when you have had a life as remarkable as your own, with such impressive giftings yourself, you are loathe to believe?"

"I just—" He was not accustomed to faltering, and came back with a booming voice, "No one lives that long!"

The Queen had an unnerving ability to stay calm when no one else could manage. "It is very rare, yes."

"Well, whoever this jester is," he caught her eye and coughed, changed his tone, "he would like an audience."

"Of course."

Just as she said this, the two guards standing like statues at the doorway, facing outward, sprung to life and each aimed a weapon at the chest of a man who now stood still and oddly unperturbed. He raised a hand in greeting to The Queen and smiled, tilted his head.

"Please! Guards! Stand aside! He is a friend." She offered a hand to him and he came across the floor, taking it for a moment, feeling the heat of the ring against his own skin. Without looking down, he said, "I see you still wear it. Or what is left of it."

If The Queen flushed at all it was just barely. "Yes, I do."

"That is just what I have come to talk to you about."

"Oh."

Jaden couldn't just stand there, gawping. "What is he going on about?"

The Queen turned toward her husband, not unkindly touched the side of his neck with her warm hand. "The magical seed. The one that saved the kingdom."

"You *wear* it? *Where?* In your crown? And what does it matter, anyhow? It's just a seed!"

"Did we not just have this conversation?"

"You may not speak to me like that!"

"Likewise." The room fell silent, but the smiling Sage, in all his fly-away, shapeless and colorless garments, shuffled forward to continue.

"Queen, King, you grow old. I need to make sure that the seed remains safe."

"I wear it, as you have said. But, only in part, as you seem to have guessed. It's power has diminished since it was nearly destroyed in battle by the blade of a Demoni."

"Where is the rest of it?" He looked very pointedly at The Queen, who gazed anywhere but at him. She took a long while to answer, but then spoke just before her husband started to make excuses for her.

"I hid it away, many years ago. Very far from here. I am sure it is not there, anymore." What she said was enough for him to read between the words, to find what was there in her memory that she was not telling. He nodded slowly.

"All right, then. I believe that the seed is most definitely *not* safe, which is what I expected. There will be much strife, much pain, much striving. In other words, nothing much will change."

"Can't we do something?" she breathed.

"No point. Like I said, nothing much will change. You put one half away the best you knew how, keeping the other close to you, but they will come out, they will re-enter the world." Jaden appeared half-curious, half flabbergasted at all the shenanigans, as if listening intently to a foreign language.

"But *why?*"

"The fate of mankind was determined a very long time ago. I merely sought to bottle some of its tears, preemptively I suppose. I thought that encapsulating story: fate and history and pre-story, would help more people turn. It turns out you cannot force fate. That is why it is fate. But that doesn't mean the seed doesn't have its place. It does. Just as the story continues without it, and has its own place. The storytellers..." he looked affectionate as he said this.

"But the Dark Leader has the stories."

"Not completely. And not forever. The stories are made to endure. The seed is just a piece of a vast, almost endless puzzle. It is a magic that is left in the world, and some people will need magic. Some will need something much stronger. Like him." The Sage gestured to the king.

The Queen was following, mostly. Jaden had never been known for his intelligence or faith, and now stood grimacing. "So, she said, "What hope is there for them?"

"Ahh—" The Sage grinned at her even more enthusiastically. "That's just it, you wise woman. Hope."

☙ ❧

When Butter received the call—in all its awkward trans-Atlantic glory—there were plenty of whoops and sighs to ease Gaby's heart into the idea of going home. They wanted her. Just the thought of it made her feel so tired she started fantasizing about sinking into layers of clean, fluffy down and thick, flouncy pillows, in a noiseless, sunny room right in the middle of the American dream. She would share lively meals around a bounteously-laid, if not a little processed, dinner table, check out fifteen books at the library, and litter her floor with Doritos and Famous Amos wrappers. In fact, she would cocoon herself in there with journals and TV (on a station other than *The Bold and the Beautiful*) and stereo with subwoofers. Sprawl out on the plastic-made carpet and just disappear with a hot bowl of Ramen noodles. Faygo Rock 'N' Rye.

Afentra was sad to see Gaby go. The evening they spent out at Second Cup having a final friend-date was mellow and they discussed if Afentra shouldn't also think about heading back to the states. Maybe she would come and visit Gaby sooner than later. Their eyes sparkled with tears shrouded in the steam from their mugs.

Stateside, it worked out well, since Annie had only been in town a few days and would be there long enough to see Gaby and to overlap the interviews. Annie was mostly holed up in the room next to what would become the Dorito cocoon, recharging *her*self with a shelf of childhood books: *Matilda, The Wheel on the School, A Wrinkle in Time, Caddie Woodlawn*; and Stellar's home-cooking and laundry services, meeting with Mercedes, daily.

Melodie and Annie had fallen into a routine; Mel came straight over from work to change into a bathing suit and sit out poolside in the back yard. They made sure they did the things that accompanied sun-bathing so well: pedicures and manicures, sipped lemonade and sangria, casually devoured chick mags and low-brow literature. And floated on the still water on fluorescent mats, sending out turquoise ripples to the perfect tile edges of the rectangle pool and out across the un-cracked cement, past the spired metal fence (also in a perfect rectangle) and across TruGreen, manicured lawns out and out and out. The blue sky shimmered above them. The sun baked them.

Annie apprehensively invited Gaby to the party a few days later and reported to Mel (also apprehensively) her visions of three young women with cotton balls between their toes and sunglasses holding back their hair. Mel looked tight, dubious. Anyhow, Gaby was flying in around lunchtime on a week day, which meant that Mel or any other normal working stiff was unable to meet her at the airport. Annie in fact had been doing a little work from Butter, just a little writing and a telephone call here or there. The day Gaby was flying in, she scheduled a lunch meeting with a fellow environmental journalist in Detroit. She told Gaby she would be there as soon as she could. Gaby might have to wait at the curb a few minutes.

Annie pulled the garment bag she had packed out of the closet and hung it in the bathroom. Cleaned up, primed her face with makeup, created good scents everywhere, mounds of glossy, blonde hair, and a sheen on her skin. She struck an impressive vision, with her stylish heels, tailored pencil skirt, her ironed blouse, her tucked clutch. And the way she suddenly walked differently, erect and with quick, deliberate steps: thwak, thwak, thwak, thwak.

She backed the car out of the driveway in much the same way, swooping into the street and then pulling off down the road with a fluid movement and not a moment's hesitation, her chin lifted up above the steering wheel and her lips and eyes set in a polished indifference.

Annie's lunch went well, the kid looked out of sorts at the pricey Greektown Casino restaurant, but she managed to extract answers loud enough to understand and encourage over the din of other business lunches. She then aimed Stellar's Sable toward the airport. Just outside, she stopped for gas. She had under-eaten at lunch in order to conduct a thorough meeting and so she left the car at the pump and went in to buy herself an iced tea and something salty. When she emerged from the convenience store, she looked like the beginning of a romantic comedy, her long legs pumping her forward, her neat clothes rippling in the breeze and shining in the sun, her arms working to hold her clutch and un-cap her tea and her right shoulder propping her cell phone to her ear, her hair thrown back over her shoulder as she turned to scan traffic in the fuel bays.

It's hard to say whether the oncoming car was going just that much too fast or whether Annie's phone conversation was engaging her more than enabling her to correctly judge the traffic patterns of those around her; these questions would be hashed out to the point of obscurity later in the judicial system and the driver of the blue Mazda would claim with candor that it was the fault of The Black Eyed Peas. Annie stepped forward, an engine gave a loud rev, Adam—on the other end of the phone conversation—heard a jumbled series of thuds and yells which ended in the mouthpiece of the phone scraping long against the cement as it went sailing away in artistic spirals.

⚃ ⚄

Gaby waited for Annie at the curb outside of international baggage claim. She tired of standing and found a place on a bench, where she huddled her luggage close to herself. She tired of people-watching and fished a book out of her carry-on, which she read under compulsion; the plot was dragging and she had already been reading it for something like five hours today. Enough, already.

She timed how often she looked up at the clock mounted above the exterior of the exit doors and wished that she had a cell phone. Gaby went back into her carry-on and dug around for her wallet and pulled it out. Opened the zippered pouch and fished around for change. How much did a pay phone cost, anyhow? And did she have Annie's number? She certainly knew home by heart. She could call collect.

Gaby stood with her nose still in the pouch, and looked up to locate a phone and calculate just how annoying it would be to drag all her luggage to it. Just then, her sight caught on an older woman, hunched over into a cane and struggling to pull a small travel case behind her along the crosswalk. She appeared to be heading for the bus stop out on an island in traffic.

Gaby didn't think, she just jumped up and jogged the ten paces or so to the woman. "Would you like some help?" she offered, reaching for the handle of the case.

"Oh!" The woman looked up into Gaby's face and took her time assessing the situation. "Well, yes, dear. I really could." She surrendered the handle to Gaby. "That's very sweet of you."

They moved slowly across the street, the woman shuffling and leaning with small steps and Gaby staying right beside her.

This one was more clear. Gaby and the woman were simply crossing snail's-pace traffic in a clearly marked pedestrian crosswalk and keeping up the fastest pace her walking would allow. The driver of the Dodge Shadow was in some kind of hurry, and its pointed nose picked them both up and violently sprawled them onto its hood. The rolling case crunched under its front, right wheel before it screeched to a stop. When the Shadow stopped, the old woman readjusted on the hood, but Gaby went rolling forward and off onto the cement.

The driver jumped out of the car and went running at Gaby, her eyes wild. Gaby knew there were several fires lit in her body but that she couldn't move, that there was a loud and blurry face weaving in front of her darkening vision, that coming to her out of the yelling and the noise of traffic was a song pulsing in the air. A track from Putumayo's *Mali to Memphis* came lilting to her from the radio of the Shadow and put her into a deep, deep sleep.

CHAPTER 28
THE ANGEL

ℰ   ℭ

They say for a moment time stopped.

The Angel stood quietly over Gaby's hospital bed. Well, in this world he was quiet, as always: unperceived, stealthy. In another realm—the realm where they wrinkled time for Gaby's sake—his face was radiant and (even with his mouth shut) his skin sang.

Mikhail also stood over Gaby's bed, calmly moving his eyes up and down the rises and falls of her body under the thin, bleach-stinking linens. He wanted to set his hands on an arm or a shoulder or at least take her hand, but even the thought of it was too awkward and inappropriate to bear so he moved it farther from the front. He laid it aside, where all of the years of discarded love lay. The graveyard was starting to take over the town.

He had a feeling he should move forward or move on now. He was shadowing over Gaby, she was in a coma, just returned from a year abroad. He imagined himself in a soap opera; what he would do right now: throw his body across hers and weep pent-up tears until her sheets were wet with them, all the while exclaiming poetic renditions of his undying love. He got a little carried away with the idea and muttered out loud, "I love you."

When he heard his own voice in the beeps and whirs of the hospital room he jumped. Then to save his own sense of dignity, he said it louder and clearer, "I love you."

His imagination again began to take over, and he was seeing Gaby move a finger, and then a hand, and then flutter her eyes open and then acknowledge him. Behind the veil of his fantasy, the beeps and whirs remained steady, the noises in the hall encroached in muffles and then receded away, the stillness of movement in the room palpable, as if cotton were filling the room instead of an unflattering blend of obstructed sunlight and industrial light, so tight that nothing could move.

The Angel felt Mikhail move his toe very slowly along the edge of the bed stand, tracing a dirt-embedded crack in the linoleum until it touched the hem of a sheet that was spilling over the edge of the bed and cascading down to it. Without him thinking, Mikhail's eyes followed the sheet back up and over and rested on Gaby's face. She looked terrible, really, with all the tubes and the lacerations and swelling in her face. Her tongue blackened from lack of saliva, he had been told, that's all. But he could see the vestiges of her beauty there: the fullness of black waves falling back from her face and stuck with medical tape; her heavy lashes—as if finally exhausted from the weight—laying almost flat. So still. He was sure he had never seen Gaby so still.

A lump suddenly pushed out in his chest and he pushed back against it while blinking his eyes. Heat rushed to his face, rushed all over his body. He folded his hands together and noticed they were shaking; each one gripping at the fingers of the other for some sort of leverage. There was none, and he was startled again to hear his voice, gasping at the air. Then a metaphorical curtain pulled back and he sobbed into the stillness, his shoulders heaved into the sobs and his hands searched for sanctuary on the bed. He took Gaby's arm under his hands, as if he was about to give her an Indian burn and the thinness and solidity of her arm sent him into a few more spasms.

Suddenly, as a surprise, his breath caught again in his throat and maintained its usual rhythm in and out of him. The lump melted inside and he put his hands to his face, erasing the hot itch that spread from his eyes and down his cheeks. He began to pat alongside her bed, looking at her face and still composing himself one lip-lick at a time.

This wasn't just shadows of something, he thought. He would do anything... and he had to break off his thought when he felt a lump building again. He gave it a minute. He would do anything to be allowed to love her freely.

αβ

Melodie stood alone beside the hospital bed, right as the sun dipped below the horizon outside and emptied the room of any sunlight that had been there. A hospital attendant reached in the door behind Mel's back and switched the lights to dim and then sidled back out, filling the room with a single click of the door jamb. Mel pivoted her chin, looked back over her shoulder and then straight back to Gaby, nothing else about Mel's body wavering: not her straight posture, her defeated shoulders, her arms slack at her side, her lips just barely parted over her teeth, her dimmed eyes. Her nose was running and she was forgetting to blink and gumming up her contacts.

"Gaby?" She felt her voice sucking into the room and away from them.

"Gaby? Please."

She stood there like this for a long time more as the hospital sounded its routine noises and The Angel stood vigil on the other side of the bed. Mel shut her eyes and wanted to fall asleep into the blackness, but instead heard someone coming down the hall outside the door. In a voice creased throughout with age, a woman called repeatedly, "Gracie! Gracie! Gracie!"

Then another voice, much younger and professional in tone approached on solid footsteps and muffled something at the other voice. There was a scuffle of bodies and feet as the older woman raised her voice in increments into a panic, yelling "Where's Gracie? Where's my Gracie? Gracie! Gracie!" This last blast of sound exerted right at the door to Gaby's room, and then the scuffle moved on down the hall and the voices washed away in receding waves until there was only an industrial hum, again.

As if a meditation were over, Mel opened her eyes. She looked down at Gaby and sighed. "Gaby? Gaby? I don't know what to do, Gaby. I'm going to talk to you. Maybe you'll hear me. What do you want to hear? What could possibly help you right now? I'll do it. I'm sorry. I should have told you about the protest, should have told you I liked Mikhail. Just come back to us. Please. Just come back. I don't know how to hold together without you, never have." Her eyes filled up slowly and tears seared their way down to her chin. Her voice cracked around the hole in her throat.

"And this whole world just won't be what it has been without you. It just won't. I don't think you should go, yet. Let's get old, yeah?"

Mel suddenly felt an overwhelming exhaustion descend on her voice. She thought she could stand there and ramble on and on just so that Gaby would have a voice to hear. Mel had visions of reading stories out to her, of telling her daily anecdotes, to get her through these long days. But now there was an unspannable break in the earth over which her voice refused to carry her. She might have felt annoyed with herself, but the exhaustion sunk further into her.

The door behind her opened and she jumped a little at the intrusion, but did not turn around. A draft of cooler air touched on her back, her shoulders, the nape of her neck.

When Andrew quietly opened the hospital door and slipped into the silence, he did not expect anyone else to be there. What he saw, there, were stray hairs lifting in a draft and flitting against a sculpted neck, shining white against auburn hair and dark clothes and the general dimness. A shiver moved down his own spine. He considered that there were many things about coming to Gaby's hospital room that might make him shiver. He considered he should have known someone else might be here during visiting hours.

"Hello?" he ventured.

"Oh." Mel turned around, her green eyes wide and still wet. She had not bothered to wipe the tears from her face. In a moment, she thought that it might be Adam or Mikhail or some other male relative who was one of many hanging around the hospital at all hours, intersecting in lines pulled taut against the unthinkable. But when she saw his face her own changed instantaneously to surprise. "Do I know…?"

"I'm Andrew." He extended his hand to her, which she took rather lamely, and the shake was completely one-sided and not a little impressive.

"Oh…" Mel was again caught with her voice stuck back. And thus they stood, for some time, studying each other's faces. Mel's thoughts sort of popped forward and a reasonable sentence presented itself. "So you're Gaby's boyfriend? I can't imagine…" it drifted off again. "I mean, it's nice to meet you."

"And you are?" he was smiling lop-sided at her to de-venom the question.

"Oh, right. Mel." She couldn't imagine how to explain her right to be here in a concise sobriquet. Had she a right to be here?

"Sure. Yeah. You don't have to go any further. I know all about you, too." He found himself staring at her again, the softness of her startled face against the harshness of the room. "And, I don't know… I'm not Gaby's boyfriend, anymore. Sounds like someone found my and Afentra's contact information in her satchel?"

"Was it right to call you?"

He hung his head and shook it a little. "Yeah. Yeah, of course. I mean, I came all the way here…"

"Must be true love," she mused and smiled crookedly back at him.

"Hm."

Ω   Ω

Betsy was in Detroit on business. She was in an office ferreted away behind the sparse beauty of the DIA and sipping on a coffee, the timing of her flight in from Phoenix making her a little early. There were remnants of a dissected weekend paper, a little outdated, discarded and spread out haphazardly on the long, chair-flanked table. Betsy sifted through them and sipped with her legs crossed, her eyes intelligent, her nails neatly manicured. And there, buried in the print and peeking out behind some Garfield comics was a headline that caught her eye. "Local Twins in Simultaneous Automobile Accidents." What surprised her more than the story, of course, was that right there buried in the first sentence was a name that she not only recognized but had been actively seeking. Sonja's Gaby was in a coma at University of Michigan Hospital.

When the rest of the smartly-dressed artsy-business people in black started sifting in, Betsy had a sort of far-away look on her face and she shook her head minutely to return to her work. She chewed on the backside of her pen during the meeting and as soon as it was over she excused herself to attend to some "personal matters." "Is everything all right?"

"Yes, fine." And then furrowed and arched eyebrows followed her out of the room.

She caught a taxi all the way out of the city and into Ann Arbor, to the hospital. What she had been thinking about—besides Gaby and the strange coincidence—was in her briefcase, which was in itself another strange coincidence, just part of a bizarre story, now, it seemed.

Her heels clicked up and down the hallways of the hospital until she learned that it was presently visiting hours and that she could go to the waiting room and talk with Gaby's ever-present family and friends about when she might go in to see her. The nurse said that someone was bound to be in with her right now, already. The family was very obliging—and surprised too—and sent word in to some cousins to go ahead and come out of the room soon because Gaby had a new visitor; a "special visitor from out-of-town" they generously labeled her.

Betsy entered timidly around the heavy door, which had been cracked only a little, and shut it quietly behind her. She stood surveying the room, the patient, the still-slender arms laying limp in the narrow bed and crossed with tape and needles and tubes. The face. Was that the face she remembered? Surely it couldn't be expected to look the same now as it did then, when Gaby was really just an innocent and so healthy despite her exhaustion and grief. The room must have been cold: the hairs on the back of her neck were rising.

She had not expected this; but the tears came to her eyes and came to her eyes so that they overflowed tears which worked their way in jumps down over her cheek bones and around her tightened mouth and to her chin, where they jumped kamikaze style one-at-a-time through the vast expanse and onto the plastic floor.

The Angel looked at the tears pooling there in the dust. To him, they looked aquamarine and incandescent. The tears on Betsy's face looked like war paint, then, in the crooked lines of the juvenile coloring. Her eyes glowed with them. Then again, her eyes were glowing anyhow, with a faint luster, like illuminated opal and amber and malachite. There was repentance behind those eyes, a mine of other things as well: loneliness and judgment and selfishness and anger and compassion. He saw into their lives through their eyes, like they could do with each other, somewhat. It was all the same, anyhow, that bentness and the need for grace. That's what angels were doing at bedsides and in conversation with young, pregnant women and in climbing up and down ladders. Grace dispensers, or glory-givers. Same thing. Just part of the big-picture job; all the hallelujahs and bowing down and an eternity of one-way glory.

The Angel reached across the bed, then, and slid his hand gently under Betsy's, guiding it inside the briefcase where she had been keeping it in stealth. He lifted, so slow that in her weak body she wouldn't know that there was any help. Not this time. The hand came up to her chin-level, palm up. She saw the ring there, and the moist, pink indentations in her flesh where she had been holding onto it. She blinked at it and blinked at it again. And then she set it down on the bedside table and left the room.

෬   ෭

The Angel completely filled the room; if not with physicality, then with presence, with light, with vibration, with energy, with heat, all emerging from another dimension and folding over onto itself so that if one were not paying careful attention, one could not see or feel these things at all. The clues were often reduced to vagaries, to moments of clarity, to arm hairs standing on end, to a cock of the head to the side and a narrowing of the eyes with questions behind them. When The Angel shifted a wing, it went swooping through half the room, its force so powerful that Afentra suddenly looked up from the book she was reading in one of the two visitors' chairs, quizzically.

A moment later Mikhail banged into the door as he wheeled Nadine in. Nadine held a flower arrangement in a vase with a card forked in the top, and another draft of air sucked through the width of the room and into the vent system. Afentra was still, watching the water slosh in the vase as Mikhail banged about awkwardly and Nadine grimaced.

"Well, hello." Nadine smiled at her. They had met, there in the waiting room. Nadine was on the verge of a discharge, Gaby's family told her. Nadine's blood count finally looked good and most of this remaining battle could be fought with a commute. Mikhail wheeled her down daily to visit Gaby. Afentra wondered if she would drive all the way in here to visit, once she was home. Afentra just wondered.

Afentra said hello, how-are-you, and good-to-see-you, released her book into her lap and adjusted as if to stand.

"Please. Don't get up on my account. I don't need to stay long. I was just bringing in these flowers."

"It's okay, Nadine. You stay as long as you like. I was just keeping her company." Afentra was at the edge of her seat. Making conversation, "Who are the flowers from?"

"Well, let's see." She balanced the vase on her lap and opened the envelope with a rip and her thumb. "Of course, they're not as beautiful as all these *other,* special flowers…" Nadine looked conspiratorially back at Mikhail and he reddened. She turned her attention to the card and sat reading to herself.

"Oh!" she moved her hand to her chest. "It seems that the mystery of the ring has solved itself!"

"Really? What does that say? Who is it from?" Afentra stood and moved toward Nadine as if to read over her shoulder, but Nadine had glanced behind Afentra and seen The Angel, standing there. She made a jump and her face filled with panic until The Angel said to her, "Do not be afraid," in a way that was indeed soothing. He quickly told her something else before dissolving from view in the corner of the room. Nadine made an odd movement and flipped the card closed, shoving it alongside her leg, away from Afentra, hoping Mikhail hadn't read it.

It was Afentra's turn. "Oh!"

"Can I ask you a question?"

"Yes, I suppose so."

"Mikhail, wheel me over there. She pointed to Gaby's bedside, where Nadine set the card down standing up in a V and scooped up the ring that was still sitting there, from a ceramic coaster that someone had provided. "Pick it up." She extended it out on her palm, toward Afentra. Afentra seemed nonplussed that this was not a question.

Afentra picked up the ring and brought it close to her face, turning it around and observing its pristine beauty. She closed her hand on the ring and closed her eyes for a moment, looked up at Nadine. "It's pretty, isn't it?"

"Look closer."

Without even opening her hand or looking. "Well, there's a little pebble inside the gem, isn't there? That's odd."

"Yes, yes it is." Nadine hadn't studied the ring herself, found her suspicions fulfilled.

Nadine watched as Afentra's eyelids flickered, as her chin made quick little movements from side to side. Afentra was in a skiff in the center of the sea of her memories and thoughts. She was rowing against the current to catch a particular drop of water. She was hoping it was not below the surface, or at least would churn back up to her, sometime. She was collecting droplets, was stringing them together on a fine wire. Was holding up the string of droplets to see it together. She closed her eyes.

She could see Gaby, sitting up in the hospital bed. She resisted the urge to turn and look to see... She saw Gaby smiling. Saw a strange wind come in and blow her hair back from her face. Saw her hold out her hands with palms up, without saying a word to her. Then she saw Gaby's elbow catch the vase next to the bed and send the whole thing falling to the floor with a time-lapsed arc and a silent crash. She saw the glass shards thrown across the floor in a pool of water and a spray of flowers, bent and bruised and throwing wild patterns of color there.

Afentra opened her eyes looking directly at Nadine and held out the ring to her. Nadine took the ring and put it back on the bedside. Afentra looked away, reluctantly, because what she had seen was amazing and cool but she was seeing something else in Nadine's eyes which she did not understand.

CHAPTER 29
THE TIMESES AND THE HERALDS REPORT
ON THE MATTER

ℰℭ   ℭℛ

The headline: "Local Twins in Simultaneous Automobile Accidents."

The first couple paragraphs of copy read: "6:30PM. June 30, 2002. Metro-Detroit Airport. 23-year-old Gabrielle LeFevre is helping an elderly woman navigate her luggage through busy airport traffic when she is hit by a Dodge Shadow and thrown onto the hood of the car. Known as "Gaby" to her friends, she is then taken to the University of Michigan hospital and admitted. She is currently in a coma.

"6:30PM. June 30, 2002. A Metro-Detroit Sunoco gas station. 23-year-old Anibel LeFevre is exiting the convenience store with her hands full of snacks and a cell phone in use when she is hit by a swerving Mazda and sent sprawling across the cement. Known as 'Annie' to her friends, she is taken to the University of Michigan hospital and admitted. She is currently being treated for minor injuries from the accident and a re-injury of her back.

"The combination of events is uncanny, at best. But when one is told that Gaby and Annie are fraternal twins, it is shocking."

 C8   8O

The headline: "Are Boonetown Sheep Populations at Risk?"

The first few paragraphs of copy read: "One of the cruel realities of shepherding is the occasional loss of a sheep to a predator. In Boonetown, where there are at least 25 separate flocks of sheep as well as a booming population of coyote, it is a common, cruel reality. For farmer Robert Hurley, June 30 was not one of those days."

"'I almost lost a couple sheep, Thursday. I was bringing them into the pen about dinnertime.' That's when Hurley noticed that his dogs were barking loudly and acting strange, followed by a half-dozen coyote emerging from the tree-line on the east side of his farm, Pine Barn Valley. Hurley watched from a distance of about 100 yards as the coyote approached quickly and were soon on the heels of the sheep, now funnelling into the open gate. The last sheep tucked itself into the pen and the gate slammed shut behind it. 'I don't know how it happened,' says Hurley. 'The gate was open and then it was shut. I was standing there watching helplessly and a shiver went up my spine. I don't know what else to say. It was a miracle.'"

C8   8O

The headline: "Dow Jones Takes a Hop, Skip, and a Jump."

Buried in the copy, it read: "It was an unprecedented day for the Dow Jones, as well as Standard and Poors and the

NASDAQ. In fact, the activity has left analysts mostly wagging their heads in confusion and wagging their fingers at various sources.

"'We just don't know what it was about that day and about that particular time that sent, well, what appears to be the business world, into such abrupt, disparate action.' says Harvard economics professor and author of *The Magic and Mechanisms of Wall Street*, James J. MacIlvoy. 'And once that happened, well it was all history, as they say.' Meaning, once the jump happened, the commercial community responded with a panic that sent numbers spiralling downward for days. Since no one has yet come up with a plausible explanation, the Dow Jones has yet to see a complete recovery."

ᙂ ᙀ

The headline: "Large Area of Indonesia's Palm Forest Saved."

The third paragraph of copy read: "Witnesses present at the signing are still baffled about what happened to change the outcome. Head engineer Joyce Waukegan has said, 'He was the engine driving everything. I don't know what made him stop the signing, but I'm sure he must be losing a ton of money.' An estimated $4 billion, according to experts. So what did happen? Truman's spokespeople have only said that he 'had a change of mind' and that Truman will remain Pelco's CEO and continue doing business as usual. This hardly seems plausible given his sudden appearance on the internet with a 'tree-hugging' agenda and a mysterious, impromptu, up-coming appearance on Oprah. Truman has said little about the event as of yet, but a later-deleted article from his website read, 'Everything about my life up until then just conspired against me and I had a change of heart, right there, with the pen poised over the paper. It felt like I had extra time just then, like someone's fingers paused over the keys writing my story, and then 'enter.' And yet, what business could possibly make sense of such a momentous decision?"

⋘ ⋙

The headline: "SJA Loses Pennant to Pickford, Thursday, 41-40."

The school paper article read: "It was an exciting game with an even more exciting conclusion. Unfortunately, the drama did not bode well for the Scranton Junior Academy girls' basketball team. It should be put in a movie. In fact, it probably already is a movie. The Pickford team was down by one with three seconds left on the clock. Pickford had possession of the ball under their own net. The ball was thrown in by Marcia Abbot to her sister, Amelia Abbot. A. Abbot went in for a layup, threw, and missed. SJA fans were nearly on their feet when a quick glance at the clock alarmed everyone that it had stopped. The head referee, William Ganny, made the judgement for a re-do. Pickford was given possession of the ball, again, under their own net, and the clock was examined and re-set. M. Abbot again handed off to A. Abbot who tried again for the layup. This time, with the crowd in the background yelling the countdown, A. Abbot made the shot. That made the score 41-40, and the SJA fans went home feeling cheated and defeated. Great season, girls!"

⋘ ⋙

The headline was: "I Saw the Light."

The conclusion of the editorial read: "There it is. Perhaps I have seen too many violent movies or just plain too many movies. Perhaps. But I am sticking to my story. Our fists, clenched tight for battle and stained already with the debris of spray paint and blood, floated in mid-air. The air vibrated around and above us, as if thousands of translucent gnats hazed between our yells, our angry stares, our fists, now paused in the trajectory of our swings. I could see it all, as slowly as I wanted to, and with the clarity of suspension. My mind raced through a run-away course of surprise and then contemplation before life snapped back into its normal bumpiness, its speed and its messiness. Both of our swings completely missed each other and levelled off out in the air. I looked down at my fist and stared hard. It was a stranger to me now that I had seen it so thoroughly. Then I was hit, from the side. I went down. And I knew then that I would never again throw another fist at anyone. Call this a pacifist's confession, a moment of impassioned lies, but I am, and will ever be, standing on the razor-thin edge of a pause in time."

CB   BO

The headline was: "The 6-30-6-30-2 Phenomenon."

The scientific paper copy read, somewhere in the middle: "Many are calling it the 6-30 Phenomenon, short for The 6-30-6-30-2 Phenomenon (sparing us all the mouthful). The name is the numerical time and date of the supposed event, which was 6:30pm on June 30, 2002. It was at that precise time that subjects claim to have each had their 'alternative experience.' The explanation most accepted by the subjects and their proponents (largely in various far-flung religious fields as well as with science-fiction fanatics) is that the space-time continuum was stopped for an unknown period. If that were true, the stoppage certainly affected the various subjects and witnesses in a multitude of ways and their perception of the 'time-jump' is not consistent one to another. Let us take a look, then, at the subjects' testimony and medical data and discover the psychological and sociological threads that bind them together."

CB   BO

The headline: "True Love, Tru Dat."

The middle of the lifestyles copy read: "He has invested an undisclosed amount of money in local flower shops, just filling her room with flowers of every shape and description. There is no space left untouched, uncolored. It is radiant, and almost overwhelmingly floral. It is a wonder the hospital has allowed this at all, but his pleading eyes are compelling. How can an institution compete with such ardent love?

"In the room filled with his flowers, Mikhail stands, shyly dragging his foot as I ask him questions. He is on day 42 of his arduous vigil. 'I just wanted to do something to let her know I love her.' Perhaps, one day, she will wake from her coma and tell him that she saw it all, behind those closed lids and through the stretch of time that they were together, but apart."

CB   BO

The Angel felt the sword heavy in his hand, a weight that was wonderfully perfect for the instrument. It was the sword he had used to slice the sky on his descent to earth, the slice that had severed time from itself. He had done it because he had been told to do it. The act was not complete. It was one that was magnanimous and wild. It was a gift for Gaby; something to contribute marvellously to her efforts, but mostly to slice her from her deeds. He could see it now, the long wound in her brain, cutting across the underside of her face and garishly red and disfiguring. If one could see it. He could. "That will leave a scar," he thought. And he held these things close to himself: he did what he was made for; he wanted her to come out severed and then cleaved in the end.

His brilliance projected from his chest upward and outward and skyward, but it grazed Gaby on the way by.

CHAPTER 30
THAT GIANT PAUSE BUTTON IN THE SKY
ဆာ   Ꮖ

Stellar had always carried her frame like an Amazon. The possession she had of her impressively grand, broad, and womanly frame made it almost deadly. If you were jealous, you might say she had "birthing hips." If you were humble, you would make way for her to pass by and suck the light from the room to recycle it out again on you. With her up-right-ness and confidence, she had aged well. But when Gaby slipped just out of reach into a vortex of silence and uncertainty, Stellar shrivelled, aging instantaneously. A saggy waistline and falling breasts, a spine curved often into a question mark under hunched shoulders, deep blueness in crescents under her eyes accenting the crazed light that was burning fires inside them.

She stood beside Gaby's bed, held Gaby's hand with one claw—all red knuckles and loose wedding rings—and patted it, almost violently in the repetition, with the other. She was blubbering, not saying anything coherent, but making a noise akin to crying. Her face squinched up and released, in turn. There were no tears, however, as she had spent all that she was allotted, already.

Annie stood on the other side of the bed, her chest feeling heavy and her stomach, fluttery. She was aware of a certain vacancy growing larger and larger with each day that she counted down on the calendar at home. Well, she had been counting. After a month, she didn't have the heart to continue. The article about Mikhail had said forty-two days. Forty-two days like this. No. Now it was worse, with Mom on an eternal fast and living continuously the projection of an infinite sadness. Forty-two days more. And then another forty-two. And forty-two. And forty-two. She shut her eyes for a moment and pulled herself back from the madness. That was another presence right there, with vacancy: insanity. The insanity she had managed to expel by tiny drops out through the skin. The vacancy was yawning wide.

"Mom?" Where this was going, she didn't know. Louder, "Mom? Mom! Mom!?"

Stellar stopped the patting, still looking at Gaby, but with a questioning look as if something had just occurred to her. Her gaze turned so slowly to settle on Annie, she felt invisible. The vacancy steamed up angry. "Mom!"

"What, Honey?" The smile was still there. Of course it was. The lines on her face that meant happy were chiseled and suspended, all through this crazy tragedy. Annie realized that with every undulation she had endured, that smile was ever-present. What a beautiful smile it had been, as it was formed in the years of youth and young love and motherhood and mature love. And now?

"Mom, quit smiling. Please."

"Annie?"

"I can't take it anymore. I can't." She gestured toward what lay between them. "This is enough, okay? I don't need any more."

Stellar now focused on her, but as if she were a quandary. The smile quivered, trying to die, but could not be compelled to give up its fight.

"Please. Please."

"Quit smiling?"

"Quit smiling," she coaxed verbally, leading Stellar like a lost child. Stellar's gaze wandered around the room, finding little holds where it stopped and her eyebrows knit together and then unknit. It was this way for a long time, Annie standing suspended in between a sigh of desperation and a scream, trapped in accidental patience that emerged from a spring of near-defeat. She, too, was looking worn, but with her it was pathos, was the crystallized beauty-sadness of the blessed. Her T-shirt and jeans hugged her, a dusty rose scarf wrapped around her sculpted collar bones, and her red lips and hazel eyes blazed through the pain in specialized clearness. Her hands rested on the edge of the bed, the fingers of one overlaying the fingers of the other.

Stellar's gaze finally settled back on Annie's face just as Annie looked back at her. Stellar's Cheshire smile was again plastered on under the crazed eyes but she was finally in the same room, Annie could feel her. "Honey... Honey." She reached out over the bed, extending her hands out in a dramatic pose. Annie laid her hands in them and they were quickly engulfed, if boniness can engulf by desire alone. "Honey, I think pain like this must either burn you to ash or purify you. I love you. I'm sorry for all this." Just like that.

Annie looked at her mom and her own eyes filled with spent tears. "Mom, I..." She pulled her hands loose and smoothed Gaby's sheets down over her, tracing the contours of her still body, but with the absence of a habit.

"She's never coming back," Annie stated.

"She's right there."

"Well, should she be? Should she be trapped forever like this?"

"I have hope."

Annie found her voice trip over a hitch in her throat. "I had no idea." And then, when anger replaced shock, "Really? What hope can you possibly have?"

"I don't know. The doctors…"

"Okay, Mom. Okay. I'm just saying I need you, too. That's all."

Stellar turned again to Gaby, stroked her hair away from her bloated and pale face. Together, with one stroking the linens over the body and the other lovingly brushing at the hair, it looked like a preparation for burial, perhaps from an Arthurian legend.

Pulling back like this, pulling way back and out into the sky but where the hospital walls were invisible as were the walls of their bodies and the walls of all their cells, they were stroking in desperation, trying to keep Gaby there with them and to warm her body back to consciousness. Gaby's neurons flashed and fluttered, her brain had some activity that would perhaps re-organize itself into the myriad patterns of self-sustainment and the turmoil and churning of normal human life. Gaby's finger twitched then, in a rapid, irregular movement. The fire in Stellar flamed up into blinding flames, and Annie was engulfed in the zip and spit of a hundred sparklers. The moving finger just barely glowed gold and left orange streaks where it had just been, back and forth in a light soup of orange and gold. Annie reached out with one long arm for the red button that would call the nurses and rang and rang and rang, pushing it as hard as she could manage.

❧   ❧

"Well, I heard you're moving a little?" Mikhail couldn't help smiling again as he repeated the news to Gaby.

"Oops. Sorry to interrupt." Adam made as if to back out the door, but Mikhail stopped him.

"No, Adam. Stay. I was just talking to her about moving. It's so great."

Adam moved into the room, added a single white rose to one of the already-full vases and then sat down in one of the chairs, patted the chair next to him for Mikhail to sit. Mikhail sat and there they stayed in silence for a time. Mikhail ventured, "It's so strange how I have gotten used to just talking to her and talking to her. Before, I did a lot less talking. But I have gotten used to feeling silly, or gotten over it. I just want her to hear me, in case…"

"I know. Me too."

Another few minutes. This time Adam risked conversation. "I suppose the trick now is to keep talking when she can talk back, when you risk everything by saying what you have to say." The two exchanged a nervous smile. It was unfamiliar territory: Adam the guru and Mikhail the lover. But it felt good, too.

"You know, I am really, really voting for you as a son."

"You mean…?"

"Mikhail!" The confused shyness was amusing even to Adam. "If you mean do I know that you love her, yes. Do I think she loves you, yes. Do I think she will discover it? Probably, if you help her. Or surprise her. I mean," and there was a time while Adam was finding his words. "Think of all the successful lovers of TV and movies and literature. You have to be bold, man! There is no conquest without a battle. Storm the castle! Okay, so that's silly. But you really do have to make her believe your love before she is going to bet the house on you."

Adam thought about this a moment. "And then you have to keep her believing."

"Hm."

"I think I need a coffee. You want something?" Adam stood up and crossed the room in a few wide strides.

"Oh, no. I'm good, thanks." And the door popped shut, loud and abrupt, but then there was the sound of a commotion and many voices outside the door and Adam came back in, holding open the door for a troupe of people as they filed in.

Mikhail looked down at his watch. "Is it that time already?"

"Well, yes," answered Annie as she led the line in and moved to the bedside table, where she set down a contraband candle and retrieved a lighter from her pocket, "But we're also cheating a little. One of the nurses has let us come in together, for once." Behind her, Stellar, Mel, Andrew, and Afentra. Then lagging behind, John and Mercedes. Mercedes—her long hair shot through with gray—came right over to Mikhail at his chair, where he stood and she swept him into a hug. "We just wanted to visit, you know?"

"Not because of the book," John added, a look of distaste on his face, as if the book had offended him. "Or maybe, in spite of the book. We're so sorry for all of this..."

"John, it's nothing you've done. Don't feel bad about the book. I can't wait to read it." John gave Mikhail a thankful smile, relaxed his brow. Mercedes took a minute to look around the room while everyone settled themselves in a sort of semi-circle, at the hundreds of roses and peonies and irises and daisies and baby's breath and daffodils and carnations and black-eyed Susans.

"Mikhail!" she breathed. "I know I read it in the paper, but this is really something!"

He shrugged it off. "Better late than never." That's something his mom had been saying a lot lately, calling shots from her hospital bed to her one-man army of Mikhail. He sent special letters, helped her find phone numbers for old friends, sold off items on Ebay so that Nadine could purchase jigsaw puzzles, a book to improve one's memory, even a new car. She had him rent movies she had never seen, borrow books she had always meant to read from the library, and had him go in the jewelry box at home to bring her that secret locket out of the back of it. She kept it in a tin by the side of her hospital bed. She said she was going to bequest it to Mikhail on the day she got out of this place.

Speak of the devil, here came Nadine wheeling into the room, now, with Ruth pushing behind. Mikhail was about to charge across the room and tell Aunt Ruth he was just about to go up there and get her for her final discharge, but when Nadine crossed the threshold—the tin holding the locket on her lap—there was a sort of explosion that hit them all, a wind that came from nowhere and moved outward at them, whipped back hair and clothes and made eyes close, cheeks turn against the spray. Flower petals flew, a couple vases fell and spilled, one hit the floor and shattered; the blinds at the window thrummed metallically against one another as the wind escaped to nowhere, through the walls, blasting straight into them and then disappearing.

Next to Annie on the bedside table, the illegal candle flame twisted sideways and then a sputter from the wick sent a rogue spark over the glass barrier and onto an unopened card that lay under it. The paper smoldered a mere fraction of a moment before small flames leapt to life and Annie turned her face, horrified. During the time it took her to locate water to throw or material to suffocate it—she ripped off her own cardigan—everyone else turned to see the fire blazing up. Annie threw her cardigan down on the flames as Adam came running with a vase of water (the de-containered flowers now adding to the mess on the floor), sprawled himself over the foot of the bed and Gaby's feet, splashing water in utter disregard of what might be on the table.

The cardigan knocked into the ruby ring and the ring went flying through the air in the direction of the bed. Eleven pairs of eyes watched as the ring sailed, the red stone reflecting the dying sunlight that was pouring in the windows into points of ruby and magenta and pink and rose and even gold, wheeling around in circles. The ring landed directly in Gaby's open mouth. For another moment, no one moved. Gaby's mouth shut, Stellar screamed, and at the foot of Gaby's hospital bed, Afentra fainted. Mel, at the opposite side and end of the bed, lurched forward and started to pry Gaby's mouth open with her fingers just as Gaby started to choke. Mel reached in Gaby's now-open mouth and pulled out the ring, held it firm in her fist just inches from Gaby's chin as Gaby opened her eyes, staring directly into the green pair hovering in front of her own.

Mel and Gaby looked fixedly at each other, Gaby confused and Mel shocked speechless, but no one else was looking there anymore, had not realized Gaby's eyes were open or that she was registering thought. From the moment Mel retrieved the ring from Gaby's mouth, they all were staring instead at Afentra, unconscious, suspended backwards, resting as if in someone's arms, in mid-air.

No one said a word or moved, or sniffed, or breathed.

The Angel realized his predicament, and very, very slowly lowered Afentra to the floor as all the watching eyes followed the body down. There was Nadine, looking curious, Mercedes, smiling, and John looking nonchalant. Stellar had gone white as a sheet, Annie was holding a scream silent on her soot-streaked face, and Adam, watching Afentra while still half-laying across the foot of the bed with a vase in his outstretched hands, was as terrified as Ruth and Andrew seemed to be. It was very hard to know what Mikhail was thinking behind his eyes as he blinked at Afentra, now on the ground and stirring.

And in the next moment, Annie finished her interrupted scream and Gaby moved, looking around the room.

CHAPTER 31
THERE SHE GOES
ℬ   ℭ

Gaby was a scrappy child with big eyes, starry chestnut eyes, and lean, pale limbs topped with a mound of curly black hair which Stellar called "wild and wonderful, like West Virginia." She sprawled out belly-down on the old, dust-colored carpeting in her grandma's bedroom, one foot turned pigeon-toed and the sun spraying in through the sheer curtains to line up across her calves, clad in pink stockings.

Her upper body was propped up on her elbows facing a giant, plastic fortress—all uncompromising turrets and flags—called Castle Rising-Moon. In Gaby's left hand she held a pale horse (of the castle) with matting hair; Quiklander. In her right hand, the dismounted rider, one Queen Northwyth, with a crooked crown and some marker embellishment on her short, white, battle skirt. The Queen was leaving the castle—being overrun with Demonis—to invoke the help of her friends, Jaden the Great and the Angel of Northwyth. Their superpowers would be needed, even more than her incredible strength, persuasiveness, and ability to hypnotize with a single glance. Who couldn't use invisibility, peace, and healing (The Angel) and Herculean strength, agility, bravery, and nobility

(Jaden) during a battle-for-good of epic proportions? If only The Sage (wisdom, foreknowledge, telekinesis, and a magical staff) hadn't been currently disappeared into the Wood of Branderby.

Around Grandma's room piles of dark things loomed, stacked and tangled and compacted along the walls and creeping out onto the open floor. The TV with rabbit ears askew was quietly tuned to a repeat episode of *Avengers of Northwyth*. Gaby—when not saving the world as Queen Northwyth—spent hours dawdling through the China cabinet filled with tea sets and a leaning tower of crates filled with books. Gaby would read anything: a Cutco cooking book, antique Nancy Drews, a Bible with a zipper and orange-rimmed pages, 1970s romance novels. On reading the latter, she probably would have been reprimanded, but an uncomfortable feeling in her stomach usually stopped her perusals, anyhow.

Squeals heard through a closed window distracted Gabrielle and she set the steed down, not very gently. She walked with The Queen suspended upside down in her giant hand, by her small feet, The Queen's hair long, a coppery-colored tangle, and swaying as Gaby tread over to the window. Gaby pulled the sheer curtain aside and then moved behind it, looking out at a world of spring green and gray and kelly green. It was drizzling, almost imperceptibly. Drops of water beaded up along the edge of the window, each containing bubbled white and green rectangles and circles and miniature alternate universes.

Outside the second-story window, below the tirelessly gray sky, red brick broke the view: the wall of the house next door, or more specifically, the garage wall of the house next door. At the top of that wall, the line of its black roof, and the clean, white gutters dripping with rain. And the source of the squeals: two boys in the muddy grass, squatting on either side of a green, tin bucket, peering down inside and yelling one at the other.

This was Bobby and Brian, a pair of brothers around Gaby's own age. While turning circles in the driveway on her bike, Gaby had been forced into awkward conversation with them. Gaby preferred to play alone or with her sister.

Now she watched Bobby's and Brian's intrigues with their bucket. First, Bobby's hand came slowly up and out of the bucket, holding a frog by one of its back legs. The frog writhed. Gaby imagined its eyes wide with terror (her own were, at that). Next, Brian placed a square board on top of the bucket so that it was sitting sturdy, and Bobby squished the frog onto it, belly up, and held it in place. Brian fished disused twist-ties from his pocket, and threaded them through holes drilled in the board at its four corners. Together, the brothers fastened the twist-ties around the frog's ankles and wrists (if a frog has ankles and wrists). The boys lifted the board with the frog attached, and giggled and skipped with it between them around the corner.

An electricity filled Gaby. She turned from the window, struggling a bit with the curtain that shrouded her. When free of its snares, she ran across the room, out the door, down the hall, down the stairs and past the wondering glances of her mom and sister and grandma, out the front door, across the porch, and across the wet, green lawn, her tights dampening and the hem of her Sunday dress sprinkling with mud. Her patent leathers ticked as she met with cement driveway, and then she came around the corner of the house and faced Bobby and Brian at their open garage. She was stupefied by what she saw.

Along their father's, tidy workbench which stretched along the left wall, six or seven similar boards were propped up among the spare screws and sawdust. Each board held its own frog splayed-legged and belly-up. Limbs twitched, stomachs rising and falling with breathing. Bobby and Brian each stood on an up-ended milk crate, pulled close together. Gaby watched, as yet undetected.

Brian had something in his hand which he touched first to one frog and then the next and so on. (It was in fact a small, metal object made to look like a Zippo, but which gave off a small electrical current meant to shock the duped borrower. Theirs had been neatly jerry-rigged to shock instead from the flame guard). As he touched each frog, it squirmed against its twist-tie restraints, pulling hard. Bobby and Brian giggled, their eyes glistening.

Gaby shouted, "You guys cut that out right now!" She lunged forward and grabbed for the lighter with the hand that wasn't still holding an upside down Queen. Brian was stunned still by Gaby in bows and frills and furious eyes and she managed to knock it to the ground. She then reached for the first wood board with frog, but had only undone one twist-tie when Bobby snatched at her hands while Brian pulled at her waist, yanking her away from the workbench and into the center of the car-less expanse. The Queen of Northwyth went spiraling off to the side, her hair arching behind her head, and landed with a slap on the smooth cement. She skidded to a stop with a scraping sound.

Gaby knocked the frog-with-board face-down on the smooth, painted cement and winced. She pulled at her arms, kicked her feet, and tried to throw her body forward at the five frogs still lined up on the bench, but she went nowhere. It occurred to Gaby that it would be nice to have the strength of Jaden, just then. Or to have Jaden there to avenge her. Or to avenge the frogs and save her, really. Maybe Jaden was there, peeking behind the warehouse shelves. Yes, she could see his steady, silvery blue eyes peeking out from over a dented tool box. What was he waiting for?

The struggle intensified. They swung as a mass around the room and with one final lunge the mess of three kids slammed against a ceiling-high shelf at the back of the garage. They scuffled some more, then hit against the shelf again. And one more time. On the third hit against the shelf, the three bodies unfrayed and separated. Bobby and Brian flew out to the sides, and Gaby stood in the shadow of the shelf, alone. A gallon of paint (half-used, with an uneven dried drip of Brandeis Blue around the rim) teetered. Then it fell, directly on Gaby's head, and she dropped to the floor, unconscious. The azure paint crawled toward her lacy frills and her patent leathers, and Bobby and Brian stood paralyzed, terror on their faces. The Angel strode out from behind the shelf and the tool box, cradled The Queen in the palm of his hand, and then blazed out the door, loosening the twist ties as he went, with the wave of his sword.

附 附

Nadine might be in remission, but she was still intent on some mental bucket list she constructed while in the hospital. She kept Mikhail on his toes and he humored her. Planning a trip down around Lake Michigan and north to the sight of the bridge was a bigger deal than Mikhail had planned on, especially since Gaby and Mel insisted on coming with them. Perhaps they should have gone through the Upper Peninsula, but then they might have gotten in trouble with snow, this time of year.

And the biggest hurdle was now, at the mouth of the bridge, finding a place to park the car, a way down to the base of the bridge, a way that Gaby—still in rehabilitation from the coma—could be helped down. Mikhail was not about to leave her in the car.

They parked along the roadside, Nadine exiting the driver's side and leading the way down a precipitous drop with a slick mud trail amongst the rocks, curving down to the water where the last landed pylon emerged. Mikhail couldn't protest, too busy with assisting Gaby out of the back door with the oncoming traffic, lifting her up and carrying her, with her arms around his neck, down the path after Mel.

Mikhail placed Gaby gently on a slab of cement encasing the bottom of the pylon, and sat down next to her, engulfing her small hand in his, twining their fingers together. He looked up at his mom, standing at the edge of the dirt and rocks so that her toes touched the icy water. Nadine strained with her whole body out at the water, binoculars pressed to her eyes as she faced out at the pylons further out.

"It's there, Mikhail." Her voice choked off and she made no move to look away.

Mikhail jumped up, looked back to make sure Gaby was secure, and then was there beside Nadine. They stood like this, shoulder to shoulder, until Nadine handed over the binoculars and Mikhail made to look in the same direction she had been.

The brass plaque was high up on the pylon, not completely sheltered in the bridge, but high enough that no water would rise to it. Alexy's name, and then his dates of birth and death, and then an inscription, "Died in the making of this bridge. Loving son, husband, and father."

"Well, I wanted to see it." She turned, looking tired. "Who's got the camera? I want a photo."

"Mom, are you sure? We don't have to take a photo of this."

Nadine wanted a photo. She saw what happened to people when they saw the clear face of an unexplained baby in the clouds. The clouds moved, changed, and then people looked away, forgetting to believe in it.

THE END

A preview of Devon's next book,

The Date and the Cockroach

SECTION ONE: UNDER A CRAYON BLUE SKY

She had a perm. John didn't know anything about those kinds of things, but he was surprised later to find out—when she came home one afternoon smelling of bitter plastic and fish—that what he had been running his fingers through and adoring splayed on his white, eyelet bed linen, was a ruse. And that *smell*. He could hardly stomach his pork chops and fried potatoes from the stink of it. Then a week later, at the academic ball, he drew her close to fit her curves to his body while everyone watched and commented on her fiery youth, and when he buried his face in her chestnut curls his nostrils were assailed and he coughed, hesitated in his waltz step.

The song ended and her warmth escaped him as she stepped back and opened up to the room, clapped. She was trying so hard to be perfect but there were things about her that eluded her careful manicuring; the things he loved most. He had seen them from the first moment she filed into his classroom, carefully lined a notebook and pencil up on the desk top at right angles. The careful color of her nail polish was a little too fluorescent to avoid notice, her pale hands never stayed completely still so she sat on them sometimes.

Like tonight, he was so proud that she had on red, even though it seemed to defy all her literary training what the red in red dress signified. Gemma, in red? He must have loosed something inside her that the young bride would choose sports car red, fitted to her form and smoothing over her tight waist with an obvious bulge, her round bottom, her ample bosom that might be the foreshadow of children, or affairs, or weight gain, but none of them with restraint.

Gemma's lips were lacquered red to match her dress. (Subtlety and Cindy Crawford had not yet happened to makeup, in the 1960s.) She turned to him with her face flashing a brilliant smile (her smile was expansive and full of perfect, blue-white teeth) which deflected quickly off of his constant watchfulness. Sparkling eyes? (Why was that? Did humans produce excess ocular moisture when happy? And why? Mating reasons? He would have to ask George.) That would signify she was enjoying herself, despite his secret misgivings. Maybe she had them, too. He took her girlish hand in his—slight, warm, ornamented with the aquamarine wedding ring that he chose to accent her eyes—and would remember that moment for all the rest of his ninety-two years, the gold of a thin chain nearly disappearing next to her whiteness, a ruby pendant (Had she planned her outfit because of this wedding present?) cradled in her clavicle.

*   *   *

The dogwood was in bloom then. He could tell by the piece pressed into the pages of her journal and taped there, dying the page in brown blotches these four decades. In his mind's eye, he could see the dark wash of East Coast evergreens with wintry bark, desecrated by the crystallized fireworks of all those dogwoods. He could smell them, feel the way they dressed up a campus, a town, a freeway, an alley.

He lay a veiny hand on the page, on the mummified dogwood sprig. He wasn't sure where else to go, just here in the bedroom. How much time did they spend together in this room, anymore? *Anymore.* Not anymore. He found Gemma here, yesterday, and now he was trapped in the domestic silence (ticking grandfather clock, heater hum) and cream voile and doilies and Hummels.

Who were you supposed to call when you found someone dead? Why didn't people talk about those sorts of details? It was mostly unexpected, but he was certain there was no foul play. You had to call the police, anyhow? Report death to the government like you had to births? *Yes sir, my wife is dead. I've filled out all the required paperwork.* And now the bulk of her was at the funeral home and he was in the bedroom.

The kids would be coming. Like him, they wouldn't know what to do. Unlike him, they would do what occurred to them. Until then, he sat in limbo, stuck between the voile and the dogwoods.

*   *   *

"When you see something more than once, it's a sign." That's what he had said to her. He couldn't have known it then, but saying that to her was like holding a newborn to your chest or inviting Homeless Pat over for Christmas dinner. Of course, it was meant ostensibly as a comment on literature, but there under the raging blooms under a crystal sky, the heat between their bodies and the shadows in their eyes were indicative of his subversive meaning. He would tell her clearly soon enough. He believed that when he saw something repeated, it *was* a sign. And that was the second time he had seen Gemma floating between classes that very day, the day of meeting her in class.

And it was spring, a season for blossoming love. The flowers were exploding, pollen erupting into the air and shifting with the winds. Flowers were making love. The earth was softening, the grass the greenest and softest it would be all year. How long had he watched these portents for other men, other women? How many times had he highlighted them in stories for dimwitted students? It is spring. The world is in bloom. The girl with the pink nail polish is seen walking under the cherry blossoms. The girl with the pink nail polish is seen sitting neatly on the lawn, her books and papers scattered about her. Then a paper breaks free of its makeshift weight and moves spastic as a butterfly until it lands at the young professor's feet. *That*, he explains, *is foreshadowing. That is a sign.*

So where was his sign, now? What did he miss that unveiled the secret of Gemma's death before it unfolded? He could not comprehend that perhaps the author of this story was cruel or inept enough not to give the proper clues to soften the blow, to create that perfect moment of "Aha!" when it became clear the ending was—although secret—always inevitable.

This in no way felt inevitable. But he had missed the signs, surely. What were they? Where were they? What weapon was hidden in the paragraphs of her life, what antagonist creeping along the pages and waiting to spring from the shadows, unbidden but practically absolute? Maybe he had just forgotten. Old age. How long ago was it that he first noticed his words tripping over each other, his thoughts hitting against the front of his skull and then falling back into his brain before he could form the word on his tongue? "It happens to everyone," Gemma said to him. They were driving in the car, sometime, somewhere. All he could remember was that feeling of plastic and glass all around, the slide of pavement beneath them and scenery around them lost in the sounds of the car, and her beside him looking forward over the dashboard. She was trying to soothe him. She knew he was thinking, *Not me.* He told her he must have lesions on his brain from a life of headaches. She sighed. He knew she was thinking, *Sometimes we are just ordinary, just like everyone else.*

*   *   *

When her fire surprised him, her ferocity erupting into his cautious life, he became full of romantic ideas. There was a plane trip to New York City to eat at a restaurant she had mentioned. There were the Poconos and all that skin and sexiness which was something he had never thought of before and was all he could think of afterwards, distracting his work something dreadful and being a bit of a scandal besides. They went rowing on the lake, and then they did it again, and again. He would pack a generous picnic basket, never dreaming of the way she would handle each food as though it were sensual. Later, he lay in bed and the food would come back to him in flashes; a red grape surrounded by her pretty lips and held in her fingertips, her nails painted lilac, her fingers ivory, so slender; an ice cube on a wave of iced tea, clinking against her pearly teeth as she struggled not to smile, pushing her tongue against them; even a chocolate cake, one bite at a time, and how her eyes would first widen with the bite and then shudder closed as she chewed, a private ecstasy.

Dusk was smearing the sky pink and a purpled gray on the far side of the lake and he had taken Gemma on another rowing picnic. He packed while she was in her perfect dorm room, or so he imagined; he had never been stupid enough to actually visit her there but he had painted in his mind's eye her small bed with ruffled comforter, her school-issue desk with drawers lined with floral contact paper and sharp pencils with unused erasers, a divider between paperclips and rubber bands, shelves with lines of Ken Kesey, *King Lear*, *Of Mice and Men*, Simone de Beauvior. And would she be bold enough to have a framed photo of them together reclining idly on the bureau next to the vase of flowers that he kept full with wildflowers and occasionally a bouquet from Anna's downtown? Maybe he was buried in with her panties, but he imagined he was on the dresser, watching her furrow her brow and bend her head over her novels and course texts until her eyes were slits and the only light left on was her desk lamp and somewhere her roommate was snoring and Gemma was slumped almost onto herself.

But that was a rabbit trail. One that he loved to take. Those old memories. On that particular day—the other one he had been thinking about—it was purpled dusk out in the row boat and he could still recall the bounty of the picnic basket. Pasta Alfredo from Vinnie's, still warm from the way he had wrapped it in layer on layer of towels. Red wine. Chilled. Fresh bread that steamed when he ripped it open. Olives, the kinds with pits still in them. And Gemma had oohed and ahhed as he wanted her to, as he needed her to. She was good at that. A skill he later learned was not a gifting of all women, but of the crafty ones. It would keep him producing, keep him fawning for their whole marriage, this rewarding him with innocent praise.

She tipped a wine glass back so that the rim fell across her wide eyes, brushing her eye lashes, the wine ebbing in between her lips. There were a few stray pieces of bread on the bench in between them, who knows how they happened to be there? And a crow came suddenly swooping from the land and the shoreline of darkling trees and right across the barely rippling water (darkling too with barely a reflection of the lazy, cloud-smudged sunset). With a raucous flapping the crow landed on the side of the boat. He snatched a piece of bread into his bill before John could wiggle his hands at him and yell "shoo!" Gemma had been cool as a cucumber, giggled into her wine. John leaned back and stared at the bench with bread crumbs, dubious. A crow? What did it mean?

It didn't matter. He went ahead with the proposal anyhow because there was nothing he could do about it. His fate was with Gemma, no matter if she was his *femme fatale* or what. He had the sense, that night, that he was walking into disaster, what with the crow and all. But he would never tell her that, would never really have the need to. She slid the ring onto her slender finger and held it out in front of them as they snuggled in the same end of the boat, his arms around her waist (with an obvious bulge, again), supporting her thin arms and draped with her chestnut curls, his nose at the crown of her head. She watched the dusk wane in the luster of the aquamarine, then the starlight twinkle there. John was looking up at the sky, watching the gods and warriors march their way toward morning, shivering as silent black bats flew between him and the infinite universe, wondering if a single crow were more ominous than bats against a waxing moon.

The Date and the Cockroach is a novel about secrets, family, and love.

John was once a young, superstitious literature professor meeting the fiery love of his life, Gemma. Now he's an aged, superstitious literature professor dealing with the sudden death of the grossly obese, shop-o-holic love of his life, Gemma. As their seven surviving kids make their way back to their East coast home for the funeral, they each uncover a secret about Gemma, and in so doing unhinge something in themselves.

Due to be published by Owl and Zebra Press in spring, 2014.

ACKNOWLEDGEMENTS

Thanks to Kevin. This is only a little something compared with what you are about to accomplish.

Thanks to Windsor and Eamon for bearing the brunt of my ultrafocus and workaholism.

Thanks to Mom and Eric for moving to North Carolina just to watch Eamon while I re-wrote a book that was dead in the water.

Thanks to my Aunt Shelly, my editor and my partner in crime. Believe me when I say this book never would have been in your hands if it weren't for her, from day one through to day 12,227. It is fitting that she helped me wrap and glue my first homemade book at age six, and is still dotting my i's and crossing my t's.

Thanks to all the people who believed in me from the beginning, and are likely to be out there, still believing. You are too many to list. Specifically, thanks to Anne Sullivan.

Thanks to my friendly support; Rebecca, Nellie, and Coran. No author can really survive and accomplish without some sort of friends at every stage, and I couldn't have made it without our ladies' nights, without our late night chats, and without your honesty and acceptance.

Thanks to everyone who fed me those short words of encouragement—whether strangers or family or somewhere in between—that serve to reanimate the fragile, dreaming soul.

Thanks to my first readers: Kevin (again), Aunt Shelly (again), Anne, and Heidi. Thanks anyways to Amy, Lauren and Mr. Brian, for other things.

Thanks for the many inspirations and good times. You probably can tell who you are by the shape of these characters and the events in their lives. I won't list you in case someone comes along and claims these characters *are* you. Except you, Linds, because you want to be mentioned and well you should be.

Thanks to my CR family, who helped me get from angry to beloved to published, as well as my WOEAIHF group, who walked with me right up to the yawning chasm's edge.

Thanks to Dwight Knoll for his photography and his opinions.

Thanks to Donald Desloge for asking me, every single Sunday from years seven to eight, how the book was coming.

Thanks to Catherine Ryan Howard and her *Self-Printed*, as well as www.catherinecaffeinated.com. I've never met you, but you became "Miss Catherine" around here, and a well-used source.

Thanks also to all the people who are about to market, promote, and sell this book, in any capacity. I can't yet put faces or names to all of you, but thank you so, so much.

Last but first, thank You Jesus. Thanks for the talents, and I only hope to do You proud.